Spring Breeze

Angela Barton

Dedicated to my late husband and best friend, Paul.

You left this world, but not my heart.

First Published in 2022 by Oxford-Harlyn Publishing Company

First Edition
Print Edition

This novel is a work of fiction. Many of the names and incidents portrayed in this book are the work of the author's imagination. However, parts of the storyline were actual events from history and some secondary characters lived during the timeline of the story. The author has included them with respect.

ISBN: 978-1-7391191-2-6

A CIP catalogue record for this title is available from the British Library.

Operation Spring Breeze took place in July 1942. Over thirteen thousand Jewish citizens, including four thousand children, were rounded up and kept in horrendous conditions in the Vélodrome d'Hiver, in Paris. After several days without water or food and in unsanitary conditions, they were transported in cattle trucks to concentration camps. Could a more contradictory and erroneous name have been chosen for such cruelty?

Do not be dismayed by the brokenness of the world.
All things break. And all things can be mended.
Not with time, as they say, but with intention.
So go. Love intentionally, extravagantly, unconditionally.
The broken world waits in darkness for the light that is you.

L.R. Knost

"These dark hours soil forever our history and are an injury to our past and our traditions ... the criminal folly of the occupier was seconded by the French, by the French state."

Jacques Chirac

Spring Breeze

1

July 1940

PARIS HAD FALLEN. It was unthinkable. It was terrifying.

The weather continued to show its allegiance to the city's citizens by offering an equally cold reception to the German troops. The streets appeared bereft with their shops boarded up, a diminished population shuffling along the boulevards, and cafés closed due to food and staff shortages.

Rain began to fall more heavily as Matilde Pascale left Lombard's Auctioneers. For five years she had researched and catalogued collectables there and had never tired of the sweet smell of aged wooden frames or timeworn jewellery. Not that she had any choice now. The auction house had closed for the foreseeable future, yet another victim of the invasion. Turning for one last look, she flicked up the collar of her jacket.

Matilde reached the edge of the food market that took place twice a week in the wide expanse of the square, in front of St. Augustine's church. Once a bustling meeting place selling a huge assortment of food, the stalls were now forlorn, the displays paltry and the food unappetizing. Stallholders were busy packing away while a handful of shoppers ambled from one meagre display to another, bartering down high prices for low quality provisions. Matilde looked at the wilting cabbage she'd bought earlier, its flaccid leaves falling into soft yellow folds.

The bells of St. Augustine's began to toll six o'clock. One. Two. Three. She counted the chimes to herself and had reached the fifth strike when the bells were interspersed by staccato popping.

Gunfire.

Instinctively she ducked and stepped inside the nearest shop doorway. Someone screamed. Footsteps clattered as people hurried away. Her heartbeat quickened. Peering around the edge of her hiding place, Matilde watched a man sprint and disappear into an alleyway a short distance in front of her. On the ground lay a body dressed in a grey uniform. A German. The deluge was diluting his blood; it flowed into the gutter. She felt sick. More footsteps. Running. Within seconds several German soldiers ran past her, each holding a gun. She lowered her head and pretended to search for something in her handbag. Then a hand grasped her shoulder. She jumped, half-expecting to see one of them. To her great relief, it was her neighbour.

'Sylvie! You frightened me.'

'Sorry. I was hurrying to catch up with you when I heard gunfire. What's happened?'

'A German's been shot.' Matilde pointed. 'Over there by the tobacconist's.'

Sylvie leaned forwards to see. 'Christ. There'll be repercussions. We don't want the curfew brought forward again. Come on. Let's go.'

'Wait,' said Matilde. She grabbed Sylvie's coat sleeve. 'Shouldn't we stay here for a while and wait until it's calmer?'

'If we don't go now, the soldiers might start asking questions.'

IT HAD BEEN six weeks since the Germans had entered Paris. Matilde remembered that day as if it were yesterday. She had been leaning out of her second-floor apartment window, the stone lintel grazing her elbows as she leant forwards to get a better view. The low vibrations of a long column of Panzer vehicles entered Paris like the tip of a blade penetrating the heart of France. She watched squat black tanks rolling past, their tracks clattering along the Rue de Rivoli. Canvas-topped lorries were packed with men, followed by smaller tanks pulling heavy weapons. People lined the streets in silence, watching as the enemy paraded into their capital city. The reverberation of the slow, deliberate invasion made a knot of anxiety tighten in her stomach.

A pall of black smoke had hung over the rooftops for days. Although people spoke openly about civil servants destroying records so that the Germans didn't have access to them, she had been told that it wasn't the burning of paperwork that was causing the dark cloud. It came from oil depots that had been set alight by retreating French troops. If the people of France were unable to make use of the fuel, then they'd make sure the Germans wouldn't get their hands on it either. The darkened skies had seemed like a fitting apocalyptic moment for Paris as the city prepared to receive its invaders.

Last month, as she had watched, she'd felt her husband's breath on the back of her neck as he leant over her shoulder. Xavier had said he wouldn't give the filthy Boches the satisfaction of an audience, but his curiosity must have proven too strong. Matilde swallowed hard. France was occupied by a foreign power. It was appalling, yet fascinating to watch. She remembered squashing an ant on the stone mullion ledge with her forefinger.

THE THOUGHT OF being interrogated, however informally, urged Matilde to link arms with her friend and hurry towards the Métro. She dipped her head to share Sylvie's umbrella.

'Do you think it's safe?' she asked.

'What?'

'Us. Walking. Do you think we're safe walking the streets after what's happened?'

'Our boys aren't about to shoot us, if that's what you mean.'

'You know I don't mean that. I don't think I'll ever get used to living like this.'

Sylvie's stiletto heels click-clacked on the pavement. 'It's amazing what we can all get used to if we have no choice. Anyway, how's work?'

Matilde looked over her shoulder. Several women were scurrying along with baskets tucked into the crook of their arms, but no Germans were close by. She turned back. 'As from today, I'm unemployed.'

Sylvie slowed her walk and looked at her. 'Oh, I'm sorry. Has Monsieur Lombard been forced to close down?'

'Yes, but not by them. No one's selling and no one's buying, so the auction house's salerooms are empty.' Matilde had to run a few steps to catch up with Sylvie who had picked up her pace again. 'Some German officials came snooping around the halls last week. I think that's another reason why he decided to close. He doesn't want them storing any equipment in his property.'

'If they want to use his building, they will. Closing it won't make any difference.'

'It's a terrible thing to lose your livelihood. I don't know what he'll do now.'

They walked down the steps to the underground where a train was pulling into the station. They ran to catch it. Once on board they made their way to where a mother and two children were leaving their seats. The fabric was still warm.

Sylvie pointed at creased tickets stuck to the seat in front.

'Have you seen these? People are folding paper into "V" shapes. They're chalking them on walls and bending matchsticks in half, too.'

'Why?'

'It symbolizes victory; secret insults aimed at the Germans.'

The train rattled out of the station and Matilde closed her eyes while the motion of the carriage rocked her to and fro. The air smelt of damp clothing and the ripe cabbage slowly decaying in her bag.

Two stops later, they emerged from the underground, squinting into sunshine. A ribbon of blue had opened up between the clouds and sunlight sparkled on the wet streets. With each gust of wind, raindrops blew like silver beads from trees and hedges. They walked down the pavement alongside the Tuileries gardens and towards Vue du Jardin, the three-storey building where they both rented apartments. The weak evening sun had turned its stonework a muted shade of pink. They stepped inside its wide arched doorway above which was a semi-circular tympanum featuring carved religious imagery. Inside the bare entrance hall smelt of stale tobacco.

'I'm done in,' said Matilde. 'I'm taking the bird cage.'

Without answering, Sylvie pulled the metal door of the elevator sideways, its bars folding like a concertina as it slid open. They stepped inside, dragging the door shut with a clang. Matilde set her bags down and pressed the button to the second floor. The metal cage jerked before beginning its ascent.

'How's Xavier?' asked Sylvie.

'Busy. As usual.'

'Is he still teaching at the university?'

'For the moment. Many of his Jewish students and several of his French ones have left. If he loses his job, we'll have to leave here.'

'Where would you go?'

'To my parents' house. They live in the south.' Matilde peered through the bars as they reached her floor. 'What about you? We haven't talked for weeks. Is there a new man in your life? You have a glow about you.'

The elevator stopped. Sylvie puckered her red lips until they curled into an enigmatic smile. Matilde often wondered what she herself would look like with a painted face, but she didn't want to be noticed these days. She had even stopped rubbing rouge into her cheeks. The Germans wouldn't notice her if she didn't wear make-up.

Sylvie gave a wry smile. 'Maybe, but that's all I'm saying.'

Matilde pulled open the cage door. She bent to gather her bags. 'Spoilsport!' Stepping outside, she turned to her friend. 'Good bye, then. Stay safe.'

'And you. Bye.' Sylvie swished the door closed and pressed the button to the third floor.

Matilde watched the elevator rise and when only her friend's legs were visible she turned towards her front door. Once inside and with the door locked, she lifted her bag on to the kitchen counter. She was often drawn to the window when she first came into the apartment. She and Xavier were fortunate that their living room overlooked the Tuileries instead of the street. The public gardens usually had a calming effect on her, but now, as she leant her forehead against the cool glass, she chewed her thumbnail until it was sore.

Xavier had told her over breakfast that he would be late home that evening, yet another secret meeting. The clandestine gatherings he attended moved around Paris in order to remain undetected. She had begged him to keep his head down now that the city was occupied, but she knew her pleas would be ignored. A fire shone in his eyes whenever he spoke of opposing the German forces and he'd developed a passion for these meetings. Once his eyes had burned for her, but in the space of six weeks, they now burned for France. Something indefinable had happened to change the balance of their relationship, and not for the better. She wanted to carry on in the face of war and make the best of a bad situation. He wanted to save his country.

Having changed out of her damp clothes, she prepared and cooked a small piece of grey meat and boiled the yellowing cabbage. She always ate her meal alone on the evenings Xavier was going to be late. The meat was tough, the cabbage was soggy and both were tasteless. She cleared her plate, sat beside the window overlooking the gardens and began to sew buttons on one of Xavier's old shirts. There would be no new clothes for the foreseeable future.

She awoke with a start when Xavier unlocked the apartment door. Her neck ached from having fallen asleep and it would have been dark except for a dim lamp that seemed to throw more shadows than light around the room.

'Sorry I'm so late,' he said, crossing the room and kissing her forehead.

Matilde stretched. 'What time is it?'

He walked to the window and closed the blackout blinds. 'Almost midnight. You forgot the blinds.'

'I fell asleep before it was dark.' She sat up straight. 'You've never been this late before. Is everything all right?'

He stripped off his jacket and battered hat and sank into the chair opposite her. 'I had difficulty getting back. Bloody Boches are patrolling more frequently. It took longer to get home because a German officer was shot near St Augustine's market and they've set a curfew in response.'

'Was he killed? I was there when it happened.'

He shook his head. 'He survived. What did you see?'

'Just a man running away and the soldier on the ground.'

'I wish I could shake the hand of the patriot who did it. It took courage.'

Matilde folded her husband's shirt. 'Be careful where you say such things. It's dangerous talk and collaborators might hear you.'

He bent forwards and untied his shoelaces. 'I need a drink.'

Matilde followed him into the kitchen. 'I'll heat dinner for you.'

'I just need a brandy. I ate earlier. Robert's wife cooked a vegetable broth for everyone at the meeting.'

Instead of feeling angry that he'd already eaten, she was relieved that she had a meal ready for him the following day and wouldn't have to search for food again. She decided that she would make do with whatever meagre provisions she could find in the kitchen cupboards for herself tomorrow.

'Who's Robert?' she asked.

Xavier laughed. 'Sorry. I forgot you didn't know. We're thinking about using aliases for extra safety. Robert is Charles's new name. We're all calling each other after kings of France.'

'So who are you?'

He winked then bowed. 'May I introduce to you, your new husband – Louis.'

Matilde screwed up her nose and grinned. 'Isn't it all a bit silly?'

Xavier's smile disappeared. 'Silly? Do you call watching our friends and countrymen clogging the roads fleeing Hitler's army, silly? Is it silly that my students have left their studies and future careers to hide instead of being imprisoned or shot?'

'I just mean the names, not …'

He threw back his head and emptied the brandy into his mouth. He swallowed then slammed the glass on the worktop.

'You can't be submissive and obedient to these people. You can't accept that we queue for hours just to be handed food coupons so we can get in another line and accept any pathetic morsel. We stand like animals at an empty trough, waiting our turn for rotting food to be thrown our way.' He grasped his hair in frustration and stalked out of the kitchen.

Hurrying behind, Matilde tried to placate him. 'I just meant the change of names. You know I hate them too, but what can I do about it?'

He turned. 'We can't be cowards. Nothing can be built on fear or shame. We need to recover our pride and if it's only by making life a little more difficult for the Germans, then we must do it. If everyone hid away, nothing would change.'

'But… '

'I don't want to talk about it.' He waved an arm as if batting away a fly. 'I'm going to bed.'

He left her looking at the bedroom door that had been slammed to. She felt her chin quiver and her throat tighten in sorrow. Then it began. At first a low moan over the moonlit rooftops and across the silver ribbon of the Seine. It sounded as if Paris was protesting. The wail of the air raid siren sounded across a city that had smothered its lights.

She was afraid and lonely. But was she also a coward?

2

AFTER THE FIRST peaceful night for several days, Matilde woke early. She opened a lounge window and felt the sun warm her skin as she inhaled the scent of flowers drifting up from the public gardens below. She decided to visit the market a La Tour-Maubourg close to the Eiffel Tower. Sylvie had told her that she had bought some decent potatoes there the previous week, not like the soft seed potatoes that were sold in St. Augustine's Square. Despite having coupons, every day was a struggle to find food. Xavier had told her that the best food went to feed the Germans and she thought he was probably right. Many of them carried paunches beneath their uniforms.

Matilde walked down the communal staircase, the grit on the dirty stone steps grating beneath her sandals as she slid her hand down the banister, savouring its coolness.

A sound. The echo of footsteps. She wasn't the only one on the stairwell.

Looking over the banister and through the spindles, Matilde caught occasional glimpses of someone running upstairs. She recognised the dark hair, rolled like a wave at the front of her head, and the click-clack of Sylvie's peep-toe shoes. Her friend was panting when they met.

'Oh, hello,' said Sylvie.

'Good morning. You've been out early.' Matilde noticed that

her neighbour's hair was unkempt with wisps escaping the usually perfect curl.

'I stayed overnight at a friend's place.'

Matilde saw Sylvie's cheeks blush pink. She raised an eyebrow. 'A friend?'

'It's early days and bad luck to talk about it too soon.'

Matilde couldn't prevent a smile. 'Your new beau?'

'Maybe.'

They both turned at the sound of a lock being turned. Madame Fournier's first floor apartment door opened a fraction and remained ajar for a few seconds before closing again. Since their new neighbour had moved in five weeks earlier, she and Matilde had never spoken; Matilde didn't even know her first name. Sylvie shrugged. 'She's an odd one. Where are you off to?'

'To that market you told me about. The one that sold the good potatoes.'

Sylvie placed her palms and fingers together and held them in front of her as if in prayer.

'Please could you pick me some up? I know it'll be heavy but I'm cooking tonight for—'

'Your friend?' asked Matilde.

Sylvie laughed. 'Yes. Do you mind? If you could just pick me up a few, I'll pay you when you come back.'

'Of course. I'm cycling. Thankfully *they* haven't confiscated bikes yet.'

Sylvie gave a tight-lipped smile. 'I'd best get back. I need to freshen up and change. Besides, I think she's waiting to leave and won't while we're standing here.' She nodded towards Madame Fournier's front door. 'See you later.'

The tenants' bikes were kept in the hallway of the Vue des Jardin, adjacent to the cellar door. Matilde threw her purse into the pannier and rubbed the dust off the seat. Now she wasn't working, she didn't need the speed of the underground.

She looked up and greeted Madame Fournier as she walked through the hallway.

'*Bonjour.*'

Her neighbour didn't answer. Her head was bowed and her walk was hesitant. Surely she must have heard her. Matilde sighed and shook her head, deciding that she didn't care if she'd been ignored. She didn't want to talk anyway. What would they discuss? How long did you stand in line with your food coupons? How hungry are you? How frightened?

Matilde wheeled her bike out of the building and cycled through the public gardens and along its winding pathways. Flowers were in full bloom with stocks and gardenias smelling of sweet sherbet while pollen danced in the warm breeze. She reached out her hand and stroked long grasses, her unexpected touch scattering ripened seeds as she pedalled.

The previous year, with the prospect of war growing closer, the Musée de l'Orangerie and the Jeu de Paume in the Tuileries had been closed. Valuable collections had been evacuated for safekeeping but larger items had been left behind, protected by sandbags. She'd told Xavier that the Nazis had re-opened the buildings and he had laughed and said he hoped they enjoyed looking at empty walls and sacks of sand.

Cycling in the sunshine, beneath boughs hanging heavy with fat leaves, Matilde found it difficult to believe that bombs were dropping over Europe. She felt her stomach grumble as she cycled out of the garden and joined a path bordering the Seine. She passed two German soldiers strolling along the banks of the river. The enemy. Life was indeed very different.

Her attention was attracted to a series of white posters pasted on to lampposts along the bank of the river. Curiosity steered her bike towards one of them. Stepping down, she moved closer to the lamppost and read the message.

"A cowardly criminal shot Captain Ackermann on the afternoon of July 25th 1940. As yet, the perpetrator has not been apprehended. To expiate this crime, five prisoners will be shot. If the guilty party is not arrested before July 30th at midnight, ten more prisoners will be executed."

Matilde closed her eyes to block out the words. Would killing innocent people exonerate the gunman? And at what stage would they stop shooting prisoners? She opened her eyes and raised her head. Across the river the Eiffel Tower stood like a giant initial A on an old manuscript. At its point billowed an enormous enemy flag, a black swastika inside a white circle on a violent red background. There was a weight of menace in the air. She looked around. No one was close. She ripped the sheet off the lamppost, screwed it into a small ball and threw it on the floor.

Her first rebellious act.

That evening, Matilde was happy to see Xavier return home early from work. She hugged him when he walked into the kitchen and was relieved to feel his arms wrap around her waist. This was his first show of affection since they had exchanged words several days earlier.

'I bought some good potatoes today. I cycled to the market near the tower.'

He placed his hat on the table. 'I'd heard that the cables to the lift in the tower had been purposefully cut before Hitler visited last month.' He sneered. 'I also heard that he declined to walk to the top.'

'Somebody walked up. There was an enemy flag hanging from the top.'

'They can cover it with as many of their ridiculous red and black flags as they like, but it won't make the tower theirs.'

Matilde decided to change the subject before he became agitated again. 'How was work today?'

In a swift movement he sat on the worktop. 'Another two students left. There are only eight in my class now. It's not looking good. I may soon be out of a job.'

Matilde bit her lip to prevent herself from worrying out loud about their earnings and how they would afford to remain in their apartment. She knew others suffered much greater hardships.

'Where do your students go?' she asked. 'How do they cross from the occupied zone into the south? I've heard there are roadblocks at every crossing point along the demarcation line.'

'Some manage to obtain passes and I know others are still here, in hiding. I've heard that Gideon Blum and his family have been arrested. He had amazing potential.' Xavier closed his eyes and inhaled, deep in thought. 'God forbid that he was killed in response to the shooting of that German scum.'

Matilde prodded the potatoes in the saucepan to see if they were softening. 'I saw the posters. It's dreadful.'

'I was speaking to the father of one of my students. He was telling me that he'd joined an underground movement.'

'What's one of those?'

'Groups of people meeting in secret to plan ways of causing disruption for the Germans.'

'Is that what you do at your meetings?'

'Not really. We just talk, but we like the idea of actually doing something to make life more difficult for them.'

'Please don't. Talking is one thing but actually doing something is dangerous.'

Xavier opened his mouth to speak but chewed his lip instead.

'What?' asked Matilde.

'We've invited him to our meeting tomorrow night.'

'Xavier! Why would you put yourselves in such danger?' She dried her hands on her apron.

'We're careful. Can't you understand that I want to do more than just talk?'

'What sort of things?'

'I don't know. Maybe we could sabotage their plans. Maybe disrupt transport or destroy stores. Small inconveniences could make a big impact.'

She retrieved cutlery from a drawer. Having placed the knives and forks on the worktop she sliced three flaccid carrots and wiped away an angry tear.

'Please don't,' said Xavier.

'How do you expect me to react?' She continued chopping. 'You're telling me that not only are you continuing to meet in secret, but you're inviting trouble along.'

'What do you want me to do? Hide? Do you want me to accept that we've lost our freedom and our right to go wherever we wish in our own country? Do you expect me to do nothing while our countrymen are being murdered? I don't understand you, Matilde.'

Matilde rested the knife on the worktop. She paused. 'They frighten me.'

She heard him sigh, and still sitting on the counter, he pulled her towards him. She felt his arms wrap around her shoulders as she rested her cheek on his chest. His heartbeat was strong.

'They are just men with weaknesses like all of us.'

She spoke against his shirt. 'But they're not weak. They have power over where we go and what we do. They kill innocent people.'

'We all have frailties – even them. Mine is fear of losing you and fear of losing my country. France has been weak and allowed the enemy in, but even though some Germans are evil bastards, they're also human. Beneath their uniforms, their buckles, badges and weapons, they have shortcomings and flaws like the rest of us. We must be careful, but I believe we can find those weaknesses and fight back secretly and silently.'

She held him more tightly, inhaling the scent of his body. She had missed his intimacy recently and the warm familiar smell of his skin felt sensual. She began to relax. When he explained things to her she always felt a little more secure, a little less vulnerable.

Loud knocking at the door made her jump.

3

MATILDE WAITED BY the stove while Xavier went to answer the door. It wasn't the soft tap-tap that Sylvie made when she visited. Standing motionless, she heard a man's voice. He was speaking French but with a distinctive accent. She squeezed the skirt of her apron until her knuckles were white.

Xavier appeared at the kitchen door. 'There's a German at the door. He wants to speak with you.'

Matilde's jaw dropped. She pointed to her own chest, her eyebrows rising in question.

Xavier nodded.

She shook her head rapidly, her eyes once again wide with anxiety.

Xavier spoke quietly. 'If you don't hear what he has to say, he will want to come inside to speak with you. Just listen to what he has to say and then he'll go.'

Matilde let go of her apron and rubbed her hands together. Her palms were damp and her heart was racing. Each step felt heavy as she walked out of the kitchen, across the living room and towards the front door.

She was startled when the German knocked his heels together with a loud click and bowed his head.

'Madame Pascale. Please excuse this interruption.'

Matilde nodded.

'May I step inside?'

She was caught off guard again. Turning, she looked at Xavier who was standing a short distance away. He mouthed, yes.

Matilde moved to one side and the soldier stepped into the room.

He smiled. 'Would it be possible to close the door? It would be good to speak in private.'

Matilde shut the front door. While the German was glancing around the room, she studied him. He was taller than both her and Xavier, with short fair hair. His face was tanned and his nose slightly sunburnt. His tapered trousers were tucked into boots and although his tunic was a dull grey, it glistened with polished silver buttons. She was shocked to think him quite handsome.

The soldier looked from Xavier to Matilde. 'Again, I must apologise for this late intrusion. My name is Sergeant Kemp. As I'm sure you must know, the museum in the public garden has been re-opened, although not to the public I must add. We will be using it to store certain items and we're in need of help to compile an inventory of objects and to record their movements. We are led to believe that you've recently left your post as a bookkeeper and we'd like to… let's say, *invite* you to take up this new position.'

Matilde wasn't sure that she had heard correctly. Was this German soldier offering her a job?

'Madame Pascale?'

'I think my wife is a little shocked,' said Xavier, stepping forwards.

Sergeant Kemp nodded. 'That's understandable.'

'When will you need this new position filling?' asked Xavier.

'Not until October, so perhaps we can speak again in a few weeks.' He looked at Matilde. 'Your close proximity to the museum and your qualifications make you perfect for the job, Madame Pascale.'

Matilde swallowed, her throat clicking noisily.

'Thank you, sergeant,' said Xavier, following him back to the door.

'I will be in touch again. Good evening.'

Matilde realised that she hadn't spoken a word since the German had knocked. Not only had she been left speechless by his unexpected visit but she was shocked to realise that he was an ordinary man: a polite, good-looking, ordinary man. Her perception had been very different because her imagination had been fuelled by rumours about these men. They were atrocity-mongers, hate-filled monsters that killed for sport. They were uncivilised barbarians who felt little or no sympathy for any living creature.

But this soldier didn't look like a monster. When she was younger, she and her friends would have nudged each other and giggled if they had seen such a man in the small village where they had grown up. Not that it changed anything. Paris was occupied and he was the enemy. There was no way that she would work for them.

She looked at Xavier who was still holding the door handle with his back to her. Expecting him to be outraged at the German's suggestion, he slowly turned with a smile stretching his lips.

'What?' she asked.

'This could be a perfect opportunity for us.'

'What could?'

'Don't you see?' He grinned and took hold of her hands, gently shaking them. 'You will have access to… who knows what information?' He let her hands drop and paced the room biting his fingernails. 'I must let Charles know.'

'Don't you mean Robert?' she said, sarcastically. 'I thought you all had aliases now.'

He looked up at her and blinked. 'Of course. You see. You're getting the idea.'

Matilde decided not to admit that she was being facetious. 'You can't seriously expect me to work for them. I'm not doing it, Xavier. You can't make such a decision for me.'

'But you must. This is a fantastic opportunity to learn more about their plans. I don't expect you to find out about any tactical military data, but you could have access to troop movements around the city and find out where they're based. This is so important. Besides, you heard him *invite* you to accept. Do you really think you have a choice in the matter?'

Matilde's head was spinning and her stomach churned. She turned, opened the front door and left the apartment. With tears stinging her eyes, she ran down the circular staircase. Once outside, she entered a side gate to the public gardens and marched along one of the gravel paths. She was angry. How could Xavier force her to work for them? He was too wrapped up in his stupid game of subterfuge and plotting. She checked her watch. It was half past six and the sun was still strong. She had an hour and a half before curfew so she crossed her legs and folded her arms, lost in thoughts of the recriminations and arguments she and Xavier had recently shared. Closing her eyes and raising her head, she saw a pattern of colours caused by the flickering sunlight. It glinted through the movement of the leaves and shone on her eyelids. Yellows. Reds. Greens.

A shadow blocked the warmth and light of the sun. Matilde's eyes snapped open. She sat up, startled at the silhouette of someone in front of her.

'Good evening,' said the shadow.

'Madame Fournier?'

'I'm sorry to disturb you.'

'It's fine. Please, sit down. It's nice to finally meet you.'

Her neighbour sat down on the bench next to her and Matilde turned sideways. She was surprised to notice that Madame Fournier was younger than she had imagined. Her eyes were green and, apart from a few creases around their edges, her skin was unlined. As always, she was wearing a scarf that covered her hair but it didn't hide the sallow colour of her face and hollow cheeks.

'I keep meaning to introduce myself,' said Matilde, 'but you know how it is. What with work and trying to buy food and, well…' She shrugged, feeling unkind for making excuses.

'I don't leave home much. I'm too afraid.'

Matilde felt an instant connection. Her immediate instinct was to help this slight, nervous woman who was sitting beside her. 'Is everything all right?' She laughed and touched her neighbour's sleeve. 'What a stupid question. Sorry. Of course everything isn't all right. What I mean is, can I help with anything?'

'My husband hasn't been home for five days. I don't know what to do.'

'Five days? Did he say where he was going?'

'He went looking for food but didn't return before curfew. I thought he might be hiding somewhere overnight but it has now been many days and I haven't heard from him.' She began to cry and wring her hands. 'I don't know anyone I can ask and the German soldiers are everywhere. I'm so frightened.'

Matilde took hold of her neighbour's hands. 'I'm not sure what I can do to help, but my husband knows many people. He could ask around.'

'Thank you. You're very kind.'

It felt good to reassure her. 'What's your name?'

'Ruth.'

'I'm Matilde. When did you last eat?'

Ruth shook her head, as if trying to remember. 'Yesterday morning.'

'Come home with me? I'll find you something and you can speak with my husband.' She could see Ruth's shoulders relax a little.

'Thank you. That would be wonderful.'

MATILDE OPENED THE door to their apartment and saw Xavier reading a newspaper. He didn't raise his head when she entered and she knew he was sulking.

'Come inside,' she said, holding the door wide. She closed it behind them.

Her invitation for Ruth to enter their apartment made Xavier lower his paper and look over his shoulder. He stood up when he realised a stranger was in the room.

'This is Ruth. She lives downstairs.'

Xavier came around the chair and stood next to them.

'This is my husband, Xavier,' said Matilde.

Xavier said hello and Ruth smiled in reply.

'I'm going to make a meal for us all,' said Matilde. 'Ruth was hoping that you could help find her husband. He's been missing for nearly a week and I told her you knew many people. Perhaps you could ask around at your university *meetings*.'

Matilde left them in the living room. Having scraped black skin from some vegetables, she chopped them up and boiled them. She could hear the hushed voices of her husband and Ruth in the living room and realised that she felt energised. She was being constructive and helping someone else, albeit in a small way.

4

October 1940

THE STEADY *KER-CHOFF ker-choff* of horses' hooves and the rumble of a cart's wheels on the Rue de Rivoli, disturbed Matilde. As she lay in bed, relaxing in that indistinct moment between sleep and wakefulness, she sensed the early morning light seeping through the shutters. Dawn had risen above the rooftops of Paris.

Her eyes snapped open. Today was the day she was starting her new job. Working for the Germans. Nausea twisted her stomach. She turned towards Xavier but his side of the bed was empty. She sat up, panicked.

'Xavier!'

Her husband appeared at the bedroom door, holding a tray in his hands. The aroma of coffee entered the room with him.

'I've scrambled you two eggs,' he said, walking towards the bed. 'I bought them from Gaston at the meeting last Friday. I wanted to make sure you ate before you left for the museum.'

'I can't.'

'You must try a bit.'

'I mean I can't do it.' Matilde wrung her hands together. 'I can't work for them.'

Xavier sat on the edge of the bed, resting the tray on his knees. 'We've talked about this for a couple of months now and you agreed that working in the museum could help many of our people. We're not asking you to do anything dangerous. You just need to do your job, but keep your ears and eyes open for any information that may be of help.' He handed her the cup of black coffee. 'Here, drink this.'

Matilde sipped the bitter drink. She rested the cup on the bedspread, her fingers still wound around its handle. 'I'm so nervous.'

Xavier smiled and rubbed her upper arm. 'Of course you are. Who doesn't feel nervous on their first day at a new job?' He placed the tray on her legs and propped a pillow behind her back. 'I'm very proud of you. Now eat your eggs, before I do!'

THE FIRST DAY of October had arrived with fog that rolled along the Seine. The air smelt of decaying leaves and damp grass as Matilde walked through the gardens of the Tuileries. She held a small lunch pail in one hand and clasped her woollen cloak around to her chest with the other. Silently berating herself for her trembling knees, she climbed the steps to the museum. Two German guards, with weapons slung over their shoulders, stood in front of the entrance door. A third man stood to one side with a clipboard. They didn't move when she approached.

Stay composed, she urged herself. 'My name is Matilde Pascale. I'm starting work here today.'

The man with the paperwork checked a list. He turned to one of the guards and gave a curt nod. He then beckoned her to go inside with a dismissive wave of his hand.

Matilde followed a guard along several corridors. Oblong shadows on walls betrayed where paintings had once hung. Now red flags with white circles and black swastikas decorated the interior. Occasionally men wearing Nazi military uniforms passed them and barked, '*Heil Hitler.*' She looked away, but the guard beside her returned the greetings.

They climbed a marble staircase and walked down a hallway before the guard unexpectedly stopped. Without knocking, he opened the door and gestured for her to go in. They had not exchanged a word in the few minutes it had taken to reach this office. Once she had taken a few steps inside, he closed the door and left.

She was standing in a small reception room. A desk stood in front of the window where a thin, middle-aged woman sat writing. She didn't look up, leaving Matilde to stand awkwardly for a few moments. A faint smell of cloying floral cologne hung in the air. Matilde walked towards the desk, already taking an instant dislike to the woman. Even with her shoes clicking on the wooden floor, the woman ignored her.

'Excuse me. My name is Matilde Pascale. I've been asked to report here this morning.'

'Just a moment.' The woman held up a hand to silence her and continued her work for a few moments. Finally, she put down her pen and looked up. She inspected Matilde with a sweeping glance. 'I wasn't expecting someone so young. How old are you?'

'Twenty-five.'

The woman sniffed. 'You look younger.' She stood up, scraping the chair on the floor. 'I suppose you must have passed all your security checks or you wouldn't be here. I hope you realise what an honour it is to work for the Germans in this magnificent building?'

The woman hesitated, maybe waiting for acknowledgment, but one wasn't forthcoming. It was difficult for Matilde to think of working for the enemy as an honour.

'My name is Gertrude Loup,' said the woman, 'and I've been asked to assist you with anything you need.'

Matilde saw Gertrude's lips purse and wrinkle, as if assisting the new employee was the last thing she wanted to do. It also dawned on her that this woman's post must be subordinate to hers, so it was likely that jealousy was playing a part in her aloofness.

'Thank you,' said Matilde.

The receptionist sniffed again and Matilde wondered if she had a cold or whether it was her way of showing her indifference. She watched the woman pat her greying shoulder-length hair and straighten her skirt, before asking Matilde to follow her. Gertrude took a few steps towards another door that led from the reception area. She knocked twice and tilted her head to listen.

Matilde heard a deep voice resonate from the other side of the door. She gripped her lunch pail even more tightly. Gertrude nodded at her to go inside.

Once inside, the receptionist smiled at a man who was standing beside the window, smoking a cigarette. The woman flexed her knees at the same time, giving Matilde the distinct impression that she was curtseying to the German. There was no doubt where this woman's allegiances lay. Matilde made a mental note not to share any information with this willing collaborator.

'Kommandant Beitel, this is the new assistant, Matilde Pascau.'

'Pascale,' Matilde corrected.

Gertrude shot her a look, her neck flushing with red blotches. She straightened her hair again and rested one hand against her throat.

'That will be all thank you, Gertrude,' said the Kommandant.

Matilde watched her leave the room a lot less reassured than she'd entered it.

The Kommandant laughed and pointed to the closed door. ‘You don’t want to make an enemy out of that one.’

The irony of his comment didn’t escape Matilde. She glanced around the room and hoped he couldn’t see her body shaking with nerves. The office was spacious. Eight dining chairs stood sentinel around a table piled high with paperwork, files and books. A sofa and two armchairs faced inwards towards a low coffee table where a half-full ashtray sat on the table. The Kommandant’s desk was set in front of the window.

‘Well, Matilde Pascale.’ He emphasized her surname. ‘Welcome to this wonderful building. I understand that you logged artwork in an auction house?’

Matilde studied him as he spoke. He was tall and impeccably dressed in his uniform. His dark hair was combed to one side, his nose was large and his lips were thick and fleshy. She couldn’t see his eyes as they were hidden behind the reflection on his wire-framed glasses. He spoke French well, but the harsh inflection of the German accent remained in his speech. The ash on his cigarette hung like a silver catkin, before falling on the carpet.

‘That’s correct.’

‘So, you should manage your new post admirably.’

Matilde nodded.

‘Did you work here in Paris?’

‘Yes.’

He moved to one of the sofas and sat down, gesturing her to sit in a nearby armchair. Matilde took off her coat, folded it across her arm and sat down. She placed her lunch pail on the arm of the chair.

‘What do you understand your new job to be?’ he asked.

‘I’m to make a record of items stored here for safekeeping.’

He chewed his bottom lip and removed his glasses. He leant

forwards with startlingly blue eyes that looked directly at her.

'Are you discreet?' he asked.

Matilde was taken aback. 'I'm sorry?'

'Can you be trusted not to talk about your job?'

'I… I believe I'm trustworthy.' She was cross with herself for stammering. For showing weakness.

He paused, still scrutinizing her. 'This job is highly secretive. You will speak to no one about what or whom you see here, or there will be consequences. Do you understand me clearly, Madame Pascale?'

Matilde nodded.

'You have passed all your security checks and have come highly recommended from an acquaintance of Officer Kemp. You will be given a pass that will allow you to access an area where we store an important collection of artifacts. Only a handful of people who work in this building and some high officials in Paris are aware of the exceptional importance attached to these items. The Führer himself wants to see this inventory and hopes to open a museum with this collection.'

Matilde could feel sweat dampen her back. Adolf Hitler had been mentioned in this conversation and she felt distinctly light-headed. She dug her nails into the palm of her right hand and willed herself to stop shaking.

'Discretion is essential, Madame Pascale?' A vein throbbed on his neck as he stared at her, unblinking.

'Yes, sir.'

He sat up straight and slapped his knees. 'Good.'

Matilde jumped, knocking her lunch off the arm of the chair. She fumbled on the floor for the metal box.

'I'll show you to your office where you can familiarize yourself. I've several meetings today, so you will begin listing the items tomorrow.'

The German stood up and she followed him back out into the reception area. Madame Loup was sitting at her desk reading correspondence. He continued out of the reception area and Matilde felt relieved that she wouldn't be sharing a room with that unfriendly woman.

THE MATTRESS DIPPED as Xavier climbed into bed beside Matilde. She'd felt his hand seek hers and her eyes grow heavy with the comforting touch of their entwined fingers. They'd eaten turnip stew earlier while discussing her first day at the museum. Despite her anxieties, imaginings about what treasures lay hidden deep inside the museum teased her curiosity as her mind drifted into sleep.

A noise. Her heart immediately beat faster as she was abruptly awoken. The air raid siren was wailing above the Parisian rooftops and in through the casement windows. Still in a state of torpor, Matilde reached for her dressing gown, slipped her feet into her shoes and clasped the hand that Xavier offered. She walked with him down to the ground floor, through a doorway and down a further flight of stone steps into the cellar.

In a matter of minutes, the residents of the building were sitting in the cramped cellar. A bare light bulb lit the interior and swayed slightly, throwing shadows around the walls. Having greeted each other, everyone was lost in their own silent thoughts. The only sound came from the occasional shuffle of people's legs, empty grumbling stomachs and a moth flitting around the bulb. Matilde and Xavier were sitting together opposite Ruth and Sylvie, each using makeshift chairs from crates or upturned buckets.

'I'll make it a bit more comfortable in here,' said Xavier, to no one in particular. 'I could find some old chairs. No doubt we'll be down here a few more times yet.'

'Perhaps we should keep a supply of water in here too,' said Sylvie. 'We could be here a while.'

'And candles,' said Matilde, patting Ruth's clasped hands.

Her neighbour gave a tight-lipped smile. She was sitting forwards on a large paint tin, hugging her knees. Since Matilde had met her in the public gardens two months earlier, there had been no news about Ruth's husband. At least they spoke to each other now, and occasionally she and Xavier would share a meal with her.

Footsteps could be heard hurrying down the stairwell. The group in the cellar looked up with questioning frowns. Only Sylvie kept her head lowered. Just as Matilde was about to ask whom it might be, thuds and vibrations from bombs finding their targets, sent cement dust falling from the ceiling. The light bulb flickered and the cellar was momentarily plunged into darkness. Within seconds, its pale yellow light illuminated the wide-eyed residents once again.

5

CORPORAL HANS ENGEL was typing at his desk when his commander opened the office door. Hans made a move to stand but his senior gestured for him to remain seated.

'You're being reassigned, Engel.'

Hans tensed. Please God he wasn't being sent to the front. 'Where to, sir?'

'Central Paris. They need your knowledge of art at the Jeu de Paume. The Führer has acquired a great number of treasures that need cataloguing. You're to work alongside a civilian who's been employed there.'

Hans stood up. 'A civilian, sir? A French civilian?'

His senior smirked. 'We're in France, Engel. What do you think?'

Before he could continue, his commander had turned and closed the door. Hans sat down with his head in his hands. He'd known it would be unlikely that he could spend the war in the quiet town of Bussy Saint-Légeron on the outskirts of Paris, but it suited him. This town was nestled in countryside and dense forests, a place that reminded him of his hometown in the Black Forest. He ripped the sheet of paper from the typewriter, screwed it into a ball and threw it at the waste paper bin. It bounced off the metal rim and rolled onto the floor.

The following week, moments after stepping off the train at

Gare D'Orsay, Hans looked across at the Seine's bridges and numerous stalls along its banks. As he walked further outside the station, the Louvre and Notre Dame came into sight, each bathed in the afternoon sunshine. Swinging his bag over his shoulder, he walked towards the Pont Royal where he stopped and leaned against its parapet wall. He watched the changing shapes of the water as it created eddies and currents around the solid structure of the bridge. He noticed a measure fixed to one of the arches and was interested to read the levels of past floods. Alongside him stood a fisherman, eyes closed against the low autumn sun and with skin as thin and translucent as the membrane of an egg. The fisherman coughed, opened his eyes and pinched a fleck of tobacco from his tongue. He looked towards Hans, curled his lips in distaste and muttered to himself.

Hans continued along towards the Latin Quarter, the sound of his hobnail boots announcing his whereabouts. Having crossed the bridge, he noticed that the streets were wider and busier with market stalls selling meagre supplies of flaccid vegetables. An elderly woman swept rubbish from between the chairs of a café, pushing debris of leaves and cigarette ends towards the gutter. She looked up at him, spat on the floor and disappeared back inside the coffee shop.

Hans knew he was despised, but what did he expect? Germany had occupied their country and his uniform revealed him as a German soldier. It didn't matter to them that he detested this war as much as they did. He had visited Paris twice before, once with a girlfriend and once on his own. On both occasions he had absorbed the beauty of the city with its history, cathedrals and architecture. He'd embraced its wildness, love songs, street artists and coffee houses. It was all very different now. Hans sat down at one of the pavement tables. None of the other cafés would welcome him either so he may as well sit here, he thought.

He ordered a black coffee and lit a cigarette, inhaling deeply before blowing out a long white cloud of smoke.

A young woman at a market stall caught his attention. At first it was her slender legs that made him notice her, but then he saw her hair. It was long and flowing, the colour of autumn leaves. Her face was pale and beautiful, even though her mouth was twisted with concentration as she bit her bottom lip. He watched her squeeze, then smell a turnip, before replacing it. A gust caught her coat, opening it to reveal a dress as blue as cornflowers.

He blinked as his coffee was banged on the table in front of him. The old woman turned her back and walked into the café without saying a word. Hans took a sip and looked up to where the woman had been standing. The breeze slipped through the linden trees and rustled the bill that had been placed beneath his saucer. She had gone.

THE FOLLOWING MORNING, Hans pushed open the shutters at the window of his hotel room. The sky was turning from white to a glorious blue as the sun rose over the rooftops. He had been ordered to stay at this rundown hotel on Rue de Lille, a road running parallel to the river, until a nearby apartment had been made ready for him. That morning he was to start work in the *Galerie Nationale du Jeu de Paume.* He lit a cigarette, wishing he could work alone instead of alongside some miserable Frenchman.

Having eaten a dark bread and liverwurst sandwich that he'd brought with him from his previous accommodation, Hans stood in front of a mottled mirror. The anxious eyes of a Wehrmacht Corporal stared back. He had been reassigned. He had no choice. Touching the lump beneath his shirt, Hans felt his ID tags before straightening the lapel on his jacket and leaving the room.

The passageway smelt of body odour and the subtle aromas of last night's meals. Along the corridors were deep gouges where luggage had been dragged removing paint and plasterwork. The threadbare carpet ended at the main staircase where the stone steps had been worn smooth over time, each tread now softened with curved edges.

Outside the sun had painted the boulevard with a broad brush, highlighting the street lamps that had been stained blue, as ordered by the German Occupation Authority. The street was empty apart from a short SS lieutenant who was reaching up to light the cigarette of his blonde companion. Hans had no interest in women who slept with men solely for their own gain. He knew that French women who allowed Germans to escort them were playing a dangerous game with their fellow countrymen, but he assumed that the lure of better food and occasional gifts made the weak and greedy succumb.

At the entrance of the Pont Royal, he passed a colourful poster announcing performances by the Berlin State Opera. Sprinkled around it on the floor were broken v-shaped matchsticks left behind by people who had stopped to read it. Once across, Hans walked along the Rue de Rivoli, a wide street vital for the movement of the city's population. And yet, apart from a German car overtaking a cyclist, it was quiet here too. On his previous visits to Paris, even narrow streets would be bustling with energy and laughter. It had been a time of interesting conversation, beautiful women to admire, fine food and wine to enjoy. Now, he was one of many to be blamed for this husk of a city.

Soon he was standing at a junction. In front of him on the Place de la Concorde was the *Hôtel de Crillon*, now German headquarters and where he had been ordered to report at nine o'clock. Hans shaded his eyes from the sun, taking in the magnificent architecture. Giant pillars of pale stone stood to attention in front of its façade. Huge windows reflected the sky, and the wide building's roof was punctuated on each end with huge triangular tympanums. German standards hung at angles from poles in front of the building.

With slight trepidation, he entered the building and walked across the marble chequered floor towards the desk, his boots clicking on the veined tiles with each step. The reception area was immense and ornate, with chandeliers, columns and beautiful furnishings. It smelt of cigarette smoke, coffee and mothballs.

'Good morning. I have a meeting with Officer Heinrich.'

A uniformed woman looked up. 'Name?'

'Corporal Hans Engel.'

She held out her hand. 'Papers.'

Hans passed her his military papers for inspection. The woman conscientiously checked them, handed them back and made a telephone call. Hans walked a short distance from the desk, his hands clasped behind his back, hoping to give the impression of a calm exterior, while absorbing his surroundings. His damp palms and increased heart rate secretly belied this. Several officers walked past him, causing him to snap to attention and salute. He was thinking about lighting a cigarette when a soldier in a grey-green SS service tunic walked towards him.

'Corporal Engel?'

'Yes.'

'Follow me, please.'

Hans followed him along wide sumptuous corridors filled with ornate panelling and walls interspersed with paintings, each framed with carved wood and decorated in gold leaf. At regular intervals hung yet more swastika flags, their dark colour in stark contrast to the cream and gold decoration. The soldier stopped at a door, saluted and left. Hans turned towards the arched door. He knocked and waited.

'*Herein!*'

Hans obeyed and entered. The room was more typically a working office, filled with filing cabinets, paperwork and books arranged along shelving.

'Engel?'

Hans saluted, bringing his heels together. 'Yes, sir.'

'Come in. Sit down.'

Hans sat in the proffered seat, his damp shirt pressing against the back of the chair.

'Where are you from, Engel?'

'Heidelberg, sir.'

The officer nodded slowly. 'Beautiful place. I'm sure you miss it.'

'Yes. It sometimes feels unreal to be occupying Paris.'

The officer's expression changed; somehow darkened. His features became more concentrated and watchful.

Hans quickly corrected himself. 'Unreal, but justified, of course. It's an honour to be chosen to work on the Führer's collection.'

The officer's smile returned. 'Indeed. Cigarette?'

Hans accepted the tobacco and lit both his and his superior's cigarettes. He heard it crackle as he sucked deeply, heady with relief.

Officer Heinrich walked towards the window, his back turned to Hans. 'Tell me a little about yourself, Engel.'

Hans pinched his nose and adjusted his position in his chair. 'I'm thirty-one. I studied French and the history of art in Munich. I worked in an art gallery for several years before conscription in 1935. Since serving in France, I've mainly been based at Bussy Saint-Légeron where I've been translating paperwork, but I've also been required to value retrieved items from raids.'

'Perfect,' said the officer, turning to face him. 'You are just the man I need to accompany a very important visitor on a tour of our collections, tomorrow morning.'

Hans nodded, once. 'Yes, sir.'

'Do you own a better uniform?'

Hans looked down at his tunic. It was a little worn at the wrists and the material had faded slightly, but his uniform was perfectly clean and functional. 'I brought a second uniform with me, sir. It's newer than this one.'

Officer Heinrich stubbed out his cigarette. 'Good. Wear it tomorrow. This visitor is one of the Führer's senior officers, so I want you to see to his every wish.'

Hans wondered who the visitor might be, but despite his trepidation, he was excited to view the paintings that were stored at the museum across the road. Gazing into a painting helped him to find himself *and* lose himself. For him, viewing art allowed time to slow, the rush of life to soften and the noise to mellow. 'When may I see the artwork, sir?'

'I will personally show you this afternoon. It is a sight to behold, Engel.'

Hans had no doubt that the artwork had been stolen from other museums or private collectors. A confusing mixture of distaste and longing churned in his stomach.

Officer Heinrich continued. 'Our leader has issued a law stating that every piece of abandoned art will fall under his direct control. He intends to display works of classical art and antiques in the *Führermuseum*, a cultural centre that he plans to build in Austria.'

'Yes, sir.'

The officer returned to his seat and leaned forwards on his elbows, his fingers held against his lips as if in prayer. 'Members of the High Command will occasionally visit the museum to choose some art for their own personal collections. Next month our first esteemed visitor will honour us with his presence and will also be choosing some pieces for himself.'

Hans tried not to show his shock at this appalling act of greed. 'May I ask who our visitor will be, sir?

'Reichsmarschall Hermann Göring.'

6

MATILDE WAS LATE for work. She hurried along garden pathways of the Tuileries having lingered in Xavier's arms a little too long before rising. As she approached the museum, swastikas snapped and flicked in the wind, their cords rattling against their flagstaffs. It seemed to her that the number of banners in the city had doubled as the population diminished. It was as if the Germans were replacing each fleeing French citizen with a flag. Parisians that remained were forbidden from using public spaces, the very same parks and squares where they had grown up. Matilde felt that the Germans had multiplied the oppressive effect of being occupied. Buildings had grown tyrannical, days longer and the Seine, blacker.

It was Friday and the end of her fifth week. Matilde's shoes clicked along the museum's corridors, yellowed with subdued lighting, before setting about her morning routine in her small office. At least she didn't have to sit with Gertrude Loup. Small blessings. She turned on an electric heater and heard it begin to click as the elements heated. She knew from experience that it would be half an hour before the room was warm enough to remove her coat.

Matilde laid out a suede mat for examining each piece of jewelry, removed the cover of her typewriter and polished her magnifying glass. She breathed on the glass and rubbed it against the hem of her skirt. Just as she was about to leave and collect another box to be sifted through, Kommandant Beitel and another man walked into her office. She had only seen the Kommandant a handful of times since their first meeting, and silently berated herself for blushing in surprise.

He looked at her, his features showing no emotion. His back was straight and his chin was raised. 'Good morning, Madame Pascale. I trust you are well?'

Matilde laid the magnifying glass on her desk. 'Very well, thank you, Herr Beitel.'

The Kommandant gave a quick nod. 'The amount of valuables we've been receiving has risen significantly. This is Corporal Hans Engel. He's been assigned to assist you.'

She looked at the tall man at the Kommandant's side and smiled in simple reflex. Immediately she felt ashamed. In that instant of introduction, she had been transported back to her life before war, where manners and smiles were commonplace. She had dropped her guard; lost her concentration. Corporal Engel didn't return her smile, in fact his expression was almost one of surprise. His hair was fair and pushed to one side at the front, like the wing of a gull. He looked young, but an ageing v-shaped frown sat between his blue eyes. He wore a look of resignation about him, as if working alongside her wasn't his idea of a substantial enough contribution for the German war effort. She blinked when he suddenly bowed his head in greeting. Something jangled in the worn leather bag he was holding.

'I have a busy morning, so I will leave Corporal Engel to show you where you'll both be working for the time being. Good morning, Madame Pascale.'

Matilde watched the Kommandant leave her office. His footsteps receded down the corridor, leaving an uncomfortable silence hanging in the air.

'Well… ' began Matilde, trying to make an effort at polite conversation. It seemed that ingrained good manners were a difficult habit to break.

Corporal Engel interrupted her. 'This way.' He turned and left the room.

She hurried to catch up with him as he marched down the corridor in the opposite direction to the Kommandant. On reaching a staircase, he shoved the leather bag beneath his arm and took a crumpled packet of cigarettes out of his pocket, removed one and lit it. Matilde followed him downstairs. Her body was turned slightly to one side because her restrictive brown pencil skirt was making movement difficult on the steps. She held on to the handrail, sliding her fingers down the smooth wood and praying he wouldn't look back at her because the hem of her tight skirt was riding above her knees as she descended. She inhaled the bitter smoke left in the soldier's wake. Three floors below, he paused and waited for her to catch up. She saw him pinch a speck of tobacco from his tongue with his thumb and forefinger before sucking once more on his cigarette's diminishing length.

Despite having worked at the museum for more than a month, Matilde still felt out of her depth. It wasn't that she couldn't organize an inventory or recognize the majority of gemstones and artists, but the sheer amount of treasures was overwhelming. Her mornings were spent sifting through jewelry: rings, bracelets, necklaces, earrings and watches. She made use of a measuring gauge, a Zeiss Ikon camera and a book filled with photographs of gems and precious stones for ease of identification. Occasionally she would come across a stone she couldn't find pictured on any page. These were placed inside a velveteen bag that was collected daily; she had no idea where they were destined, presumably to be examined by a more qualified eye. It didn't stop her puzzling over where they'd come from, especially when she prized open lockets with her fingernail to reveal sepia photographs of family members. Perhaps their owners had sold them in order to feed their families.

Every afternoon she would type up the inventory that she had scribbled on sheets of paper and at the end of each day, Gertrude Loup would collect these typed lists. Occasionally Matilde would make her wait in front of her desk, as she herself had been made to wait on her first day. It amused her to see Gertrude's jaw tighten with annoyance, her lips pursing and stretching as if sucking sherbet.

At the bottom of the staircase, two guards opened double doors and stood to attention, arms extended and palms straight. '*Heil Hitler*.' They spoke in unison. Corporal Engel responded. She prayed that she wouldn't be spending too much time with this ill-disposed German. He marched ahead, lithe and square-shouldered. His uniform fit him well and was pressed sharply, with just a frown of wrinkles puckered behind the knees of his trousers, disclosing the fact that he'd been sitting earlier.

They walked along a corridor lined with empty display cases and shelves covered in layers of dust. The walls were studded with oblong smudges of accumulated grime, ghosts of missing paintings. Eventually the passage widened into a foyer where more armed soldiers stood at intervals around the tiled space. Corporal Engel walked towards a solid mahogany desk behind which sat a double-chinned soldier lost in his own cloud of tobacco smoke. The walrus of a soldier coughed and the two men exchanged a few sentences.

Corporal Engel turned and beckoned to her. She followed him to a wide, metal door. Two armed men moved aside as he removed the bag from beneath his arm and retrieved a ring of keys from inside. He inserted one in the keyhole and turned it.

There was a loud click. He pushed open the door and walked inside, turning to look at her by way of asking her to follow. She stepped through the doorway.

An aroma of beeswax, old books and damp material hung in the air as her eyes slowly adjusted to the dim light. The soldier's footsteps echoed with each stride, leading her to believe that this was a large room. But when he pressed several switches and light flooded the space, Matilde caught her breath. The room was vast. It was even bigger than Monsieur Lombard's main saleroom at the auction house. It was two stories high and as wide as the *Vue du Jardin* building where she lived. Makeshift shelving and storage racks had been erected in long rows, each one laden with objects.

'What is this place?' she asked.

The German spread his arms wide. 'This is one of many storage facilities ordered by the Führer.'

'One of many?' She took a few steps further, stopping at an ornate table with barley twist legs. Red material had been draped over its surface, but much of its colour was hidden beneath a pile of glistening valuables: gold fountain pens, silver cutlery, goblets, watches, picture frames, candlesticks and oddly, spectacles. She turned to the German.

'Where has all this come from?'

He gave her a look that she couldn't decipher, before walking towards the far side of the room. 'This way.'

Matilde hugged her arms against the chill and followed him. She could hear grit scrape beneath his soles. He stopped in front of different sized boxes, each draped with thick sacking. He pulled a length of hessian away with a flourish, as if wielding a bullfighter's cloak. They weren't boxes. They were paintings stacked against each other. Some had ornate frames of polished wood or feathered with gold leaf. Others were frameless, paint exposed on naked canvas. Wherever would she begin?

LATER THAT DAY, Matilde was ordered to leave work early due to a visit by a high-ranking member of the Gestapo. She supposed they didn't want the possibility of a Parisian eavesdropping on their secret plans and anyway, she was relieved to escape the claustrophobic atmosphere of the basement and the questioning eyes of Corporal Engel.

Outside the sky was the colour of watered-down milk and a breeze carried the scent of wood-smoke. Before the war Matilde had loved autumn with its glow of streetlights reflecting on rain-drenched boulevards and the promise of Christmas, but now, Paris in November simply appeared insipid and dirty. Windows wore a coat of neglect and paintwork was dulled with grime. Even the railings of the *Tuileries* reminded her of ribs instead of ornate metalwork. Perhaps this time next year the war would be over. Maybe festive lights would illuminate the avenues with colour once again.

Matilde wrapped her coat tightly around her body and hurried home with thoughts of Xavier and hot onion soup cheering her mood. But as she approached the entrance to the Vue du Jardin, she slowed her pace. She saw a French gendarme salute a German officer with submissive servility. Stiff and mechanical, already infused with German traits. It hadn't taken that Frenchman long to surrender. With her next breath, a creeping realisation made her stop and clutch a railing. Who was she to condemn this French policeman? Didn't she work for the Germans? She was as bad as him. Yes, it was against her will, but she was still collaborating. France *must* fight back. *She* must fight back. If everyone relied on others to retaliate, nothing would change. France would willingly succumb to the enemy, one person at a time. She vowed to support Xavier more actively from now on.

A shout. Her head shot up. Sharp, guttural commands were being barked nearby. The sound of an engine grew louder. She pressed her back against the railings. A truck sped past and braked sharply outside the entrance door to her apartment building. Raised voices echoed inside the doorway. Matilde's breath came in gasps and she could feel her heart thumping as she pressed her knuckles to her lips. The French policeman and the German officer ran across the road towards the noise. So, their meeting hadn't been a coincidence. They were working alongside each other. She stayed where she was, partly hidden behind a large evergreen shrub and skeletal branches that draped over the metal fencing. What was happening inside the building where she lived? Had someone run inside to hide and had been discovered?

She watched wide-eyed as several Germans scuffled with a man. They had found who they were looking for. The man was bare-chested and hunched forwards. He stumbled despite being grasped by uniformed men. They dragged him to his feet. Blood covered his body. The French policeman opened the back door to the truck. *Traitor!* The prisoner gave one final attempt to retaliate and as he did so, he raised his head.

Xavier!

7

MATILDE RAN ACROSS the road into the path of a cyclist, leaving him shouting abuse beside the kerb after a near collision.

'Xavier! No. No.' She could see the men dragging him towards the back of the van. She wouldn't reach him in time. Fear jabbed at her chest. 'Wait. Xavier. No.'

He had heard her. She saw him look up and shout something back. He looked different. His face was swollen.

'Xavier. I didn't hear. Where are they taking you?'

With her arms outstretched she reached the group of arresting officials, but before she could touch her husband, a sudden impact and blinding pain caused her to reel sideways. Her legs buckled beneath her and for a few seconds she lay dazed on the ground. When she looked up, the French policeman was jabbing a finger towards her.

'Get up before he's gone and you'll join him.'

Xavier was shouting expletives at the man who had assaulted her and across the road several people had stopped to observe from a safe distance. Matilde watched her husband being shoved backwards, but he held onto the truck's doors and shouted, 'Mon chapeau.' The door was slammed shut and Xavier was driven away.

Too shocked to cry, Matilde stayed on the freezing pavement

feeling numb. The crowd lowered their heads and dispersed. Moments later, a warm hand took hers. She could smell Sylvie's expensive perfume before she saw her friend. Floral scents seemed out of place at this moment – almost an insult.

'Let's get you inside,' said Sylvie.

With some effort, Matilde stood up and allowed herself to be led upstairs. The lift had been out of order for several weeks with little chance of repair in the near future. Matilde felt the area of skin between her right cheek and temple. It ached and felt sore from the impact. 'They've taken Xavier away.'

'I know. I saw. It's awful.'

'Why? Did they say why?'

They reached the first landing and Matilde stopped. Ruth's door had been forced open and was hanging from its hinges. Splinters littered the floor and she could see that furniture had been upturned. Not waiting for Sylvie's answer, she rushed inside.

'Ruth.'

'Matilde,' called Sylvie.

'Are you here, Ruth?' She ran into the bedroom. The bed was unmade. The pillows still indented.

'Matilde, she's not—'

'She might still be hiding from them. Help me look.' She pushed aside a bedside table that was lying on its side. A watch fell to the floor. Xavier had one similar.

'They arrested her, too,' said Sylvie.

Matilde turned. She looked at her friend and slowly shook her head.

'I'm sorry. I tried pleading with them but they threatened me,' said Sylvie.

'What happened?'

'Come upstairs. You need a brandy.'

The two women walked up to the next floor.

'You go inside your apartment and sit down while I run upstairs and fetch the bottle,' said Sylvie.

Matilde turned the key, surprised that the door was still locked. She'd expected to find devastation similar to Ruth's apartment, but everywhere was in order. She undid her coat and took it off, throwing it across the arm of a chair before sitting down. Her head ached. She leant forwards and covered her face with her palms. Had they found out about Xavier's meetings? How could she find out where he'd been taken?

Finally the shock of the last ten minutes hit her. She felt a wave of heat followed by a bitter taste in her throat. She flung herself out of her chair and ran to the bathroom where she fell to her knees in front of the toilet basin and retched. It was several minutes before she felt well enough to rinse her mouth and leave the bathroom.

She heard Sylvie's footsteps coming down the stone steps before her friend entered, carrying two glasses and a bottle of copper-coloured liquid.

'I don't understand how our apartment is untouched,' said Matilde. 'Xavier was struggling and covered in blood. It doesn't make sense.'

Sylvie sat down and poured a measure into each glass. 'He wasn't here when they came.'

Matilde grimaced as the brandy stung her mouth. 'Where was he?'

'He was downstairs in Ruth's apartment.'

Matilde stood up. 'So it was just bad timing that he was arrested? That means they'll release him as soon as they see his identity papers.' She began to pace the room, feeling more hopeful. 'He must have taken Ruth some food. He does that sometimes while I'm at work. Not that it's much but if the Jews don't have it tough enough already, they're now being forced to shop at the end of the day when the food's gone.' She stopped pacing and turned to Sylvie. 'Surely they're not taking Jews from their homes now?'

'Don't be naïve, Matilde.' Sylvie tipped her head back and drained her glass. 'And there's no need to look at me like that. You work for the Germans so don't tell me that you don't know what's going on. Jews are being sent to work camps and their valuables confiscated. What do you think you're making an inventory of every day?'

Matilde looked at Sylvie. 'I'm not naïve. I know the Germans have stolen them from abandoned houses. I know they're heartless thieves.'

'For God's sake, they're not taking things from deserted buildings. There's a campaign of organized theft from Jewish houses and businesses. The Nazis are killing or arresting Jews then seizing their property and taking their valuables.'

Matilde sat down slowly. She had kept a low profile at work, keeping her head down for a quiet life. She never asked questions. What Sylvie was saying would explain the strange expression on Corporal Engel's face when she asked where all the treasures had come from.

'My God,' she whispered.

Her breaths came in short, shallow gasps. The jewellery, paintings and artefacts stored beneath the museum, were family heirlooms belonging to victims. She sorted through them each day as if she had bought a job lot at an auction house, admiring many items before logging and wrapping them. Not only that, but she was being paid for sifting through their personal treasures. Paid by the Germans.

'My God,' she repeated.

'You seriously didn't know?'

Matilde snapped. 'Of course I didn't. She held her head

again. 'I have a headache. I need a little time alone for to make sense of things. Thank you for helping me and for the brandy, but I need time to think.'

'Of course.' Sylvie stood up. 'Do you know any of Xavier's associates? Maybe I can get in touch with them for you and find out why the Germans are interested in him.'

'He hasn't worked at the university for months. Who knows where his colleagues have gone now? South if they have any sense.'

'I remember you telling me that Xavier met friends some evenings.'

Matilde tried not to show her surprise. Surely she hadn't mentioned Xavier's secret meetings to Sylvie. To anyone. 'I've no idea what he does when he goes out.'

'Don't worry. It was just a thought. Let me know if I can help with anything. I'll call in on you tomorrow evening and see if he's back home. Keep your chin up.'

THE FOLLOWING SUNDAY afternoon Xavier had still not arrived home. Matilde now realised how much she'd underestimated the situation both at the museum and with the harassment of the Jews. Had she pretended not to notice things escalating on the streets or was she just as guileless as Sylvie was suggesting? She had befriended Ruth and shamefully felt as if she was doing her bit for the Jews, but she may as well have been trying to douse an inferno with a cup of water. She should have done more to help both Xavier and Ruth.

Sylvie's accusatory remark about her working for the Germans had made her feel more ashamed than ever. But hadn't it been Xavier's idea that she took the job so she could pick up small bits of information to pass on to him? It was all such a mess.

She began to run through the images of Xavier's arrest once again, touching her sore cheek as she did so. She relived the screech of the police van's tyres, Xavier's struggle and his rough manhandling as he was pushed inside the vehicle. Why had he mentioned his hat at such an inappropriate moment?

Matilde leant against the back of the armchair and closed her eyes. She could hear the tap dripping in the kitchen and the pipes gurgling as if someone was running a bath in the building. It must be Sylvie. Who else was left?

The more she thought, the more she realised just how incongruous the mention of his hat had been. It was either a message for her or he'd been knocked senseless during his beating. He kept his hat on the bedpost. She stood up and went into their bedroom. There it was. She picked it up and turned it over several times. It was a worn cloth cap in a herringbone pattern in many shades of brown. Matilde turned it inside out. Nothing seemed out of the ordinary, but when she turned it back again, she felt a thickness on one section of the hem. She hurried into the kitchen, retrieved a penknife from a drawer and began to unpick the stitching. She laid the hat on the counter and eased a piece of card out of the hem. There was a telephone number written on it.

8

MONDAY HAD BEEN a strange day at work with Matilde being unable to concentrate. Not only had she struggled with the thought that Xavier and Ruth were still missing, but the previous evening she had used a public telephone to call the number found in her husband's hat. She was to meet someone at six that evening and that thought had taken her appetite all day.

It was 11th November and Armistice Day. A day when Parisians commemorated the end of the last war and remembered those who had died for their country. Xavier had always taken flowers to the Tomb of the Unknown Soldier at the Place de l'Etoile on this day, so Matilde decided to go in his place and hopefully she would be able to tell him about it in a few days' time. She'd make him proud.

Matilde knew she was taking a risk. For the past few weeks, anti-German inscriptions had been scrawled on walls and leaflets had been pasted on buildings calling people to unite on this day. The German authorities had responded with a ban on all forms of commemorative demonstration.

She left the museum at five, surreptitiously picking several stalks of ruby Photinia hedging. The remaining flowers in the borders of the Tuileries looked withered and brown and she wasn't prepared to spend money on flowers instead of food. She hurried towards the Place de la Concorde, surprised at the number of people on the streets. She knew that many Parisians were returning to the capital and schools were reopening, but it was still startling to see so many people in one place.

Surprisingly, most of the crowd was chanting and laughing, but perhaps the fact that they were all disobeying German orders made them a little giddy. A siren startled her as it erupted on the far side of the Seine but she kept walking, jostling through the crowd. The atmosphere was similar to that of a carnival rather than a sombre protest. Somewhere a single soprano voice was singing *La Marseillaise*. Matilde's throat tightened, overwhelmed with sadness and affection on hearing France's anthem. A ripple of voices joined in and suddenly she was surrounded by singing and joined in the last few lines herself. She vowed silently that whatever happened in the future, she would always remember this moment.

Many demonstrators wore blue, white and red, waved tricolour flags and held banners aloft, declaring, '*Vive la France.*' The crowd continued to grow as students left schools and universities, and spilled from smaller side roads into the path of the growing demonstration. Matilde was moved along by the footfall of the crowd. Slogans had been drawn in chalk on pavements along with symbols of the Cross of Lorraine; white etchings of defiance on black tarmac. Cafés were closed and their street furniture stacked inside locked front doors. Were they expecting violence?

'Matilde!'

Matilde scanned the heads of the crowd until she saw a hand waving. It was Adrienne, a teacher who had worked at the same university as Xavier. Matilde weaved and jostled her way sideways, across the flow of people. Adrienne grasped her hand and pulled her away from the maelstrom of moving bodies. They gasped for breath on the pavement and hugged each other.

'It's so good to see you,' said Adrienne.

'And you. How have you been?'

Adrienne shrugged. 'Hungry. Angry. Worried sick. It looks like we've both lost weight.' Her friend lifted her cardigan to reveal a length of string tying her loose skirt around her waist.

Matilde nodded but didn't reveal her waistband that had been hastily pinned that morning. It was so good to see a friendly face. Adrienne was an attractive woman with naturally fair hair; only the fact that her nose was a little too big for her face prevented her from being beautiful. Matilde wiped away an unexpected tear.

'Whatever's the matter? Is something wrong?'

'I wouldn't know where to begin.' It was ironic, thought Matilde. People become used to a different way of life so quickly. Their city had been taken over by an enemy and Adrienne was asking whether something was wrong. Yes. Her life had been shaken like a child's snow globe. Her husband and friend were missing, she was always cold and hungry and somehow she was now working for the enemy. 'It's just so good to speak to someone I knew before all this.' Matilde waved her arm in an expansive arc, as if encompassing Paris in its entirety. 'Xavier was arrested last Friday.'

Adrienne's fingertips went to her lips. 'No! Why?'

'He was taking some food to a neighbour. Her husband went missing months ago. She's Jewish, so was too afraid to venture out much. I think he was in the wrong place at the wrong time.'

A group of students walked past them, one of them shouting into a crackling loudhailer. 'De Gaulle. De Gaulle. De Gaulle.' His friends repeated his chant so that Matilde and Adrienne were silenced by the commotion. They stood and watched as more people converged on the Champs-Élysées and the Place de l'Etoile, marching in small groups or in processions that were quite dense one minute and fragmented the next. Voices of hostility were directed at the occupier and cries for General de Gaulle were shouted with passion. They watched a man climb onto the base of street lamp for a better vantage point in order to throw leaflets into the crowd.

Adrienne called over the noise, taking Matilde's hand. 'Come this way.'

The two women hurried along the pavement where Matilde noticed German soldiers posted in several cafés and a cinema foyer. Watching. The mayhem subsided when she entered a narrow alleyway. It smelt of urine but it was quiet enough to hear each other.

'Let's get out of here. Come back with me. I've made soup from a chicken leg and turnips,' said Adrienne. 'Albert and I broke up last year. I could do with some company.'

Matilde was torn. The thought of chicken soup made her mouth water and she swallowed involuntarily. The thought of friendly company was equally as appealing. But she couldn't. She needed to find out more about the men that Xavier used to meet, but something prevented her from telling Adrienne. No one trusted anyone these days; yet another consequence of war.

'I can't this evening. I have to be somewhere at six. I can make tomorrow, though.' Matilde was thankful that Adrienne couldn't read her mind. Her main thought was that her friend might have some soup left over the following day.

Adrienne looked disappointed. 'Tomorrow then. You know where I live, don't you?'

'Are you still on the Rue de Lille?'

'Yes. Shall we say four?'

'I don't finish work until five.'

'Oh yes, I'd heard the auction house had closed. Where are you working now?'

Matilde felt her cheeks grow warm. How could she say that she was working for the enemy? 'Locally. I'm in administration.'

'Good for you. I'm back at the university now things have settled into a routine and people are returning to the city. Come along after work, then. I can't wait to catch up and you can tell me what happened to Xavier. Maybe I could help you try to find out some information.'

'Thank you. I'll see you tomorrow.'

The women kissed each other on each cheek and left the alleyway in different directions. Matilde checked her watch. It was half past five and due to the crowds, she'd have to hurry if she was to take the red foliage to the Arc de Triomphe and then make the meeting point on time. She noticed more German uniforms mingling with the demonstrators. It seemed that the police no longer seemed happy to just channel the crowd or advise youths to clear off home. They were now using force.

There was the sound of breaking glass and a moment of silence. A scuffle broke out in front of the cinema. The mood of the evening immediately sharpened. People began to flee. Some dived for cover in cafés or started running into side streets. Chairs were kicked over and tables upturned. Someone ran into her, knocking the sprigs from her hands. She bent to retrieve them but was knocked to the floor by two uniformed men in pursuit. Hands appeared as if from nowhere to lift her to her feet but she didn't see who had helped her. Panic started to spread through the crowd. The leaves were trodden underfoot. The street had become a battleground.

Matilde turned and struggled against the tide of people. She saw groups of students disperse and regroup according to the intervention of the police. More fights broke out, with the Germans making arrests. She cowered as Wehrmacht soldiers armed with pistols, machine guns and grenades, ran past her and began to violently disperse the demonstration. Some soldiers charged from Avenue Georges V to the roundabout on the Champs-Élysées wielding clubs and pistol grips and others fired randomly into the crowd. Matilde cried out, head bowed, pushing towards the edge of the crowd. She needed to get away. Military vehicles appeared and swept the pavements by driving in zigzags. It was utter confusion. She was jostled along at a run, her hands resting on a stranger's shoulder in front of her to prevent her from falling. Having almost cleared the Champs-Elysées, German soldiers began charging into crowds, pursuing those who were fleeing down side streets. Police vans and military lorries arrived in large numbers.

Matilde ran. The wail of sirens and the crack of bullets made her flinch and momentarily squeeze her eyes shut. She was leaving the mayhem behind now, but everywhere people seemed dazed, injured or just stood transfixed in disbelief. Ambulances began arriving in convoy, sirens blaring.

Before long, Matilde turned into a square and was reminded of the old Paris, the city before it had been suffocated by swastikas and stiff uniformed men. Ivy clung to painted masonry and orange leaves draped themselves across intricate trellises of ironwork. Pale blue shutters covered windows, shut tight like squeezed eyelids hiding from the truth. It was all a masquerade. The exteriors hid the hunger and fear of the household within. Perhaps many of them were caught up in the chaos behind her. The gardens masked the misery of suffering and the loss of loved ones. Grief for those carefree times unexpectedly caught in Matilde's throat.

She took a deep breath and straightened her back, continuing down narrow alleyways and cobbled lanes. Eventually, she reached a much smaller square, edged with boarded up cafés and a huge carved arch, the entrance to L'église Sainte Madeleine.

It was five to six. Following instructions she'd received on the telephone, she waited. Children were playing hopscotch, jumping on chalked squares while squabbling, and a barmaid from one of the few remaining open cafés, stepped outside and rubbed out the words, "cold beer" from the black board. When five minutes had passed, a man entered the coffee house. He fitted the description she had been given. His beard was grey and he wore a long beige coat. She waited a few moments before following him in through the door. Her contact was sitting at a table in the far corner of the room. She ordered a café crème and sat down at the table adjacent to him. As instructed, she addressed him with a memorized greeting as she passed him.

'Hello. They say a storm is on its way.'

The man gave a slight nod and sipped his coffee. Five minutes later, she heard his chair scrape on the floor. As he passed her, he dropped a coin and bent to retrieve it. Before standing up he whispered for her to follow him. Matilde waited until he'd gone before draining her cup and leaving.

She followed the billowing coat for fifteen minutes, trailing at a distance, turning this way and that until she realised they had walked in a large circle. Her feet ached and her head hurt. Her contact bent to tie his shoelace, looked right and left along the road, unlatched a gate and disappeared through it. Matilde bit the cuticle around a fingernail, tasting metallic blood in her mouth. She crossed the road and copied what the man had done by looking up and down the road. A mother and child had turned into the street, but she couldn't see anyone suspicious. She slipped through the gate. The man was waiting for her in front of a large wooden door, its red paint flaking like diseased skin.

'Sorry about the walk. You can't be too careful,' he said. 'Did you get caught up in the demonstration?'

'Yes. It was awful.'

'Filthy Boches.' He held out a hand. 'I'm Pierre.'

Matilde took it in her gloved hand. 'Xavier told me you used aliases.'

He leant forwards until his face was centimetres from hers. 'We decided against it. What we do isn't a game. It's life or death. We don't use names at all in public.'

Matilde nodded.

Pierre turned and gave three slow raps on the door. He waited ten seconds before repeating three faster knocks. Footfall could be heard coming towards them. The door opened a fraction.

'Trouble?' a man asked.

'No.'

The door opened wider and Matilde followed Pierre through. Flakes of the peeling paint caught her coat as she stepped inside and followed the two men down a narrow corridor towards muffled voices. The conversation stopped when the door was opened. Several men looked up at them standing in the doorway. They were sitting around a kitchen table, leaning over an unfurled map. The air was foggy with tobacco smoke and there was an unpleasant smell of blocked drains. Cigarette papers, spent matches and empty coffee cups were strewn across the table. A dark-haired man in his late thirties stood up.

'Matilde?'

'Yes.'

He left the table and walked over to her.

'I'm Henri. Come in, come in.' He shook her hand firmly. 'You're very welcome. Comrades,' he said, turning to his friends, 'where are your manners? This is Matilde Pascale.'

Matilde nodded in response to the men's greetings. These were the men she had resented for taking Xavier's time and attention; the same people she had imagined being broad-shouldered, roughly spoken brutes who were always on the lookout for an argument. From what she could see from the unkempt, undernourished bodies sitting in front of her, they were like her, ordinary victims of the occupation. This made her feel out of place, because like many Parisian women in work, she had vowed to remain as elegant as she could. Her clothes were now too big and faded through repeated washing, but by setting her hair and now indulging in adding a little colour to her cheeks, she felt as if she was showing the Germans that they couldn't take away her dignity. However, here in this small grimy kitchen, she felt overdressed and a little embarrassed that she was well turned out in front of these men.

Henri winked. 'Don't be frightened. We only bite the enemy.' He paused while the others either laughed or made disparaging remarks about the Germans. 'This motley crew are Philippe, Francis, Pierre and of course you've met Charles.

'Pleased to meet you all,' said Matilde.

Henri removed his hat and batted a chair seat to remove any dust. 'Please, sit down and we'll fill you in with what we've found out.'

Matilde sat down. A fresh cup of coffee was poured and pushed towards her through the detritus of cigarette papers and leaflets.

'Thank you.' She tasted the warm bitter liquid, thinking that wartime coffee should be given a different name, but she drank it thirstily all the same.

'We've located Xavier.'

Matilde looked up. 'Where? Is he safe? Did they say when he was being released?'

Henri raised a hand. 'Slow down. I said we'd found him. We know where he's being kept but there's no way we could speak with anyone there. He's… ' Henri rubbed his palms together making a shushing sound, 'he's at Gestapo headquarters.'

Matilde understood what that meant and placed her cup on the table. Xavier had told her that not all German soldiers carried the same weight of authority or were feared equally by the French. The largest section was the Wehrmacht. These soldiers were the regular army who did most of the fighting and showed a modicum of decency towards the French people. Next was the Waffen-SS. They were an elite army unit of the Nazi Party who not only fought in combat, but were also responsible for rounding up Jews. Xavier was in the hands of the Gestapo. They were the secret police and the worst of the Germans. They tortured, mutilated and murdered anyone, including fellow Germans, for crimes against the Reich. And that included helping Jews. It was the worst news.

'How bad is he?' Matilde asked.

'Pretty bad, but he's alive.'

'How do you know?'

'One of our men makes food deliveries and the headquarters is one of his stops. He's not permitted to enter the building but occasionally manages to exchange information with a French policeman whose job it is to patrol the grounds. This policeman is working undercover and unbeknown to the Germans, he speaks enough of their language to report the latest news. He's a great asset, as you can imagine.'

Matilde looked up at the men. 'Do we know why Xavier was arrested? Did they find out about these meetings?'

Philippe pushed his chair back in order to turn towards her. He was the oldest of the group with lined, leathery skin and he spoke with a strong voice. 'The word is that he was believed to be living with a Jew as he was in her apartment when they came to arrest her.'

'You mean Ruth.' Matilde leant forwards and laid her palms flat on the table. 'But he was taking her food. And how did they know where Ruth was? She has more or less been in hiding since her husband went missing.'

'We've been thinking the same thing. There must have been an informant who told the authorities.'

Matilde rested her fingertips on her lips. She couldn't think straight. Who would have told the Germans that a Jewish woman was living at Vue Du Jardin? How could she go to work tomorrow without knowing how Xavier was? She ached to hold him. He must be terrified.

'Is someone going to tell her the truth, or are we all going to pretend it hasn't happened?'

'Shut up, Francis,' said Henri, shooting him a warning glance.

Matilde dropped her fingers from her mouth and looked at Francis. He was a thin man with a cigarette wedged into the corner of his mouth. 'Tell me what?'

Francis lowered his eyes against Henri's glare.

Matilde turned to Henri. 'Tell me what?'

Henri took a deep breath. 'I will speak with you later about a matter regarding Xavier that was passed on to our informer at the headquarters.'

'What matter?'

'It's not a concern for the moment and—'

'What matter? If it's news about my husband I want to know now.' Matilde noticed a couple of the men shuffle uncomfortably. 'I need to know everything. I don't need protecting. I need honesty.'

Matilde saw Henri throw Francis a look of scorn before he reached for his chair and drew it alongside her. He sighed and looked straight into her eyes. She noticed his eyes were the colour of tree bark, brown with flecks of green and hazel.

'Xavier's arrest wasn't as straightforward as it might have appeared,' said Henri.

'In what way?'

'In so much as he hadn't taken food down to Ruth.'

'What had he taken her?'

Matilde heard a grunt from one of the men, but didn't turn from Henri's gaze.

'They were found together.'

'Together?'

'Yes.'

'What are you saying?'

'In bed.'

'In bed?'

'I'm sorry.'

Matilde paused. 'In bed?'

'I'm really sorry. Please understand that you're not alone. We'll look out for you.'

'There must be a mistake.'

Henri pointed to the bottle of Pastis and beckoned with his fingers. Immediately some was poured in to a glass and it was pushed his way. He splashed some water into it and held it out to Matilde. 'Drink this.'

Matilde obeyed. She felt the liquid burn her throat when she swallowed. As Henri spoke, it seemed as if his voice grew distant. As if she was listening to an echo.

'The French patrolman I mentioned, is allowed access inside the Gestapo's headquarters on Avenue Foch. He didn't see Xavier but he managed to read a report of the arrest. I'm sorry, Matilde.'

9

SLEEP ELUDED MATILDE. She'd spent the dark hours trying to reconcile her heartache at missing Xavier with the knowledge that he had betrayed her. It had also rained all night and by morning, it felt as if the chill had permeated the apartment walls.

Having stepped into her petticoat and pulled a blue woollen dress over her head, Matilde walked into the kitchen still fastening her belt. She lifted a damp stocking from the rail in front of the stove door, balled the cold resistant mesh and stretched it up her leg, leaning back against the kitchen door for balance. She pointed her other foot ready to slip on the second stocking, when another image of Xavier and Ruth intruded. Matilde whimpered, dropped the length of nylon and clasped her hand to her mouth. She mustn't cry again. Not now. Not before work. She'd already re-applied her mascara following her last bout of tears.

She turned to face the kitchen door and rested her head against it, before slowly banging her forehead a few times. The thudding was dulled by the folds of her apron hanging from a hook on the back of the door, but the repetitive movement helped to dispel the unwanted images. After a few moments she stood up, pulled on the second damp stocking and slipped her feet into her shoes. The apartment was quiet, its silence expanding until it enveloped her. For once she was thankful to leave the building and go to work.

Matilde hadn't even walked the short distance to the Tuileries' gate before a black car pulled up beside her. The passenger door opened and a uniformed German stepped out. At first she was confused, wondering why they had stopped the car here and not a little further along the road where the pavement was clear. An emblem of an eagle on the man's lapel caught her eye when he blocked her path. She felt a twist in her stomach. He'd stopped to speak to her.

'Madame Pascale?'

Matilde squeezed her handbag a little tighter. 'Yes.'

'Get in the car, please.'

'I work for the *Reich*.' She pointed towards the museum. 'I'll be late for work.'

'Inside the car, Madame Pascale.'

His leather-gloved hand opened the back door. Matilde stepped forwards, dipped her head and was gently pushed into the back of the German staff car. The man walked around the back of the vehicle and sat beside her. With the notebook in his hand, he tapped the driver's seat and the engine started. She removed her scarf and undid her coat. Despite the bitter weather, her back was damp with fear. She looked across at the soldier.

'Where are you taking me?'

'We need to ask you a few questions.'

'What questions?'

He ignored her and began to write in the notebook.

Matilde looked out of the car window as they crossed the Pont de la Concorde, all the time twisting the scarf on her knee. People on the streets walked with their heads down, as if contemplating their feet. War has done this to Paris, she thought. The less you knew, the better off you were.

The car stopped outside a drab building in Saint-Germain. Men were coming and going through the front door and she recognized their grey uniforms as the German police, the same uniform as the men in the car. The door was opened and another man gestured for her to get out. She was jabbed in the back and escorted up several steps towards the entrance.

Inside, Matilde was directed up a flight of stairs, the growl of hobnail boots ever present beside her. She was led to a stuffy reception room with badly painted white walls on which were pinned several notices printed in German. Could Xavier have been brought here? She scanned the room hoping to find traces of him, or simply some reassurance for herself. Perhaps there would be some flowers, or maybe a smile on someone's lips. But there was nothing.

After speaking with a man behind a desk, the policeman escorted her down a corridor and towards a door. He opened it and nudged her forwards. Inside, a woman was sitting at a small table, its surface just wide enough to hold a typewriter. She was feeding a sheet of paper through its roller. An older man was sitting in a chair behind an ornate desk. A smoking tower of ash balanced on the upright cigarette that he held between his fingers. He wore wire glasses and had a rim of grey hair around his head, leaving a shiny central pate. He nodded for her guard to leave.

Matilde swallowed.

The German snapped his fingers. 'Identity card.'

Matilde fumbled in her pocket and retrieved her documents. She took several steps forward and handed them to him. He studied them before laying them on the table.

'Madame Pascale?'

'Yes.'

'Yes, sir.'

'Yes, sir,' she repeated.

'I see you work at the museum.' He squeezed the bridge of his nose. 'A very important job. A job that requires the utmost loyalty and secrecy.'

'Yes, sir.'

'Your husband has been arrested.'

'Yes, sir.'

'He was found with a Jew.'

'Yes, sir.'

He frowned. 'Does this not concern you? Are you aware of the circumstances in which they were discovered?'

'Yes, sir.'

He scraped his chair backwards, stood up and thumped his fist on the table, startling both Matilde and the typist. 'Are you unable to say anything else?'

With her body shaking, she bit back a repetition of her previous replies. 'I'm aware of the circumstances.'

He thumped the table a second time. 'Sir!'

He walked around the table and leaned against the front edge, folding his arms. 'The Jew's husband was executed several months ago for sabotage.'

Matilde's mouth opened in shock. She wondered if Ruth had been told.

'We want to know who he was working with. Several men were seen attempting to derail a train. The Jew was shot but the other rats escaped back in to their holes. We believe his wife knows and if his wife knows, surely her lover has been told.' The German smirked, showing straight, nicotine-stained teeth before continuing in his poor French.

'How do they say these days… pillow talk?'

Matilde momentarily closed her eyes. She felt physical pain in her chest.

'Did your husband ever mention this man?'

'Never.'

'What did you both know of him?'

'Nothing. Our neighbour told us her husband was missing. We never met him.'

The German's jaw stretched with a suppressed yawn as he rubbed his neck, moving his head from side to side as if easing a pain. 'It's funny how no one knows anything or anyone. It would be far better if you co-operated.'

'I'm telling the truth. I never saw him. *We* never saw him.'

'I'm tired. Perhaps if we continue this conversation tomorrow, you may remember something.'

'Can I leave?'

There was a pause. The only sound was the clatter of the typewriter keys.

'I think your thoughts will be more focused on helping us find a solution if you were to remain as our guest.'

He clicked his fingers towards the typist. She immediately stood up and hurried towards the door, opened it and spoke a few words in German. Matilde's guard reappeared, carrying a bunch of keys. She noticed a blue-black tattoo on the back of his hand but couldn't decipher what it was. He gestured for her to follow.

Down two flights of stairs, Matilde was shown into a small room containing a single metal bed with a stuffed straw mattress. There was a bucket with a lid in one corner of the room. The stale air and smell of bodily waste made her wince. A light bulb hung from the ceiling on a thin wire, gently swaying in the draught and casting shadows around the room. She was shocked to see two female scarecrows slouching on the thin mattress, staring at her. One of them coughed.

Matilde looked at her guard and raised her eyebrows in an

unspoken horrified appeal. He grinned and pointed inside with a nod of his head. She tentatively took two steps inside and the door was slammed shut. She tucked a stray wisp of hair behind her ear and pulled her coat tightly around her body, aware of how ridiculous she must look in her smart clothes.

'Bonjour. Je suis Matilde.'

'Bienvenu, Matilde,' said the older woman.

Neither of the women moved and Matilde knew that the welcome she'd received was sarcastic. She was shocked to see that the other person was a young girl of about ten. She tried to smile at her but her mouth seemed to twitch instead.

'What are your names?'

The older woman pointed to herself. 'Sandrine, and this is my daughter, Celeste.'

'She's very young to be in here.'

'Twelve.'

'Very young.' Matilde had never felt so uncomfortable making conversation. No doubt they were wary of this new, overdressed woman. They each wore a shabby dress, thin shawls pulled tightly around their shoulders with wooden clogs on bare feet. 'Would your daughter… would Celeste like my coat? I have a wool dress and warm cardigan—' She stopped talking, aware how pompous she sounded in describing the quality of her clothing.

'Thanks.' Sandrine held out her hands.

Matilde removed her coat, at once feeling the chill. She handed it to the woman and watched as she spread it across both of their torsos.

'Why are you here?' asked Matilde.

'Caught thieving food.'

'They're arresting people for scavenging for food? Soon everyone in Paris will be locked up if that's the case.'

'A man put his bag of shopping down. Celeste grabbed it and we ran. Turns out the man was one of them out of uniform.' She bent her head in the direction of the door to indicate whom she was talking about.

At the mention of food, Matilde remembered her plan to meet Adrienne after work. She also recalled the promise of chicken soup. Would she be free by this evening? Not if the man who had questioned her had been serious about her overnight stay. How was it possible that in the space of twenty hours, she'd discovered that Xavier had been unfaithful and Ruth's husband had been executed and she herself was locked up in a cell?

'What about you?' asked Sandrine.

'Sorry?'

'Why are you here? You don't look like you need to steal.'

Matilde could have answered by saying that she regularly went without meals and was starving. She could undress and show this woman her ribs and hipbones, but what would be the point? Now wasn't the time to compare hardships.

'Nothing.'

Sandrine let out a laugh that erupted into coughing. She looked at Matilde. 'We said that when we first arrived here.' She paused. 'It doesn't take long to tell the truth.'

'They think I have information about a man. But I don't.'

'Tell them something. Make it easier on yourself.'

Matilde's feet were aching from standing for so long. There were no other seats except a space on the bed alongside her cellmates. 'May I?' She gestured to a gap beside them.

'No. This is our bed. Wait your turn. We've spent three nights on the floor before they took the other woman away. It's ours now.'

Matilde nodded. 'I understand.' But she didn't. She didn't understand why she was here. She didn't understand that their so-called crimes now defined who they were. There was no mention of family, home or work. She didn't understand that she had given her warm coat to them, but they couldn't share a corner of the mattress. She felt her eyes sting with tears, but busied herself by settling on the floor.

Matilde woke up with a jolt, surprised that she had nodded off. Sandrine and Celeste were asleep, leaning against each other and wrapped up in her thick winter coat. Matilde looked around the cell. The room had grown darker and colder. She shivered. A light tapping on the high window drew her eyes upwards to where snowflakes were sticking to the window, before melting and dripping down the glass in silver rivulets. She was freezing. Every part of her body ached. Despite her misgivings, she wished Xavier were there.

Matilde unfurled her legs and stretched them in front of her, grimacing in pain. Somewhere in the building, someone screamed. She held her breath and listened. A guttural voice shouted, too far away to discern what they were saying, but it was shortly followed by another wail.

'Interrogation,' said Sandrine.

Matilde looked towards the bed. Celeste was still asleep against her mother, but Sandrine's dark eyes were looking at her.

'Aren't you afraid?' asked Matilde.

'They won't question us. We've admitted our theft. We're waiting to be moved on somewhere. But remember what I said. Tell them something and make it easier on yourself.'

Matilde leaned forwards and hugged her knees. Would she be tortured? Why had Xavier put her in such a position? He could be so selfish, always wanting to do things his way despite her protestations. He'd refused to give up his meetings undeterred by the danger. He'd continued to come home after curfew and risk arrest. He'd been unfaithful and because of that, she was sitting in a freezing cell waiting to be questioned further.

A violent shiver shuddered through her body. Her back ached and she'd lost so much weight that her bones dug into the concrete floor. She lay down sideways, curled her legs up and folded one arm beneath her head, grateful for the temporary cessation of pain. She dozed, her body having been deprived of sleep the previous night.

It was dark when she woke again. By now it was certain that the German had been serious about her spending the night in this place. She lay there shivering and hungry for several minutes before she heard the footsteps. Her heart quickened and she wondered if Sandrine and Celeste were awake. The footsteps stopped outside their door. Keys rattled in the lock. The door opened and two beams of light crisscrossed the room. The torchlight was directed towards the bed.

'You two, out now,' a man's voice ordered.

Mother and daughter unfurled their arms and legs and hobbled towards three men waiting at the door. They didn't speak a word. The door closed, the light disappeared and the sound of footfall slowly diminished.

It was silent again and after a few moments, with the help of the moonlight, Matilde's eyes adjusted to the darkness. She needed the bathroom. With some effort, she stood up and limped towards the darkest corner of the cell. Stretching her arms in front of her, she crouched, feeling for the bucket. She found it to her left. Turning her back to it, she pulled down her underwear and felt between her knees for the metal container. She squatted and relieved herself.

How had it come to this?

10

HANS WALKED INTO Kommandant Beitel's office, trying not to look annoyed that his rare day of rest had been interrupted. Earlier, he had been lying in bed and musing how he might spend his free day, maybe call in to a gallery or wander the cobbled streets of the Place du Tetre. He doubted the artists would be painting outside in this bitter weather, but maybe they were selling some of their canvasses.

Within minutes of getting up, an envelope was pushed beneath the door to his room. Inside were instructions ordering him to report to his superior's office. He cursed before washing and dressing in his uniform. Once at headquarters, Hans was anxious to get whatever was expected of him out of the way.

He raised his arm with fingers outstretched. 'Heil Hitler.'

Kommandant Beitel was looking out of the window. He turned and repeated the greeting, his arm bent at the elbow, seemingly distracted.

'Madame Pascale has been arrested,' he said. 'I want you to take this release order so she can return to work.'

'Yes, sir.' Hans took the sheet of paper, pleased that this order wouldn't take too long but also surprised to hear this news. He wondered what she had done to be arrested. He hadn't been working with her very long, but Madame Pascale didn't appear to be self-assured, let alone capable of stepping out of line.

The Kommandant sat at his desk, his chair groaning in protest. He reached for his glasses and cleaned each lens before speaking.

'Reichsmarschall Göring is visiting next Wednesday and I need you both to select and organize the best artwork for him to view. I don't need my staff locked up when there's important work to do. Tell Madame Pascale that I expect her to be at work on Monday.'

'Yes, sir.'

'One more thing, Engel.' He reached for an envelope lying on top of a pile of paperwork, hesitating for a second before holding it out to Hans. 'This is for her. It's important. Please make sure you pass it on.'

A NEARBY CLOCK struck ten o'clock as Hans walked across the Pont de la Concorde. Curious to know what the message contained and noticing the envelope wasn't sealed, he quickly scanned the note, his steps slowing before momentarily stopping.

'Christ!'

He slipped the paper back inside its envelope and pushed it inside his jacket pocket, letting out a long sigh. The bastard was passing on his dirty work.

Once in Saint-Germain it only took a few minutes to reach the austere building that had been appropriated by the Gestapo. He took the steps two at a time and entered through the main door. After speaking with a soldier behind the reception desk, he was shown down two flights of stairs and along a windowless corridor. Ceiling fans thrummed overhead and it appeared to Hans that the fans were wafting the stench of urine and damp along the passageway, rather than diffusing it. The sound of doors slamming and the occasional distant scream caused the muscles to tense in his jaw. He was shown into a small room where a grey-haired soldier with heavy jowls and drooping eyelids was writing at a desk. The room was airless and very warm due to a small heater rattling in the corner.

Hans gave the customary greeting and placed the official release papers on the desk. The soldier read it, licked his forefinger and leafed through the paperwork in front of him.

'This prisoner hasn't been questioned yet.'

'My orders are to escort Madame Pascale from here so she can return to important Reich business,' said Hans.

'I see it's signed by Kommandant Beitel.' The middle-aged man pinched his nose with his thumb and forefinger. He hollered a name and waited.

Hans took this opportunity to ask what offence she had committed.

'What's it to you?'

Hans shrugged. 'Nothing. Curiosity.'

'She's a looker. You interested?'

The soldier grinned and Hans was reminded of a childhood visit to a zoo's humid reptile house with his parents.

'My interest is to carry out my orders and for her to return to work.'

The man leant back on his chair, raised one leg at a time onto the desk and shouted once again, 'Schmidt!' He looked steadily at Hans. 'Her husband was fucking a married Jew. The Jew's husband was shot for sabotage. She may know the names of others involved.'

Schmidt hurried into the room, saving Hans from replying. The lanky German was given instructions to escort Hans to a particular cell.

Hans bowed his head towards the seated man, brought his heels together with a click and followed the younger man out. He welcomed the chill in the corridor after the suffocating heat of that small room and obnoxious man. This place was awful. He put his hand in his pocket, feeling the envelope with his fingertips. He pulled it out and sealed it, knowing he was taking the coward's way out of this situation.

They stopped at one of the arched doors along the corridor. The soldier turned a large key in the lock and swung the cell door wide open. Hans stepped inside, his hand automatically going to his nose. The cell was dark and cold with a nauseating smell of vermin and ammonia. The stone walls were damp and a small window, crisscrossed with iron bars, lit the room with spikes of sunshine. A shape stirred on a dirty mattress and Madame Pascale sat up. Dark shadows underlined her eyes and strands of hair had escaped from a dark ribbon she wore to tie her hair back. Hans tried not to show his shock.

'Madame Pascale?'

'Yes.'

'Follow me, please.'

Hans watched her attempt to straighten her hair and reach for her coat.

'Am I free to leave?' she asked.

'I've brought your release papers.' He gestured towards the door.

Matilde stood up unsteadily. She saw Corporal Engel make a move as if to catch her, but she turned away pulling her coat around her shoulders. Despite being relieved to see a face she recognised, he was one of them. She didn't want anything from him, even his support. She was freezing, starving and dirty. They had taken Xavier away. She worked for them yet hated them. Thank God it was Saturday so she could go home and shut them all out.

By the time she had walked to the main entrance, Matilde was light headed and every joint in her body ached. It was with huge relief that she watched Corporal Engel signal to a bicycle-taxi. The cyclist steered towards them, stopped on the side of the pavement and dismounted.

'Here, let me help you,' said the Frenchman. He guided her by her elbow into the narrow wicker seat set inside a small handmade open carriage that was attached to the back of his bike. Then he laid a blanket across her legs.

Matilde closed her eyes as if to escape the moment, but was still aware of the two men speaking. She presumed Corporal Engel was giving the cyclist directions because the next minute she was being swayed and jostled as the cyclist rode across the bridge and along the embankment of the Seine. Despite shivering beneath the blanket, Matilde felt huge relief that she was free without having been interrogated. She opened her eyes. The city was grey, yesterday's snowfall having melted. A low mist hovered above the river as a flock of birds took flight from a clump of chimneypots and wheeled across rooftops tinged golden beneath weak sunlight.

With a squeak of brakes, the cyclist finally stopped outside the Vue du Jardin. He dismounted, took her hand and helped her from the seat.

'You okay?'

'I will be, thank you.' Matilde opened her handbag and searched through the paltry contents: a powder compact, a handkerchief and a comb. No purse.

'My purse. It's gone.'

'You can't trust anyone nowadays.'

'But I can't pay you.'

'The German paid. He also said to give you this.'

'For me?'

'That's what he said.'

Matilde took the envelope.

'I'd help you inside, but some bugger would steal my bike.'

'That's all right. I might spend a few minutes in the gardens. I need some fresh air.'

'You won't find any fresh air while the Germans are here.' The Frenchman swung a leg over the bike, adjusted his hat and cycled along the Rue de Rivoli.

Matilde watched him until he was lost amongst military vehicles that clogged the street. She looked up into the skeletal canopies of trees lining the road. Her tears welled up unexpectedly, threatening to fall. She yearned for the old Paris and longed to see Xavier again, despite his infidelity.

Turning, she walked through the iron gates into the public gardens, sitting on the first bench she came to. She sat at one end, trying to remember when she'd last seen her purse. She had packed it in her handbag yesterday morning before being arrested and had been allowed into the cell with it. Of course. Sandrine. Hadn't she been arrested for theft?

Matilde leaned sideways and touched the crisp brown edges of dead leaves on a bush. She pulled at one until it came away in her fingers and squeezed it in her palm, making it crackle.

The sound of laughter disturbed her. A woman was pushing a black perambulator and talking to a child who skipped along beside her. What was her story? Where was her husband? Matilde absentmindedly looked down at her wedding ring, twisting it around her finger. It moved easily now that she'd lost so much weight. She must be careful it didn't become so loose that it fell off.

Remembering the envelope on her lap, she picked it up, recognizing Kommandant Beitel's handwriting on the front. It simply read, Madame Pascale. Sliding a finger inside one corner, she ripped along the top edge imagining it to be an apology for her unwarranted arrest. Unfolding two sheets of paper she scanned the first page, also written in the same handwriting.

Madame Pascale

It is with regret that I enclose the following information, but as a member of the museum staff I believe you should be informed prior to leaflets being distributed throughout central Paris tomorrow morning. I have only been aware of this news myself for the past hour. Despite the distress this knowledge will cause, it is essential you attend to your duties on Monday to prepare for our esteemed guest, Reichsmarschall Göring.

Anxious to find out what news had led the Kommandant to send her a personal note, Matilde read the typed bulletin.

NOTICE

In accordance with my publication of 22nd November 1940, in which I stated that five prisoners would be executed if the perpetrator of the cowardly assassination of the Lt. Col. Holtz on 17th November 1940, did not surrender, the following French prisoners were executed on the evening of 13th November 1940. If the murderer of Lt. Col. Hotz does not surrender within 24 hours, ten further prisoners will be shot.

Signed
Gauführer Kistler.
Pierre Blanc
Astor Dubois
Guido Mathieu
Xavier Pascale
Hubert Brodeur

Matilde read the list. She read Xavier's name. A jolt of adrenalin shot through her body making her heart race. She could feel the *thud-thud* against her ribs. The sheet of paper began to tremble in her hands. Breathing became difficult.

Somehow, she stood up. Movement felt clumsier than before. She'd lost her sense of coordination and direction. It was as if her limbs had been detached and re-assembled incorrectly. There was no rhythm to her walk or equilibrium to her thoughts. She stumbled back out through the gates, across a side road and lurched inside the Vue du Jardin's hallway. By now she was breathless and weak, clinging to the worn patina of the wooden handrail. A sob erupted from her chest, followed by another. She climbed a step. A guttural groan emanated from her throat, surprising her and causing her to slap her palm across her mouth. She climbed another step then stopped. Her legs couldn't carry her weight and her knees buckled. She sank onto the cold stone steps and sobbed.

11

'PLEASE TRY AND eat,' said Sylvie. 'I traded a pair of stockings for half a dozen of them.'

Matilde sat at her friend's kitchen table and looked at the egg in front of her. She had felt too sick to eat since discovering Xavier's fate two days earlier, but also knew there was already too little flesh covering her hips and ribs.

'I'll try. Thank you.'

Sylvie sat down beside Matilde. 'I'm worried about you. Must you go in today?'

'I have no choice.'

'You've just lost your husband.'

Matilde looked up. 'He's not lost. They murdered him.'

Sylvie closed her eyes and slowly nodded.

'Besides,' continued Matilde, 'I can't disobey orders because I can't afford not to work, especially now. At least I'll have something to think about other than… '

Sylvie gave a tight-lipped, sympathetic smile. She patted Matilde's hand and stood up.

'You must come straight back here afterwards. I'll make us some dinner.'

Matilde scooped a spoonful of yolk from her egg and slid it between her lips. It was warm, smooth and comforting. She repeated the action, ashamed at experiencing pleasure from its taste. How could she possibly enjoy anything at this time?

'There's no need. You've already been so kind,' she said.

'Nonsense. You're in no state to look after yourself. You've been walking around this place in a trance and you haven't shed a tear since I found you on the staircase. I've no idea how you're going to manage at the museum and I've a good mind to go and tell them that.'

Matilde shook her head and swallowed the last piece of dry bread on her plate. 'I haven't been in a daze, I've been thinking. I can't hide behind Xavier or anyone else any longer. I can only rely on myself and that's what I intend to do.'

'What do you mean?'

'I'm not entirely sure yet, but Xavier believed that things wouldn't change if people didn't help make a difference.' She wiped a crumb from the corner of her mouth. 'I wanted to hide for the duration of this war, but now it's too late to tell him.'

'Tell him what?'

'That I understand.'

'You're talking in riddles,' said Sylvie.

'He used to say, live free or die.'

Matilde scraped the firm white of the egg from inside the shell then carried her plate to the sink. She wrapped a scarf around her neck, picked up her handbag and kissed Sylvie's cheek.

'Thank you for looking after me, but I'll be fine.'

'Matilde—'

'I know what I'm doing.'

'But—'

'Trust me. I'll be fine.'

Sylvie rolled her eyes. 'You know where I am if you need me.'

Matilde nodded, lifted her coat off the door hook and left

Sylvie's apartment, knowing that the life she had known had been upended and a new one must begin.

WHEN SHE ENTERED the main office at the museum, even Gertrude Loup's face was sympathetic. Matilde refused to engage with the Kommandant's secretary and walked past the desk and into her own room. She closed the door behind her, leaning her back against it. She just had to get through this day and then she would visit Xavier's friend, Henri, and tell him her plan. She wanted to be more than a messenger who fed them small pieces of information now and again.

She walked to the window and looked out over the gardens. Dull. Insipid. Dead. She heard the door click and footsteps enter, but she didn't turn around. The last thing she wanted was to hear Gertrude Loup's pretence at sympathy, but instead of the secretary's voice came the smell of leather and tobacco, together with a subtle aroma of citrus soap. Corporal Engel stood beside her.

'I'm very sorry to hear about Xavier.'

Matilde was taken aback on hearing him use her husband's name. It was almost as if she'd been violated; as if he'd just stolen something precious from her. She felt him touch her shoulder and she stiffened. Her hand went to her mouth as if to stop herself from speaking. She wanted to shout that it had been his people who had murdered Xavier, but she knew she wouldn't dare.

12

MATILDE REMEMBERED THE code; three slow taps, pause, followed by three faster taps. She flicked raindrops from her coat.

'Who is it?'

'Matilde.'

A key turned in the lock and Matilde stepped inside, chin raised and ready to argue with anyone who stopped her from taking on the Germans. She followed Henri into his kitchen, which smelt of burnt fat and tobacco, almost expecting to see the men sitting around the table like before. She remembered Henri being kind to her while breaking the news of Xavier's infidelity.

'We're all so sorry to hear about Xavier. We've lost a good man.'

'Why do people keep saying he's lost? He's been murdered.'

Henri slowly nodded.

'I want to take his place.' She knew she sounded rude and overzealous but she was determined not to appear weak or cowardly. In fact, Xavier's absence made her feel as if she now had permission to fight back.

Henri opened his mouth to speak, but he sighed instead.

'What?' she asked. 'You don't think I'm capable? You don't need me?'

Henri lifted a hand. 'I assure you that isn't the reason. Please take a seat.'

Matilde sat down. A black coffee and slices of dry bread were pushed towards her. She accepted immediately. The bread was dense and dry, but very welcome.

Henri lit a thin, bent cigarette, billowing smoke towards the ceiling.

'Let's take things a little slower. I know you met everyone briefly last time you were here, but let me tell you a little more about us. We're just a group of Parisians who are shaken by the sight of our occupied city. Like you, we have lost loved ones.'

'Not lost. Tortured and murdered.'

'You're right. Our remedy against our anger is to act together. We meet and swap news, write and distribute anti-German leaflets and plan small but important ways in which to fight back. We're not under any illusions of the practical effects of our limited acts, but they help us to stay sane under this occupation. Small seeds of resistance may blow in the wind but grow stronger elsewhere, like cutting telephone lines or sabotaging transport. But it's not just sabotage. There are even smaller ways of fighting back. If a German speaks in his own language, pretend you don't understand even if you get the gist of what they're saying. If they ask you a question in poor French, tell them a lie. If they ask for directions, send them the wrong way.' He leant back in his chair.

'Can't we do more?'

'It may seem petty,' said Henri, 'but if one of them drives in the wrong direction because of your inaccurate directions, it may give a fellow French man time to escape. We keep contact with Germans to a minimum. We show outward indifference. We don't make eye contact unless absolutely necessary. As a woman you could refuse offers of seats made by Germans on the Metro. Small victories, but victories nonetheless.'

'I want to join you. I want to do more.'

'Undeniably, having a member of the team working at the museum would be a great asset. We'd be grateful if you could safely give us details of anything you think may be of use, but not if it means putting yourself in danger.'

'When is your next meeting? Where are the others?'

'They're at work. Charles is a doctor. His wife and young daughter moved south last year to live with his mother. As you can imagine, his skills have been invaluable.'

Matilde nodded.

'Philippe is a retired mechanic. Without him a lot more German cars would be running smoothly around Paris. His specialty is sabotaging transport. He lives with his wife, Lisette, who magically conjures up meals for us out of nothing. Francis is an undertaker. He takes over when Charles's services arrive too late, sadly all too often. Then there's young Pierre. He was a journalist before everything changed, but has access to printing machines and knows many contacts.'

'And what about you?'

'I'm a tailor, or I was when there were clothes to buy and alter. I'm good with these,' said Henri, raising his hands. 'I can do a bit of joinery, paint and I can wield a spade in the garden.'

Hearing about these ordinary men had a calming effect on Matilde. 'Sorry. I didn't mean to be so rude when I came in. It's just that I feel so powerless.'

'In our own small, quiet ways we try to disrupt them and impair their plans. The important words here are small and quiet. We plan carefully. We watch and listen. We stay invisible. You can't be effective if you're angry and seeking revenge. It leads to mistakes and mistakes cost lives. For this reason, you're not ready to join us yet. Grieve for a while and we'll speak again in the summer.'

13

March 1941

HANS STEPPED OUT of the car. Despite the dour March morning he could sense a hint of spring in the air. He breathed deeply, momentarily closing his eyes and recalling the smells in the woods behind his home in Germany. The scent of damp earth and sun-warmed wood were early childhood memories.

'Engel?'

Hans snapped his eyes open. His commander was a lean, vulpine man, with grey hair, probably twenty years his senior.

'Coming, sir.'

Hans slammed the car door shut before catching up with several other German soldiers. They walked on to Rue des Grands Augustins where tall buildings were daubed with a hard northern light that seeped over the rooftops and dripped between chimneystacks. Pigeons perched on windowsills, heads tucked under wings against the buffeting wind. Despite having been granted a rare day off, Hans had been ordered to accompany the group because he had an eye for art.

The artist they were visiting lived in a top tenement in one of these old houses. This was Hans' first visit here, but he had heard that this Spanish painter was regularly given a hard time, but never arrested. It was said that his widespread fame protected him from the Nazis.

The commander paused at the door and turned to the men. 'We'll set fire to the painting in question, here, for the people to see.' He pointed to the cobbled rectangular courtyard that was overlooked by numerous windows.

Hans followed the men up a narrow wooden staircase, leaving a smashed door behind them. Their footsteps echoed along passageways as they hurried up another flight of steps. His superior hammered on the door of the top apartment.

A small, almost delicate man opened the door. 'Yet another visit? Such an honour.'

He stood aside and allowed the soldiers to enter. The studio was littered with objects: sculptures, paintings and equipment that Hans longed to explore. A floor-to-ceiling stove stood in the centre of one wall. He looked at the artist, who returned his gaze with the piercing black eyes of a hypnotist. The commander broke the silence and spoke in competent French.

'Monsieur Picasso. We have come for the black and white painting. News has reached us that it's still here.'

Hans was mesmerized. He couldn't quite believe that he was standing next to this great man. He could reach out and touch a man whose work he had studied at university. He watched the Spaniard smile, self-assured and composed.

'As you see,' said Picasso, 'this is my studio, so naturally my artwork is here.' He splayed the fingers of his right hand and indicated his work with the sweep of his arm.

Hans could feel his heart beating fast. The smell of paint, rags soaked in oil of turpentine, and wood smoke, all awakened something that had long since been dulled by war. He knew that the control of art and other cultural expressions was an important part of German power, but control of an artist's creativity was abhorrent to him. He also knew why Adolf Hitler found the power of so-called degenerate art so detestable. It probably made him feel insecure. It had the capability to undermine him and influence people. Challenge authority. It could embody the identity of a person. A community. A country.

Not for the first time, Hans wondered what he was doing here. Fate had him standing on the side that were trying to eradicate this modern type of art. Paintings were being destroyed and books burned. This cleansing was supposed to mark the beginning of the rebirth of German culture, but Hans didn't agree with these ideals. He lowered his head and studied the paint-splashed floorboards. He felt ashamed. He was weak. He was too afraid to cross the invisible line and stand beside this artist. If he did, he would be arrested and disposed of like an abstract painting.

The commander turned to them. 'Search for the black and white canvas in all these rooms. It's large and likely to have been separated into several sections.'

Hans was drawn to smaller pieces of work propped on chairs, hung from walls and stacked in rows. He moved pieces of wood, small bones and wine corks to one side of a table in order to study a picture that lay beneath. It depicted a self-satisfied cat triumphantly holding a wounded bird in its mouth, a wide gaping hole obvious on the bird's body. Besides that painting, lying on a crumpled cigarette box was a small canvas of a grimacing skull with clenched teeth, set against a background of dreary greys. Cubed features of a face were painted in black onto a sheet of newspaper. Hans turned and walked around a sculpture of a head that captured the same brutal intensity of Munch's *The Scream*. For an artist with an engaging smile, Picasso painted oppressive and melancholic scenes, thought Hans. Everywhere stood or lay canvasses portraying gloom, sorrow, pain and foreboding. It was all so overwhelming yet beautiful to Hans.

Hans looked towards the apartment door where Picasso continued to share his unassuming charm with the commander. The artist's shirt was open at the neck, revealing a polka-dot neckerchief beneath. His hair was greying and severely parted just above his right temple and brushed across his receding hairline. His cheeks were sunken, highlighting lines that ran from his nose to the corners of his mouth.

After a search of the apartment, the painting hadn't been found but as Hans sorted through paperwork on Monsieur Picasso's desk, he found a small printed postcard of *Guernica*, the painting they were here to destroy. Painted in black, white and grey, it showed flailing bulls and horses, bodies of men lying prostrate on the floor or screaming in agony. Hans knew it to be a depiction of the Nazis' bombing of the helpless civilians of Guernica in Picasso's country of birth, Spain. He took the postcard to his superior who was now standing alone, looking out of the window into the courtyard below. The commander studied the print while chewing the inside of his cheek and took a few steps towards the artist, who was now stoking the fire. He held up the card that represented breathtaking indictments of war, meaningless death, pointless suffering, destruction and government hypocrisy.

'Did you do this?' asked the Kommandant.

'No sir. *You* did.'

'What?'

'Take it as a souvenir,' replied Picasso, straight-faced.

Hans could see the German's lips become thin lines and the muscles in his jaw tighten. The commander screwed up the postcard, threw it on the floor and ordered his men to leave.

14

HANS CLIMBED THE steps of *Pigalle*'s Metro station, welcoming the warmth from the weak sun that shone on his neck. He walked with his head bowed, reading from a leaflet pinched between his fingers. A thin spiral of smoke rose from a half-smoked cigarette nestled in the corner of his mouth. 'Montmartre, the hill of martyrs,' he read.

In front of him were steep, narrow streets that were glistening from a recent cloudburst. The insipid sunshine was casting shadows on buildings that were decorated with posters advertising cabarets of swing and jazz. Women offering their bodies slunk in doorways beside market traders who were selling rotten vegetables mounded high on rickety carts. The smell was overpowering. Stale urine, unwashed clothing and the putrefying smell of fetid cabbages. Hans pinched his nose, crossed over the cobbled road and hurried along the Boulevard de Clichy.

A German soldier and a French woman hurried past him, laughing. The woman had the same hair colouring as Matilde and he wondered what she was doing at that moment. As hard as he tried, he couldn't forget the image of her appearing from beneath her coat in that cell. It had been several months ago now, but for some reason, from that day he had felt drawn to her. Did he want to protect her? Or was she just a member of staff he had something in common with – their love of art and its history? Whatever the reason, she occupied his mind frequently of late.

Ahead of him was the Moulin Rouge. Pale blue sky filled the gaps between the open wooden fretwork of the windmill's sails, its red paint seeming to sneer at the drab grey buildings surrounding it. A woman with heavily rouged cheeks smiled as he approached.

'Dancing girls, sir? Perhaps some food?'

Hans had intended to walk by, but the invitation piqued his interest. His gait slowed. He'd never been inside before, despite hearing from his comrades that this cathedral of vice was *the* place to visit while in Paris. Perhaps he could just look inside. He nodded, pinching the fingertips of his leather gloves, easing them off.

The reception area was sumptuous with expensive perfumes lingering over a backdrop of red and gold opulence. Plump cushions reclined on upholstered benches, chandeliers glistened above heads and paintings hung from crimson walls, the antithesis to Picasso's apartment he'd visited last week.

The vestibule was full of activity. Small groups of German soldiers loitered with off-duty dancers and couples came and went through the door to the dance hall. Hans still found it unusual that French women happily draped themselves on the arms of their country's occupiers. Civility was one thing, but surely sleeping with the enemy was a step too far.

Each time the door to the dance hall opened, effervescent laughter spilled from inside. Hans followed a group of four soldiers through to the entertainment. Cigarette smoke softened the colours of the room but the bright red, orange and gold of the decor seeped through the haze. Someone was playing a piano, and at the far end of the room was a stage where a line of dancers swirled and danced, lifting their petticoats to reveal short lace bloomers and black stockings. Several soldiers sat at a nearby table and encouraged by drink and comrades' coaxing them, one of the group whooped and blew kisses at the girls. The men spotted Hans.

'Hey, Corporal. Join us!'

Hans didn't feel tempted to sit at the table or enter into their banter. He raised a hand in thanks and pointed to his watch, hoping to indicate that he had to leave. Back in the entrance hall, he noticed a framed black and white photograph in one corner of the room. It appeared to show a huge elephant standing next to this very building, but surely the dimly-lit area was playing tricks on his eyesight. Curiosity drew him closer. It *was* an elephant and it was as tall as the sails of the windmill. He shook his head in disbelief.

'Incredible, isn't it?'

Hans turned to see a young dancer standing beside him. Her face was painted with thick make-up and she wore a long shawl around her shoulders, covering her costume.

'Sorry,' she said. 'I shouldn't intrude but I thought you might like some company. I'm Nina.' She held out her hand.

Hans swapped his gloves from his right hand to his left and shook her hand. 'Was this elephant really here?'

Nina laughed. 'It was. I bet you didn't even know we have a garden here?'

He smiled instinctively. She was open and friendly. All the other Parisians he'd met had either treated him as if he was invisible or else they were openly hostile with their sneers.

'I didn't.'

'It's not here now, of course. The original building burned down over twenty-five years ago, but the elephant was here during the earlier years of this place opening.'

'Why would someone build such a huge statue?'

Nina grinned, showing a smudge of red lipstick on a front

tooth. 'It wasn't a statue, and the owner didn't build it. They bought it from the Paris Universal Exhibition late last century.'

'You don't look old enough to remember,' said Hans with a laugh, surprising himself to be flirting.

Nina giggled and playfully slapped his shoulder. 'We're all told to read about the history of the place before we start work here, just in case our customers ask us about it. Not that any of them do. You're the first. The others are more interested in what time we finish work.'

'So if it wasn't a statue, what was it?'

Nina shook her head and frowned. 'You're a strange one.'

Hans raised his eyebrows in question.

'A pretty lady is paying you attention and you seem to be more interested in a boring photograph, so that either makes you happily married or… ' she looked behind her before whispering, 'homosexual.'

'For your information, I'm neither. I'm simply fascinated by it. I can appreciate your beauty, but also the magnificence of this structure,' he said, pointing to the photograph.

'I've finished my shifts for the day. How about you buy me a drink and I'll tell you all about the luxurious opium den that was built inside the elephant, where for a single franc, gentlemen could enter by way of a spiral staircase inside the leg.'

Hans extended his elbow towards Nina and gave a small bow. She slipped her arm through his and together they walked towards the crimson velvet bar. One drink, he told himself. He had no intention of taking part in any other form of amusement. He just wanted to relax with a pretty lady and dilute the memory of his visit to the Spanish painter, and of Matilde.

TWO HOURS AND too many drinks later, Hans left The Moulin Rouge feeling light headed and a little unsteady. He hadn't intended to spend so long indulging in good wine and delightful conversation, but time had slipped by as smoothly as the glasses of wine had tasted. Towards the end of their conversation, amidst unrestrained laughter and loud *shushing* with fingers pressed against wine-stained lips, he and Nina had devised an elaborate dare.

Chuckling to himself and emboldened by alcohol, Hans concentrated on walking in a straight line while following Nina towards a clothes stall not far from the windmill. He stood a short distance away while Nina bartered in French for an off-white shirt, a pair of trousers, thick-soled shoes and a faded trench coat. She winked at Hans who fell in step beside her, back towards the Moulin Rouge. Inside, she gave him his change and the bundle of clothing.

'I dare you,' she said.

Hans smirked and walked towards the gentlemen's lavatory and entered a cubicle, sitting down on the lid of a toilet. He grinned while pulling off his jackboots and trousers, wondering why undressing felt so arduous. When he'd finally changed from his uniform into civilian clothing he sat once again on the lid, waiting until the last person had flushed a nearby chain, washed their hands and left the room. Having folded his uniform, he left the cubicle and hid his clothing where Nina had suggested, in a cleaning cupboard that wouldn't be opened again until the following morning. He looked in the mottled mirror, straightened his collar and ran the palm of his hand over his hair before leaving the building.

Paris smelled of horse manure, tar, diesel and coffee. With the sun on his face, a smile on his lips and alcohol in his bloodstream, Hans felt invincible. He could almost convince himself that the war did not exist as he walked towards the Latin Quarter.

It had been Nina's idea to change his clothing. Hans had complained of how people saw his uniform instead of him and of how he was made to feel unwelcome wherever he went. So when she suggested changing out of his stiff grey-green jacket and trousers, it had seemed like an exciting idea. However, having walked for fifteen minutes, the haze of excitement was gradually diminishing and the reality of his position was growing clearer. It was illegal for him to go out in public without his uniform on. He would be hauled before his superiors and have to answer for his actions should he be caught.

Hans lowered his head when two German soldiers crossed the road ahead of him with arms full of shopping bags and shoeboxes; it seemed his countrymen were the only people who could afford to buy these days. Hans held his breath. The military men walked closer and passed by him, continuing their conversation. A surge of adrenalin raced through Hans' body and once his heartbeat had calmed, he felt excitement begin to grow again. He could do this. He would continue, spend some precious time admiring paintings and hurry back to change once again. He decided that this would be a one-off. It was just too risky.

Music drifted from an open window but the majority of shops were closed, their shutters closed. He passed a bakery with a queue winding out of the doorway and his stomach growled at the thought of bread. The line moved forwards one step when a woman left the shop cradling a wrapped loaf. Hans decided to stop and wait behind an elderly man, who in turn, touched his beret in greeting. Hans nodded in reply, astonished at the gesture. It felt good to be noticed as a man, not an enemy.

Ten minutes later he was standing inside the shop. He pulled a blue and white five-franc note from his pocket, noticing the words, *Vivre Général de Gaulle* scribbled at one corner. Clever, he thought. Even the French who supported Pétain couldn't afford to destroy money. As he waited his turn, Hans looked past the counter and into the kitchen. The wooden table used for kneading dough looked scrubbed and the gaping mouth of the oven door spoke volumes; bakers were forbidden from baking bread every day.

Hans left with a small flour-dusted bun. It was bland and dry, but he ate it quickly. Turning the next corner, he saw a sign above an arched doorway. *Bertrund Rosenberg's Art Gallery.* A man, arms browned by the sun, played on an old accordion to one side of the doorway and a thrill pulsed through Hans as he crossed the road towards the building. It was like entering a church. He felt as if he should whisper with reverence in this darkened place and the sweet, dusty smell of books reminded him of incense. It was a large room with strategically placed carved Breton chairs, each one facing a wall where paintings hung beneath angled lighting that beckoned him as if he were a moth.

'What do you think?'

Hans turned to see a smartly dressed man standing beside him. He was a balding and middle-aged with a friendly smile. Hans guessed he was the gallery owner and knew he had to use his best French accent.

'Are you Monsieur Rosenberg?'

'Indeed, but please call me Bertrund. I haven't seen you here before.'

'I don't live here. I'm visiting family.'

Bertrund nodded, knowingly. 'We are lucky to have family nowadays. So many of mine have moved away and a few have been arrested.'

'I'm sorry.'

'It's not our fault. It's theirs.'

Bertrund pointed to a non-specific place out of the bay window. Hans knew who *they* were. Germans. Him.

'Aren't you afraid of remaining open?' asked Hans.

'Afraid? No. Sensible? Yes. I'm closing the gallery this weekend, storing my collection and joining my family in the south. They're escalating the number of raids on Jewish homes and businesses so sadly it's time to go. Last October they confiscated our wireless and bikes. They even disconnected the gallery telephone. Can you believe we're also banned from using public telephones so how do they expect us to contact family? There are even rumours that we're to be prevented from entering public places. I was born here as was my mother, but that doesn't seem to count for anything these days.' He shrugged his shoulders, palms upturned. 'I'm sorry, my friend. You visited my gallery to look at my beautiful paintings and here I am making your heart heavy. Here, what do you think of my Van Gogh?'

Hans knew the painting well, having studied it along with many more at university. *Painter on the Road to Tarascon* hung in emblazoned blues, yellows and greens before them. It was a self-portrait of the Dutch artist walking in the midday sun, carrying his art materials. The vivid colours and distant Cyprus trees hinted at a Mediterranean climate.

Hans imagined the heat of the day and sound of the leaves rustling in the painting. 'I can smell the scent in the air and feel the sun on my back.'

Bertrund bellowed with laughter and slapped Hans on the back. 'I knew you looked like a man with art in his soul. I'll leave you in peace to enjoy their beauty.'

Hans thanked him and imagined being good friends with him in another lifetime. Bertrund was right, he thought. His heart *was* heavy, not only because of the man's story, but also because of this war. It was difficult to believe that he had been in

Picasso's apartment to find and remove a painting instead of admiring the man and his work. And now here he was standing in this gallery, out of uniform and pretending to be French while wishing he could get to know this Jewish gallery owner better. The Führer called these paintings degenerate art, yet to Hans they were intoxicating. He could see textures, each dab, drag and swipe of brush marks. He could see the shapes of daubed oil paint, the vibrant colours juxtaposed against plain, dark areas.

For a moment he was reminded of a visit he made in 1937 to an exhibition in Munich. The paintings on view had been accumulated from museums around Germany with the intention of ridiculing modern art before banning its sale. The paintings had been deliberately hung next to drawings by children or mentally handicapped adults: Marc Chagall, James Ensor, Henri Matisse, Pablo Picasso, Léger, Dalí. They were displayed with the intention of humiliating the artists, yet here in this small gallery tucked away in the heart of the city, they were shown for their individuality and brilliance.

Hans was just wondering how long he would dare to stay out of uniform, when a figure at the bay window caught his attention. It was the man who had been playing the accordion by the doorway. Did the man look to his left and nod? Hans felt uneasy. If he was signaling, to whom was he signaling? Instinct told him to leave immediately. He walked as nonchalantly as he could out of the building and crossed the road without looking right or left. He stood leaning against a lamppost and lit a cigarette before daring to look up. The accordion player was walking away and Hans was just beginning to feel as if he was being paranoid when a German lorry and car arrived at speed, stopping outside the building.

It all happened very quickly. Three men exited the car and six soldiers climbed out the back of the lorry. Guns drawn, they hurried inside the gallery. Within seconds, Hans heard raised voices. He felt sick. He needed to return to the Moulin Rouge and get back into uniform as quickly as he could. How could he have been so reckless? And what would happen to Bertrund?

He threw his cigarette into the gutter knowing that he couldn't intervene. He began to walk quickly back in the direction he'd come from. Noise drew his attention back across the road but he continued walking while glancing towards the commotion. Betrund was being manhandled out of his doorway and thrown into the back of the car. It was immediately driven away, leaving the soldiers to seize the paintings. Hans stopped, his eyes wide in horror. The first German was carrying the *Painter on the Road to Tarascon* upside down under one arm. He cringed as it was roughly scraped along the floor of the lorry. Next came a Renoir, a Gauguin, Delacroix…

Hans turned away, unable to watch any longer. Of course he knew that art theft had been orchestrated by the leaders of his nation for a long time, but to see Bertrund Rosenburg being removed from his gallery with such force and the paintings thrown into the back of the lorry, was too much. Anger grew inside him as he hurried back past the bakery and towards the windmill. He cared little at that moment for his own safety. He hated the war. He hated his uniform and, at that moment, he hated his nationality.

15

May 1941

IT HAD BEEN six months since Xavier's execution. Time had passed in a blur of drawing up inventories, searching markets for edible food and moving home. It hadn't been Matilde's choice to leave her marital apartment, but the Vue du Jardin building had been requisitioned by the Germans to accommodate soldiers. She had been given two days to vacate, a luxury afforded to her because she worked for the Reich. She supposed that she should be thankful, as civilians were normally told to leave their home immediately with what they could carry on their backs.

Matilde had asked for help from the underground cell and both Henri and Philippe helped her move furniture and clothing in Philippe's van. She had taken Xavier's clothes with her, detesting the thought of a German wearing them if she left them behind. There had been no sign of Sylvie on the day of leaving, which Matilde found odd, but at least speaking with Henri had given her the opportunity to ask once again, how she could help.

For the past month Matilde had been living with Adrienne, the schoolteacher she'd met on Armistice Day during the demonstrations and who had worked alongside Xavier before the war. Adrienne had welcomed her warmly on the doorstep saying she would be glad of the company. But before Matilde had stepped over the threshold, she knew she had to reveal where she worked and for whom. She would never forget the look of horror on Adrienne's features before her friend tried to close the door in her face, but Matilde had quickly looked over her shoulder and whispered that she was working for the Resistance. The door had tentatively re-opened and now, four weeks later, Adrienne was aware of everything. Matilde knew it couldn't have been any other way and she trusted her. Since that day, a comfortable friendship had grown between them and although no one could replace Xavier, Adrienne's company had certainly eased her loneliness.

MATILDE ARRIVED AT work at half past seven, early enough to enter her office before Gertrude Loup, but not too early to arouse suspicion. As usual she showed her *auswiss* to security as she entered, although she found this a pointless exercise because she'd been working at the museum for seven months now and all the guards recognized her. The corridors and stairwells were quiet apart from a couple of officers who didn't appear to notice her. Once inside her office, she hung up her coat, turned on a small electric heater and uncovered her typewriter.

Kommandant Beitel had been summoned to Berlin so she was taking this unexpected turn of events as a good opportunity to look for information in his office. She hadn't slept well, but that had come as no surprise, being the night before undertaking her first act of subterfuge.

Matilde opened her office door and paused. There was no sound in the main reception room where Gertrude Loup usually sat. She walked to the Kommandant's door and pressed her ear against the wood. Silence. She knocked, just in case his meeting in Berlin had been cancelled, then a sudden thought made her panic. What if he answered? She didn't have a reason for knocking. Coffee. She could ask if he would like a coffee.

There was no answer, much to Matilde's relief. She gripped the handle and turned it. The door opened with the gentlest of pushes. The room smelt of ashtrays and leather. Leaving the door ajar, she hurried to the desk and began reading loose paperwork despite knowing he wouldn't leave important information on top of his desk. She glanced towards the door. Next she tried a drawer but it was locked. She looked around for a key, lifting books, moving two dirty glasses and opening a small box on the table. There were only cigars inside. She ran her fingers along the underside of the desk edge, scanned the bookshelf, looked inside an empty pewter tankard and ran her fingers through the soil of a potted plant. She bit her lip. Time was running out and who knew when she would have access to this office again? She looked over the desk again, her gaze settling on the cigar box. Maybe… She moved the tubes of tobacco to one side and something glinted. A key! She picked it up and unlocked the drawer. It clicked loudly. She paused again, scanned the room and listened, almost expecting to see Kommandant Beitel standing in the doorway with a gun pointed in her direction. No one. Silence.

Matilde opened the drawer and began to sift through the information inside. Her hands were shaking uncontrollably. Although this was the third time she had entered this office alone, it was the first time she'd dared to open his desk. A voice in her head begged her to leave the room before it was too late, but she remembered Xavier and all the other men who had lost their lives trying to help their country. She continued searching despite her heart thumping and perspiration dampening her back.

Matilde read extracts from different pages: invoices, business activities, dates for official visits and menus for restaurants. Then she felt something, a folder at the bottom of the pile. Could this be what she'd been looking for? She slid the folder from beneath the stack of paper. Opening it, she read an inventory of paintings; a list that she herself had made. But someone had written additional notes beside each title, the addresses in Germany where the artworks were being shipped.

Matilde knew that the amount of treasures being stored in the *Jeu de Paume* was increasing to such an extent that the Nazis had to move them on for safekeeping elsewhere. She already had a good grasp of German from school and from working at the museum for months, but some words meant nothing to her. She needed to make a copy for Henri, but did she dare take the paperwork to her office and then home? Matilde looked at the clock on the wall. She had quarter of an hour before the Kommandant's secretary arrived at eight o'clock. She didn't have time, so tried to at least memorize a date and station. Then she felt the sheet of paper shift between her fingers. It had a carbon copy attached to it. Surely the Kommandant wouldn't notice if the copies were taken for twenty-four hours? And even if he did, he'd think Gertrude Loup had filed them elsewhere.

Matilde moved quickly. She removed the carbon copies from three sheets of paper, placed the originals back in the folder, closed the drawer and replaced the key.

Back in her office, Matilde felt exhilarated both with relief and at her own bravery. Who would have thought that the timid woman, who was afraid of making eye contact with Germans last year, would have trespassed in a high-ranking Nazi's private office? Could the dead look down on the living? Would Xavier be proud of her?

She couldn't concentrate on anything. The adrenalin was wearing off, leaving her terrified that her actions would be discovered. Hearing the door to the main office open, she glanced at her watch. One minute to eight. Gertrude Loup had arrived. Matilde walked out of her own door, determined to brazen out her fear in front of the moody secretary. She stepped into the reception area to say good morning and to make it clear that she had been working in her office, but Gertrude's desk was empty and the Kommandant's door was open. She chewed a fingernail and walked towards the open door. Just as she was about to look inside the room, Corporal Engel walked out, bumping into her.

'Oh! Excuse me,' said Matilde.

Corporal Engel steadied her by grasping her upper arms. 'It was my fault. I'm sorry, I didn't know anyone was here yet.'

Why had she assumed that the corporal had gone to Berlin, too? A stupid mistake.

Before Matilde could answer, she was perturbed to notice him looking at her chest. Embarrassed she looked down and was horrified to see a corner of the Kommandant's paperwork sticking out of her cardigan. Her cheeks burned. She couldn't breathe. She had been caught. It was all over before she had even passed on any relevant information.

The main door opened and Gertrude Loup walked in carrying her bag and lunch satchel. She stopped and stared at the two of them in the Kommandant's doorway.

'Good morning, Madame Loup,' said Corporal Engel, then turning to Matilde, 'and thank you for your assistance, Madame Pascale. You may return to your office now.'

Matilde frowned and looked at the Corporal, questioningly. Astonished, she saw his eyes flick in the direction of her own door. She stepped inside her room and closed the door behind her.

Once inside she felt dizzy with nerves. What had that meant? Would he report her in his own time or had he not realised what was hidden in her clothing? Any exhilaration at her bravery had vanished. Matilde felt scared and sick. She sat in her chair, her body rocking in rhythm with her hammering heartbeat. What if he blackmailed her? No, she was being silly. She pulled the carbon copy from her clothing and looked at the corner the corporal had seen. No visible writing. Unless he searched her, he knew nothing, she told herself.

For the next hour, Matilde found it impossible to concentrate on her work. The stolen paperwork was now at the bottom of her handbag hidden beneath her scarf, gloves, purse and hand cream, but it was may as well have been mounted on plinth due to its presence in her mind. Why had she been so stupid? At any moment the Gestapo could barge in and drag her away. Should she hide the documents in the office somewhere?

She stood up and walked towards her office window. Roses sprinkled colour around the grounds, contrasting with the drab uniforms of the guards standing at the razor wire surrounding the *Jeu de Paume*. Matilde had only been at the window for a moment when she heard her door creak open. She didn't dare move. She rested her forehead on the cold glass, taking one last moment before being arrested and dragged into an awaiting car.

'I have sent Madame Loup on an errand.'

Matilde didn't answer.

'You need to be more careful,' Corporal Engel said.

Matilde remained silent, her back to him.

Before he turned and shut the door she heard him speak again, more quietly this time. It left her stunned. His sharp German accent had softened as if its edges had been smudged.

'Not all of us want this war. Not all of us agree with what's happening.'

By the time she'd steadied her breath and turned around, he had gone.

16

MATILDE WALKED IN through Adrienne's front door just before six on the evening she'd taken the paperwork from the Kommandant's office.

'How did it go?' asked Adrienne, wringing her hands. 'I've been worried sick all day.'

Matilde dropped her bag and slumped in an armchair. 'I found some important information.'

'Really? What?'

'Details of where paintings are being sent.'

'Thank God you're safe and no one saw you.'

Matilde grimaced.

'What?'

'It's not as simple as that.'

Adrienne perched on the arm of the chair opposite, her clasped hands pressed between her knees, looking intently at Matilde. 'What do you mean?'

'Corporal Engel knows something's going on.'

'The German you work with?'

Matilde nodded.

'*Merde!*' Adrienne hurried to the windows and peered through the curtains into the dark evening. She looked over her shoulder back at Matilde. 'Does he know what you've got?'

'No. Not exactly. He knew I was hiding paperwork but he

doesn't know what.'

'I don't understand.' Adrienne returned to the chair's arm. 'Why did he let you go? Did he ask questions? Could they come here?'

'He told me to be careful.'

'A warning?'

'I don't think it was a warning. It was the way he said it. He came into my office and said he didn't agree with what was happening. It was as if he was confiding in me.'

'God, Matilde! How can you be gullible? Don't trust him. You can't trust any Germans. He's probably waiting to catch you in the act of stealing confidential documents to make an example out of you.'

'Then why didn't he ask to look at the paper he saw tucked in my clothing or ask to search my bag?'

Adrienne gripped two fists of her hair close to her scalp. 'He saw the paper on you?' She got up and paced the room. 'I don't think I can cope with this anymore. It's too dangerous.'

'I'm sorry. You're right. I was careless, but it's a huge lesson learnt. I've worked with Hans for a while now and he seems different to the others.'

'You mean he's sweet on you and trying to get you in his bed. And you called him Hans. How long have you been so familiar with him? What better way for him to blackmail you?'

'I really don't think he would, and I don't call him by his name at work. I don't know why I said it just then. I wish you knew him. It's as if he's ashamed that they have a huge warehouse packed with stolen treasures. I catch him looking at watches and rings with a sad expression. I've seen him stare at a painting for several minutes without moving. He actually cares about those pieces.'

'Have you ever thought that maybe he's planning to steal

them for himself? You're playing a dangerous game if you start to trust him, and don't forget, if they arrest you then they arrest me too.'

'I don't forget. I won't.'

'Good.' Adrienne stood up and straightened her skirt with her palms. 'I presume you're going out tonight if you've got the information?'

'Yes.'

'I'd better put our dinner out then.'

AN HOUR LATER, Matilde slipped out of the front door. She had almost two hours to accomplish her mission before curfew. It was raining and fat droplets sank into the fabric of her coat. She hurried on.

Eventually she crossed the square and passed the café where she had first met Charles. It seemed like such a long time ago now. She could see dim lamplight and figures drinking inside the café, their outline obscured by condensation on the windows. A few people crossed the square in the opposite direction to her, so she was alone when she reached the narrow alley that led to Henri's house. Her footsteps echoed against the end walls of tenement blocks on either side of the thin passageway. She tried to walk more quietly on the balls of her feet.

The end of the alley opened out on to a road. She had to cross it in order to reach the solid gate leading to Henri's front garden. Although the road seemed clear, Matilde did as she'd been instructed and walked across the road and past Henri's garden gate.

She continued for several minutes before stopping between two lampposts and pretending to tie her laces. If anyone had looked closer, she thought, they would see her touching her low-heeled court shoes without a lace in sight.

The road was still clear so she made her way back towards the gate. As she neared it a dog barked nearby, startling her. She let out a long breath through pursed lips and stopped. Again she checked up and down the road before entering the gate.

Inside the front garden she paused to catch her breath, only now realizing how soaked she was from the unexpected May downpour. Nerves had masked her discomfort until now. Through the obscured glass window, Matilde could see a door open at the end of the hallway, a pale lemon rectangle of light shining from the kitchen doorway. She wiped raindrops off the end of her nose with the back of her hand and tapped out the code on the glass.

'Hello.'

'It's Matilde,' she replied, softly.

Henri let her in and she followed him into the kitchen.

'You should have come tomorrow night,' said Henri. 'The weather's dreadful. Here.'

Matilde peeled off her wet coat and accepted the proffered towel.

'I had to come tonight because I need to return some paperwork before the Kommandant returns tomorrow.'

Henri's eyes opened wider. 'You've brought some paperwork from his office?'

'Yes, from a locked drawer in his desk.'

Matilde withdrew the paperwork from the sleeve of her cardigan. It was limp and damp so she opened it carefully on the table. Henri leaned forwards to read it.

'Are you sure it was safe?' he asked, running his finger down the list of paintings to be transported from the museum.

'As safe as anything can be nowadays.' Matilde had already decided not to mention her conversation with Hans.

'You did well, Matilde. Right, I need to find a pencil to copy this transportation information.'

17

June 1941

LYING IN THE damp undergrowth, Matilde could feel the train's thrumming pulse vibrating through her body. The headlight on the track ahead grew closer. As the locomotive's brakes squealed, she tucked her chin against her chest and squeezed her eyes shut. Daring to look up, she saw yellow sparks showering the tracks as metal scraped on metal. She was panting in fear at the realization that the train was actually stopping. The plan that she and Henri had made with the others was actually happening, thanks to the information she had gathered.

Looking along the railway line in the opposite direction, she could see Henri still swinging a makeshift warning sign from side to side. Thankfully, darkness and distance had prevented the driver from noticing that the red light was emanating from a thin coloured scarf inserted inside a simple lantern.

No one moved. They were waiting for the order. If the Germans discovered too soon that it was an ambush and not simply a warning of danger on the track ahead, they would have time to pick up speed, taking with them priceless artwork to different destinations.

The wind was strengthening, stirring trees and whipping up loose leaves. As the train slowed, moonlight highlighted someone holding a lantern inside the engine's cab, leaning out, trying see along the line ahead.

The locomotive drew closer. Indistinct shapes merged in the night as the wagons clanked and creaked. Matilde fumbled with her torch as she descended the embankment leading to the railway line. The bag of tools she was carrying dug into her bony hips through the thin fabric of her dress. Flashes of torchlight from fellow Resistance members appeared in a line alongside her, creating shadows that sprawled over hedgerows and bushes. Gingerly making her way through low-lying shrubs, she gasped as something grabbed her ankle. She fell forwards, arms outstretched into a bed of nettles as her torch rolled a short distance away. After taking a second to catch her breath, Matilde stretched forwards, her fingers inching towards the small beacon of light. She retrieved the torch and shone it towards her foot, relieved to find that it was only a tree root that had tripped her.

She limped a little further, stopping where the ground changed to jagged stones at the edge of the railway track. Carriages passed in front of her, rattling and groaning as they slowed. Steam hissed and a stringent odour of creosote and belching coal smoke filled her nostrils. She could taste soot.

Matilde's skin prickled with nettle rash and she could feel her heart thudding against her ribs. The wind blew her hair across her eyes and a light rain spat on her face. Disorientated, she remained still.

'Now!' came a shout.

Shots rang out. The man in the cab dropped his lantern seconds before he toppled from the engine. As previously planned, a flurry of small fireworks exploded. Together with staccato cracks of gunfire, the aim was to fool the Germans into thinking that they were outnumbered. Instructions and warnings hung in the air amidst a hail of bullets and the hissing of pistons.

'Look out, to your left.'

'He's running away, shoot him.'

More gunfire. Matilde was petrified. She crouched lower. The train gasped and sighed, its carriages clunk-clunking until the engine finally stopped. Shots were exchanged and orders barked on both sides. Someone howled in pain and fell with a dull thud. Footsteps ran past. She remained still as she'd been instructed, watching shards of white torchlight cut through the night. Mayhem continued until she recognised Charles's voice calling to the men from the front of the train.

'No passengers. Seven dead Germans and two escaped. We'll have to be quick. They'll alert the Gestapo.'

Matilde stood up and joined the group of men congregating by the engine. Henri appeared at her side. 'Well done, everyone. The two who escaped have got half an hour's run ahead of them to sound the alarm, and then we'll have roughly ten minutes before vehicles arrive. We'll have to get a bloody move on. Matilde, which numbers?'

Matilde shone a light at a sheet of paper with carriage numbers and their contents listed, valuable information she'd obtained by theft. 'Numbers 2419 and 2420 contain paintings and valuable artefacts.'

Men followed Henri as he hurried along the track, holding a lantern above his head while looking at the wagons. Half way down the length of the train, he stopped and turned before addressing everyone.

'These are the ones. Place the lanterns up the bank. Those who are to form a chain, get in line now. Drivers, wait in your vehicles. Matilde, pass the bolt cutters to Pierre. Get these doors open now.'

Everyone got to work. Matilde emptied her bag of tools and lanterns were spaced at intervals leading up the embankment. Their vehicles were parked on a dirt track at the top. Francis had brought his hearse and Philippe his truck. It had been a risk driving here tonight as only Germans and emergency vehicles were allowed on the streets of Paris these days. Being a doctor, Charles could legally drive his car, but strictly speaking, only when he was on duty. It was doubtful that sabotage was considered being on duty.

Someone cursed.

'It's taking too long to cut the wire securing the bolts.'

'Try bloody harder, then.'

Matilde bit her fingernails. Why had she demanded that she should come too?

'We're in!'

The door was dragged open and torches shone inside. White beams highlighted wooden crates piled one on top of the other. There was a moment's pause in disbelief before men climbed inside and began to crowbar the boxes open. Frames were extracted, each wrapped separately so it was unknown which masterpieces were being handed from person to person. The paintings were passed along a chain of men along a line snaking up the embankment, followed by bulky packages. Who knew what treasures lay inside?

Due to the information Matilde had discovered in the Kommandant's office, three separate resistance cells had merged to plan this assault. As she watched in the dim light of the moon and oil lanterns, it seemed incomprehensible that she was the catalyst for this attack. She felt a pride for these brave men who were risking their lives to save priceless treasures, works by Picasso, Matisse, Chagall, Braque, Vermeer, Rembrandt and many more incredible artists.

A calm descended on her. As she watched these courageous people pass the last of the items up the chain of men, she no longer felt limp and cowardly. She determined not to be governed by this invader or ordered by an enemy. She would fight for France and her countrymen, even if the battle would one day take her life. Xavier would be proud of her. She knew in her heart that she was here, facing this danger, for that very reason. Even though he was no longer here, she wanted to prove to Xavier that she wasn't a coward.

And what about Hans? How would he react if he knew she was actively resisting? Where would his loyalties lie?

'Matilde! Quick! It's time to go.'

18

'DIAMOND ENCRUSTED SILVER tobacco box,' said Hans, squinting into his magnifying glass. He measured the box, gave it a number and relayed the information to Matilde, who wrote it down.

'Silver picture frame with leaf motif.'

Before he placed it to one side for packing, he looked at the family depicted in the sepia photograph. Three generations looking uncomfortable, unused to having their picture taken, but evidently happy due to the closeness of their bodies and linked arms. Where were they now? He slowly laid it face down.

'Mirror. Giltwood. Oval. Probably 19th century from the Belle Époque era.'

'Belle…?'

Hans looked at Matilde. Her brown eyes searched his for a second before she looked away. Could she really not face looking at him for more than a second? Hadn't he tried to communicate his, if not his solidarity, then understanding? He knew he had been treading a dangerous path when he told her that he did not agree with what was going on here, and maybe she hadn't understood, but did she think of him as evil?

'Belle Époque. The good old days. A time between wars.'

He saw her nod before writing in her notebook. Her fingers were slim and she still wore her wedding ring. He liked the gentle slant of her handwriting.

'What did you do before the war?' Hans held his breath. Had he really spoken his thoughts out loud? He felt as if he had broken a rule. Her face was in shadow when she answered, so he couldn't see her expression.

'I worked at an auction house.'

There was a pause before Hans asked, 'What did it sell?'

'Mainly paintings and valuables, a bit like here, except—'

'Except they weren't stolen.'

'I didn't mean—'

He held up a hand. 'It's all right. You really don't have to explain. We work together every day and I hope you can sense that I hate this… sorry. I shouldn't. What I mean is, I've visited Paris several times before. I love this city: its narrow, cobbled alleyways, its broad boulevards, its music, its architecture and atmosphere.'

Was that a hint of a smile he saw stretching her lips?

'Madame Pascale sounds so formal,' said Hans, trying to lighten the atmosphere still further. 'Can I call you Matilde when we're working like this? Alone.'

He was relieved to see her give a slight nod but disappointed when she kept her eyes on the notepad instead of making him feel more at ease, but what did he expect? She owed him nothing at all, not even conversation. He watched her doodle a circle, round and round until it was filled in with pencil lines. He was surprised when she looked up at him.

'What did you do?' she asked.

Hans rubbed his chin. 'I studied French and the history of art in Munich. I worked in a gallery for several years with the dream of opening my own. Then other people made decisions that altered the course of my life and here I am. But it's like that for all of us, isn't it? We can't be where we wish to be.'

Hans saw that Matilde held his gaze for a while longer, long enough for him to notice flecks of amber in her brown eyes and a constellation of tiny freckles across her cheeks. He lowered his head. Had he said too much? It was safe enough here in the vast storeroom, but he should be more careful in the rest of the building. You never knew who was listening.

'We'd better continue,' he said.

Matilde turned from him and smoothed the paper with the back of her hand.

'Ruby and diamond bracelet… '

On the 24th of July, the day before the next transfer of art from the museum, Reichsmarshall Göring was due to visit the Jeu de Paume for the third time since Xavier's death. Matilde now measured time by that date; the time when her old life had ended and a new one had begun.

As usual, the building was busy with preparation. Extra cleaning staff had been drafted in to make the windows sparkle, the marble shine and the wood gleam. Swastikas were removed, washed and pressed ready for rehanging. Framed photographs of the Führer were polished and straightened, floors were swept and mopped, cigarette boxes were filled to bursting and plenty of wine was stocked.

In addition to listing valuables, Matilde and Hans had spent the last couple of days retrieving the paintings that Göring had specifically requested to view. Depressingly, she realised that a copy of her itinerary must have been given to the Reichsmarshall, or how else could he ask for each particular piece by number and title? It made her feel sick that in some small way she had helped the country's treasures be picked over by senior members of the Nazi Party, as if they were pieces of fruit on a market stall. But it strengthened her resolve to keep track of these items. It was too soon to risk stopping another train, but at least she would have a record of the destination of the art chosen today, for when the war was over.

By two in the afternoon, everyone was nervously busying themselves at their desks. Even Kommandant Beitel couldn't sit still. Matilde was typing up the list she had made with Hans that morning and could hear him pacing up and down his room. He stopped every now and then, and she imagined him checking the window for their so-called esteemed guest's arrival. It was difficult to believe at this moment of stressful anticipation that she had dared to rifle through the desk drawers in his office. Matilde had found it equally as terrifying to replace the carbon copies of transportation dates as it had been taking them. She had arrived early the following day, but as she now knew where the key was hidden, the missing paperwork had been returned within one nerve-racking minute.

Unable to concentrate, she left her office and walked into the reception room. Gertrude Loup was chewing her lip and looking at the telephone. She was like a cat watching a bird, full of expectation and ready to pounce. The secretary looked up and sniffed. Matilde knew that Gertrude was finding it difficult to contain her satisfaction that it was she and not Matilde who was waiting for the all-important telephone call to announce the arrival of Reichsmarshall Göring.

Hans walked into the anteroom with a bundle of paperwork under his arm.

'Madame Loup, could you take these through to the Kommandant. He's waiting for them.'

The secretary looked at the telephone and then at the bundle of paperwork. She tutted irritably, stood up and almost snatched the pile from Hans. She hurried to the Kommandant's office, knocked and walked straight in without waiting for a reply. Matilde could hear a few words being exchanged before the telephone rang. Gertrude almost ran out of the office as Matilde picked up the receiver.

'Yes sir. Thank you. I'll inform him.'

She walked past the secretary who wore a look of utter contempt on her face. Matilde knocked, waited until summoned and pushed the door open.

'Reichsmarshall Göring has arrived, sir.'

'Thank you, Madame Pascale.'

Matilde closed the door and joined Corporal Engel, as they were to meet the entourage in a library where the art had been displayed. They walked side by side down the corridor, Matilde's shoes click-clacking on the floor trying to keep up with his long strides.

'I don't think you improved Madame Loup's countenance by answering the telephone. It will take her weeks to get over the disappointment.'

Matilde glanced sideways and caught his grin. She smiled back.

HERMANN GÖRING ENTERED the room. His coat was as big as an eiderdown and stretched across his huge belly, the material held in place by three straining buttons. His stomach seemed to have expanded since his last visit, but Matilde supposed his menu wasn't restricted like hers and her fellow French citizens. And why was he wearing a coat? It might be cloudy outside, but the weather was dry and warm.

His face was sweating beneath a felt hat and he held a baton in his fat fingers, using it as a walking stick. Matilde guessed he was about fifty, but his thickset features and limp made him appear older. He walked beside Kommandant Beitel, up and down many lines of artwork that she and Hans had displayed. Occasionally the leader of the Nazi Party leaned forwards to take a closer look at some brush marks or he would point out something to the Kommandant during conversation. Each time he chose a painting, a sticker would be placed on the back of a frame.

Matilde looked sideways at Hans. Above him a grey cobweb thread trailed in the draught, having been missed by the legion of cleaners. He was standing against the far wall, hands clasped behind his back while looking at the Reichsmarshall. If Matilde could describe his expression, she would call it hatred. His face wore a haunted look and his features seemed to have set and darkened.

It took an hour for Göring to acquire eleven paintings for himself. Eleven paintings that were other families' heirlooms. Eleven paintings that were created by talented artists to share with the world. Eleven paintings that were to be secreted away by an overweight, greedy thief who believed himself to be important enough to deserve them.

Matilde was desperate for fresh air, but knew she must first wrap the chosen artwork. Security guards would then pack them in crates for transportation. More importantly, she needed to record exactly what the German politician had chosen. It would be too dangerous for Henri's resistance cell to intervene and stop this exchange, as only museum staff knew of it, but at least she could document his address.

19

August 1941

FOR SIX WEEKS Paris had sweltered in oppressive heat. The ground shimmered with a disorientating haze that was trapped in narrow cobbled streets and permeated wide boulevards. High temperatures lingered in the shadows and slowed the city by day, until each evening, a tangerine sky ushered in the relief of cooler air.

It was a Tuesday, and the day before, Matilde had been told that she would not be needed at the museum for forty-eight hours. This forced absence was happening more frequently now that the war had taken a firm grip on the country and more meetings were being held at the Jeu de Paume. Gertrude Loup would sidle into her office and sneer with assumed dominance, informing Matilde that highly secretive meetings were to be held at the museum and her services would not be needed for the time being. Not that Matilde minded, it always came as a relief to be asked to leave. What did surprise her though, was how often her thoughts wandered to Hans when she wasn't at work.

With the sun's rays pinching her skin, Matilde turned a corner onto the Boulevard Saint-Germain, on her way to the butcher's. Paris smelled different. It looked different. She surveyed the length of the road, its buildings scarred with blood-red flags, its pavements clattering to the sound of Germain jackboots and the shrill ringing of bicycle bells. Street signs were painted in bold Germanic words and even the church clocks chimed to German time, having all been altered by one hour on Hitler's orders. She noticed that yet another shop had been boarded up as she stepped into the road to cross.

A car horn sounded.

Startled, she jumped back from the gutter. A black Mercedes passed her, red and black miniature swastikas fluttering from prongs on its fenders. Taking more care, she waited for several more vehicles to pass. First a green military lorry, its canvas sides tied back to reveal two rows of German soldiers sitting in the back. Then a motorbike with sidecar followed by a horse and cart. The horse lifted its tail and deposited a mound of manure.

Matilde crossed the road, sidestepping the latest obstacle. On the other side she walked in front of a group of Nazis drinking coffee under a striped awning. She tilted her sun hat to cover her face while inhaling the aroma of real coffee as opposed to the disgusting chicory coffee available in the shops. She passed iron railings to the entrance of the metro station before turning into Place de la Madeleine.

Matilde grimaced. A queue had already formed outside the butcher's shop although it wasn't due to open until eleven o' clock under German rules. She had to meet Henri in half an hour and had been told not to be late. She counted nine women, stood in line behind them and hoped she wouldn't be long.

Eventually the queue swayed with the movement of bodies as the shop door opened. Wicker panniers were tucked into the crooks of arms and feet shuffled in anticipation of moving forwards. It took fifteen minutes but finally she was standing at the shop counter in front of Madame Lamond.

'Hello, I haven't seen you for some time. How are you?' asked the butcher's wife.

'As well as can be expected, thank you. I've been given a day off from work.'

'That's nice. Are you still at the auction house?'

'No, I'm working at the… I'm working in administration now.'

What was she thinking? She usually shared all her news with Adrienne but had forgotten for a split second where she was. How stupid to let her guard drop. Imagine what the queue of women would say if she told them that she worked for the local Kommandant who was meeting someone so important that only security guards and the most trusted members of the German military were allowed in the museum that day. Not only would she be refused service here, but would probably be sworn at and spat at by everyone in line.

'Is everything all right?' asked Madame Lamond.

'Yes. Sorry. I just remembered something.' She adjusted her hat and surveyed the cabinet where a meagre supply of insipid looking meat that lay in metal trays.

'If it's flavour you're looking for, I'd suggest the ham hock bones,' said the butcher's wife. 'There's still some flesh left on them and they'd make a tasty soup with some carrots and turnips.'

Matilde held out her coupon. 'I'll take one, please.'

She left the shop and noticed the queue now snaked along the pavement and was overlapping another line outside the bakery. Some women exchanged a few cordial words but most fanned themselves with food coupons or slumped against the buildings' walls. A single tree stood between the end of the line and the butcher's doorway, and here a group of women huddled in the hot shade. The tree's leaves were yellowing and looked as flaccid as old lettuces.

Everyone was suffering in the heat. The bare blue sky offered as little protection to the enemy as it did to Parisians. German soldiers appeared defeated in the scorched streets as they walked more slowly in their heavy, wool, grey-green uniforms, wiping their brows and necks with handkerchiefs.

Matilde walked through the wooden arched doorway of *Église de la Madeleine* into the cool air of the stone porch. The relief from the sun was intoxicating. She dipped two fingers in a semi-circular dish of holy water, made the sign of the cross and walked a short way down the aisle. Every footstep echoed around the stone pillars and archways before she genuflected and edged into a pew close to the confessional box, where she'd been instructed to wait. She placed her shopping bag on the ground and knelt on a small velvet cushion that was lying on the tiled floor. Matilde leant forwards, rested her forehead on her clasped hands and waited.

Would Henri come? Was it safe here?

The nave smelled of incense and the bitter sweetness of wooden pews. Two candles stood sentinel on the altar, their flames dancing in the kaleidoscope of colour from sunlight streaming in through stained-glass windows. Several people were scattered among the pews waiting their turn to receive the sacrament of reconciliation. A dark-haired woman came out of the confessional box, an unfastened scarf draped over her hair and hiding her face. She sat on the bench in front of Matilde and lowered her head in prayer. After a few moments, the woman glanced up at the huge crucifix hanging above the altar and closed her eyes, her lips moving in silent prayer. Her profile caught Matilde's attention. Was that an old acquaintance? The writer, Irène Nemirovsky? Matilde leant forwards and whispered her name.

'Irène.'

A familiar oval face, with mahogany brown eyes, turned and

looked at her. The woman's face softened in recognition and she shuffled along the pew. They kissed each other's cheeks and spoke at the same time.

'So lovely to see you.'

'How are you?' asked Matilde. 'It must be almost a year since we've spoken.'

'Yes, it must be. I think it was last autumn's harvest festival, not that there was much to offer by way of food if I remember.' Irène's laugh was soft and light.

'How are Michel and the girls?' asked Matilde.

The smile disappeared. 'We're managing. It's hard for everyone. They wouldn't let Michel continue working at the bank and my writing can no longer be published.'

'Why? You were doing so well.'

'Because of this.' She pulled open a thin shawl that was draped around her shoulders to reveal a yellow felt star pinned on her blouse.

'But you've all converted to Roman Catholicism.'

Irène shrugged. 'Yes, a couple of years ago now, but they won't accept it. Our Jewish ancestry is recorded everywhere so we can't become French citizens.' She leant towards Matilde and whispered, 'Thankfully the newspaper *Gringoire* still publishes some of my work under a different name.'

'But are you safe here? Shouldn't you try and leave the city?'

'Our daughters are safe. We went to stay with their nanny's parents in Issy-l'Evêque at the beginning of all this, but Michel and I occasionally return to check on our home and collect a few more personal bits and pieces. We're going back down south in a few days' time and we'll stay there and wait out the war in the village.'

'That's very wise, but how will you cross into unoccupied France without papers and wearing a star?'

'Let's just say that money buys many things. We know it's dangerous which is why this is the last time we're coming back to Paris for a while, probably years. I have to believe we'll be safe and when this wretched war is over we'll come back home with our daughters again.'

'I hope so, Irène. The end can't come soon enough.'

'How are you? Has Xavier managed to keep on teaching?'

Matilde closed her eyes for a second or two. 'He's dead.'

'No! How? When?'

'*They* executed him.'

Irène gasped. She laid her hand over Matilde's. 'I'm so sorry. How dreadful. I simply can't imagine… '

'It was last October. It's difficult to believe it's nearly a year ago. They shot him in retaliation for someone else's crime. He just happened to be in the wrong place at the wrong time.' She shook her head, unsure how to continue the sentence. 'I live with a friend now because the Vue du Jardin is being used for soldiers' accommodation.'

'Oh, my dear. You've lost your husband and your home. How on earth are you coping?'

'I manage. I have an office job that keeps my mind occupied. It's just a matter of taking one day at a time, isn't it?'

'I suppose you're right. Is there anything I can do? Do you need anything?'

'You're very kind, but I'm fine.'

'I'll pray for you. Well, I suppose I must hurry and see if I can pick up some bread before it gets too late. They make us wait until the afternoon before we're allowed to shop, you know? The shelves are usually empty by then, but as I say to Michel, we're luckier than many.'

'Writing must help you escape from all of this, if only in your mind.'

Irène laughed. 'I'm afraid not. I'm writing about what's happening here in France at the moment. Who knows, when the war's over maybe it'll be published so the world will know of this inhumanity.'

'We can pray it won't last much longer. I hope all goes well for you all.'

'And you.'

'Be careful, Irène.'

Matilde smiled as her friend patted her hand before leaving. She listened to Irène's echoing footsteps as she walked towards the back of the church, the sound fading as she walked outside. She wondered if she would ever see her again.

20

A MAN TURNED to her and pointed to the confessional box. 'Excuse me, it's your turn.'

Matilde smiled and shook her head. 'Oh, I'm not waiting. You can go in next.'

'No, madame. It's *your* turn.'

There was a look in the man's eyes that conveyed a silent message. It must be part of the plan. Matilde nodded her thanks, shuffled along the pew and entered the confessional box. It was just big enough to turn, close the door and kneel down. She rested her clasped hands on a small shelf in front of her, and waited. Would he give her a message? A few moments passed and she began to wonder if she had imagined the intent look on the man's face. She could see the shadowed outline of the priest through a square of wire mesh in the wooden panel that separated them. She decided she must have been mistaken and began to make her confession.

'Bless me, Father, for I have sinned. It's been several months since my last confession.'

She could see the priest make the sign of the cross before speaking.

'Bless you, my child. In the presence of the Lord, please make your confession.'

Matilde wished she'd given her sins more thought, but meeting Irène and not expecting to be in this position had left her feeling unprepared.

'I've been untruthful at times. I've felt envy. And anger. Sometimes I've been impatient. Occasionally I've taken the Lord's name in vain. I've had bad thoughts about the Germans … wishing them ill.'

Matilde paused and thought of Hans. He was a German soldier. An enemy. But she knew that she didn't wish him any ill. Sitting there, in the middle of receiving the sacrament of reconciliation, she realised that she cared what happened to him. She cared a lot. Should she confess this? Wouldn't it be untruthful not to? 'Oh, and one more thing. I missed Mass last Sunday.'

'Thank you for a thorough confession. May the Lord grant you absolution from your sins as you say an act of contrition.'

Matilde began. 'Oh my God, I am heartily sorry for having offended Thee. I detest all my sins because they offend Thee. With the help of Thy grace I will amend my life. Amen.'

'The Lord has absolved you of all your sins. Please say three Hail Mary's for your penance. Go in peace to love and serve the Lord.'

'Thank you, Father.'

As Matilde moved to stand, the priest whispered.

'There's a parcel behind the statue of the Madonna and Child.'

'Father?'

'Take it into the sacristy and open it.'

Matilde didn't know whether to ask what it was or who it was from. Instead she left the confessional box and walked slowly to the front of the church where she took a seat next to the statue. She closed her eyes and recited her penance to herself, realising that she had muttered her prayers verbatim, without thought. It was nerves. Her mind was fixated on the parcel.

Matilde waited a few moments longer before standing and turning to pick up her handbag and shopping. With a swift glance towards the back of the church she could see three worshippers praying with lowered heads. It was safe if she acted now. She stepped out of the pew, felt for the package and picked it up. It was wrapped in brown paper with a length of fraying string holding it together. She didn't look behind her but walked straight to the sacristy.

The small room was thankfully empty. It smelled of candle wax and old dusty tomes. Vestments, church furnishings, prayer books and sacred vessels were stored in boxes and on shelves. There was a table placed beneath a small round window that was piled high with hymnbooks, candles, leaflets and rosaries. She pushed aside several candles and placed the parcel on the tabletop. Her heart was racing. She jumped and took the Lord's name in vain when a candle rolled onto the floor with a loud clatter. It had only taken five minutes to sin again.

Matilde unwrapped the package. It felt soft. Inside was a roll of black material. She frowned, perplexed. She lifted it up in the air and it unfolded into a recognizable shape. It was a nun's habit. Still lying in the brown paper was a stiffer white fabric. She picked it up. A nun's veil and wimple. Where was Henri? This was ridiculous.

It didn't take long to change. Without a mirror, Matilde had to guess how straight her wimple and veil looked. The length of the habit skimmed just above her ankles but she wasn't convinced her brown peep-toe shoes were suitable footwear for the outfit.

There was a knock on the sacristy door.

Matilde quickly gathered her clothes together, wrapped them in the ripped brown paper and pushed it under a rail of vestments. Would it be a member of the congregation or Henri? She opened the door and was surprised to see a priest standing in front of her with his head lowered. He quickly guided her back inside the room.

'Oh… ' Matilde thought she'd been caught. Was this a trap? Would he hand her over?

'Shhh! It's me.'

'Henri?'

'Follow me. Don't speak.'

'But—'

'I said, don't speak.'

Matilde followed Henri out of the sacristy, past the pulpit, behind the altar and through an internal door at the back of the church. Stone steps, lit by a lantern hung from a nail on the wall, led down towards a room hewn out of rock. Broken benches, cracked statues and general detritus were strewn around the room.

'Where are we?' asked Matilde.

'Take this.' Henri switched on a torch and handed it to her. 'You'll need it.'

She took the metal box-shaped torch by its handle and directed the beam of light around the claustrophobic space. Small pebbles and grainy earth crunched beneath her feet with each tentative footstep.

Henri moved a metre-high wooden crucifix away from a corner of matting on the floor, to reveal a trap door. He leant the cross against the wall.

'Follow me.'

'What?'

'It's quite safe. Just be careful and hold on tight.'

Henri disappeared into the darkness beneath the floor. She could see his torchlight bouncing off the walls as he descended. She peered inside the void and saw a ladder attached to one side of the shaft. Gathering her habit around her knees, she turned and stepped backwards on to the first rung. She was more scared of a German discovering her than descending into a black hole.

On reaching the bottom, Matilde was surprised to be able to stand up straight with ample headroom. She aimed the beam of light around the tunnel, illuminating limestone walls and small crystals that sparkled in the torchlight.

'This is incredible. I'd heard there were such passages beneath Paris but I had no idea how big they were.'

'If Paris is the heart of France, these are its arteries. Hundreds of miles of them.'

'Hundreds? It's unbelievable.'

'Follow me and be careful.'

'What about the trap door?' said Matilde, looking up at the square pale gloom of the room's lamplight.

'Father Aubry is going to close it and wait to let us out again.'

Matilde fell into step behind Henri. 'Is it safe?'

'It's safer than up there,' he said, flashing his light upwards.

Matilde shivered despite the comfortable temperature. There was a constant drip of water echoing in the tunnels. She began to feel more uneasy, claustrophobia gnawing at her thoughts as they walked further into the underground corridors. 'Are we alone down here?'

'If you don't count the six million Parisians buried down here.'

Matilde stopped walking for a moment before hurrying to catch up with Henri. He carried on walking and continued to speak.

'Who knows how many people are hiding down here, but with hundreds of miles of passages, it's unlikely we'll see anyone else.'

They walked on in silence. Matilde's thoughts were a tangle of apprehension. This was where they were hiding the paintings from the train. This was where many treasures were going to be stored for their owners' safekeeping – if everything continued to go according to plan.

'Come on. Not far now. I have to warn you that there are many bones piled up ahead of us.'

'I'd read about these long mazes of dark galleries at school. The teachers told us that the human bones are arranged in macabre displays.'

Henri stopped walking and shone his torch along the passageway ahead. 'See for yourself.'

Skulls and bones were arranged into towers, crosses, arches and rows over two metres high and five metres deep on both sides of the path. There was a bizarre symmetry and style to the whole scene as if it were an art exhibition. Matilde shone light on disassembled femur bones stacked like cordwood alongside lines of skulls, their empty eye sockets gaping blindly ahead. Some skulls were caked in sediment while others revealed the history of a violent end with bullet holes and broken craniums. All anonymous. All individually forgotten.

'Imagine having to hide down here. It must be awful.' Matilde shivered.

Henri turned from examining a skull and walked towards her still carrying it. He held it in front of his body, a palm on each temple. 'More awful than up there?'

Henri rotated the skull so its gaping orifices faced her. Small chippings of bone and dust fell from its jagged nasal opening. He handed it to her and she took it without thinking. It sat in the palms of her hands, her fingers not moving, not wanting to feel its texture. A film of limestone dust lay on its surface.

He turned and pointed to a large dome made from dismantled skeletons. 'We've hidden the artwork from the train, inside there. Several of us hollowed out an area in the middle of it. They'll be safe there until this bloody war ends and hopefully they'll be returned to their rightful owners.'

The weight of the skull in Matilde's hands revolted her. She hadn't moved since Henri had placed it there and was finding it difficult to concentrate.

Henri turned his attention back to the cranium and pointed to an eroded area. 'See this pitted area of bone? That's a sign of leprosy. Nothing changes. Centuries later and here we are with groups of society still being ostracized and segregated.'

Matilde's breath quickened. Everything seemed surreal and dreamlike to her. Thirty metres above them, people were walking through sun-drenched parks, Germans patrolled streets, and cafés bustled with customers. Here she stood holding the head of a leper while Henri was discussing prejudice. She stretched her arms, willing Henri to take the skull. He took it from her and she wiped her hands down her black robes.

21

February 1942

THE FIRST SIX weeks of 1942 were particularly cold. Leaden skies and bitter weather made Paris look as if an artist had abandoned his paints and left a colourless canvas sitting on an easel. Ice shards floated along the Seine, Paris's statues wore fresh white coats and pavements were crisscrossed with footprints. There was a muffled silence around the city, a stillness that only snow can bring.

The previous week Kommandant Beitel had arranged secretive meetings in his office, where high-ranking visitors had attended. Matilde had been ordered to stay at home last Thursday and Friday. She wondered if Hans knew what the meetings were about. It was doubtful. A young Wehrmacht corporal, who listed paintings as a job, would not be deemed important enough to have such information shared with him.

Now that the weekend was over, Matilde stepped outside into the bitter morning earlier than usual, her focus being to see if she could discover anything about the secret talks. Their underground group had already retrieved and stored more artworks having run a lorry off the road, thanks to Matilde's information about transport, routes and dates. Despite the tremendous danger, she regularly took small pieces of treasure home without cataloguing them; that way there would be no record of them. She had sewn an invisible pocket in the lining of her coat, so when she was down in the cold storerooms, a watch, several rings, small gold clocks or pearl necklaces would be slipped inside her coat. These were buried in the soil of a garden plant pot in Adrienne's back yard, until Charles would visit in his doctor's guise and take the valuables to be hidden in the catacombs.

It had started to snow again and the streets felt silent and empty. The wind that had been rattling the windowpanes earlier was now making her shiver as she leant into it. A layer of fresh white had settled over greying ice to make walking difficult. She wrapped her scarf more tightly around her neck and tensed her muscles to keep warm. Her boots were old and the soles were worn to a smooth surface that made her slip and slide every few footsteps. Wherever she could, she held onto gates, fences and railings as she battled on towards the Jeu de Paume.

As she did every day since moving to Adrienne's house, she had to walk past her old apartment building on the way to work. She had learned that it was less painful to pass if she turned her head away from its roadside façade. As she neared the entrance door, face purposefully turned towards the Seine, she heard voices and playful laughter. In the next moment she collided with two people running out of the building. Matilde struggled to stay on her feet. A man's strong grip took hold of her elbows to keep her from falling. He wore a German uniform.

She wiped snowflakes from her eyelashes, and gasped in surprise.

'Sylvie!'

'Hello, Matilde.'

Matilde was confused. How was Sylvie still living here? Why did she sound defensive and look away? And she recognised the man, too. He was the German who had come to their apartment to speak with her and Xavier. He was Officer Kemp, the soldier who suggested she work at the museum. Matilde immediately noticed that he had a small smudge of scarlet on his lips, the same colour lipstick that Sylvie was wearing.

'Do you still live here?' asked Matilde.

Sylvie pulled the collar of her fur coat higher around her chin and looked uncomfortable. It was a new coat and looked very expensive. Matilde looked down at her old friend's feet clad in warm suede boots. In that moment she understood the situation clearly.

Officer Kemp intervened. 'I have been billeted to the apartment where this lady used to live at. She called by to collect some belongings she had forgotten.'

It was so obviously a lie that it was insulting.

'But it's seven-thirty in the morning. And we were evicted last May. Nearly a year ago.'

'I'm not sure what business it is of yours, madame. If you would kindly carry on with your journey, I need to get to work.'

He held Sylvie's elbow and guided her towards a car waiting by the roadside. Matilde's old friend climbed inside and closed the door, without once looking back at her. The car pulled away and picked up speed as it moved along the Rue de Rivoli.

Matilde was stunned. Thoughts and memories flashed through her mind like the changing patterns of a kaleidoscope. She walked slowly through the skeletal Tuileries' gardens where the trees stood starkly against the dawn's pink sky. Her mind was slowly unraveling information that had previously been unexplained. She remembered the Kommandant saying that an acquaintance of Officer Kemp's had suggested her for the inventory job. Who better than Sylvie would know that she had an interest in art, its history and value? Matilde also remembered the footsteps they would hear coming down the stairs in a hurry after all the tenants had settled in the cellar of Vue du Jardin during an air raid. It must have been him.

Matilde stopped walking as a thought occurred to her. No. Surely not Sylvie. Was it her friend who had informed her German lover about Ruth? Had he passed on the information to the Gestapo? Ruth used to stay in her apartment all day. Being a Jew she didn't dare venture out so both she and Xavier used Ruth's coupons to buy food for their neighbour. It must have been Sylvie's collaboration with the Germans that made it possible for her to stay living in her own apartment with her lover.

Matilde continued to walk towards the museum as if in a trance. A headache had started to throb at her temples. She stopped again, her hand flying to her mouth. She remembered Sylvie asking after the names of her husband's friends while she was supposedly comforting her after Xavier's arrest. Had she suspected Xavier of resisting because she saw him leaving and returning at strange hours? Everything fell into place.

Sylvie was a collaborator who was living with a German officer.

HAVING SHOWN HER papers to the two guards at the main door, Matilde stepped into the warmth of the museum's entrance lobby. She shook the snow from her coat and scarf, wincing as snowflakes fell inside her blouse collar. Folding the damp material over one arm, she hurried up the staircase to her first-floor office. Once in the reception area, she switched on the overhead light and looked at the clock hanging on the wall opposite Gertrude Loup's desk. It was seven-forty-five. Had bumping into Sylvie made it too late to attempt looking inside the Kommandant's desk? And was she in the right frame of mind, having pieced together Sylvie's involvement in Xavier's death and the direction her own life had taken; homeless, widowed and working for the enemy?

In the six weeks since New Year, Matilde had been mentally noting the arrival times of Madame Loup, the Kommandant and Hans and any early morning visitors, such as the delivery of letters and parcels. No one had arrived before eight. She decided to go ahead.

Laying her coat on her desk, she placed her handbag and lunch pail on the floor and picked up an inventory list that needed the Kommandant's signature. She took a deep breath, then squeezed and turned his door handle. Stepping inside, the room smelled as it always did: stale ashtrays, leather and coffee left in half empty cups. Hurrying straight to his desk, she placed the sheet of paper awaiting a signature in the middle, on top of some blotting paper. She slipped her fingers into his cigar box, wishing her hands were not so cold and stiff. She felt the key. Careless. Surely he should change the hiding place occasionally, but then again, he probably didn't believe that one of his French female staff members would be reckless and audacious enough to look inside his drawer of private papers.

Matilde turned the key and pulled open the drawer. She leafed through several sheets, moved aside a French dictionary and policy documents. Two bold red words caught her attention. *Streng Gehei.* She knew enough German to know that this document was top secret.

She checked the desk clock in front of her. She was running out of time. Deciding to spend only a few seconds scanning this private document, Matilde turned over the top sheet. With her fingers shaking, she lifted out the paper beneath and began to read. It was titled, *Operation Spring Breeze.* What could be so secret with such a pleasant-sounding heading?

Her breath caught in her throat. This new information was

devastating. It was inconceivable. She wanted to read more but it was too dangerous to delay. Having memorized the dates she had read, Matilde replaced the paperwork, locked the drawer and replaced the key, ensuring that it was covered over by cigars.

She heard the reception door open and close. Gertrude must have arrived. Straightening the sheet of paper she had placed on the desk, she looked up to find Kommandant Beitel standing in the doorway to his office, the breadth of his body filling the opening.

'Good morning, Madame Pascale. Do you need me for something?'

Matilde avoided eye contact with him, lowering her head and letting tendrils of hair act as a shield. She twisted her wedding ring to keep her hands from trembling at such a near miss, trying to sound unconcerned.

'I've left this list,' she said, pointing. 'It needs a signature, please.'

He walked towards the window where he took off his leather greatcoat and draped it over a chair used for visitors. Matilde sidled towards the door.

'Wait!'

She stopped and turned, dreading that she had left an obvious clue to what she had just been doing. He picked up a pen and signed the paper.

'If I don't do it now, it will be pushed aside.' He held the sheet at arm's length, so she had to retrace her steps to accept it.

'Thank you,' she said.

They both heard the reception door open and close.

The Kommandant startled Matilde by shouting. 'Madame Loup!'

Gertrude Loup popped her head around the door's opening before taking a step inside. She was stick thin despite wearing a coat, her greying hair piled high in a bun and the expression of an inquisitive rodent on her face.

'Good morning, Kommandant Beitel.'

That half-curtsey again, thought Matilde. The woman had no shame.

'I'd like a strong coffee and remove these dirty cups first, will you?'

Matilde and his secretary exchanged a glance. Gertrude Loup's was a mixture of contempt and embarrassment that Matilde had witnessed such a derogatory order.

'Thank you, Madame Pascale. You may go now,' he said.

Matilde edged past the middle-aged woman and went inside her office, closing the door behind her. She sat at her desk and sank her head into her hands. Her heart was hammering and she had a sour taste in her mouth.

MATILDE LET HERSELF into Adrienne's house and placed her empty lunch pail and handbag on an armchair. The first thing she needed to do was talk to her friend. Adrienne was the only person she could confide in.

'I'm back. Where are you?'

'Upstairs.'

The aroma of food cooking was welcoming, and smelled good too. She shook her coat and scarf and hooked them on a peg by the front door. The room felt bitter, but what did she expect in snowy February without coal to make a fire? She reached for a blanket draped over the back of a chair and wrapped it around her shoulders. Pushing escaped wisps of hair behind her ears, she ran upstairs. Adrienne was sewing a button on a blouse while sitting in bed with blankets pulled up to her chest. She looked up and smiled.

'Hello.'

Matilde shivered. 'They say it's bad luck to sew in bed. Apparently it means someone will be bedbound through illness.'

'Thankfully I'm not superstitious. The weather's been dreadful, hasn't it?'

'Yes, at least it's stopped snowing for now. Why are you sewing up here?'

'This lamp's brighter here. How's your day been?'

Matilde sat down beside her friend. 'It's been eventful.'

Adrienne rested her sewing on her lap, looked up and gave a half smile while momentarily closing her eyes. 'Why am I not surprised?'

'I've discovered there's to be a round-up of Jews this summer.'

'Aren't they doing that already?'

'To some extent, but this is going to be on a different scale. Many thousands over two days.'

Adrienne frowned. 'It's only February. Can't they all be warned?'

'Impossible. How can we know where every Jewish family lives in Paris? I need to talk to Henri about it.'

'Don't say you're going out tonight.'

'No. I'm exhausted and it's too cold and dark, plus the streets are treacherous with ice.'

Adrienne laughed. 'Huh, so you can make *some* sensible decisions.' She paused. 'Are you thinking of getting mixed up with this… round-up? It sounds as if it's too big and too dangerous for Henri's little group.'

'Small groups are more likely to go unseen, but I'm not sure it's possible to help this time. It would be a gargantuan, almost foolhardy task.'

'Matilde Pascale! I do believe you're growing wise in your old age.'

Matilde gave her friend a gentle shove. 'There's something else that happened this morning, and I don't feel wise at all about it.'

Adrienne began sewing again. 'I'm listening.'

'I bumped in to Sylvie on the way to work.'

'She was your neighbour at Vue du Jardin, wasn't she?'

'Yes, and she still lives there.'

Adrienne looked up. 'But I thought the building was forcibly taken to house German soldiers.'

'It was. She's living with a German soldier in her apartment.'

'She's in a relationship with one of them?'

Matilde nodded. 'I believe she's been giving information to them, too. The man she's living with is called Officer Kemp. It was him who told me about the job at the museum. I'm certain she gave him my name. And we used to hear footsteps coming down the stairs while we were sheltering in the cellar. Sylvie was the only one who never commented on it. He must have been living above us for a while, which would have been terrifying had we known. Xavier was always in and out from meetings with Henri and the others. He could have been followed.'

Adrienne had now abandoned her sewing and had turned, wide-eyed, towards Matilde.

'But that's not the worst of it,' Matilde continued, feeling her throat constrict with emotion. 'Ruth lived like a hermit in her apartment. I don't think Sylvie ever spoke to her. I told Sylvie that Ruth was a Jew and that Xavier was helping to find out about her missing husband.' Matilde wiped away an angry, guilty tear. 'It was me. I gave her information that had them both arrested.'

Adrienne moved closer and took Matilde's hand. 'No. You were having a conversation with a friend that you trusted. How could you have possibly known that she was a sneaky, whoring collaborator? She is totally to blame.'

'But her treachery led to Xavier's death. I know we were having problems in our marriage and that he had betrayed me in his own way, but I would never have wanted him to die. Never.'

Matilde leaned against Adrienne and cried. She could feel her hair being gently stroked and heard soothing noises coming from her friend.

After a couple of minutes, Matilde sat up, sniffing. She wiped her eyes.

'It's not just the guilt of giving information to Sylvie. I feel guilty for having feelings for… for… '

'Your German friend.'

'Yes.'

'You're human, Matilde. Feelings can't easily be controlled. You've had a dreadful year and he's offered friendship and shown a little support. You're not going to act on your feelings, so just accept them.'

Matilde looked into Adrienne's eyes. 'If he felt the same… if the chance arose… I'm not sure I wouldn't act on it.'

Adrienne grasped Matilde's arms. 'That would be a very dangerous game. You would be vilified by people you knew.'

'By you?'

'That's not fair. I know you're a good person and that you're helping your countrymen as best you can. I know you wouldn't purposefully give information that would hurt anyone, but that's the point. What if you accidently said something about your missions? It would be the end of both of us and your imagined relationship with… what did you say his name was?'

'Hans.'

'With Hans.'

'I wish you could meet him. He's kind, funny and intelligent. He hates this war as much as we do. I feel safe when he's near.'

'You must snap out of it. You sound like a daydreaming schoolgirl. We imagine how we want people to be, how wonderful life would be with them and how we would be perfect together. But daydreams aren't real. In reality you'll be beset with problems, mundane jobs, irritating habits and difference of opinions.'

'Isn't that the same with every relationship? Xavier and I weren't perfect.'

'Xavier was French. We are at war with Germany. Hans is the enemy.'

Matilde stood up clenching her fists and stomped to the bedroom window, acting every bit like a schoolgirl. All she could see was her own reflection looking back, so she drew the curtains with more force than necessary.

'Don't you think I know that? How can I disapprove of Sylvie having feelings for a German, when I do too?'

'I'm not saying I agree with you for having those feelings, but she is working against France and you are fighting for France. There's a big difference.'

'You're right, but I wish I didn't feel these emotions for him.'

Adrienne climbed out of bed. Wrapping a blanket around her shoulders, she beckoned for Matilde to follow her. They went downstairs and into the kitchen.

'Sit down,' said Adrienne, pointing to the small dining table laid with cutlery and two glasses of water. 'I was early to the shops with my coupons and have made a meat hash with onions, potatoes and carrots, and there's enough to last for two days. It's a bit grey, but smells quite good. I think it's lamb.'

'Thank you. I thought it smelled wonderful when I opened the door,' said Matilde.

The two women sat eating at the table and didn't speak for

the first half of their meal.

'What are you going to do?' asked Adrienne. 'About Sylvie?'

'I'm going to protect my countrymen and give her name to Henri. If she was just living with a German, I wouldn't. But she's dangerous.'

'I agree. You must intervene. It could be us arrested next.'

Having washed the dinner plates and cleared away, they both moved to the living room. Matilde sat in the armchair, wrapped in a blanket with her feet tucked beneath her thighs. Adrienne curled in one corner of the threadbare settee and straightened a shawl across her legs.

'Do you remember playing *Le Collin Maillard* as a child?' she asked.

'Of course. Someone was blindfolded and they had to find the other children who were moving just out of their reach.'

'I hated playing that game,' said Adrienne. 'When it was my turn to be blindfolded, even though I knew I was safe at home with my friends, I still felt uneasy. I'd touch familiar furniture and run my fingers along my bedroom walls knowing their contours, but I'd still be nervous. That's how I feel now in my own home. Everything is the same, yet different.'

'Because I'm here?'

'Not you, but what you're involved in.'

'I know.' Matilde leant forwards and touched her friend's hand. 'You've been amazing and I can never thank you enough. Without you I'd have nowhere to live. I don't know where I'd be without your help.'

'But gratitude won't save us. I find myself thinking of where you would escape to if there were a loud knocking on the door. If they found you, they'd presume I was involved, which I suppose I am by letting you stay here and knowing what you do. I know it sounds cowardly, but letting you live here means I'm in danger, even though I'm not actively helping your group. I think you should talk to them about it. I'd feel happier if we had a hiding place or escape plan; somewhere to go to in an emergency.'

'I'll mention it, but you know that I'd deny that you knew anything if I was ever caught.'

'That's a bit naïve.'

'I would!'

'I believe you, but do you think the Gestapo would listen to you? You're already playing a dangerous game getting too friendly with that German at work.'

Matilde thought of Hans and immediately felt defensive. 'He's… '

'Yes, I know. He's different from the others.'

Matilde heard the sarcasm in her friend's voice. 'I'll speak with Henri. We'll make a plan.'

22

HENRI STOOD IN his kitchen looking at her. He seemed tense.

'You're not in trouble, are you?'

Matilde shook her head. 'Not me, but thousands of people are going to be.'

'I'm listening. You've discovered more than artwork destinations, haven't you?'

'Thousands of Jewish families are to be rounded up and held in the *Vélodrome d'Hiver* before being transported to internment camps. It's planned for July.'

'Christ!'

'I know stolen valuables are important, but what's more important than human life?'

'What are you suggesting?'

'Helping in some way.'

'By doing what exactly? We are a few men against an invading army. I understand how inhuman it will be for those families, but what you think we can possibly do?'

'There must be something. I'm not suggesting we can alter their plans, but surely we can help *some* families? We can warn as many as possible.'

Henri scratched his head. 'Yes, Pierre can get leaflets printed.'

'And maybe help some people to escape on the day.'

'No. Definitely not. It would mean certain death for whoever went near the stadium. How can so few men organise something that will be so heavily protected?'

'I'm not suggesting we stroll in and pull a few people out in front of the Germans' eyes. Besides, from the small amount I managed to read, they're putting the French police in charge of the operation.'

'Cowardly bastards, passing their bloodstains on to French hands.'

'There must be some way, some disguise we could use to get inside and bluff our way out with some of the sickest people. These people are suffering so much already, before they've even been shut inside that arena for God knows how long.'

Matilde noticed that Henri was deep in thought and wasn't replying. 'What?' she asked.

'Nothing. Just mulling over an idea.'

'What idea?

'I need to speak with the others. July, you say?'

Matilde nodded. 'Do you think it's possible to do something?'

'I'm not promising anything.'

'Are you going to ask the underground cells who helped us stop the train, to help?

'No. The fewer people involved, the less likely we'll be noticed.'

'Are we going to try and rescue some of them, then?'

'Slow down. I said I'm not promising anything. Charles is a doctor and maybe we can get some of them out on medical grounds. You know that we have a mechanic in the team and he's been converting his vehicles to run on compressed natural gas instead of gasoline. So we have a medical opinion and transport.'

Matilde smiled. 'So you *do* have a plan?'

'A seed of a plan.' Henri cupped the side of her face like a proud grandfather. 'I'm going to be grey by the end of this war but I'm proud of you. I remember you bursting in here after Xavier's death, demanding to help save your country. You listened and waited until time played its part in making you think and act more clearly. Now you are a valuable member of our team.'

Matilde smiled at him. 'I'm glad you think so.' Then she paused.

'You haven't finished, have you?'

'Adrienne, well, I suppose we both are—'

'Come on. Tell me.'

'We wondered if you could help us create a hiding space in Adrienne's house. If something goes wrong I would have somewhere to hide, which will give her more protection from being arrested.'

'I think it's a sensible idea. I'll speak with Francis and arrange a day to visit and have a look around the house. There must be somewhere to create a hidden area.'

'Thank you, you're very kind. It will mean a lot to us.'

'Not at all.' He clapped his hands once and rubbed his palms together. 'Now if there are no further outrageously dangerous plans you want me to make, I'll see you another time.'

'Well, there is one more thing I have to talk to you about. Her name is Sylvie.'

23

April 1942

VIOLENCE, RESTRICTIONS AND hunger continued into spring. Matilde felt Paris shrinking by the day. The occupying forces prevented Parisians from using public spaces. They restricted free movement and reduced spatial freedom. Denying the French people their liberty seemed to multiply the oppressive effect of being occupied. Queues snaked along pavements and curfews restricted movement. German soldiers had taken over the city. They strolled along pavements, sat in restaurants and attended the theatre. Uniformed groups were always found at the Eiffel Tower, the Sacre-Coeur and Notre-Dame, having their photographs taken as if on vacation. Many were weighed down with bags of fabrics, silk stockings, perfume and women's shoes, gifts to be sent back home to family and loved ones back in Germany.

Silence rang in the ears of Parisians and sadness pressed against their throats. It was as if the buildings had grown taller, the streets wider and the Seine darker. There were psychological changes too. Ever since Matilde started to resist the Germans in her own small ways, she had grown suspicious of everyone she met for fear of speaking with *les collabos*; French collaborators who would turn you into the authorities for the slightest infraction. Trust had become as rare a commodity as fresh fruit;

consequently her conversations grew dull and mundane. She purposefully kept her topics to housekeeping, the weather and recipes, not daring to risk sharing her opinion on even the most trivial of subjects regarding the city's occupation.

However, both Matilde and Adrienne felt a little more relaxed at home. After Henri and Francis had visited the house and discovered a metre-deep space beneath the floorboards, they had started work on creating an area in which Matilde could hide should the worst happen. Now a rug and dining table covered sawn and removable floorboards, beneath which had been placed an old mattress from Adrienne's spare bedroom. This small adjustment to the house helped both women sleep more peacefully each night.

One Saturday morning in early spring, Hans was lying on his bed looking up at patterns of damp stains on the ceiling. He knew the repetitive thumping was his neighbour Jürgen throwing a small rubber ball against the adjoining wall before catching it. It sounded like a metronome keeping beat to the seconds of boredom. When he was first stationed in Paris, eighteen months earlier, he'd been told that this accommodation would only be temporary. He placed his hands behind his head, looking up at the cobwebs hanging from the fraying lampshade. It didn't really bother him. It was a single room and he didn't have to share, unlike so many other soldiers. There was no need for polite conversation for talking's sake and no irritating habits to put up with, apart from audible disturbances.

He turned his head towards the window. The sky was bruised with rain clouds, their outer edges gleaming gold and silver as the sun shone from behind them. He thought of Matilde, who seemed to be stuck in his mind like a sticky burr these days. When he worked alongside her, a simple room could become an enchanting space. When he was away from her, he counted the hours until he saw her again.

He sat up, irritably, and banged on the adjoining wall. The ball bounced one more time against the wall then stopped. He needed to do something other than lie here on his day off. Despite the threat of rain showers, it was warm. Perhaps he could wander the market stalls alongside the Seine, or catch the Métro to Montmartre and take the funicular up to see if any artists were braving the showers. Better still, maybe he could arrange to *accidentally* bump into Matilde. If only he didn't have to wear his loathsome uniform.

After a few seconds, Hans slowly raised his head. Of course!

He jumped up from the bed and swung open his wardrobe doors. The beige felt fedora with a groove in the crown, left behind by the previous occupier of this room, still sat on a shelf to one side. He threw it on the bed then pushed aside his uniforms and pulled out two pairs of boots, a folded blanket and spare pillow from the bottom of the cupboard. The bag was still there. He tore it open. Inside were the civilian clothes he had worn on his drunken walk to the art gallery after his bet with the woman at the Moulin Rouge. He would take a chance and maybe even linger for a short while on the street where Matilde lived with her friend.

An hour later, Hans stood beneath a large oleander bush, its cerise, star-shaped flowers and waxy leaves serving as a temporary hiding place. He lit a cigarette. The bush was growing out of a patch of soil a few metres down the driveway of a small abandoned family-owned garage. A rusting fuel pump stood in front of a broken shop window with worn tyres and faded children's toys scattered around the forecourt. In the distance, church bells rang out.

He walked towards the door of the garage. The lock had been broken. Probably thieves, he thought. Civilians were forbidden from driving by the authorities, the only exceptions being ambulances, hearses or vehicles whose owners had obtained a pass. The majority of fuel was saved for themselves now – the Germans. He felt shame. Few cars meant little money for a garage business. This family would have had no option but to leave their garage and flee.

The door opened without force. Hans stepped inside and looked over the empty shelves, stripped of whatever had previously filled them. A plank of wood sat on top of two sets of drawers, fashioned into a table. A chair lay on its side behind it. Litter covered the floor along with dead leaves blown in during winter through a missing window. A decomposing rat lay feet pointing upwards, its beige ribs curving into a dozen white grotesque smiles.

Hans kicked the rat across the room and retrieved the chair. He placed it by the dirt-streaked front window, positioning it so that he was concealed from view but could see the front door of the house where Matilde lived with her friend. He checked his watch. It was nearly ten.

Even as he sat looking towards Matilde's front door, he shook his head. This was ridiculous. He must look a fool. He would wait no longer than half an hour to see if he could catch sight of her, and if not, he would head to the Métro. After twenty minutes, a skinny dog sniffed around the outside of the window and spotted Hans, but cocked a leg before limping away. Another twenty minutes passed, Hans having waited longer than he had planned to. He tutted and decided he wasn't going to act like a lovesick teenager any longer. He stood up, pushed the chair aside and went to leave. Standing in the garage's forecourt he took one last look at the house, noticing that the front door of the house was ajar. He stood still, his attention fully focused in anticipation.

Matilde stepped out and closed the door behind her. He felt his heart quicken at seeing her. She straightened her moss green dress, adjusted her wicker basket and patted her hair while looking up and down the street. A rouse, Hans believed, that enabled her to check the area before setting off. He wondered why she would feel the need to do that.

Hans adjusted the beige felt hat on his head. It was a little large, but that was no bad thing as he was hoping to shield his face from view until he was able to contrive a situation where he could bump into her and suggest having a coffee with him. Keeping a safe distance behind, he followed her across the Pont-Neuf, the stone bridge crossing the Seine in the direction of the Tuileries. Was she going to work? He couldn't follow her to the museum. It was against the rules for soldiers to dress in civilian clothes without good reason. Feeling relieved on seeing Matilde turn right at the end of the bridge, walking away from the Jeu de Paume, he picked up his pace. She stopped to look at a vegetable stall so Hans leaned against a tree trunk and waited. Several shoppers occasionally blocked his view, but he could still see green flashes of her dress behind drably attired older women. He watched her choose several potatoes and onions, which were placed directly into her woven basket. He smiled to himself when he saw her drop an onion. She retrieved it from the floor and laughed with the stallholder. If only she would laugh so openly with him.

Matilde continued along the row of food and bookstalls running along the edge of the river, occasionally stopping to look inside a book or squeeze and smell a vegetable. It was almost eleven o'clock when Matilde left the market and wandered along the embankment. After a short time, she descended a few steps and sat looking out into the Seine. Hans stood on the highest step, far enough away not to be noticed. The sun was warm on his back and the river smelled of the sweet decay of vegetation and fish-tainted water, strangely pleasant. He daydreamed of sitting beside her, planning their future, professing their love as they gazed over eddies and currents. The rainclouds had passed and the river was calm and blue. A gentle breeze occasionally rippled its surface but the water was still enough to reflect the buildings running along its opposite side. Now was a good time to approach her and feign surprise.

He stepped down twice, then stopped, doubting his actions. Surely it was too obvious to pretend to recognise her from the back and away from the market? She would know he had been following her. Sighing deeply, he looked from her into the water. He was a fool. She would never love him. Whenever they worked together, she spoke with him, but always appeared distant. Sad. And why wouldn't she be? She was a widow, her country had been occupied, she had been evicted from her home, forced to work for the enemy and he could never overcome the fact that he *was* that enemy.

Hans rubbed his face roughly, deciding to catch the funicular up to the Basilica of Sacré-Coeur. Just as he turned to leave, he noticed a man walking down the steps towards Matilde. The man was in his forties, dressed in baggy trousers and shirt, braces and a dark beret. On reaching the same step as her, he walked closer and sat less than a metre away. Hans was rooted to the spot.

Was the man a friend? A stranger wanting to talk? Maybe a secret lover?

He was too far away to hear what they were saying, but when they stood up together and climbed the steps to the pavement, he decided to follow, out of intrigue and jealousy. He was relieved to notice that they didn't hold hands or link arms as they walked beneath the perfumed avenue of trees, and neither did they continue their conversation.

The avenues and boulevards appeared to buzz with invisible friction. Ever since the Renault factory had been bombed a couple of weeks earlier by the British, everyone seemed more alert and agitated, wondering where and when the next raid would take place. Hans had seen how agitated his superiors had grown now that the local assembly of tanks and trucks had stopped, and it seemed that the same apprehension had been passed down to those on the street. As he looked around, he noticed a definite increase in soldiers patrolling on foot, wearing black uniforms. They were no doubt keeping a look out for saboteurs and resisters, but he still felt uneasy being out of uniform.

To his right, Hans could see Notre Dame Cathédrale on the Île de la Cité, its gothic architecture and flying buttresses dark and majestic against the blue sky. It was at this point that Matilde and her companion turned left and crossed the road, walking away from the river. Hans hurried along the main Quai de Gesvres, keeping pace and hiding behind a moving pony and trap. He stopped behind a newspaper stand before crossing the road. Where had they gone?

A shout! '*Halt! Was ist in deiner tasche?*'

Hans slipped into a doorway. A little further along the road a skinny boy of about fourteen had been stopped by two German policemen. The teenager clutched a bag to his chest and was being asked what was inside it. The boy was shaking his head.

Hans cursed. He had lost sight of Matilde and the man. What a waste of time.

Slowly, people began to pull away from the scene like an ebbing tide. No one wanted to get involved.

'Don't run, boy,' whispered Hans, to himself. 'Stand still. Drop your bag.'

One of the Germans repeated that the boy should open his bag, but instead, the boy turned and even before he took his second stride, a shot rang out. The boy fell forwards. A woman screamed. Hans momentarily screwed his eyes tightly closed against the sight. A dog ran into the road, barking and snapping at the boots of one of the soldiers. It gave a yelp when a boot made painful contact with its ribs. The other soldier pulled the bag from beneath the body. He pulled out a bundle of leaflets. Probably anti-German, thought Hans. The unfortunate boy would just have been a courier taking the bag from a printer to a group of partisans.

Within five minutes, the boy had been thrown into an open-topped truck, the policemen climbed inside the cab and all had been driven away. Like many others, Hans ventured out of his hiding place. A couple of men went over to where the boy had fallen and inspected the red pool of blood staining the cobbles. Others muttered or shook their heads.

A green dress!

Matilde and the man stepped out of a street café a couple of doors away. They seemed agitated as if they'd been waiting for the police to leave instead of relaxing over a coffee. Hans turned away, pretending to read propaganda posters pasted to a wall of a boarded-up shop. He followed as they crossed a small square passing a waterless fountain where a woman sat begging, a child in her arms. Just before they left the open expanse, Hans saw something fall from Matilde's basket and float to the floor. When he reached it, he bent to pick it up. It was a piece of onion skin, as thin and translucent as tracing paper.

He hurried past a terrace of narrow houses and kept his head down as he sidestepped a queue of men and women waiting outside a tobacconist. Turning the next corner into a larger market square, he watched them walk toward Église de la

Madeleine and enter its large wooden entrance door. He would have to wait and hope they didn't exit from a different door. He couldn't risk coming face to face with Matilde if she wasn't alone.

Sheltering from the sun beneath a broad-leafed tree, Hans batted a fly away while watching the church's arched door. His stomach churned. He was starving, having not eaten anything all day. A mother and young son walked past, the boy letting go of her hand and chasing after a group of scrawny pigeons. Hans lowered his head, leaning awkwardly against the trunk as several soldiers passed nearby, his heart beating so hard he could feel it against his ribs.

Why was he doing this? Why was he putting himself in danger just to be close to Matilde?

Ten minutes passed and a bird began to sing in the branches above him: whistling, trilling and gurgling. It was beautiful. Hans wanted to seek out the bird, almost certainly a nightingale he thought, but he couldn't risk losing concentration.

After fifteen minutes, Hans decided that if he stayed where he was any longer it would look more suspicious than stepping inside the church. If he kept his head lowered, as if in quiet contemplation, he could observe them inside from a distance. Matilde wouldn't recognise him out of uniform and wearing a hat.

Hans stepped out of the shade, crossed the square and walked towards the entrance. He rubbed the sweat from the back of his neck before lifting the latch of the oak door. Swinging it open, he stepped inside. It was cool and dark. He could smell candle smoke and incense. The noise outside sounded like a muted echo, but inside the church itself was silent.

Raising his head, Hans looked from beneath the brim of his hat into the nave. The pews were empty. He checked the time.

Nearly half past eleven. A sign read that all women must cover their heads and men must remove their hats. Damn. His fair hair would be instantly recognisable.

Hans decided he had broken enough rules already and that one more would not make much difference. He would stay close to the walls on either side of the nave with his hat firmly in place. He walked with difficulty along the back pew where small knee cushions littered the floor.

Sunshine shone through a huge stained-glass window, throwing reds, blues and greens across the altar and spreading onto the first three rows of pews. Candles flickered and huge beams in the rafters occasionally creaked, but it was so quiet Hans could hear his breath. He felt nervous. His palms were damp despite the cool of the building. He moved towards the front of the nave. There was a door to the right in front of the altar steps. He pressed his ear to it and listened. Nothing. Hans slowly wound his fingers around the handle and turned it. It clicked open and he pushed. It was a storeroom: candles, hymnbooks and religious gifts. He closed the door again.

He scratched his right temple, knocking his hat askew. The church was empty. Matilde must have left from different a different exit. Disappointment *and* relief surged through him. He straightened his hat and walked to the centre of church, each step echoing in the silence. He looked up at the elevated sanctuary where the altar stood. Christ hung suspended on a huge cross that was attached to the back wall of the building. The tabernacle's small door was open, empty of consecrated hosts until the following morning. Hans noticed a statue of the Madonna and Child to the left of the altar, positioned next to a door. He saw her halo, her loving gaze, her robe as blue as the sky outside, and her bare feet. He thought of his mother and wondered what she was doing at this precise moment.

Hans narrowed his eyes. Something had caught his attention on the floor next to the base of Mary's statue and close to the internal door. He turned and looked behind at the empty pews before stepping up onto the sanctuary. Stopping at the object, he knelt, his eyes widening when he recognised it. A flake of golden onion skin.

From his crouched position, Hans looked up at the door. Had Matilde passed through this door? He stood up and wiped his damp palms down his thighs. He took a deep breath and carefully opened the door. Stone steps led downwards, the space lit by a lamp hooked to a nail. He couldn't hear any voices or movement. Should he go down?

The grit beneath his shoes crunched on each step. It grew cooler and mustier the lower he descended. At the bottom, he slowly peered around the edge of a wall into the room. It was empty. It appeared to be hewn out of rock and used for discarded church items. A further lamp sat on the floor, highlighting broken statues and chairs, a rotten pew, snapped altar candles and kneeling-cushions spewing out white filling. Then he saw the wicker basket containing several potatoes and onions. The basket sat beside a square plank of wood lying on the floor. The plank had a handle on it. He crouched to see more clearly.

No! It wasn't a plank of wood. It was a trapdoor.

He whispered. 'Matilde, what have you done?'

24

MATILDE STROLLED, BOOK in hand, along the Seine's riverbank. She had reached a place by the water where it curved around the city as if embracing a lover. It was the first of June and a beautiful day. Aged trees swayed in the shifting breeze, their leaves changing hues as one moment they faced the sun, the next bent into submission towards the shadows by a gentle breeze.

She sat down on a bench and took a deep breath. Matilde had brought a book with her to give her an excuse to sit quietly and to think. The week before she had met Henri by the river close to Notre Dame Cathédrale. He had shown her where they were going to hide people they managed to rescue next month. The men had done a wonderful job. Deep in the catacombs were thin mattresses, blankets, tinned food and rudimentary toilet facilities – lidded buckets. She felt a wave of both fear and excitement bubble up inside her stomach. In five weeks, people would be rescued and living down there.

Henri had organised the printing of large quantities of leaflets to be distributed around Paris. The notices told of the planned arrest of Jews living in the city, and if possible, to find any way of escaping. The act of distribution was only like a ripple in the river, but hopefully that ripple would swell and surge through word of mouth.

With anxiety tightening her chest, Matilde opened her novel by Daphne du Maurier. She began to read, freeing her mind and escaping into another world. At the end of chapter one, she paused, feeling as if she had visited Manderley. If only she too could be possessed by a dream's supernatural power and pass like a spirit through a barrier. She closed her eyes and lifted her face to the sun, imagining passing through time where she was living in a life of story-book perfection with Xav…

No. With Hans.

Matilde looked across at the far bank's mirror image reflecting on the water, outlines receding with each ripple and undulation. What was Hans doing now on this Sunday morning? She lay the open book on her knees. There always seemed to be a frisson of invisible static when he was close; she even felt it to a lesser degree now, in his absence – just thinking about him. She breathed deeper, slower and more steadily. She knew that Hans had found a way into her heart, and the thought softened her lips into a smile.

But it was impossible. She sighed, her even breaths now disturbed. She raised the book to her eyes, letting it press on her eyelids. This wasn't a happy-ever-after story. This was war.

'Is the book that bad?'

Matilde jumped and dropped the book on to the seat. The voice was hesitant, yet safe and familiar, but the sun was behind the figure and all she could see was a silhouette. He stepped forwards out of the glare. Hans.

'May I sit with you?'

Her heart was now racing with a mixture of excitement, disbelief and anxiety. She shouldn't be seen with a German. He was wearing his Wehrmacht uniform and Matilde knew how it would be perceived by fellow Parisians to be seen sitting with him.

'Hello. I… I would like you to but I'm not sure… ' She looked up and down the bank where small gatherings of people were browsing riverside stalls set up on rickety tables.

'I understand.'

'Maybe if you sit at the far end… '

Hans sat down. The breeze carried a soapy scent towards her, as if he had recently showered. She felt immediately shy, as if he had been reading her mind and her thoughts about him.

'I wasn't following you, if that's what you're thinking.'

She shook her head. 'No, of course not.'

'It was your dress.'

'My dress?'

'You were wearing that bright blue dress the very first time I saw you. It stood out on the first day I came to Paris two years ago, just as it has now.'

She turned sideways to face him along the length of the seat. 'You must be mistaken. I've never worn this dress to work.'

'Oh, we hadn't met at that point. I had stopped for a coffee at a street café the day I arrived. You were browsing the market. I noticed your auburn hair and admired you from a distance.'

'Really?'

He smiled shyly at her. It felt like a gift.

'Yes. And when I discovered that you were the French woman who I was to be working with, well, suddenly the war seemed… better.'

'You've never mentioned it.'

Hans leaned back against the bench and his body turned in her direction. 'It's easier to talk outside, don't you think?'

Matilde realised that they were both facing one another and leaning inwards. She turned to face the river and sat up straight. 'Yes, I suppose it is.'

'What are you reading?'

'Rebecca.'

'What do you think about Maxim de Winter?'

Matilde was surprised. 'You've read it?'

'Why do you sound so surprised? It's been published a few years now.'

'I just didn't expect… '

'… a German soldier to enjoy reading.'

'No, I didn't mean that. I don't know what I expected. Anyway, I've only finished the first chapter so I haven't met Maxim de, who?'

'De Winter.'

Matilde tried to subdue a laugh. 'I presume he's the wonderful hero who makes everything all right.'

'Well, actually… I won't spoil your story. It's a good book.'

They sat in silence for a few minutes, both gazing out across the river.

'You're in uniform. Are you on duty?'

'No, but we're not allowed to wear civilian clothing outside our rooms without good reason.'

Silence again. There were a myriad of unspoken words that seemed to cross the distance between them. So many emotions kept in check by the barrier of being on opposite sides of the war, as well as the bench.

Hans spoke again. 'Did you know that Manderley represents buried secrets? The house is beautiful, but it hides a dark mystery.'

Matilde tensed. Was this a test? He knew that she had taken some paperwork from the Kommandant's office, so was this a gentle questioning? A soft inquisition?

She tried to act unconcerned and shrugged. 'As I say, I've only just started it. Don't give the story away.'

He wasn't looking at her at that moment so she watched him

freely. He seemed pensive then rubbed his forehead and ran both hands distractedly through his hair. He seemed uncomfortable. Matilde looked away just before Hans spoke.

'I want you to know that I didn't have any choice in this war. I hate it as much as you. My memories of Paris are of a city of beauty, art and history.' Hans paused. 'I care about you. I worry about your safety. I know you're probably trying to help your countrymen, but be very careful. This isn't a warning from a German soldier. This is a warning from a friend who cares for you. Do you understand?

Matilde nodded but didn't dare speak.

'You may be encouraged to put yourself in danger. You can trust me if you wish to tell me anything. Maybe I could even help in some way.'

'I'm not sure what you mean. Everything is fine at work and home.'

Matilde thought he looked sad, even disappointed.

He nodded slowly. 'I should go.'

Hans leaned across the bench and picked up the book she had dropped earlier. He stood up and took a few steps towards her, holding out the volume for her to take. As Matilde reached up and took hold of the book, he moved one of his hands and covered hers with it. It felt warm and safe, lingering for a moment. Then he turned and walked away.

25

July 16th 1942

A HEAT HAZE shimmered above the pavements outside the Vélodrome d'Hiver, July's oppressive weather seeming to pull the nerves of Parisians ever more taut. Green and white buses had been arriving since the early hours and from each of these vehicles trickled lines of forlorn men, women and children, each identified as being Jewish by the yellow stars sewn onto their clothing. Mothers held babies, children cried, men carried meagre belongings and the elderly stooped and stumbled. All were being roughly ushered inside the stadium.

Hans walked the outer perimeter of the sporting arena in Paris's fifteenth arrondissement, struggling with the difficult undertaking of remaining unnoticed and at the same time appearing confident in front of other armed soldiers and policemen. He knew he had no authority to be here at this mass confinement of families, and questions would be asked if he was challenged. He noted that there were only a handful of Germans patrolling the area, with the vast majority of the police being French. The High Command could now point a finger elsewhere if protests and fighting broke out, he thought.

Hans was looking for a way inside the sports arena without arousing suspicion. But then again, he thought, who would suspect a uniformed German soldier of duplicity? He wasn't here to constrain these people, but to make sure one person remained safe. He wondered if Matilde was already inside or if he had guessed wrongly. He knew he should not have searched her office, but it had only taken five minutes after work one day to find a notepad tucked away in a drawer. Although the top sheet was blank, small indentations from a pen had been left on the following page. When he had carefully rubbed a pencil over the impressions, the words Vél' d'Hiv could be seen alongside some illegible markings. After her suspicious meetings with a man, and the Kommandant receiving a letter informing him that she was sick, he realised that she must be involved in a dangerous situation. He hoped he had jumped to the wrong conclusion.

An elderly woman fell to his left, bringing him out of his reverie and causing a commotion. She lay in a pitiful heap with arms raised to her face to protect her from being trampled by the stream of people who hadn't noticed her on the floor. Instinctively Hans made towards the old lady but not before a soldier's boot kicked her in the ribs. She groaned, was roughly pulled to her feet and quickly swallowed up in the steady flow of bodies being herded inside the arena.

A memory of Hans's grandmother sprang to his mind. He remembered her podding peas at her kitchen table, occasionally winking as she passed him a tiny, green ball. He could remember the sound each one made as they rolled across the work surface and even sensed he could taste their sweetness.

He leaned against a wall to regain his composure. If his grandmother had been living in Paris, would she have been arrested for being a quarter Jewish? Did his superiors differentiate between full, half or quarter Jewish when they gave their orders to rid the city of this so-called vermin? Would she be shuffling in pain through the main entrance towards an unknown fate? Would he? However diluted his lineage, it was still in his blood.

'You!'

Hans turned automatically. A German officer was beckoning to him. He felt sick. If he hurried away now it would automatically arouse attention. He reasoned that all he was guilty of so far this morning was of being here without orders. He wouldn't be missed at work because his orders today were to deliver paperwork to various offices around the city for signing, which he intended to do later. He strode assertively towards the man, thankful that no one was aware how fast his heart was pounding.

Hans saluted.

'You're needed.'

The soldier turned and beckoned for him to follow. Hans hesitated before hurrying forwards. The officer opened a door in the perimeter wall of the Vél d'Hiv', wedged it open and pointed to the ground.

'Stay here and shoot anyone who attempts to escape. All the windows inside have been locked so no one can get out. I need a gun on each exit. Keep a low profile. We're letting the French authorities take the lead in this mission; letting them believe they still have some independence.'

As Hans walked through the doorway, the noise emanating from inside the arena was dreadful. There were screams from lost children, wailing, cries for help, coughing and shouting, all with a background thrum of conversation. At first he was dazed. The heat was unbearable inside the stadium. Above him the domed roof had been painted dark blue for protection against bombing raids, similar to street lamps, but it didn't prevent the heat of the sun from making the stadium insufferably hot. It also gave off a glaucous light that reflected on the faces beneath. The smell of dirty bodies and excrement hung heavy in the air. People were urinating in corners or against walls because there was nowhere else to relieve themselves.

Hans' shirt stuck to his back with sweat and he fought the urge to turn his back against this inhumanity, but the thought of finding Matilde made him stay. He remembered sitting with her by the river last month and they were now less self-conscious with each other at work. He longed to be alone with her, even if they were simply valuing lists of objects. The scene he was witnessing here was a different world to the tranquility of the river.

'Please help me. My baby hasn't had a drink since yesterday.'

Hans looked at the woman in front of him. She could only be in her twenties but her face bore the lines of lack of sleep and food. She was grasping a small, listless child to her hip while holding out her other hand.

'There's no water,' replied Hans, in French. 'You shouldn't be here long. They're moving you on later.'

'But she's sick'

A French policeman appeared from Hans' left and slapped the woman. She stumbled backwards into the crowd, dropping her child to the floor. People around her jostled for balance with several standing on the child's limbs before her mother scrambled to pick her up. With the woman's nose bleeding and the child now screaming, they disappeared into the mass of bodies.

Hans looked around. The middle of the arena was full of families, their eyes wide with fear and confusion. Above him the galleried seating areas were filling up as crowds were continually being pushed inside from all districts of Paris. Someone vomited nearby, adding to the atrocious smell. The Paris of his memory was of sophistication and romance. This was more like his interpretation of hell.

He felt inadequate. Outraged. Strange. Something was shifting deep within him. It was as if each cell, organ, thought process and instinct had retracted. He felt as if he was literally on the wrong side of everything he stood for. Despite this roundup being carried out by French police, the orders came from the High Command. His nationality. Yet he never gave his permission for it to be allowed in his name. If he were faced with a dangerous man trying to kill him in the street, he'd shoot, but not these people. Never these desperate, abandoned people. He felt suffocated. It was difficult to breathe in such heat. He could no longer be part of this. Not only would he find Matilde, but he would also do what he could to help her. Help these people. How could he take part in this atrocity and live with himself?

26

MATILDE AND CHARLES made their way to the stadium. Charles was the doctor she had met in Henri's smoky kitchen and she had spoken to him several times since. Her instructions were to stay by his side and act as his assistant until he had chosen those in most need of care. Previously, Charles had supplied her with a nurse's uniform from a local hospital that she had dressed in that morning. As the mechanic in their resistance cell, Philippe had provided a van and two cars on which large red crosses had been painted; hopefully to avoid unwanted German attention. Being an undertaker, Francis would be driving his aged hearse. These would be waiting around the back of the building ready to carry as many people as possible to safety. Water, bread, blankets and mattresses would be waiting for the rescued families deep below the city in the catacombs.

She and Charles arrived early, but already crowds were being pushed inside the stadium.

'Are you all right?' asked Charles.

Matilde nodded.

'No second thoughts?'

Matilde shook her head.

'Remember to stay close. If you're questioned on medical matters, just direct them to me.'

She straightened her cap. It was sliding to one side and she wished she hadn't washed her hair last night. She followed Charles towards the main door. The large capital letters above the stadium's main doors, read VEL' D'HIV. The Winter Stadium. The austere, concrete building had high walls, very few windows and the gaping entrance appeared to be devouring the lines of people walking from rows of green and white buses. Matilde continued in trepidation.

'Raise your chin,' said Charles. 'Act like you're meant to be here.'

Soon they were walking alongside families, before finding a gap and passing between them. Matilde was confused by what she saw.

'I thought they were arresting men and sending them to work camps in Pithiviers and Beaune-la-Rolande. I thought that children younger than sixteen and their mothers were exempt from the round up.'

'Never believe what the Boche say.'

'But there are babies, children, women and old people here? They can't work. This isn't what the paperwork said. Look, that old man is in a wheelchair. How can he work? I thought we were going to try and free some sick men and teenagers. What are we going to do?'

Charles caught Matilde's arm and stopped walking. He pretended to look in his medical bag while talking.

'Listen. There'll be enough time for questions later. Have no doubt about the danger we're in by being here. I've noticed that the bastards pushing and shoving these people are French. They may be acting on German orders, but they don't appear to have a conscience about it. No more questions. We'll see the most needy when we're inside. If we get inside.' He snapped his bag shut, gave her a tight-lipped smile of encouragement and walked towards a French policeman standing at the entrance.

'We're medical staff,' said Charles.

'What?'

'I'm a doctor,' he repeated. 'I'm here with my assistant.'

The guard's eyes lingered on Matilde. A smirk stretched his lips.

'I can think of better things to do than help these animals.'

'I have orders and this bag is heavy,' said Charles, raising his leather holdall a little higher.

The guard's smile disappeared. He jerked his head in the direction of the stadium's entrance.

'Your choice.'

They walked alongside several families who were shuffling in through the wide doorways. Matilde looked back. She could see the top of the Eiffel Tower behind some buildings and the huge swastika flag at its tip that lay limp in the still air. She turned her back on it and stepped inside the vast interior.

Thousands of people were crammed inside, everyone searching for some space to sit. The stench and the heat were suffocating and the thought of offering help to such a huge number seemed impossible. It was overwhelming. People pulled at her arms begging for help. Charles wore an old suit so wasn't noticeably a doctor, but her nurse's uniform made her stand out as someone who might provide some hope. Charles took her hand and led her through the throng. A folded sheet was forced into her arms as she struggled to follow the doctor. She clung on to it thinking it could be ripped into strips and used as bandages if necessary.

'Where are we going?'

'I'm looking for the back exit where the others will be parked and waiting. I've been here before to watch the cycle racing so I've a fair idea of the layout. Philippe knows where to look for us there when he arrives.'

Eventually they reached the back wall where a line of five lavatories had been boarded up. Despite her anxiety she asked a French policeman nearby, why that had been done.

'There are windows inside them. Can't have them escaping, can we?'

She turned to Charles who was looking pale despite the beads of sweat on his face. 'This is barbaric. It's wicked,' she said.

He pointed to an area by the back wall where several metal chairs were stacked.

'That'll do,' he said. On reaching the wall, he dropped his bag to the floor. 'Let's place these chairs in a row and arrange a makeshift bed.'

'Hello. It's good to see you.'

Matilde and Charles turned in surprise. A nurse stood in front of them. She looked disheveled and a smear of blood coloured the top of her apron like a brooch.

'It's dreadful, isn't it? Are there any more of you coming to help us?'

'I'm not sure,' said Charles. 'Where are you set up?'

The nurse pointed to the far corner. 'Over there. We have two Red Cross doctors and three nurses for all these people, so thank you for coming. I presume you're a doctor. Have you been sent by the local hospital?'

'Yes,' lied Charles.

'Three Jewish doctors have come forwards from the crowd. They've left their families somewhere in this hellhole to help us. The sanitary provisions are non-existent. There are four internal lavatories open in the far corner, but you wouldn't want to see what state they're in. They're all blocked.'

'What about food and water?'

The nurse shook her head. 'There are a few Quakers wandering through the building looking for undernourished children, but if you ask me, they all look that way. They have jugs of water and are giving out crackers to the most needy.'

'The most needy? Isn't that everyone here?' asked Matilde.

'Those that can stand and talk are considered strong enough. Those too weak to move are offered what the Quakers have. We can only do so much.' The nurse pointed to the sheet that Matilde was still holding. 'What happened there?'

Matilde looked down at the folded sheet and saw there was blood on it. She hadn't noticed before.

'I've no idea. Someone pushed it into my arms as I walked through the crowd.'

She began to unravel the layers of material, the bloodstain growing larger as the folds untangled. As the covering was unwrapped, Matilde felt a solid object in her hands beneath the final few pleats of fabric. Charles stepped forwards and turned back the final fold. Matilde gasped. A tiny, purple-mottled baby lay in the sheet. It was dead. The infant's skin was translucent with minute blood vessels decorating its body like intricate lace. It would have been too tiny and frail to survive in a hospital, let alone in this wretched place.

'Poor mite,' said the nurse. She held out her hands. 'Give it to me. It won't be the last body we see over the next week. We've made provision for those who are too sick to survive.'

Matilde passed her the little body. She felt tears well up in her eyes, but crying wouldn't help these people. She cleared her throat. 'I thought people were staying here for a couple of days. What makes you think it'll be a week?'

'It'll take two days to round everyone up, but it'll take longer to disperse them all to other places.'

'My God,' said Matilde. 'How will anyone survive here for a week?'

'We'll do what we can,' said Charles.

'That's all we can do,' said the nurse. 'Good luck. You'll need it.' She turned and walked away, carrying the bundle in her arms.

For two hours, Charles and Matilde saw a constant stream of people. All were malnourished, many had impetigo, dehydration, or were sick with an infection or a stomach ailment. They had yet to hear from Philippe and the other drivers and as their orders had been to wait until contacted, they continued working in the intense heat. They treated a woman for burns to her leg where someone had dropped a lit cigarette onto her dress. It had gone unnoticed until she had felt the pain and saw a flame. They helped a man who had his lip split by a guard, another who had fallen and broken his arm. Charles could do no more than splint the man's bone and inject him with a hypodermic syringe of morphine. The limited supply of penicillin Charles had brought with him had already run out.

Just before midday, Philippe found them. He had brought two glass bottles of water with him and offered one to Matilde. She was desperate to drink from it, but couldn't bring herself to raise it to her lips.

'The children need it more than me.'

'If you faint from exhaustion, fewer children will be rescued,' said Philippe.

He lifted her hand and helped the bottle to her mouth. It was warm but she took several gulps. Charles drank his so quickly he choked. He wiped his eyes and sat down on a chair, exhausted.

'What was the hold up?' he asked.

'The roads in this area are blocked with vehicles bringing Jews here. After the buses, German cars and trucks had priority. When we said we were sent to aid the sick here, they made us wait longer. Bastards did it on purpose.'

'So, we have four vehicles outside?' said Charles.

'Three. One of the cars wouldn't start.'

'Damn. I've placed a few families with very sick children against that wall,' said Charles, pointing. 'They're priority on our list. Now, if you can—'

Someone screamed. A shrill, harrowing sound that made the noise in the arena grow quieter. People were looking up and Matilde followed their gazes. A man and woman had climbed over the railing of the balcony seating. They were holding hands. A deep breath later, they leaned forwards and fell. It took a second before a sickening thud was heard. There were more screams and shouting.

'Christ,' said Philippe. 'Poor bastards.'

Matilde clasped her fingers to her mouth. She found it difficult to breathe properly. Finally her lungs filled with half sobs, half gasps.

Charles held her upper arms and looked into her eyes.

'Stay strong. I know it's difficult, but put it to the back of your mind for now. We need to concentrate on the plan. Can you do that?'

Matilde couldn't speak. She nodded.

Charles turned and walked towards a family that were waiting where he'd placed them. A lethargic toddler lay in their father's arms while the mother was trying to clean vomit from her baby's clothing.

'Come with us. Let me carry your daughter,' said Charles. 'Give the baby to the nurse.'

Matilde had glanced over towards the area where the young couple had fallen. They were being stretchered into a corner.

'Nurse. Take the baby.' Charles raised his eyebrows at her, conveying the message that she needed to pay attention.

Matilde held out her hands and the small child was handed to her. The baby's eyes were closed. Her pink lips pouted and her tiny hands were clasping and unclasping. Her clothing was wet and smelled of urine and something more unpleasant. The group walked towards the back exit. Three armed French policemen had been talking between themselves, but stood up and faced the group as they approached. Charles took charge.

'We've been granted permission to take some prisoners to the local hospital under the proviso that we bring them back by the end of the day.'

'Whose permission?'

'Kommandant Kramer.'

Matilde didn't know if Charles had made this name up or if such a man existed. She watched the men frown at each other.

Charles continued. 'The sooner we get treatment for the children, the sooner they can return.'

The guards looked at the baby and the filthy child. One of them took a step forwards.

'Just the nurse can leave with the child and baby. They seem well enough to stay,' he said, nodding towards the children's parents.

The baby's mother begged. 'Please. We can't be separated from our children. Please let us travel to the hospital with them.'

People nearby overheard her pleading.

'If they're leaving, we need to go, too.' A man pointed to his young son. 'He's sick. He's in a lot of pain. He needs help.'

More people took notice. They began shouting out. 'Us too.'

'My husband can hardly breathe.'

'Our daughter needs help.'

A growing number of people had started to gather and the guards began to fidget. One of them raised his gun.

'Get back!'

The other two policemen also pulled guns from their belts. One shot into the air. The sound reverberated around the interior, silencing almost everyone in the stadium.

'Move back or we'll shoot whoever comes near these doors. Everyone move back. That includes you.' The man was looking from Charles to Philippe. 'No one's leaving now. It'll cause a riot. Move back.' A gun was aimed at the doctor.

Charles stepped back, arms raised. He nodded and backed away further to calm the policemen. The families retreated and the guards appeared to relax a little, their guns still pointing towards the crowd. The medical group moved back to where they had been, next to the line of metal chairs.

'Now what?' asked Philippe.

'We'll never get out of the front entrance so we need to check the smaller exits to the sides,' said Charles. 'If I remember there are doors half way down the length of the building. Philippe, you see how many guards are at the far wall. Matilde, can you walk past the exit on this side. Don't stop or speak to anyone, simply make a mental note of how many policemen are blocking the exit. I need to stay with the sick baby.'

Matilde began to weave through the crowds. She felt a trickle of sweat roll down between her shoulder blades. The heat was unbearable. The atmosphere was suffocating and the stench was growing worse as people relieved themselves against the stadium walls. She kept going, stepping over sleeping bodies and neglected belongings. Ahead she could see a single doorway, but still the number of people squashed into small areas meant she couldn't see how many guards were manning it. She side stepped an elderly couple who were sitting on a sheet leaning on their bags, the legs of a pair of black trousers spilling out of one bag like necrotic snakes.

As she neared the exit, a slight breeze ruffled her hair. It was intoxicating in this baking atmosphere. She stepped closer to the exit, waiting for the next waft of fresh air. Then she saw a uniform. A German uniform. The soldier had his back to her and was holding a gun. She instinctively turned, but in her rush, she tripped over the trouser legs dangling from the bag and fell to the floor. In the next moment, a man's hand reached out to help her to her feet. She noticed the grey-green sleeve of the German soldier's uniform. All she could think was please God, don't let him ask for my identity papers.

She stood up and reluctantly looked into the soldier's face.

'Hans!'

'Matilde!'

'Oh, God.'

Although they were being watched, families had moved away from the soldier with the gun. From a distance it must have seemed as if they were having an argument, but no one could hear what they were saying. They were speaking quietly.

Hans held her wrist firmly. 'You must stop this. It's too dangerous.'

'How—?'

'You weren't careful enough. Where did you get this uniform from?'

Matilde looked down at his gun. Had their growing friendship been a ruse? She glared at him.

'Are you working here?' she asked.

'Not officially.'

'What does that mean?'

'I haven't had orders to be here.'

'Then why are you here?'

Hans looked over his shoulder then back at her before saying something quietly. She could see his lips move but couldn't hear him over the mayhem.

'I can't hear you.' She remembered what Charles had said as they entered the stadium. Never believe what the Boche say. 'Are you going to arrest me?'

'… still don't… '

'I can't hear you,' she said.

Hans leaned forwards. 'You still don't trust me.'

'But I don't understand. Why are you here? How did you know…?' Matilde began to panic. She felt confused. She mustn't forget who he was. The boundaries between friend and enemy had become blurred. She didn't know him *that* well. Would he turn her in?

Matilde pleaded. 'I need to go. I beg you not to say anything.'

She turned to leave but he grabbed her arm. She fought to free herself. How could she have been so stupid as to trust him? His grip remained firm. People surrounding them were watching the struggle between a nurse and a German soldier, but no one dared intervene.

Matilde felt him pull her arm towards him. Her body fell against his. He smelled of soap. It disorientated her, but even more so when he whispered sharply in her ear.

'I came for you. I came here to make sure you stayed safe.'

She stopped resisting and looked at him. He appeared earnest, but…

'I don't believe you. You didn't know I'd be here.'

'I guessed.'

Matilde stared at him, speechless. 'How?'

'Come over here,' he said.

He led her towards the doorway, guiding her rather than holding her. People knew not to come close to the exit with a gun on view.

'I know you're part of a resistance cell. I'm afraid you don't hide it too well, or maybe… maybe it's because I notice you more than others do.'

'You spy on me?'

'No, not like that.' He gently shook her forearms. 'I have feelings for you, can't you see? That's why I notice you. I saw you meet a man by the Seine. You took paperwork from the Kommandant's office. You left an indent of the name of this place on your pad at work.'

Matilde was confused. She was hyperventilating. He said he had feelings for her. Could she believe him? Was he pretending to find out more information? She doubted him. She doubted herself.

'What are you going to do?' she asked.

'Help you, but I need to know the truth.'

'What?'

'I don't want any part of this,' he said, looking around. 'I'm not going to watch innocent people suffer without doing something about it. I want to help you and the others.'

Matilde didn't know what to say. It had to be a trap. Adrienne had begged her not to trust him.

'I'm here alone.'

Hans closed his eyes and sighed. 'I understand. Why would you believe me?'

Matilde didn't reply. She was wringing her hands.

Hans continued. 'I didn't report you for taking the paperwork, did I? I didn't tell my superiors about my suspicions. I'm here without permission. I could be arrested for not reporting the missing paperwork.'

Matilde knew that she had little choice but to trust him now he had seen her, but could she divulge the names of the others? Putting her own life in danger was one thing, but to jeopardize the resistance cell was unimaginable. Another gust of air blew in through the doorway.

'I can't… '

Hans released his soft grasp from her arms. He looked disappointed. Matilde didn't know if it was because she hadn't trusted him or because he was unable to claim the arrest of a group of resistance fighters.

'I'll be here for thirty minutes,' said Hans, matter-of-factly. 'Then I have papers to deliver. It is up to you whether you trust me or not.'

He turned and walked to the exit, not making eye contact with her again.

27

MATILDE HURRIED BACK towards Charles, weaving in and out of groups of people sitting on the stadium floor. Every so often she looked towards Hans, but he wasn't following her or even watching her. Surely he would be if he were hoping to arrest the group. It was true he had kept his suspicions to himself. She remembered the earnest look in his eyes when they shared a bench and discussed Manderley. Matilde didn't understand why, but she suddenly felt a certain belief that he was genuine. If the group was going to help save some people from this madness, what choice did she have?

Charles was trying to give the last of the water to the baby.

'What did you find? How many guards?'

'One.'

'I presume he's armed?'

'Yes.'

Charles nodded, thoughtfully. 'That's good. I expected more to be watching the exit. We just need to think of a distraction and let Philippe know where to park the vehicles.'

Matilde knew she had to choose her next words carefully. She needed to maintain Charles's trust, but also needed to persuade him to trust a German.

'I need to speak with you, privately.'

She saw him furrow his brow, but the look on her face must

have conveyed the urgency of what she had to say. He handed the baby to her mother and explained how to tip a few drops at a time into the baby's mouth.

Guiding her by her elbow, Charles led Matilde to a space behind the stacked chairs.

'What is it?' he asked. 'Is our mission compromised?'

'This is going to be difficult for you to believe and it will take a great deal of trust. Please listen before speaking.'

'You're worrying me.'

'I work with a German called Hans Engel. He… he's sympathetic to… '

Matilde wrung her damps hands together.

'Matilde, we don't have time for this. Just tell me.'

'He knows I'm here. I'm sorry. I didn't know he was coming. He has helped me before and kept a secret that could have had me arrested.'

'What secret? Are we in even more danger than simply being here? Do we need to leave?'

'No. He wants to help us.'

Charles took a step back, an incredulous look on his face. 'You told a German about what we're doing here?'

'No! He guessed why I'm here. He knows I took some paperwork but didn't report me. I trust him. He's going to help us get through the exit.'

'And you believe him? You've jeopardized our plan. You do what you must, but I'm getting the men out of here.'

Charles turned and hurried towards Philippe and Francis. Matilde took several deep breaths, and fought the tears stinging her eyes. She knew she could have explained things better than she had. Now Charles had questioned her judgment and was leaving without having rescued a single person. She couldn't let this happen.

Matilde fought her way through families, pushchairs and belongings. The sun continued to blaze in through the glass roof and sweat dripped down Matilde's back and between her breasts. She could see Charles talking urgently to Francis. When she reached them she was horrified to realise that they looked afraid of her.

She had one last chance to convince them.

Matilde raised her forearms, showing her palms to the men. 'Give me two minutes. Please. I understand you not trusting the Germans. I feel the same. Remember they murdered my husband. Do you think I would collaborate with such monsters? But look around you. Look at this suffering. These people aren't being treated as human beings. The human race does not exist here. These people are cargo, supposedly to be transported to Germany to work. There are thousands of children, frail, elderly and disabled people in wheelchairs. Do you believe they are all going to be cared for and given work in Germany? The very country that is killing our loved ones? And you ask how we can trust this German who's willing to help? I'll tell you how. Do you see those policemen? There.' Matilde pointed over the heads of families. 'Over there by the entrance. Over there by the back exit. The bus drivers who brought them here. The armed police outside, pushing more and more vulnerable people inside here. Who sealed the ventilation system, locked the lavatories and denied these people food and water? Do you know what nationality these cruel men are? French. French Milice obeying German orders.'

Charles and Francis didn't reply.

Matilde placed her palms together in front of her, as if in prayer. 'If you can see with your own eyes that the French can be so cruel towards their own people, why can't you believe a German man with a good heart can be trusted?'

Charles looked at Francis.

'This is our one chance to help,' said Matilde. 'Please help me to save some families from this living nightmare.'

Charles bit his lip. Francis nodded slowly.

'Thank you. Thank you,' repeated Matilde. 'Bring one family at a time to the side exit. Let the drivers know they have to park on Rue Nélaton. Let them know that the fair-haired German is working with us. I'm going to let him know our decision.'

Matilde found Hans standing by the side exit, wiping sweat from his brow. He appeared surprised and relieved to see her.

'Have you spoken to the others?' he asked.

There was no point in pretending she was alone. She either trusted him wholeheartedly, or walked away.

'I have.'

'They trust me?'

'Let's just say, I've persuaded them you want to help.'

'Good. How are you transporting them?'

'We have a few vehicles. The doctor has a car he's allowed to drive. There's also a hearse and a van. They're making their way to this side of the building.'

'A hearse?'

'Francis is a funeral director.'

Hans nodded. 'I'll wait for them to arrive.'

'I'm going back to collect the first family.'

Within minutes, Charles's car pulled up alongside the exit. Matilde arrived a short time later carrying the sick baby, followed by a wide-eyed child and their parents. The mother looked confused while the father looked alert, eyes darting in all direction looking for further danger. They stopped abruptly when they saw Hans. They were terrified at the sight of his uniform and weapon.

Matilde intervened. 'Please. Trust us. We need to get you out of here.'

They tentatively stepped forwards on seeing Hans step back and direct them towards the waiting vehicle. They walked past him, looking incredulous that they were leaving without being apprehended.

Matilde noticed many families looking on. It was heartbreaking to see the longing on their faces, but it was impossible to rescue everyone. Not one person tried to take advantage of the open door. They were like captured animals, believing they had no choice in the matter. They were thirsty and starving, dirty and exhausted, and probably wouldn't have the energy to escape, even if they were yearning for it.

Matilde guided two unmarried sisters in their forties, towards the exit. One of the women was heavily pregnant, having been raped by a German soldier. They were escorted to the car where Hans shut the door. He checked up and down the road before signaling for the car to leave.

With no time to waste, Matilde looked for another family. How could she possibly choose one over another? Vast crowds were filling the stadium, writhing bodies everywhere. Children wailed, adults wept, shouted, rocked to and fro or stared disbelievingly around them. How could she choose from so much suffering? Should she choose younger people who were stronger than the elderly, or the elderly because they were less likely to survive hardship? It was an impossible decision to make.

A young girl tugged at her uniform. She looked about five years old, with wide brown eyes and tangled dark hair. The little girl held up her forefinger.

'I've hurt my finger.'

Matilde knelt down to the little girl's level. 'Let me see. Oh, it is a little red and swollen. What happened?'

'Somebody trod on it when I was sitting down.'

'What's your name?'

'Eloise.'

'Is your mummy here, Eloise?'

'Just there.' Eloise turned and pointed to a couple who were resting against one another, each holding a young boy on their laps.

'Are they your brothers?' asked Matilde.

'They're twins. They're three now.'

'Can I have a word with your daddy?'

Matilde followed Eloise, side-stepping a couple huddled together on the floor. The girl's parents looked up, apprehension creasing their faces.

'I'm sorry. I told her not to bother you,' said the woman.

'It's no bother. I can get you out of here. There's no time to explain, but trust me and follow me.'

The couple looked at each other in disbelief and began to rouse the sleeping boys. Their father lifted his son and picked up a small bag. The mother was too weak to carry the other little boy, so she pulled him gently by the hand. They followed Matilde, who was holding Eloise's hand. The five-year-old little girl had saved the lives of her family without even knowing it.

Hans was waiting for them at the exit. Relieved to see Philippe's work van parked on the road, she led the family to its back door. She lifted Eloise up and pointed to a seat.

'Sit there. Mummy and Daddy are coming too.'

'And my brothers?'

Matilde smiled at her. 'Of course.'

As she turned, she saw two French policemen approaching. They both held guns, pointing them at Matilde and the family waiting to step inside the vehicle.

'What are you doing?'

'I'm a nurse and I've been given permission to let this sick family visit the hospital. They're returning shortly.'

'I don't care. Get them out of here and back inside. Our orders are that no one should leave.'

Eloise began to cry. She stood up from her seat and went to her mother who was waiting beside the van door.

Hans stepped forwards and faced the men.

'The nurse says she's been given permission.'

The policemen looked taken aback to see a German soldier confront them, but remained resolute.

'By who?'

'It's not your job to question procedure. Remember who's in charge here. You may be guarding this place, but don't forget where your orders came from in the first place. If you want to keep your job and not be reported for disrupting the High Command's decision, I suggest you move on and let us carry out our work.'

The policemen looked uncertain. They looked from Hans to Matilde.

'Very well. These people must be returned here as soon as possible.'

Having acquiesced without further protest, they turned and left.

Hans let out a long sigh of relief. 'Let's hurry things up.'

Matilde settled the family in to the back of the van. She returned moments later with two more groups of people, including children, their parents and elderly grandparents. With the vehicle full, its engine started and moved away.

Within fifteen minutes, the hearse was also full with children sitting on parents' knees, and two further families squashed into the space reserved for coffins. The curtains around the windows had been drawn and they were urged not to move and disturb the material that was hiding them from view.

Matilde turned to Hans. They held each other's gaze. No words were necessary. She turned and opened the passenger door before climbing inside.

AS ARRANGED, THEY drove towards a small side road running parallel to Église de la Madeleine. When Francis turned into the road, Matilde frowned. Henri was shaking his head and hurrying towards their vehicle. Francis wound down the window.

Henri was gasping. 'There's a service taking place.'

'What?'

'I don't know what's gone wrong. Father Aubrey knew we were coming today, but another priest is taking a service.'

Matilde's hand went to her open mouth.

Henri looked up and down the road. 'We can't stay here, and until I speak to Father Aubrey we can't go into the church. Can you think of *anywhere* we can hide everyone overnight?'

'The funeral parlour is empty, but it has a glass frontage,' said Francis. It would be useless as a hiding place. What about Philippe's garage?'

Henri shook his head. 'He says it's full of car parts, dangerous and there's only enough room for one family.'

Matilde suddenly began searching in her pockets. The men watched her; so frantic were her movements. She pulled out her set of house keys, looked at them and triumphantly held them up in the air.

'The auction house. I still have the keys attached.'

'Thank God,' said Henri. 'Lead the way and I'll tell the others.'

THE SHORT JOURNEY to Lombard's Auction House was

harrowing. Although Hans had mentioned that there were fewer German soldiers on the streets today, they crossed paths with several enemy vehicles and kept their heads lowered whenever they drove past soldiers on foot. Being caught would mean the end for all of them.

Matilde chewed a thumbnail as she directed Francis past St. Augustine's square. The food market on their right had already closed, its empty wooden tables waiting for a paltry amount of decaying food to be unloaded the following day.

'Turn left just after that stack of sandbags,' said Matilde.

She turned around. No one was moving in the back. They had fear etched on their faces.

The hearse pulled into the forecourt of the auction house.

'Keep going and turn left at the fence. There's a small car park around the back.'

Once parked Matilde climbed out of the passenger seat, the heat of the sun stinging her bare arms. She pulled Adrienne's house keys out of her pocket, still dumbfounded that she had kept her work keys attached.

A bedraggled array of traumatised people climbed out of the vehicles, still clutching their flasks of water. The elderly were offered arms to lean on and the children were subdued and quiet. Matilde stood at the faded blue door. She inserted the key and sighed with relief when it turned with ease. She pushed it slowly until it was wide open, brushing aside a blanket of dusty spider webs from the entrance. She beckoned everyone to follow.

It was cooler inside as she stood in a small office where her boss used to sit. There was a desk and chair, a dirty sofa leaning against one wall and a second desk chair used for visitors. The light was dim due to the dirty windows covered in dust and grime and the interior had a sweet musty smell. As the families stepped in from the heat of the sun, wide-eyed and curious,

Matilde could now smell unwashed clothes, body odour and children's soiled undergarments.

The floor was littered with yellowing newspapers, broken picture frames and dead flies. A skeleton of a bird, wings spread like ornate fans, lay in the entrance to an internal door. Matilde moved it to one side with her shoe.

'Follow me. Be careful where you stand. This is the main auction room. As you can see there are lots of chairs, but be careful, they may not all be in good condition.'

She walked into a smaller room that had several doors leading off.

'In here you'll find two lavatories.' She stepped inside and pulled at the hanging chain; surprised at the thrill she got from seeing they still flushed. 'In here,' she said, opening another door, 'is a storage room, and for some mysterious reason, there's a sink.'

The tap squeaked when she turned it, giving a trickle of light brown water that ran into the bowl.

'I can see lots of sheets and blankets at the back, here. We used to cover and protect paintings and large ornamental items with them, so although dusty, they'll be fine to use for bedding, ripped to use as cleaning cloths or other personal use.'

One of the two sisters half raised a hand. 'We will never be able to thank you enough, but what's going to happen to us now?'

Henri stepped forwards. 'We won't be able to move you today, so you need to rest and we'll try to get hold of some food.'

A woman stepped forwards. 'Must we move? With lavatories and water, chairs and blankets, this is like heaven to where we've been.'

'We understand,' said Matilde, 'but although you probably won't be missed because of the numbers of people involved, there are regular German patrols here. Look.'

She picked up a cigarette butt with the letters T and R still visible on its white paper. 'These are Trommler cigarettes. They're German. Neither Monsieur Lombard, who owns this building, or myself smoke and we certainly wouldn't have left it in this state.'

'Matilde's right. You're to stay here until we can get you underground.'

A man holding a sleeping child stepped forwards. 'Underground? Where are you sending us?'

'We've found a safe place at the back of a church. There's an entrance to the catacombs there.'

The pregnant woman shook her head. 'I can't. I've heard there are dead bodies down there. And it's dark. I can't.'

'What's your name?' asked Matilde.

'Matya.'

'We'll keep you safe, Matya. And your baby.'

'I don't want it,' she said, shaking her head. 'It belongs to a Nazi. I want it out and never want to see it.'

'I'm so sorry. I can't imagine… Listen. You will have outwitted the men who planned this evil round-up. You need to focus, fight and survive. There's a comfortable constant temperature in the catacombs, you'll have lanterns, blankets, whatever food and water we can gather. The main thing is that you'll all be safe.'

An elderly man spoke up. 'You've put your own lives at risk for us, people you have never met. I thank you for your courage and for saving us. I will climb down to the pits of hell if I can outwit those bastards.'

Others murmured their support.

'But what about the dead bodies?' asked Matya.

'They can't hurt you. They're just a pile of bones. The danger lies on the surface.'

Matya nodded and placed her palm on her swollen stomach. 'I will go. I will outlive those monsters and the mongrel who did this.'

Matilde suddenly felt nauseous. She wanted to say that not all of them were monsters; that she had grown close to one. What would they think of her if they knew what was in her heart? She wanted to say that it was a German who helped them escape and the French police had forced them into the stadium. But they wouldn't believe her and besides, now wasn't the time.

Henri stepped forwards. 'We'll talk more later. For now you need to rest and find somewhere to settle down. There's water for your personal needs and make use of the chairs and blankets. It's important for you to keep as quiet as possible and take it in turns to keep someone watching the road. Hopefully, now the Boche know there are no valuables here, they won't regularly patrol it.'

'We need to go now,' said Matilde. 'One of us will be back before curfew with fresh water and whatever food we can find.'

28

HANS COULDN'T SETTLE. He sat on his bed with his head in his hands. He had crossed a line earlier today. It had felt right at the time but sitting alone in his room, it felt reckless. Stupid. He stood up and went to the window. He should have talked her out of such a dangerous plan. Through the thin glass, behind rooftops and spires, he saw red ribbons of the setting sun in the western sky. It seemed nature's beauty cared little for the abhorrence of war.

He had collaborated against the High Command's orders. He remembered how he'd felt at work today. Fear in his bones, waiting for a door to be thrown open and the Gestapo, or even SS soldiers arresting him for interrogation. God, what had he done?

Hans banged his forehead against the pane several times, but the action didn't ease his turmoil. He was falling in love with a French woman and in doing so, making life dangerous for himself. Why hadn't he simply focused on his job and seen out this war in his undemanding role at the museum?

A knock at the door. His heart raced. Had they come for him?

'Who is it?'

'Günter.'

Hans sighed, relieved it was only the soldier billeted in the next room. If it wasn't Günter's snoring, tuneless singing or throwing a ball against the wall that disturbed Hans, it was a squeaking bed frame as he grunted on top of his latest conquest. Hans opened the door, stealing himself to appear undistracted.

Günter was as loud as he was overweight. He exhaled tobacco smoke as he strode into the room and slapped Hans on the back. 'What's all the noise?'

Hans took a step to find his balance, not missing the irony of the comment. He tried to make his conversation light and teasing.

'My noise? You snore like a suffocating hog at night unless you're wheezing over some unfortunate woman.'

Günter bellowed with laughter. 'You're only jealous,' he said, his ample belly wobbling. He leaned forwards, laughter turning to a fit of coughing. When he regained his composure, he sucked on his rolled cigarette and asked again, 'What were you doing, trying to fight your way out of this pit of a place?'

Hans obliged his comrade with a wry smile while he fought for time to explain his actions. He was hardly going to admit to banging his head against the window because he'd fallen for a French woman and collaborated against the Reich. That would certainly remove the grey-toothed grin from the fat man's mouth.

'I was moving my bed away from the wall. Perhaps I might get some sleep tonight.'

Günter belched and thumped his fist against his own chest. 'You'll sleep. I'm leaving for work.'

'Now? It's nearly ten.'

'A unit of men has been ordered to work through the night looking for missing *Judenschwein* from the stadium.'

A shiver of dread spread down Hans's spine. 'Some are missing?'

'They were seen leaving in several vehicles, supposedly on orders, but when reported it was discovered that no such orders had been given. Then of course, none of them returned later that day. The bloody audacity of it. It's thought they'll try and move on during darkness, like the rats they are. When the Jews and medical staff are discovered, there are orders to execute them in the streets to show how collaborators are punished.'

Hans smelt soured garlic sausage from Günter's belch. He felt nauseous, but not from the stench of this man's stomach contents.

'Were the rescuers seen? Perhaps it was just luck they escaped?'

'Luck? They're Jews! Their luck ended the day they were born.'

Günter removed a fleck of tobacco from his furred tongue. 'They were seen by two French policemen who reported the activity. Apparently a man in German uniform was part of the escape. Was he a soldier, or someone who'd stolen the clothes? Who knows? Christ, I wouldn't like to be him when he's found. We've been ordered to find out the names of who were officially helping in the stadium: the Red Cross, the Quakers and the medical staff. Then there's the list of soldiers working there, mostly French but a few Germans. We'll find the perpetrators. People talk if they're scared enough.'

Hans felt slightly relieved. He knew that his and Matilde's names weren't on any official list.

'They'll be sorry when the photographs are delivered tomorrow morning,' said Günter. 'Pictures don't lie.'

Hans felt a rush of adrenaline. He reached out for the brass bedstead to support his unsteady legs. 'Photographs?'

'An official photographer was there; orders from above.' Günter looked at his watch. 'I've got to go. Stop rotting away in this room and go and have some fun. Try the Moulin Rouge. That's where I'd be instead of staying in.'

Hans closed the door behind him and lay on his back on the bed, his forearms folded in front of his eyes. If he was photographed, he was done for. He licked his lips. Fear had made his mouth dry. He felt sick at the thought of being arrested, tortured and surely executed. Should he try and escape, just in case he had been photographed? But if Matilde had been photographed, she would be recognised as working for the Kommandant and he couldn't let that happen. He must warn her. She mustn't return to the stadium tomorrow but should go back to work. Perhaps she could intercept the photographs when they were delivered to the Kommandant's office and she could view them first? If their image had been captured, she could dispose of the picture. Matilde needed to know before morning, which meant speaking with her tonight.

He sat up and chewed the skin around his thumb while he thought. He would have to wear his uniform as it was past curfew. A man in civilian clothing would be questioned or arrested.

He wondered if Matilde's friend knew anything of the role she played at the stadium? How close were they? Her friend might report her to save her own skin. He pressed his palms against his temples where a gnawing pain was growing.

Hans stood up and got dressed. He left his room shortly after ten. German soldiers were patrolling in front of him but Hans walked purposefully past them, hoping to appear to be on an urgent errand. Deep in conversation, the soldiers paid him no attention. He slowed his walk and exhaled noisily. Subterfuge did not come easily to him.

A short time later Hans reached Rue de Lille, deciding that the best thing to do was to walk straight up to the doorway without delay. He just needed to warn Matilde about the photographs and return quickly. He had decided on the way that if a senior rank questioned what he was doing, he would say that he'd heard a rumour that an illegal wireless had been heard coming from the house.

He lifted the latch on the small wooden gate, closed it behind him and climbed several stone steps before knocking on the door. A charcoal-fired car growled past. His heart was racing. He was going to see Matilde again.

'Who's there?' came an unfamiliar voice from the other side of the door.

'Open the door please, Madame,' said Hans, stressing his German accent with a firm voice.

After a few clicks, the door opened just wide enough for a woman to peer through the opening. Her pale brown hair was scraped back from her face and he saw that she was shaking despite the warm evening.

'May I step inside?' He asked the question as if it were a statement, gently pushing the door so she had to take a step backwards.

Hans could see she was thin and pale. Her clothes hung from her, the material of her dress falling from her neck to her calves, without curves from breasts or hips. Culpability. Sorrow. Shame. He felt them all in that instant.

'What's your name?' he asked.

'Adrienne Beaulieu.'

'I need to speak with Mademoiselle Pascale.'

Adrienne hesitated.

'I know she lives here, so please fetch her immediately.'

Hans saw Adrienne swallow before turning and scurrying upstairs. A door opened then closed before he heard a frantic mumbled exchange. He looked around. Thick curtains, walls painted in deep maroon and dark mahogany furniture made for a dim living space.

He turned at the sound of movement. Matilde was walking barefoot downstairs, wrapped in a shawl. He could see she wore a white nightgown beneath it. Her hair tumbled around her shoulders, her eyes wide and fearful. Instead of bringing her worrying news, he wished he could return to her room with her and…

'Hans!'

He noticed a small sigh of relief when she recognised him. Was she happy to see him or just thankful he wasn't the Gestapo? He felt an immediate compulsion to put her at ease.

'Everything's all right. So far.

She stood before him. 'Why are you here? What do you mean, so far?'

'Your friend. Madame Beaulieu.' He nodded towards the back of the house. 'Does she…?'

'She knows everything. I've known her for many years and I couldn't live here without trusting her. Why are you here, Hans?'

'They took photographs inside the stadium.'

Both Matilde's hands went to her mouth. 'Who did?'

'Official photographers.'

'Are we—?'

'I don't know. I've discovered the photographs are being delivered to the Kommandant tomorrow morning. We need to get to them before he does. Just in case.'

'But we need to get more people out—'

'No. Forget that. There'll be more soldiers and police guarding the building. It's impossible. You've done your best. You have to say you're feeling better and return to work.'

Matilde wrapped the shawl more tightly around her shoulders as if subconsciously protecting herself from the news. 'Yes, of course. But Madame Loup—'

'I'll create a distraction that'll get her away from her desk. I know the Kommandant has a meeting on the Champs-Élysées at ten, so we must pray they're delivered after that time.

Matilde nodded.

'Did the families make it to safety yesterday?' asked Hans.

'They're safe, but at the auction house. There was a service taking place at the church?'

'But I thought it had been arranged with the priest.'

'It had. A different priest was taking Mass.'

'So what happens now?'

'Tomorrow Pierre and Francis are going to find out what happened to Father Aubrey and try to organise the families' relocation underground. I was going to meet Charles again at the stadium. I need to let him know if it's too dangerous now.'

'I'll do it. It's past curfew. I'll get word to Henri that plans have been changed. What's his address?'

Matilde told him Henri's street name and number.

'Right. I must go.'

He turned to leave, but Matilde reached out to him.

'Hans. Thank you.'

Hans was surprised when both her hands encased his fingers to emphasise her gratitude, leaving her shawl to hang around her shoulders like broken wings. Five minutes later, as he walked towards Henri's house, he believed he could still feel his skin tingling from her touch.

MATILDE ARRIVED AT work at eight o'clock the following morning. She hadn't slept well due to the news Hans had delivered, but it was more than that. She'd touched him; taken hold of his hands. But what she hadn't foreseen was the soft warmth that had sent a jolt through her body. She had thought about that moment again and again throughout the night, reliving the exhilaration despite the possible devastating outcome of the message he had brought.

Madame Loup was already sitting straight-backed and tight-lipped at her desk, filling her pen with ink.

'Good morning,' said Matilde.

The Kommandant's secretary nodded her head curtly, continuing with her task.

Matilde walked past her, stepped into her office and closed the door. She leant her back against it, lowered her head and took three deep breaths. Life had been so much simpler before the war: listing items and their price for sale in the auction, writing a few sentences of description and provenance, then walking home to cook dinner and spend the evening with Xavier. Now it seemed as if she was living a contradictory life as a different person. She was risking everything. Not just her job and her freedom, but her life. Even understanding that, she realised that she never felt more alive than when she was with Hans.

The hands of the clock seemed to pass more slowly than usual. After an hour, she heard Kommandant Beitel walk into the reception area and exchange a few words with his secretary. Thank God. He was about to leave for his meeting. His jackboots clattered once more on the wooden floor as he returned to his office and closed the door. That was odd. She bit the cuticle around one of her thumbs. Why hadn't he left?

Time continued to drag. Quarter to ten. Five to ten. Something was wrong. Hans hadn't arrived at work and the Kommandant hadn't gone to his meeting. At one minute past ten on her wall clock, the nearby bells of Notre-Dame-de-l'Assomption tolled the hour. She stood up and walked quietly to the door, pressing her ear against the wood. It smelt of vinegar. She could hear the clickety-clack of a typewriter. What should she do?

Matilde heard a sharp knock on the main reception door followed by the sound of Madame Loup's chair being scraped backwards on the floor. Not being able to stand the anxiety any longer, she turned the handle and stepped into the reception area. Madame Loup was returning to her desk carrying a parcel. She placed it on the corner of the table before noticing Matilde.

'Can I help you, Madame Pascale?'

'I'm… I was wondering where Corporal Engel is. We should be working on the inventory by this time.'

'Kommandant Beitel has informed me that there's been an incident at the Arc de Triomphe. A shooting I believe. His meeting has been cancelled and Corporal Engel has been ordered to join other soldiers to calm the situation there.'

Matilde could not stop glancing at the parcel on the table. It was covered in tan-coloured paper with thin string wound around its bulk. It was small, about the size of her lunch pail and certainly a possible shape to contain photographs. Its presence was almost palpable.

Matilde jumped when the Kommandant came out of his office.

'Good morning, Madame Pascale.'

'Good morning.'

He nodded once, looked at his watch then addressed his secretary.

'I'd like coffee and this file from the storeroom.' He handed her a piece of paper. 'As soon as possible.'

'Right away, Herr Kommandant.'

He disappeared back into his office while Madame Loup stood up, pushing her chair back beneath her desk. Matilde walked towards her own office but when she heard the secretary close the reception door, she stopped and turned. The parcel sat like a time bomb on the corner of the table. She wouldn't have long.

Tiptoeing, she picked up the parcel and returned to her room. Without pausing she untied the string and unfolded the paper. A stack of fifty or so monochrome photographs sat in a pile. Matilde immediately began to sift through the images.

Her hands shook, her fingers seemingly incapable of holding anything still. Her breath came in short gasps as she scanned picture after distressing picture. Pitiful human beings: blood-stained faces, crying mothers, pleading fathers, listless children. A sob came from deep within her chest. No, she mustn't cry. Tears would blur the images. The photographs included wider images of the building, groups of people on the balcony or lying around the stadium's cycle track. A nurse helping a collapsed man… no, it wasn't her. French policemen patrolling the perimeter. Quakers giving out crackers. A rabbi comforting an old woman.

Charles!

The picture was so clear she could see his greying sideburns. If Charles was identified he would be questioned, perhaps tortured. Not having been officially employed that day, he would be a definite suspect. And if he were followed, Henri's house could be raided, perhaps even while there was a meeting in the kitchen. She had to destroy it.

With her hands still shaking and her back feeling clammy, she set the photograph aside and continued to sort through the pile. It has taken less than two minutes but had felt as if she had been in possession of the package for an hour. It had only been Charles' face she had recognised. Not remembering what order the photographs had been in, she tapped them on the table to make a neat bundle. The Kommandant would have no idea that they had been replaced incorrectly. Matilde folded the paper in the same creases and retied the string. She placed the photograph of Charles in her pocket, picked up the parcel and carefully opened the door just wide enough to see through. She could hear the Kommandant opening then closing one of his desk drawers in his office and Madame Loup's desk was still empty. Pulling the door wide enough to slip through, she crept to the table, replaced the package and hurried to find the ladies' powder room.

Once inside a cubicle, Matilde took the photograph of Charles from her pocket, ripped it into tiny pieces and flushed it down the toilet. She stood in front of the cistern with arms outstretched on either side, holding on the walls while she panted, looking to see that all the pieces had disappeared into the sewers. She took several deep breaths, trying to calm her nerves and stop shaking.

29

BACK IN HER office, Matilde began type up her handwritten lists of treasures she had made the day before she had pretended to be ill. Thoughts of Hans slowed her fingers on the keys or caused her to make mistakes, then, cursing under her breath she would have to start from the beginning again with a fresh sheet of paper.

Damn! Another mistake.

Unable to concentrate, she left her desk and walked towards the window. A huge lorry had parked alongside the building, where men were unloading wooden crates. Yet more stolen belongings, Matilde assumed. She rested her head against the cool window that was now in shadow due to a mature tree obscuring the sun. Perhaps she would walk around the gardens to clear her head before starting on the lists once more.

Then, through the window, Matilde saw a group of German soldiers walk out of the building's side door and gather at the back of the lorry. She leaned to one side to get a better view. A long, wrapped package was eased out of the back into the arms of the first two men. Every few feet, as the thick roll was pulled out, two more men took its weight. Eventually, the package was carried into the building and out of site.

There was a sharp knock on the door. Matilde turned to see Gertrude Loup standing in the doorway.

'The Kommandant wants to see you in his office.'

'What for?'

'I don't concern myself with the Kommandant's business unless instructed to do so.'

Matilde tightened the pins in her hair and ran her hands down her hips to straighten her skirt. She took three slow breaths before walking out of her door and into the reception area. She noticed that the tied package of photographs had gone from the desk. Kommandant Beitel must have them.

Had she missed an image of Hans or herself?

Gertrude Loup was sitting back at her desk seemingly absorbed in some paperwork. Would this be a good opportunity to leave quickly and quietly? She could say she was going to tidy up in the ladies' room before seeing the Kommandant. But then what? Within an hour someone would be sent to find her. And what if he wanted to see her for some benign reason? She'd have put herself and Adrienne in danger of a visit for no reason.

In an instant she decided to knock on the door.

'Herein!'

Matilde stood up straight, turned the handle and stepped inside his office.

'Ah, Madame Pascale. Please, sit down.' A wisp of cigarette smoke escaped his lips as he motioned towards a chair placed opposite his desk.

Feeling both anxious and uncomfortable, she sat straight backed on the edge of the chair.

'You must forgive my manners earlier,' he continued. 'I should have asked after your health. You've been ill, have you not?'

Was this a genuine question or was he playing mind games? 'I'm well now, thank you.'

'Good, good.' He stood up and walked to the window, turning his back to her. His hands were clasped at the small of his back, his cigarette resting between two fingers. 'I've been watching you.'

Matilde's pulse raced. Her mouth was dry.

He turned suddenly, making her start. 'I think you deserve a reward for your service to the Reich.'

'Oh.'

'There's to be an evening of entertainment at La Coupole restaurant next month. We like to occasionally thank staff working here and I'm informed there are two vacant seats. I've taken the liberty of inviting both yourself and Madame Loup. A rare privilege, I assure you.'

Matilde was speechless. She physically couldn't say simple words of thanks. Not only had she been invited to eat with the enemy, but Gertrude Loup would likely be sitting next to her. It was a nightmare.

The Kommandant spoke again. 'You do understand what an honour this is, don't you? I'm giving you a chance to eat good food and dress in your finery. Do you have nothing to say?'

Matilde quickly reasoned that any prospect, however unpalatable, was preferable to being arrested for having had her image found on a photograph.

'Herr Kommandant, I *am* deeply honoured. It's just come as a surprise, that's all. Thank you.'

He looked appeased and smiled indulgently. 'Good. That's settled.' He ground his cigarette end into an ashtray. 'Oh, and one more thing. We've received a valuable asset and I need you to log its arrival. You will go downstairs when instructed. That will be all.'

Sitting at her desk moments later, Matilde knew she should be relieved. *Of course she was relieved.* But now one anxiety had been replaced with another. She inwardly winced when she recalled that he was rewarding her for her service to the Reich. Would she ever have believed such a statement could refer to her? She would be sitting in a restaurant full of Nazis. It was incomprehensible. Then again, two years ago the thought that she would be working for the Reich would have been just as inconceivable. He had said he was giving her a chance to dress in her finery. Was he joking? She had taken in and mended her clothing so many times that her wardrobe looked like everything was made up of patchwork blankets.

She wondered how the families had slept last night. It was difficult pretending that all was normal when her head was throbbing with anxiety. Where was Hans? Had he got a message to Henri about the photographs? Were plans arranged to move the families underground tonight?

Matilde forced herself to concentrate and completed her work just before Madame Loup informed her that the package was ready for inspection and logging. She followed the familiar route downstairs into the basement carrying her notepad, pen and gloves, before pausing at the doors to the vast storage area. Her documents were checked, a procedure she thought was ridiculous as she came downstairs most days and was obviously recognised.

She was granted permission to enter. Tables, shelving, boxes and crates were labeled with her green stickers to show that they had been documented. These items were gradually moved to another secure storage facility in Alsace or across the border into Germany. She knew that those items were probably lost forever, but she had addresses for all the other stolen treasures.

Matilde turned as a soldier walked towards her.

'The new delivery has been stored in that side room,' he said, pointing. 'You are to touch it as little as possible. It is priceless. You have no more than half an hour and then the room will be locked.'

She nodded her head once and stepped slowly towards the gaping side room door. Two light bulbs hung from the ceiling casting artificial light on the giant mound of rolled material. It smelled of old tomes and dusty cupboards. A moth flittered around one of the bulbs, tapping against the hot glass and causing tiny shadows to flicker on the mound in front of her.

Matilde placed her notepad and pen on the floor and walked towards the object. Whatever could it be? She touched it. It felt solid. She peeled back its wrapping and saw material that had been rolled tightly. She found one end but it was too heavy to unroll. She followed a fold, running her fingers along its length and gradually teasing out the material until she had enough to fold it back. Slowly she peeled back a corner to reveal embroidery. The workmanship was exquisite, in vibrant colours and Latin inscriptions. The material felt like linen and smelt musty, like walking into an old church. Looking closely she could see that it had been sprinkled with moth powder. She unfolded a little more: a horse, a man with a sword, arrows. The figures were immediately so individual and so identifiable that her mouth fell open. Her eyes, now wide with wonder and horror, took in what lay before her on the floor.

It was the Bayeux Tapestry.

30

THERE HAD NOT been enough time to fully examine and log the tapestry, so the following morning Matilde returned to the cellar. When she opened the storeroom door, dust particles swirled in the air. Astoundingly, the faint aroma of cigarette smoke mingled with the sweet smell of wood and aged artifacts. Who would have been so careless to smoke in this highly combustible room full of priceless pieces of treasure? Perhaps she should report it to the Kommandant.

Earlier she had been surprised at the depth of disappointment she felt on hearing that Hans would be absent from work for a few days. It would not have been appropriate to have asked after his health, so she had nodded at Madame Loup and hoped that he'd simply been given duties elsewhere.

It was quiet in the basement, apart from occasional echoes of footfall from the floor above. Shadows cast strange dark shapes due to several bare light bulbs suspended at intervals from the high ceiling. Matilde made her way in excited anticipation towards the tapestry. Yet again she had slept badly, this time due to the excitement of seeing this remarkable piece of history again. It was almost a thousand years old and proudly told the story of Normandy's conquest over England; a precious French treasure.

She reached the storage area and frowned. Yesterday she had wrapped the end of the tapestry very carefully to keep it protected from the air. Although it had been covered over, the end was not as tightly sealed as she had left it. She would definitely inform the Kommandant that not enough care was being taken in the basement.

Matilde knelt reverentially before the giant roll of fabric and pulled on her gloves. She gently lay her palm against the cloth, leaned forward and smelled it. A frisson of awe forced her to close her eyes and wonder at the history this tapestry had seen. It had been associated with such bellicose men as William the Conqueror and Napoleon Bonaparte. It had survived the French Revolution in the 18th century and withstood examinations and transportations.

'It's quite something, isn't it?'

Matilde started and opened her eyes. Still on her knees, she looked up at Kommandant Beitel. She stood up and removed her gloves.

'I didn't mean to startle you,' he said.

'Sorry, I thought I was alone.'

Incredulously, he took a final suck on a cigarette and ground it into the floor with the tip of his boot. So much for informing the person in charge of the building, thought Matilde.

He pinched his nose and sniffed. 'So what are your thoughts on this magnificent roll of sewing?'

If she dared to roll her eyes, she would have done. To call the tapestry, sewing, was like saying the Seine was a stream.

'I don't believe that the term, sewing, quite fits this precious and revered piece of art. Its history goes back to William the—'

'I'm not asking for a history lesson, Madame Pascale. I'm asking for your thoughts on the condition of the piece.'

Put firmly in her place, Matilde slipped her hands into the gloves and knelt before the tapestry again. She examined its surface on both sides, gently studying the frayed ends.

'Essentially, it isn't a tapestry,' she said. 'The threads aren't woven together but instead this woollen yarn sits on top of the backing fabric. A more accurate description of it would be an embroidery. The end of the fabric, here, is perished in parts and frayed in others. The scene is also incomplete. I think this would suggest either damage, in which case the length would have been even longer, or lack of care in moving it over the centuries.' She automatically glanced at the squashed cigarette butt on the floor. 'Overall, considering its age, it's in remarkable condition. In all honesty, I don't think this area of the basement, close to a quarry rock wall, is the best place for it to remain for any length of time.'

The Kommandant rocked on his feet several times. 'It's all in hand. It's being transported to Chateau de Sourches, near Le Mans. It will be safe there until Europe finally realises it can't win this war, then I believe Reichsführer Himmler has requested its safe storage in his castle at Büren.'

He seemed to daydream for a few seconds, perhaps imagining his homeland. He blinked a few times and inhaled deeply.

'I shan't keep you any longer. Continue with what you're doing. And remember, this is top secret. No one must know what is down here. Do you understand?'

His steely eyes glared at her.

'Yes, Herr Kommandant.'

'Good, carry on.'

She watched him walk towards the door, stroking the top of an elegant black Steinway grand piano as he passed it. He inspected his fingers then wiped them on a trouser leg. He left the room.

Matilde sat back on her heels. His arrogance and that of his superiors made her angry and resentful. The Bayeux Tapestry was not theirs to pass around to whoever wished to decorate their houses – or castles. She would pass on its destination details to Henri, who in turn knew someone who would track its movement.

Continuing with her report, she gave the tapestry an inventory number, description and made a note of where it was stored and where it was being transported. She just needed to check daily when its likely move to Chateau de Sourches would be.

IT WAS TUESDAY and there had been no sign or word of Hans since last Thursday night. Matilde continued to itemise valuables that were brought in daily and regularly checked to see if any date had been identified for the movement of the tapestry. Twice she thought she had seen Hans at a distance, but realised she had been deluded when one soldier had turned to face her and the other spoke to a fellow German, his voice unrecognisable. Her disappointment had been palpable. Hans's absence was making her wistful.

On the fourth day, her continued disappointment at his absence meant she had to ask after him, even if it meant making conversation with Gertrude Loup. Matilde gathered several sheets of lists together and carried them into the reception area. Gertrude was typing, her wire-rimmed spectacles perched precariously on the tip of her nose. Placing the sheets of paper in a tray, Matilde waited until the Kommandant's secretary had finished typing her sentence.

Eventually the older lady looked up, but didn't speak.

Matilde gave a half-hearted smile. 'This week's lists are shorter than usual due to Corporal Engel's absence.' She ventured the question. 'I was wondering where he is.'

'He's in Germany.'

'Oh. Is he staying there?'

'I really can't say. Was there anything else, Madame Pascale?

I really need to complete this before lunchtime.'

'No. Thank you.'

Matilde returned to her office and sat down at her desk. Had he moved back to Germany permanently? Why hadn't he let her know he was going?

She knew she had grown accustomed to having him keep her company, noticing his blue eyes during conversation, the way he tilted his head slightly to his right when asking a question and… the scent of his skin. A jolt shot through her body at this last thought. It unnerved her. It was as if her body and mind were separate entities.

She rested her cheeks on her hands. He wouldn't be at the meal, either. Perhaps she had imagined their growing connection. Maybe it was simply the stupid infatuation of a grieving widow.

As the afternoon wore on, she reasoned that his remoteness was a good thing. He might be a good man, but he was German. He was the occupier. The enemy. Her feelings for him were wrong and it was good that things ended before they had even begun.

Yet, she missed him.

EARLY THE FOLLOWING morning, Matilde was once again summoned into the Kommandant's office.

He was sitting at his desk studying paperwork. He looked up at Matilde but there was no invitation for her to take a seat. Despite her mouth being dry from nerves, she forced a smile.

'Good morning, Madame Pascale.'

'Good morning.'

'You have a busy day ahead of you, especially in the absence of Corporal Engel. This is of great importance and highly confidential. Do you understand?'

She nodded. 'I do.'

He looked at her with a steely glare.

'Are you sure? Do you understand that you could be shot if you discuss anything associated with your work here?'

Surprising herself, Matilde replied calmly. 'Only a fool would ignore the risk of talking.'

He nodded. 'Good. Reichsmarschall Göring is making another visit. He's arriving on Monday by private train and will be here by midday. Madame Loup is arranging a lavish luncheon in his honour but beforehand he wishes to view two-dozen pieces of art. Here is the list.'

The Kommandant picked up a folded sheet of paper from his desk and handed it to her. Matilde tried to keep her features expressionless.

She hated the overweight, greedy Reichsmarschall. He liked to pretend he was a Renaissance man and art connoisseur. He had visited the museum eight times already, each time studying masterpieces with eyes watering with avarice, cigar in one hand and a flute of champagne in the other. Each time leaving with sealed masterpieces he had chosen for himself; or stolen, as Matilde thought of it. She hoped the Kommandant could not see the contempt on her face.

'I shall locate these paintings immediately,' said Matilde.

'Wait. As I've said, you have a busy day.' He shuffled his papers, pushing his wire-rimmed spectacles further up his nose. 'Ah, here it is.' He smoothed a sheet of paper. 'Our esteemed Führer is planning another exhibition, this time in Linz. Indeed, I shall be travelling to view it myself. He has requested one particular painting.' He looked down and ran his forefinger down the page, stopping at a particular point. 'The Astronomer. A work by the artist Vermeer. I need you to find it and pack it safely. Please mark the crate, H13.'

'Yes, Herr Kommandant.'

The Kommandant stubbed out his cigarette, and leaned back.

'In his letter, the Führer has noted that this piece of work appeals to him because it reminds him of our country's nationalistic ambitions and Germany's scientific achievements. A great choice, don't you think?'

'Yes, sir.'

'And finally, we are to entertain our honoured visitor with some light amusement. You and Corporal Engel have stored the work of degenerates elsewhere in the building. Is that correct?'

'Yes, sir. Any art not favoured is taken to three large storage rooms on the first floor.'

He gave a deep laugh and sat forwards. 'They are not just unfavoured, Madame Pascale. They are works by sub-humans, disgraceful monstrosities that offend the eye. I want a large pile of modern rubbish taken into the front garden where we will light a bonfire for our esteemed visitor to enjoy. I imagine he will return to our great leader and inform him of our exemplary work here in Paris.' He paused in thought. 'I must ask Madame Loup to organise an official photographer.'

Matilde bit her bottom lip.

The Kommandant lit a cigarette. 'Thank you. That will be all.'

Having found the paintings requested by Hermann Göring, made all the easier due to her careful record of where items were stored, she tracked the location of The Astronomer and found it wrapped in material inside a large box of other paintings. She read the paperwork attached to it, which was in her own handwriting.

Title – The Astronomer
Artist – Johannes Vermeer (Dutch)
Date of arrival – February 1941
Previous owner – Edouard de Rothschild
Size – 51 cm by 45cm
Medium – Oil Paint
Support – Canvas
Relocation date and address –

Matilde made a private mental note of its destination in Bavaria so she could record it when she got back home to Adrienne's. She knew better than to write down any information while at work. She filled in the space left blank for relocation date and address, and then took time to study this masterpiece in her gloved hands.

It was a fairly small canvas, not protected by a frame or glass. Matilde could smell the painting's sweet mustiness of age, reminiscent of an old chocolate bar, if her memory served her correctly. It had been a long time since she had tasted the delicacy. She turned the canvas over, disgusted to see a small swastika had been stamped on the back in black ink.

Turning it back round, she studied the image, knowing it would most likely be the last time she would see it. Even if it were rescued one day, it would probably be stored somewhere secret. A solitary man wearing a robe was sitting at a table gazing at a celestial globe, his thumb and middle finger resting gently on a particular spot. Warm amber sunlight spilled in through a window, highlighting the globe, the man's features and the book in front of him. It was exquisite.

Matilde lowered the painting on to an area of a table she had cleared. She had a feeling of slight panic over its impending loss.

There was also a sense of bewilderment and guilt. Was she collaborating in packing up this treasure to be sent to that mad man in Germany? No. She wasn't a collaborator. She was feigning collusion in the hope of benefitting her country. If she could help families escape, track the movement of stolen treasure and feel as if she was resisting the enemy in a quiet and secret way, then she could sleep with a clear conscience at night. It would be hunger that kept her awake. Had the families been moved the previous night?

She began to carefully wrap the painting, folding it in paper and cloth before sliding it into a narrow wooden frame. Using black paint, she daubed H13 onto a baton of wood. She guessed the H stood for Hitler.

BY FOUR O'CLOCK and not having had time to stop for lunch, Matilde sat at her desk. She had closed the door so she was able to lean forwards and sink her head into her arms, unseen. It had been an exhausting day, both emotionally and physically. Her latest job had been to wheel fifty pieces of modern art down to the ground floor level of the building, but not before she had taken several canvases out of their frames and hidden them beneath rolls of papers. Hopefully she had saved a few pieces of art, and if she faced the wooden frames inwards on the bonfire, no one should notice. She stored the modern paintings in an empty room near the main entrance of the building and would move them all outside on Monday morning.

Matilde heard some movement and conversation in the reception area. It was normal to have interruptions throughout the day, with deliveries, visitors, staff comings and goings and official guests. For this reason, Matilde stayed resting on her forearms, in fact, her eyelids were growing heavy and she was beginning to feel quite sleepy.

She was lying on her back in a field of grass. It was a dark, clear-skied night and she was searching the constellations for star patterns. But instead of finding their famous shapes, stars and planets were colliding and bursting into flames.

'Matilde.'

Matilde stirred. She had fallen asleep. Had someone called her? The voice had been gentle, so perhaps she was mistaken. No, someone repeated her name and she recognised his voice.

'Matilde.'

She sat up, not yet focusing, and wiped the haze of recent sleep from her eyes. Hans was standing in her office. He turned and closed the door. They were alone. Her heart had gone from a steady slow beat, to hammering in her chest.

'You look like you've had a busy day.'

'Yes.'

She felt emotional static in the air. Why did she suddenly feel so shy? She had thought about him every day of his absence and imagined what she would say to him if she saw him again, but now he was here, she had been rendered inarticulate. The pause must only have lasted a few seconds, but her embarrassment made it seem like several long minutes.

'You're back.' Matilde felt her cheeks blush. Did that suggest that she had missed him?

'My mother was sick. Heart attack. I was given immediate leave.'

Matilde looked up at him and gasped. 'I'm so sorry.'

He pressed his lips together in a tight smile, as if holding back emotion. 'Thank you.'

'How is she?'

'She's comfortable. It could have been a very different outcome if her neighbour hadn't called around to see what the noise was. Mother had fallen and dropped a pan.'

Matilde nodded slowly. She would give a friend a hug after hearing such news, but…

Unspoken words hung in the air between them as her fingers played with her belt. Hans gave her the slightest of smiles. She felt silly sitting behind the desk while he stood by the door. She tried desperately to find her composure. She felt clumsy pushing the chair back and standing up. She straightened her skirt.

'It must have been frightening news,' said Matilde. 'When did you hear about it?'

'Friday, first thing. It all happened very quickly. As soon as I'd packed a few things, my transport had arrived to take me to the station.'

'It's good they allowed you to go.'

'Yes.'

'Is your father alive?'

'He was killed in the last war when I was young. I don't really remember him. I don't think I've asked about your family.'

Matilde rubbed her damp palms together. Why were they talking so hesitantly?

'Both my parents live in Languedoc-Roussillon, near the coast. I haven't heard from them for a while now, but I can't imagine La Poste is reliable these days.' She gave a short laugh and noticed his eyes soften in reply.

He paused, looked over his shoulder at the closed door and took a step forwards. He spoke more quietly.

'The photographs. Were they delivered?'

'Yes, on Friday morning.'

'Was there… anyone… '

'Charles. I destroyed it.'

She saw him take a deep breath then slowly exhale.

'Well done. That must have been nerve-racking.'

She nodded.

'I have something,' said Hans, taking a travel bag from his shoulders and searching through it. Matilde took the opportunity of watching him freely when his head was lowered. The top of his hair was a little longer than the back and sides. His shoulders were broad and she could see the shape of his arm and thigh muscles through his uniform. She swallowed hard and pretended to straighten some paperwork on her desk when he looked up.

He stepped towards her and held out something white in his hands.

'For you.'

'For me?'

Matilde reached up to take the gift from him, intensely aware of his hand being close to hers. It was an embroidered handkerchief. The edges were scalloped with a lace edging, and pale blue forget-me-nots danced around a dark blue letter M.

'It's beautiful. Thank you so much.'

'My mother's name is Mitzi. I thought as you shared the same initial… '

31

MATILDE STEPPED FROM the car on to the Boulevard Montparnasse and was greeted by a light August rain. Unaccustomed to heels, she touched the back wing of the Mercedes for support while Gertrude Loup, Hans and two other members of staff climbed out.

She walked beside Gertrude towards the restaurant, wishing that she were by Hans's side holding his arm for moral support. They reached the pavement in front of the brightly lit building just as Kommandant Beitel and several other senior German officials arrived.

'Ah, good evening, Madame Loup.' He turned to Matilde. 'Good evening, Madame Pascale.' He nodded towards Hans before extending his right arm, fingers straightened in front of him. 'Heil Hitler.'

When Hans acknowledged his superior by returning the salute, doubt taunted Matilde. It seemed such a repugnant, arrogant gesture to her. As she stood beneath neon lights on the boulevard, a repetitive gnawing anxiety replayed in her head; she felt guilty by association. She was standing with the enemy, dressed in borrowed shoes and dress, about to eat food she could only have dreamed about and most damning of all, she was in love with a German. However, seeing Hans dressed in his pristine uniform decorated with German insignias and giving the

Nazi salute, felt like a slap in the face. She fought an urge to run. Could she feign illness and leave? But she loved him. She pressed two fingers against her right temple as a headache threatened.

Matilde suddenly became aware of being watched. She looked up to see Gertrude Loup's narrow, grey eyes observing her. The woman's thin lips were set in a straight line, made all the more severe because they were smeared in red lipstick. Matilde steeled herself, remembering what Xavier used to say. Fear is wisdom in the face of danger. It's a good thing to feel like this, she told herself. To be aware of the danger but remaining calm, would give her the time to watch and plan. Was that bravery? She wasn't sure, but if Xavier could see her now, he would certainly not call her a coward.

The Kommandant beamed as he looked up at the sign positioned above the main entrance, which read, La Coupole. He continued to speak in French, no doubt showing off to the ladies present, thought Matilde.

'Only the best for the Reich, eh? This is the grandest of the Parisian brasseries. In fact, our regular esteemed visitor to the museum, Reichsmarschall Hermann Göring, has dined here. Did you know that they can cater for five hundred Germans at one time?'

Matilde felt nauseous. The thought of eating delicious food that the majority could only dream of, had not whetted her appetite either. Adrienne and hundreds of thousands of people were at home making do with minimal, unsavoury provisions. It felt obscene to be here but maybe she could learn something of value for Henri and the others.

Once inside, Matilde stared wide-eyed at the vast room with its bright avant-garde embellishments. The decor and lighting resembled a shrine to the new *style moderne*, with its smooth lines, geometric shapes and streamlined forms. The walls were covered with framed paintings, many of which were being admired by high-ranking soldiers with pretty girls clinging to their arms. No doubt off-duty chorus girls, thought Matilde.

Ahead of them, the maître d' led the way up a staircase to the dining area which was equally immense. Numerous square pillars stood floor to ceiling at different points around the room, their top halves covered with images in vibrant colours. Someone was playing a piano in the background and the room was filled with the heady smell of rich food, cigarette smoke and sickly pink oriental lilies. The excitement Matilde felt being in the most glamorous place she had ever visited almost matched the guilt she felt for being there at all.

They were shown to their table where other members of museum staff were waiting. She was wondering who she would be sitting next to, but her attention was distracted when she felt Hans lay a warm hand in the small of her back, gently guiding her. If only she and Hans were alone, the war was over and…

'Madame, s'il vous plait.'

A waiter pulled back a chair and was waiting for her to take a seat. She obliged, shifting awkwardly and feeling out of place. She lifted her serviette and began wringing it between her fingers beneath the tablecloth. Relieved to see Hans sit down beside her, she laid the serviette across her thighs as chairs were scraped backwards and twelve people settled themselves.

A seemingly constant line of museum staff took their places at surrounding tables. Conversation hummed around the room alongside the clattering of cutlery and chinking of glasses, all interspersed with occasional laughter.

Hans leaned sideways and spoke softly in her ear. 'Are you comfortable?' He was smiling at her, no doubt trying to put her at ease.

'It's a little over-whelming.'

'I'm here. In a few hours it'll be over.'

Matilde returned his smile, careful to show anyone who happened to see their exchange, that they were simply colleagues being cordial with one another. Falling in love with Hans had been the easy part; admitting it to herself had been much more difficult. The thought of him filled her with joy, yet also pain and fear.

A waiter appeared at her side, pad and pencil in hand.

'Que voudrait boire, Madame?'

She fidgeted, adjusting the shoulder strap of Adrienne's dress. She couldn't resist one glass of wine. It had been so long since she'd enjoyed a glass. 'Du vin, s'il vous plait.'

'Vin rouge ou blanc?'

'Champagne,' interrupted the Kommandant. 'Tonight is a celebration of our success and progress at the museum.'

No sooner had the sommelier turned his back, than another member of staff appeared offering her a basket of bread. She smiled politely, took one and thanked him. Following the example of others at the table, she tore the warm roll in half. The aroma of the soft bread made her mouth water. She couldn't remember when she had last eaten the real thing, instead of the hard, dark loaf that was available to buy on occasions. She spread thick yellow butter on one half, forcing herself to pause before taking it to her lips. In the privacy of her bedroom she would have stuffed it into her mouth, groaning aloud with pleasure. Instead, she took a small bite. The creamy butter with a hint of salt melted on her tongue. It tasted ambrosial, truly a guilty pleasure in these times of hardship. She forced herself to eat slowly before surreptitiously slipping the second half of her roll in her handbag, for Adrienne.

Matilde's champagne arrived just before waiters brought appetizers to the table. She was relieved that this was a set menu and she didn't have to choose the food for herself. She took a sip from the glass and the burst of bubbles together with the taste of dry, fruity alcohol, flooded her mind with memories. Happier times. Celebrations. Freedom.

She dabbed her lips with her serviette, trying to blink away tears. She wiped them away as nonchalantly as she could, only to look up into Madame Loup's scrutinizing gaze. Could the collaborator know something about her secret life?

A plate of glistening pale ravioli stuffed with wild mushrooms and a creamy cheese was placed in front of her. Each perfect square parcel was exquisite. The warm softness of the filling along with the delicate taste made it difficult for her not to groan aloud. A small sound escaped her throat as she chewed, quickly covered with a quiet cough to hide her embarrassment.

Matilde looked around the table. Diagonally opposite but no longer observing her for the moment, was Gertrude Loup. She looked gaunt in her black, oversized dress. Her pale skin, sharp nose and small mouth all helped to make her appear like a rodent as she nibbled on her unbuttered bread roll.

Kommandant Beitel sat opposite Matilde, much to her disappointment. It was difficult to glance up from her food without directly looking at him, adding to her discomfort. She watched him lick his fleshy lips, smearing an oily sheen across them. It seemed to her that those who had plenty to eat paid little attention to food.

Halfway through her first course, Matilde felt a burning sensation growing in her chest. She laid her palm against the skin below her throat, as if her touch might eradicate her indigestion.

'How do you find the pasta, Madame Pascale?' asked Hans.

She knew he was making polite yet formal conversation for the sake of other diners who could hear, which proved to be the case when the Kommandant entered the conversation.

'Yes, Madame Pascale. What are your thoughts on this splendid food?'

Matilde felt her face flush as she dabbed the corners of her mouth. She took note to remember that despite the hum of conversation around them, the Kommandant had sharp enough hearing to listen in on her and Hans.

'It's delicious, but maybe a little rich compared to my normal meals.'

'Spoiling oneself occasionally is essential in these difficult times. I try to eat here each week.'

Matilde moved the remaining squares of ravioli around her dish, squeezing her fork handle in anger. Was this arrogant man unaware that it was his presence, and that of all Germans, that was creating the difficult times he spoke about?

A waiter leaned between her and Hans and filled her glass before she could say no. Then again, she thought, it was delicious and two glasses would be all she allowed herself. She raised her glass and took a sparkling mouthful. The two men opposite continued their conversation in private, suddenly looking up at the ceiling and pointing. She followed their gaze to see a large brightly coloured dome hollowed out of the ceiling above the table. She felt dizzy at the sudden movement of her head. She must not drink any more wine.

Matilde looked down at her lap, thinking that the overlapping tablecloth would make a great ally in secreting covert movements to hide more food for Adrienne, but bravery escaped her. A bread roll was one thing, but ravioli was quite another. She jumped when Hans touched her hand to gain her attention. He leaned towards her and whispered, 'You're doing well. One course over.'

Matilde gave a small laugh, still acting for her fellow diners. If anyone were to suspect their growing closeness, questions would certainly be asked. Just knowing he was in the same room as her seemed to strengthen her resolve, but she could not risk the secret of their close friendship becoming public knowledge, or he would be reassigned elsewhere.

Matilde pushed her chair backwards. 'Please excuse me while I visit the powder room.'

She stood up, laid her napkin on her chair and left the table. Having seen the sign to the washrooms on entering the restaurant, she made her way directly towards them. Occasionally she would take hold of the back of a chair or touch a pillar, her heels and the effect of champagne not helping her balance. She wound her way between tables, the rich aroma of food, loud laughter, the scent of expensive cologne and women's sequined gowns sparkling under chandeliers, all added to the clamour.

Once inside the ladies' room she entered a cubicle, locked the door and sat on the lid of a toilet. Leaning forwards she sank her head into her hands and took several deep breaths. It was cooler in there and she could drop her charade for a short time. Several giggling women came and went while Matilde remained where she was. Feeling a little better, she felt it was time to leave before someone became concerned for her absence. She took a deep breath.

On her way back to her table she stopped at a pillar and studied the painting on the top half. It was unlikely she would be dining here again and the décor was so dramatic if would be a shame not to take a closer look. The image was of a bespectacled, bald man playing the flute, with an unrecognisable black animal on his shoulder. Above him was a black and white-faced woman holding a swaddled baby.

The maître d' who had shown them to their table earlier in the evening, paused beside her. It was a relief to hear her native language with a perfect accent once again.

'Madame, I see you are admiring the painting.'

'Yes. They're colourful and very unusual.'

'They were painted by local artists like Chagall and Brancusi, fourteen years ago when La Coupole first opened. It's said they were paid with drink, which might explain some of the more bizarre images.'

Matilde smiled politely.

'May I help you with anything else?'

'No, thank you.'

The man gave a small bow and continued with his duties. Painting whilst drinking would certainly explain some of the more macabre images, she thought.

Back at the table, Hans seemed anxious to tell her something.

'Do you see that man over there?' He pointed to a small group sitting at a nearby table.

'The man with the white shirt and cravat?'

'Yes. He's an artist called Pablo Picasso. We visited his studio recently to remove a particular painting of his.'

'Which one?'

'It's called Guernica, but we didn't find it.'

'Who wanted it?'

The Kommandant interjected, speaking once again in French. 'No one wanted it. That's the whole point.' He laughed. 'It's disgusting. It was to be destroyed. Obscene degenerative art deserves no place amongst the great artists of today. Modern monstrosities make no sense.'

Matilde knew what most Germans thought of modern art but was suddenly outraged at the hypocrisy of these greedy men. She knew that Göring himself chose an occasional so-called piece of degenerate art for his own collection. Whether it was the champagne or sudden anger, Matilde answered the Kommandant, before immediately regretting it.

'But surely it's only a matter of personal taste? I believe the Reichsmarschall has chosen one or two pieces of modern art.'

The Kommandant's smile faded. Discussion around the table stopped. Matilde swallowed deeply, her face flushing hot with anxiety. Had she really said that out loud at the Kommandant's table?

The Kommandant's cheeks and forehead grew red and blotchy. He thumped his fist on the table, causing cutlery to bounce. He stood up and leaned towards her.

'Works of art which cannot be understood in themselves but need some pretentious instruction book to justify their existence will never again find their way to the German people. It is most likely that this so-called art is the product of Jews and Bolsheviks. The honourable Reichsmarschall would not have chosen such atrocious work.'

Conversation in the vicinity grew quiet as diners became aware of the Kommandant's voice growing louder. Matilde twisted the serviette tightly on her knee as he continued. Why had she spoken her private thoughts out loud?

The Kommandant continued with his rant. 'There's no telling what was in the sick brains of those who wielded the brush or the pencil in the paintings and drawings of the horrors they call art. It is not a matter of personal taste, Madame Pascale. They are blasphemous, they criticise Germany, they offend the honour of German women.'

Waiters stopped in their tracks as his voice boomed louder than surrounding conversations. Matilde's heart pounded against her chest. All eyes were upon her and Kommandant Beitel. Beneath the tablecloth she felt Hans touch her hand. He gave a gentle squeeze.

Hans stood up and raised his glass, extending it to the middle of the table.

'Let's raise our glasses to this sick, poisonous art. Without it we would be much less entertained, for where else could we laugh at such debris? Where else could we deride such atrocity? The paintings wallow in filth, by portraying human beings in a state of putrefaction. They draw idiots as symbols of motherhood or representations of mankind in the shape of cubes. They entertain us before they are burned and destroyed. Here's to entertainment!'

After a moment's pause, the Kommandant stood up straight and lowered his shoulders. He looked around the table as if only just noticing that everyone was hanging on his every word. They were all waiting for his next move. He ran the palm of his hand across his hair, looked at Hans and raised his glass.

'To entertainment,' said the Kommandant.

The rest of the table stood up, scraping their chair legs against the wooden floor. They all raised their glasses, cheered and laughed while those closest to Hans patted him on the back. Everyone drank to the entertainment of modern art, allowing the waiters to continue with their duties and conversation to return at nearby tables.

Hans had saved the evening with his impromptu speech, but Matilde's indigestion continued throughout their main course of sole in a hollandaise sauce. She didn't dare look up at the Kommandant or Gertrude Loup and prayed that the evening would end soon.

The meal continued calmly, with only one curious incident occurring. As plates were collected, a dispatch rider walked into the restaurant and stopped beside Kommandant Beitel. The man's khaki coat was dark on the shoulders, highlighting the fact that it was still raining outside. He bowed his head and clicked his heels together as he offered a package to the Kommandant.

'This is the information you urgently requested, Herr Kommandant.'

'I'm sure it can wait until I've finished my meal.'

With the unopened parcel sitting on the table, the diners enjoyed pastries filled with cream and exquisite fresh fruit. Matilde was too scared of repercussions and regret to eat such delicacies.

An hour passed without further upheaval while a cheese course was lingered over. Further bottles of champagne were brought to the table and sat amongst the debris of overflowing ashtrays, used serviettes and empty plates. Diners had begun to mingle, changing seats and wandering over to nearby tables. The Kommandant had picked up the parcel once or twice during this time, but as he remained in deep in conversation with others, it appeared to be more of an idle movement rather than a genuine interest in its contents.

Hans leaned towards Matilde. 'Would you like some fresh air? There's a balcony at the back of the building.'

'Yes please. It's very warm and noisy in here.'

'You go first, and I'll make small talk with a colleague at that table before I join you.'

'That's sensible. Madame Loup is watching me like a predator ready to pounce.'

They waited a few moments before Matilde placed her serviette on the table and walked towards the back of the restaurant. Once there, she pulled aside swathes of delicate drapes that ran the length of the glass windows leading to the balcony. The double doors were open, allowing fresh air to enter the heady atmosphere of the restaurant.

Outside, the air was cool and refreshing. She closed the door behind her. The rain had stopped and the air smelled of damp earth and blossoms. Matilde took several deep breaths before finding a powder compact in her bag. She powdered her nose and chin then walked towards the edge of the balcony. She stopped at a hip-height stone wall that overlooked a small square of grass and mature trees. The clouds had parted to reveal a constellation of stars.

Matilde heard the door open and close. Turning, she saw Hans smiling whilst walking towards her.

'Is it as bad as you'd imagined?' he asked.

'It's difficult. I feel like this is the first time I've breathed properly since arriving. Thank you for saving me earlier. I can't believe I was stupid enough to give my opinion.'

'It's a dangerous time. There are so many secrets and unspoken thoughts and emotions people aren't able to voice. I will try and smooth it over tomorrow, but hopefully he'll just put it down to naivety and you feeling out of place.'

They were standing arm's length apart. A gentle breeze ruffled Hans's fair hair. He was looking directly at her, making her catch her breath. Half his features were in darkness but half were highlighted in the restaurant lights.

'It's unusual to be so cool on an August evening, isn't it?' said Hans.

Matilde looked down and instinctively rubbed her palms on her upper arms. 'I suppose it is.'

'Matilde… '

She raised her head.

Hans took a step forwards and took hold of her forearms. 'What you're doing is growing more dangerous by the day. You're too exposed because you work for the Reich at the museum. You're more likely to be recognised if you're out.' He looked around at the empty balcony. 'You understand what I'm saying, don't you?'

Matilde couldn't breathe properly. He was touching her. The

sensation overwhelmed her. Nothing else mattered at that moment but his warm, tender touch.

He shook her arms gently to encourage an answer.

Matilde blinked. 'You know I can't stop now. I'm in a position to help people. My people.'

'I can't let anything bad happen to you. You mean too much to me.'

'And you to me, Hans, but I won't sit back and be held prisoner in my own country by—'

'By me.'

His grasp of Matilde's arm loosened. In the dim light she could still see his pained expression. She was shocked to see tears glistening in his eyes.

'No. By your country.'

Hans shook his head. 'You're wrong. Germany is beautiful. I love my country. It's our leaders who thrive on power, greed and destruction—'

'Hans! There wouldn't be a war if it were only the leaders who thought that way.'

Matilde saw the expression in his eyes change from sadness to anger. He let go of her arms.

'I'm not an idiot. Of course there are cruel and brutal men. Women too. But they're not solely German. You'll find evil on every continent on earth. Do you think we all wanted to leave our home and our families to kill, destroy and brutalise? The military oath demands unconditional obedience to Hitler and many thousands of men have been executed for desertion alone, while many others killed for smaller acts of insubordination. War is terrifying. We want to live so when our lives are threatened, fear and self-preservation make soldiers of every nation carry out orders they don't want to.'

'I understand, but it's your country that has invaded mine.

Your soldiers who are killing my people. It's because of that… We can't… It's impossible for us…'

'Please, Matilde, see me as a man and not my nationality. I didn't want this war any more than you did.'

Matilde closed her eyes and rubbed her forehead with her fingertips. A band of pain was tightening around her head. 'I'm scared. I'm terrified to give in to my feelings. My life depends on your silence. You know so much and I'm frightened to give you more.'

'I'm dressed as your enemy, but I love you. I would die for you. If you insist on helping Henri and the others, I'll do all I can to protect you all. In the end, there's no you and me. Only us.'

She felt dizzy. Was it the champagne or his words?

HE LEANED TOWARDS her and she involuntarily moved forwards. His lips pressed against hers, hard and warm. His mouth tasted of champagne and exotic fruits. At that moment, beneath the stars, nothing in the world mattered except their embrace.

The door to the balcony was flung open. They pulled apart. Gertrude Loup stood looking demonic in black, panting and wide-eyed. She had seen them.

'You need to hide. Now!'

It took a second for them to acknowledge what she had said.

'What do you mean?' asked Hans.

'The delivery. The parcel. He's opened it. It was a second batch of photographs that had gone missing. The Vel d'Hiv. You're both on them. They're searching for you. Run! Now!'

Hans looked around the balcony then held out his hand to Matilde. 'Here, quickly.'

Matilde couldn't move. Was it a trap? Why was Madame

Loup aiding their escape? Was she a secret patriot pretending to be a collaborator? If it was the truth, she was putting herself in danger for them. Despite her doubt, Matilde could hear a commotion inside. Orders were being shouted and furniture upturned.

Hans called out. 'Matilde! Now!'

'Go!' cried Gertrude.

Madame Loup's urgent plea enabled Matilde run to the far end of the balcony where Hans was waiting, arms outstretched.

'We need to climb down. Quickly!'

Matilde looked at the gnarled wisteria branches that had been fixed to the wall. The coiled bark was as thick as her wrist, but would it hold their weight? She had no choice. She sat on the wall, kicked off her shoes and took hold of a twisted branch. As she lowered herself, she glimpsed Gertrude disappearing back inside the building.

32

Hans and Matilde stood panting in the doorway of a boarded-up shop having run for ten minutes through empty backstreets. Matilde had grown up in Paris and knew all the shortcuts and alleyways the Germans were ignorant of. Hans pushed her behind him before checking up and down the narrow road. Apart from a few dim blue-tinged streetlamps, the path ahead was clear.

'I need to get you to safety. You say there's a hiding place at Adrienne's?'

'Yes. You're coming too, aren't you?'

'No. We've got to be realistic. I can't ask her to put her life in danger for me.'

'Hans, she's in danger hiding *me*. She says it's her way of resisting. What difference will one more person make?'

'You'll be safer on your own. Trust me.'

Hans could barely see her face in the shadows, but her voice was urgent and fearful.

'Where will you go?'

She clung to him and he held her tightly in return. Hans didn't answer. This was not the time for discussion.

'We have to move,' he said. 'We've got to get to Adrienne's and there's only twenty minutes left before curfew. We don't want to give the police any reason to stop us and ask questions.'

Just as he was about to take her hand and move on, the purr of an engine focused their attention. He held his breath and turned to face Matilde, turning his back on the road. He leant against her, his nose pressed against the dirty glass of the front door. From the gloom of the doorway he couldn't resist turning slightly to watch a sleek car glide past and continue down the narrow side street. A German patrol.

Once again all was quiet.

He took Matilde's hand and they tentatively stepped from their hiding place. He thought how small her fingers felt. They moved a short distance at a time, stopping regularly in recesses and alcoves to reassess the danger. They hurried along cracked pavements, passed walls plastered with political posters or scrawled with smudged chalk slogans. Thoughts tormented him. He had an unsettling premonition about losing Matilde. His mouth was sour. Was it the taste of fear?

Footsteps.

They were the hard, threatening sound of military jackboots; a noise he recognised because he owned two pairs. He guided Matilde with urgency down the side of a building. It was pitch black. With a dull thud he cracked his temple on something hard. He leant forwards, squeezing his eyes shut in pain and forcing himself not to cry out. He held his wound as warm blood oozed through his fingers.

'What happened?' whispered Matilde.

'I walked into something. I'm all right.' He reached out in the darkness to try to discern the object and touched intricate ironwork. It felt like a staircase attached to the side of the building.

The footsteps were growing louder.

'Quick, climb the steps.'

Hans followed behind Matilde, catching her once when she

tripped. The fire escape was blocked by boxes on the first floor, so they huddled together and waited.

More footsteps came from the other direction. They were calling out in German that they had not found "them."

As they crouched in the darkness, Hans could hear Matilde's laboured breathing. He could feel her body shaking in his arms. Again he asked himself what he was he doing here? Instead of living a less stressful existence in an office as a way of navigating his way through this bloody war, he had fallen in love with a French woman and become involved in her altruistic principles. Holding tightly on to Matilde, he could smell her perfume as his cheek brushed hers, and knew that if he had to choose again, he would accept the same situation.

The two groups of soldiers converged from different ends of the street and congregated at the entrance to where they were hiding. A torch was shone backwards and forwards at ground level before one of the Germans pointed out the fire escape. Hans could see a beam of torchlight travel up the staircase, slowly growing closer and closer to where they were cowering. He held his breath, one hand on his Luger pistol, waiting for the beam to discover them.

The light disappeared and conversation faded as the soldiers moved on. He let out a long sigh. They had been saved by the debris on the first-floor platform, safely hidden behind several large discarded boxes and rolls of cardboard that had once supported reams of material.

They waited a further ten minutes. The rain had started once again. Slowly they negotiated the slippery iron steps and approached the pavement. The street was empty. Matilde was having difficulty walking on her bare sore feet, so Hans supported her around her waist.

'I think my feet are cut. They hurt.'

Hans looked down but it was too dark to see. 'We're nearly there. Can you manage?'

'If you help me.'

They continued further into the 6th arrondissement, two crouched figures stumbling forwards past curfew. If was a huge relief not having to cross a heavily guarded bridge, although Hans could smell decaying moss growing along the side of the Seine. Not far now, he thought. One more corner and they would be on Adrienne's terraced street. All was quiet.

They edged towards the last corner. Hans wiped raindrops from his eyes, his other arm supporting Matilde. A few more steps and they would turn and see the house.

In an instant a German soldier stepped from the shadows in to the dim light of a nearby streetlight. The smell of fresh urine explained why they hadn't heard any footsteps; the man had been standing still emptying his bladder in a doorway.

'Halt!' The German lifted his hand in a precise, abrupt manner.

They stopped dead. The man wore a trench coat and had a rifle slung diagonally over his shoulder. He shone a torch from Matilde to Hans, blinking in surprise at seeing Hans's uniform.

'Oh!'

'I'm escorting this lady home. Good evening.' Hans hoped he could brazen his way past the man and took a few more steps, almost dragging Matilde.

'Warten Sie!'

They had passed by the German and had their backs to him, but Hans did as they had been commanded, and waited. The soldier took a few slow deliberate steps around them until his was facing them both once again.

'It's past curfew.'

'Yes. Madame was taken ill. She needed some assistance.'

Hans believed this man did not know they were being hunted. He would have been given their description. It was unlikely he would be patrolling on his own if he were searching for them, and he certainly would not be having a conversation.

The German clicked his fingers in front of Matilde. 'Papers.'

Matilde appeared to panic. Hans watched as she ran her hands through her wet matted hair.

'I left my bag. My papers were in it. I don't have it.'

Alarmed, Hans tried another tactic. He began to speak in German to his countryman.

'To be honest I picked her up on the corner, back there.' Hans turned slightly and pointed down the street they had just walked along. 'I think she's enjoyed a bit too much to drink and I thought that maybe I could spend an easy ten minutes of fun with her now I'm off duty. What do you think? Man to man. Let us pass.'

The soldier stood quite still, staring at Hans. 'Out after curfew and without papers. Do you think I should ignore my orders?'

'Maybe just ease them, this once?'

'What's your name? Where do you work?'

Hans sensed the man was becoming irritated. It was now raining heavily. He had to get Matilde to safety. He could make a lunge at the soldier and tell her to run, but she could barely walk.

The soldier followed Hans's glance and shone his torch down on Matilde's bare feet. They were bloodied and dirty. He took a step back and cocked his head to one side.

'There's something not right here.'

He moved his right shoulder and began to slide the strap of his rifle down his arm. Hans moved quickly. He hooked his right foot behind the German's ankles and pushed him backwards.

The man fell on his back to the sound of air being knocked from his lungs. The torch rolled a short distance away but shone in their direction. Hans jumped on him as they struggled together, the soldier trying to reach his weapon while Hans wrestled his arm away. They rolled over several times before the heavier man had the advantage and sat on top of Hans. He threw a punch and the blow landed on Hans's eye socket. The pain was excruciating and momentarily dazed him. A second jab hit him on the jaw, inadvertently clenching his tongue between his teeth. He groaned and spat blood from his mouth.

Hans tried to shout out when he saw Matilde pulling at the German's arm, but she was thrown to one side with ease before the soldier started fumbling in his coat pocket. Hans feared it was a handgun and tried in vain to release his arms that were pinned to his side by the man's knees. The soldier took what looked like a tube from his pocket. Hans recognised the shape of a Bakelite whistle, about the length of his middle finger. They were all issued with one. Just as the German raised it to his mouth, Hans released one of his arms and with the flat of his hand, pushed hard against the whistle.

With the discarded torch shining on them as they writhed on the ground, Hans saw the soldier's eyes grow wide in horrified surprise. The violence of having the whistle rammed to the back of his throat had loosened his grip and given Hans a chance to take the upper hand. He pushed the large man off him and then sat astride him in return. The man had his hands at his mouth, coughing and trying to retrieve the obstacle, when Hans punched him. The soldier protected his eyes giving Hans the chance to push the whistle deeper. He felt it hit bone at the back of the man's throat. Using his fingers, he pushed it further while the soldier clawed in panic at Hans's shirt. Blood oozed from the man's lips and dribbled down his cheeks towards his ears. Hans kept the pressure on, blocking the soldier's airway until he stopped struggling and lay limp beneath him.

Hans spat a mouthful of blood next to the dead man then stood up. His eye throbbed and had swollen to such an extent that it was almost closed, but he could still see the soldier lying on his back with his eyes and mouth wide open.

HANS HALF CARRIED Matilde towards Adrienne's door. He knocked with urgency, noticing a pale yellow light from inside the house as curtains moved. Adrienne opened the door with a horrified expression on her face. She beckoned them inside and hurriedly shut the door.

'What's happened?'

'They know we were at the Vel d'Hiv,' said Matilde.

'Dear God!'

'We were nearly caught.'

Adrienne's hands covered her mouth, her eyes wide with horror. 'How?'

'There was a new batch of photographs. We were pictured.'

'No!'

Hans gently pushed Matilde forwards. 'You have to hide her quickly. They'll have this address in the office.'

He saw the colour drain from Adrienne's face, but she beckoned them towards the back room.

'Quickly, in here.'

She dragged a small dining table to one side of the room then moved a rug that had been underneath it. With the floorboards exposed, she hooked a finger underneath the edge of a plank and lifted a long piece of wood to one side. She continued until there was a metre-square hole in the floor. Hans could see that an old single mattress had been squeezed inside and laid over rubble.

'Get in. Be quick,' said Adrienne.

He guided Matilde towards the opening but she turned and held him tightly.

'Please stay. They'll kill you and—'

'I'll get in touch, somehow. If I can somehow get to my room, I have civilian clothing there. I don't imagine they'll think I'll go back there now. I know a gallery that's deserted so I'll try and break in there.'

He helped Matilde below the floorboards and onto the mattress, then stood up and touched Adrienne's arm.

'Thank you.'

'Your plan is impossible. You need to hide here.'

'There's no room. Matilde stands a better chance alone.'

Adrienne shook her head. 'There is room. Look.'

Hans looked down. Matilde certainly did look small and thin, shivering on the mattress.

'I must go now. Time is running—'

Aggressive knocking interrupted him. The house seemed to vibrate to the sound. They all froze, holding their breath. Raised voices came from next door. Muffled orders were being shouted in German; then a woman screamed.

'There's no time,' said Adrienne. 'Climb in next to Matilde. They'll discover they've got the wrong house in a minute.'

Hans lowered himself on to the edge of the hole and slid his legs underneath the floor, before manoeuvring the rest of his body onto the mattress. Adrienne threw a shawl on top of them and began to fumble with the floorboards. He watched as she replaced one plank at a time until they were lying in darkness. Then there was shuffling and scraping as the rug, table and chairs were moved back into place.

Hammering returned, but this time it was louder. They were pummelling and shouting at Adrienne's door. He reached out and took hold of Matilde's hand. She squeezed it tightly.

33

MATILDE AND HANS listened to the pounding of jackboots reverberating through the house while soldiers searched every room. Lying in the darkness magnified every sound. Furniture was being scraped along the upstairs floor and loud crashes accompanied raised voices. Imagining everyone was in other parts of the house, Matilde was shocked when she heard voices above them.

The man's voice was loud and guttural. 'Where are they?'

'Who?' asked Adrienne.

Matilde squeezed her eyes tightly shut when she heard a slap, followed by someone stumbling.

'Where are they?'

'If you mean Matilde, she's at a restaurant with the museum staff.'

Her friend sounded strange, speaking an octave higher than usual.

'She left with a German,' said the man. 'A traitor. We'll deal with him when he's found.'

'I didn't know. I don't know where they are.'

'What's your name?'

'Adrienne Bisset.'

'Papers.'

Matilde couldn't hear anything. She presumed he was inspecting her documents.

The noise of footsteps resounded once again as men came back downstairs.

'No one's up there.'

There was silence for a few moments.

'If they come here, phone this number immediately. If you shield them we will find out and you'll face the same fate as them. Do you understand?'

Matilde didn't hear her friend answer. Perhaps she had nodded in affirmation.

'Be assured, we *will* return.'

Shuffling. A muffled order. Movement. The front door slamming.

Matilde could feel her whole body shaking with fear. Hans's breath was rapid and shallow. Silence. Then, when she strained to listen, Matilde could hear the slow, hesitant tread of her friend walking upstairs.

HANS WOKE UP with Matilde's head lying on his arm. It only took a second of staring into the black space in front of him to remember where they were, lying three feet beneath the floorboards under Adrienne's living room.

The single mattress they were lying on was lumpy and flattened, but it afforded them some protection from the hard stone beneath them. He shifted his weight, causing Matilde to groan and stretch. He felt her rub her arm.

'Sorry,' he said.

'It's fine. It's numb, that's all.'

Hans pulled the shawl up around her ears to protect her neck from the draught, which seemed to be whipping around the foundations of the house. The uncharacteristic depressing weather echoed his present thoughts. Yesterday he was a free man with hope and ambitions of owning an art gallery after the war. Today, he was a hunted man.

He pulled Matilde close to his chest. He noticed that if he looked down towards his feet, or turned and looked behind his head, spikes of light shone through the gaps between the floorboards. But for the rug directly above them, they would be afforded more light.

He imagined they had lain awake talking quietly for almost an hour before he heard the chairs and table above them, being moved. The rug was dragged to one side and one by one the loose floorboards were taken up. Light flooded the hiding place making him squint.

Adrienne peered down at them. 'Are you all right? I'm sorry. I didn't dare lift the boards last night in case they returned.'

Matilde and Hans sat up and stretched, their necks level with the floor.

'Of course. You did the right thing,' said Hans.

He held his neck, moving his head from side to side. 'I'm sorry we've put you in this position. Hopefully it won't be for too long. We need to get word to Henri. I know he'll think of a way to get Matilde out of Paris.'

'Both of us,' said Matilde, turning to him. 'Oh, your face.' She gently touched his cheek.

Hans could feel that his left eye was closed and the cut on his lip was tight and sore.

'Don't worry. The swelling will go down in a few days,' he said.

'It needs cleaning,' said Adrienne. 'I'll check that the back yard is clear and you can each use the outside washroom. You'll have to be very quick. They could return at any time. I've brought some of your clothes down from your bedroom,' she said to Matilde. 'I hope you don't mind, but I've brought some of Xavier's clothes down too, for Hans.'

'Of course not,' said Matilde.

Hans laid his palms flat on the floorboards and pushed himself on to his feet. 'How are you?' he asked.

Adrienne touched her cheek, as if remembering the pain of the previous evening's assault.

'Scared. I managed a couple of hours sleep, I think. I was so worried for you both.'

Hans helped Matilde to stand up and they stepped out from their hiding place. He saw her wincing and taking unsteady steps towards the kitchen, following Adrienne. Her feet were filthy, her soles cut and streaked with dried blood.

While Adrienne cleaned and bandaged Matilde's feet, Hans crept outside into the private yard. The sun was warm, but a strong breeze whipped around the enclosed space, bending the flowers in their pots in one corner of the enclosure.

Inside the washroom he emptied his bladder then stripped to his waist to wash at a small sink. He used a small, dried and cracked bar of soap to freshen up, before drying himself with a rough towel. After wetting his hands, he ran them through his hair to lay it flat.

Back outside, Hans paused in the yard and looked up. Ribbons of white clouds were racing across the sky chased by unseasonal winds. With his face still upturned, he closed his eyes and took a deep breath. What had he done?

In the kitchen, Adrienne was kneeling on the floor in front of Matilde, bandaging her feet with a length of material, ripped from a bed sheet.

'What can I do to help?' he asked.

'Can you finish this off?' said Adrienne. 'My hands are shaking so much that I keep dropping it. I'll make a dandelion root drink.'

Hans knelt before Matilde and rested one foot on his thigh. He glanced up at her. Her features were delicate but lines of worry were etched on her face. She smiled at him, or perhaps it was a tremble of her lips. He leaned forwards and rested his forehead on her knee. He felt the gentle touch of her palm on the back of his neck, and knew he had made the right choice.

With Matilde's feet clean and wrapped, Hans lingered in the kitchen while she limped out to the washroom. Adrienne had her back to him while she prepared a hot drink.

'Thank you.'

Adrienne turned to look at him. She nodded slowly in recognition of his gratitude.

'This is very dangerous for you,' he said.

'I know.'

'We need to get Matilde to safety and both of us out of the house as soon as possible to limit the risk of you being implicated. This will mean you contacting Henri and his men.'

'I'll do what needs to be done.'

'Matilde will let you know the accurate details for making contact. I understand someone waits for contacts each Friday. Make sure you're not followed. Take your time.'

'It's only Sunday. Can't I contact them sooner?'

'Matilde knows Henri's address, but it would put the whole group in danger if you're seen knocking on his door. We'll have to be patient and wait.'

'What about food? I'll need to buy for three people and it'll look suspicious if I bring more than enough for one person back home.'

'Staying safe and not arousing German interest is more important. Speaking form experience, I've never felt the need to inspect a woman's shopping bag!'

That raised a smile of relief from Adrienne, as Hans had hoped it would.

'Why do you think the second batch of photographs took so long to arrive?' asked Adrienne.

Hans shrugged. 'There are numerous reasons: lack of printing paper or ink, broken machinery or perhaps simple incompetence. Paperwork goes missing in the museum and turns up weeks later in the wrong office. I must admit it came as a shock. I thought we'd missed that bullet, so to speak.'

They turned when Matilde stepped through the kitchen door.

'It's windy out there.'

'I'll keep busy and wash the bedding. It'll be dry in no time,' said Adrienne.

Hans knew the women were making mundane conversation to ease the tension, but it was important that they understood the gravity of their situation.

'Matilde, can you explain the procedure for making contact with Henri? I know it won't be until Friday, but Adrienne needs to go over the correct steps in her mind until she feels confident.'

'Of course,' said Matilde, touching her friend's forearm. 'Every Friday afternoon at four o'clock, one of the men sits in the café on the corner of Église de la Madeleine square. Take a ten centimes coin with you and arrive ten minutes before he does. You'll know it's the right man to approach because he'll order a café express, will light a cigarette, but will also place a pipe and open tin of tobacco on his table. Walk towards him and pretend to pick the coin off the floor beside him and place it on his table. Walk outside and wait on the west side of the church. There's a stone wall and several trees there, which helps to avoid attention. He will come and join you after ten minutes. If for some reason you're late, he'll only stay in the café until half past four, then you'll have to wait for another week.'

Adrienne nodded. 'I understand.'

'I'll go over it again before Friday.'

Adrienne nodded and turned to pour out three cups of mud-brown liquid. 'Here's your drink. Perhaps you should have it sitting on the mattress. You've been out for twenty minutes now and I'm feeling nervous. I'll need to open the front curtains soon, as if it were just any other day.'

'I think it would be better if we came out during the night. It'll be a nuisance for you to set an alarm for the early hours, but it'll be safer,' said Hans. 'Hopefully it'll only be a couple of weeks before Henri has a plan in place.'

34

THE FIRST WEEK in hiding passed slowly, interspersed with visits to the washroom and simple meals shared with Adrienne. Crockery was washed and put away immediately because no one knew when they would need to rush into hiding again. Fear had taken hold and was not letting go of its grip. It was spreading like bindweed, weaving its way into conversation, thoughts, dreams and imaginings. Knocks, creaks and gurgling from pipes would momentarily silence the household as they waited like statues, listening for the affirmation that the enemy had returned. The irony that a German was sitting among them held no fear for the women. A good man was a good man; his place of birth was inconsequential.

It soon became apparent that it was impossible to expect that Matilde and Hans only came out from beneath the floorboards for a couple of hours at night. The underground space was too small and too claustrophobic. Although they would talk quietly in between hours of dream-filled sleep, nothing felt as good as stretching aching limbs or standing at the window together, looking up at the clouds and birds. They would watch the linden trees casting long shadows at the far end of the yard, changing the hues of the washroom door from cornflower-blue to violet and teal at different times throughout the day.

On the fifth day in hiding, the three of them had pulled

dining chairs next to the window overlooking the back yard, having allowed themselves a half-hour washroom break. It was late afternoon and the low buzz of aircraft grew louder, compelling them to lean forwards and gaze skywards. A formation of planes roared directly overhead, black crosses on their wings plainly visible. As soon as they were out of sight, the sound of their engines changed pitch as they banked over the Seine.

'Messerschmitts,' said Hans.

'I wonder where they're going?' said Matilde, her forehead resting on the cool glass. Her question sounded like a thought she had spoken out loud, as if she wasn't really expecting an answer.

Hans rubbed the bristles on his chin. 'Sounds like they turned east heading across the Channel.'

A minute or two of silence passed.

'I hope Henri can come up with a plan before the bad weather arrives,' said Adrienne. 'Last winter was so bitter that I burned all the furniture I could spare.'

Still looking through the window, Hans said, 'We'll be gone in a couple of weeks. They're a resourceful and resilient bunch of men.'

'Why don't you come with us?' asked Matilde.

'It'll make things more complicated. Besides, this is my home. I'll be out of danger when you're moved to safety.' She twisted the skirt of her apron between her fingers. 'They can search as much as they want when you've gone.'

Matilde and Hans exchanged glances. They both knew that she was risking her life to keep them hidden. They could see that, like them, she was struggling.

'Two more days until you contact Henri,' said Hans. 'Then it'll be a matter of a week or so until some plans are drawn up to move us on.'

Matilde laid her hand on top of her friend's. 'We'll never forget what you've done for us. Without you… '

Adrienne took a deep breath and forced a smile. 'I know, I know. Shall we have one more drink?'

'I couldn't possibly,' said Matilde. 'I'll need to go to the washroom again!'

Their restrained laughter was interrupted by abrupt knocking on the front door. Matilde and Hans immediately replaced their chairs. They scrambled back on to the mattress. They had practiced it every day and now knew the quickest way to hide, knocking precious seconds off their actions: step on to the middle of the mattress, clasp the floorboards with your hands and slide legs to the bottom of the mattress, then lie down.

They lay flat as Adrienne threw their cups on the bottom of the mattress and nimbly replaced the floorboards and the rug. The knocks were repeated before Matilde could hear her friend's clogs clattering on the wooden floor towards the front door. It was difficult to estimate how many men entered, but once again, heavy footfall could be heard climbing the stairs and walking about upstairs. There didn't seem to be the urgency that was present before. Furniture wasn't upturned and loud orders weren't barked. It sounded quite orderly.

Matilde pressed her lips tightly together and squeezed Hans's fingers. Heavy footsteps ran downstairs. The sound of boots entered the room and moved towards the window. The person paused then returned to the hall. Matilde felt dreadful. She had led the Germans here. Perhaps Adrienne should come with them after all.

They heard the front door close.

'I'm scared.' said Matilde.

Hans turned on to his side to face her. 'I'm sure they believe we've long gone by now.'

Adrienne's voice came through a gap in the boards above their heads. 'I'm going to give it a couple of hours before I open up, is that all right?'

Hans raised his chin so his voice would be directed towards her. 'Of course.'

He leaned towards Matilde and kissed her forehead, trying to reassure her. She felt it did to some degree. She certainly couldn't imagine spending all these hours alone beneath the floorboards.

'Stay strong,' he said. 'Another week and we'll be heading south.'

35

TWO MONTHS PASSED. It was now early November and every day and night merged together, hour after monotonous hour, week after week spent in a cold uncomfortable tomb, while outside the weather was embracing early winter with its cooler temperatures and foggy mornings. Lying beneath the floor with movement restricted, Matilde and Hans's limbs and extremities often grew numb with cold, despite the blankets provided.

Adrienne had been successful in contacting one of the cell members in August, but Henri was having difficulty making contact with the owners of the safe house south of the demarcation line. There was some anxiety that they might have been arrested; there were plenty of French collaborators who, for the price of a good meal, would betray their countrymen to the Germans.

The narrow gaps in the floorboards above their heads shed a paltry amount of light during the day, and even less during the evening when Adrienne left a candle on the dining room sideboard for them. Whenever they were hiding during the day, Matilde could see areas of Hans' shadowed face when they spoke quietly together, the light falling on the bridge of his nose or the curve of his mouth.

Sleep became a precious commodity. Any routine had long since disappeared. Night and day fused into one, with thirty minutes of disturbed sleep followed by three hours of clustered anxiety and accelerated thoughts racing through her mind. In her dreams she was free to run, swim, sing and explore her beautiful city. But when she awoke, the colours of her dreams darkened into a black reality, where each minute became an endurance to bear.

During the past eight weeks of forced proximity, they had learned everything about each other and their lives before they met. They professed their love to each other and had grown physically intimate, stopping short of making love. They had tried once in eager passion, but it had proved impossible. Neither Hans nor Matilde could physically lay on top of the other, thanks to the wooden flooring above them.

Hans squeezed her hand and she opened her eyes. She must have drifted off again. Creaking floorboards above them and the sound of a dull clang from the metal latch of Adrienne's bedroom door, told them it was two in the morning. Her friend set an alarm each night so she and Hans could be free to move, wash and eat for two or three hours, as well as snatched half hours during the day.

A few moments later the living room door opened and the sound of Adrienne's shuffling footsteps moved closer to their hiding place. After some scratching, the rug was pulled aside and the floorboards lifted. Candlelight illuminated the interior of the hiding space and Adrienne was a welcome sight. Matilde needed the bathroom and was stiff and hungry.

Having relieved herself and washed at the sink, Matilde returned to the back room while Adrienne had gone to heat some food and Hans took his turn in the washroom. She sat huddled in a blanket on one of two small armchairs covered in faded coral velvet, while looking around the neat candlelit room. Brass mantel candleholders stood on either end of the stone fire surround, next to which was a carved walnut sideboard. The rug that covered the sawn floorboards was turned back with sections of removed planks sitting on top of it.

An Aubusson tapestry hung on the wall and often caught her interest. As she did a couple of times a week, she stood before the woven material, lifting the candle in front of the image. A group of figures was sitting in the foreground conversing on grass adorned with flowers. Birds sat in tree canopies and in the background were glimpses of towers, spires and small villages. She imagined the freedom of walking through this bucolic scene and picking flowers without a single drab, grey-green German uniform in sight.

'Did you hear?'

Matilde turned. Adrienne had placed a bowl of watery soup on the table.

'I said I'd made an artichoke and potato stew. It won't put fat on our bones but it'll keep us all alive another day.'

Hans walked into the room. He had a few days' stubble, his hair was parted and darker than usual, being still damp from his wash. Matilde could see how much weight he had lost now that he wasn't eating German rations.

'Thank you,' he said.

'This is wonderful,' said Matilde, spooning chunks of potato into her mouth.

Hans ate hungrily before pausing. 'Aren't you eating with us tonight?'

'I couldn't wait,' said Adrienne. 'I ate mine before I went to bed. I thought it might keep the heat in my body, but I still couldn't get warm. But never mind that, I've got some news.'

Matilde and Hans looked up.

'Has Henri been in touch?'

'Someone posted a note shortly before curfew. Apparently

there are roadblocks and armed soldiers everywhere. The Germans are planning to cross into southern France. No more Free Zone. Vichy won't be in charge for much longer. The note says that British and American forces have landed in French North Africa and that plans to move you both have been compromised.'

Hans lowered his spoon.

'Gott verdammt.'

Matilde was surprised to hear him speak German with them. Anxiety knotted her stomach. First some bad news and then that direct and guttural language spoken by the man she loved.

He reached out and took hold of her hand. 'I'm sorry. It was just the shock. I was cursing the news in the note.'

Appeased, Matilde asked, 'What does the news mean for us?'

'Not much will change here, but the rest of France will find out what life has been like for… you.' Hans lowered his head.

'And you, now,' said Adrienne. 'You took a stand against your countrymen. You chose right from wrong. Matilde knows that I doubted you at first, but you put yourself in danger to help French citizens and I can see that you love her, which makes you a good man in my eyes.'

Hans gave a tight-lipped smile of thanks. 'I wonder what prompted the move south?' He looked thoughtful. 'The Brits landing in Africa will have strengthened the Soviet Union's hand. Hitler must have ordered the invasion of southern France as a show of power. The only thing worse than an angry wild animal is an injured, angry wild animal. Sorry. It seems like we may be here a little longer, but although I haven't known Henri for very long, he has great determination and many contacts, so I believe he won't stop trying to get us out. It's just a matter of time. One day I hope to repay the kindness you've shown me.'

'There's really no need, and besides, I think we've got quite a routine going, haven't we? Right,' she said, standing up. 'If there are more troops walking the streets, I think we have to be even *more* careful. I'm going to sit and read by the front window and keep a look out while you two stretch your legs, get a wash and get some fresh air. It's cold and blustery out so you'll need to take your blankets.'

Matilde and Hans stepped out of the kitchen door into the enclosed yard. They took it in turns to visit the washroom then began to walk around the perimeter of the outside space, draped in their blankets. Matilde had counted her footsteps around the circuit many times over the past weeks. Seventy-two steps. They walked in wide circles, holding hands and occasionally remarking on the stars, or straining to see the shadow of an owl hooting in the darkness, or lowering their gaze to watch their feet highlighted in moonlight, crunching on crisp autumn leaves spiraling in the wind.

'Hans.'

'Yes, my love.'

'What if they can't get us out?'

He let go of her hand and wrapped his arm across her shoulders, pulling her closer as they continued to walk.

'Something will happen. It might just take a little longer than we expected. We're being careful, we can wash, eat, have a hiding place and most importantly, we're together. Things could be so much worse.'

Matilde rested her head against his shoulder. The vast black sky made her feel the fragility of life despite his comforting words. She glanced upwards at his profile in the moonlight, and beyond him, at the constellation of stars that had witnessed countless millennia of wars and mankind's hatred towards fellow man.

When they reached the trees, Hans stopped walking and

turned her to face him.

'Do you believe me?'

'I believe things could be so much worse.'

'Exactly. We're alive. We're in love.'

Matilde felt his fingers lift her chin. He kissed her gently on her lips, his hand slipping behind her neck to support her as his kiss became more urgent. She clung to him as if he were a refuge, hope in a time of turmoil. He pulled her closer until their bodies were pressing against each other, their kisses becoming more fervent. She gasped as his fingers found the skin of her stomach.

'Cold!'

Blankets fell from their shoulders. There was little romance during their lovemaking, just the chattering of teeth, gasps of white breath that dissipated into the cold night, awkward movements and a passion that came from knowing this could be the only time they would be so intimate. Matilde lay on the blankets and autumn leaves, lifting her skirt. This was a momentary escape from their worries, a sanctuary from restrictions and a temporary haven from danger. For the first time since they had been in hiding, they found comfort in each other's bodies.

Twenty minutes later, they stepped inside the kitchen and closed the door behind them. They walked quietly into the front room where Adrienne had fallen asleep, an open book leaning against her chest.

'Poor thing. She's exhausted but we must wake her,' said Matilde. 'She'll need to hide us.'

'We've only been out for half an hour, let's sit for a while.'

They settled on the bergère sofa in silence, arms entwined. Matilde buried her nose in Xavier's old wool jumper, and inhaled. It smelled of night air, musty leaves and comfort. She felt Hans kiss the top of her head, a smile playing on her lips as she remembered the words of love he had spoken ten minutes earlier.

Something rattled outside the front of the house. They sat up straight, wide-eyed and looking at each other. Hans slowly stood up. He leaned forwards and placed a hand across Adrienne's mouth and gave her a gentle shake of her shoulder. She opened her eyes immediately and he placed his forefinger on his closed lips. He pointed to the window draped with curtains and then tapped his ears to convey that they had heard something. Adrienne was immediately alert and sat up. They all waited and listened. Matilde could hear their breathing and occasional gusts of wind blowing against the windows.

The rattling returned. Hans blew out the candle.

Adrienne whispered. 'Quick. You'll have to feel your way. Hurry.'

Matilde moved along the walls. The house was in darkness. She felt her way, sliding fingers along embossed wallpaper. She reached the door jamb. Now she was crawling, inching forwards towards the hole. A splinter pierced her knee. With arms outstretched she felt the sawn edge of the floorboards. She lowered herself down and heard Hans climb beside her. They lay down on the mattress and pulled the blanket over themselves. Adrienne lit the candle in the back room and replaced the floorboards before pulling the rug back into place.

Matilde tried to steady her breathing, listening to the sound of Adrienne's clogs as she walked to the front of the house and opened the door. Matilde strained to listen, but all she could hear was the scratching of mice and gusts of wind outside.

After a few moments had passed, Matilde dared to whisper.

'I can't hear voices, can you?'

'Shhh. They may be listening.'

Matilde guessed that ten minutes had passed before Adrienne

returned. Shards of yellow candlelight shone through the thin gaps in the floorboards. One wooden board was lifted and her friend's face peered down.

'It's all right.'

'What happened? Who was it?'

'It was nothing. It took me a while to work out what the noise was, but then I noticed a German street sign had broken free from one of its bolts in the wind. It was banging on the lamppost outside. I fixed it again so hopefully that's one less thing to worry about.'

'That was terrifying,' said Matilde, climbing out of the hole.

'Good practice,' said Hans.

But a quiver in his voice didn't go unnoticed by the women.

THE MONTH OF November crept slowly on the calendar, laden down with heavy slate skies and short days. There had been another unexpected visit by Wehrmacht soldiers; fortunately Matilde and Hans had been beneath the floorboards listening in trepidation as men searched the house and yard. Their captivity meant a continual carousel of anxiety filling their waking hours. At times Hans felt as if a sheet of cellophane had been stretched across his face, preventing him from breathing. He would gasp and have to mentally pierce the invisible film with holes so he could inhale deeply once again.

One afternoon in the middle of November, Matilde began to mumble. Hans presumed she was dreaming as she had been suffering from nightmares more frequently. As Hans lay close to her, he gently shook her arm before realising that she was already awake.

'Are you all right, my love?'

He could hear her breathing rapidly and in the gloomy darkness he felt her pushing on the timbers above their heads.

'What is it? What are you doing, my love?'

'Need to get out. I can't breathe. I won't die down here.'

Hans felt her legs moving. She was now kicking the underside of the floor in panic. Please God, don't let there be a raid now, he thought. She began to speak more loudly, the need to whisper forgotten.

'Let me out. I can't breathe. Open.'

Hans leaned sideways to try and calm her but she pushed him away.

'Get off me.' She was now hammering on the floor above her face. 'Open up. I can't breathe.'

Hans sensed movement above. Shards of light entered their space though gaps in the floorboard, which must mean that Adrienne had pulled back the rug. One by one the boards were lifted, Matilde struggling to get out before all the timbers were removed.

Adrienne looked shocked. 'Whatever's the matter? What's happening?'

'She's panicking,' said Hans, climbing out.

Even before Hans had stood up, Matilde had hurried from the room. He picked up a blanket and seconds later, he found her outside. She was bent double with her hands on her knees, gasping for breath. He watched Adrienne step forwards to hug her friend but Matilde kept her at a distance with outstretched arms.

'Just talk to her,' said Hans.

Both he and Adrienne stepped back and tried to calm her with words.

'Take deep breaths.'

'We're here. You're not on your own.'

'You can come out of hiding at any time. You're not stuck down there.'

'You're safe.'

Hans knew that not all of these assurances were true, but he had seen such attacks before in training and in his military accommodation earlier in the war. The person suffering needed to feel safe and reassured.

'I'll check the road,' said Adrienne.

She turned and stepped back inside the house. Matilde's breathing was still rapid. Her hands were trembling as she pushed her hair away from her face, revealing tear-stained cheeks.

Hans spoke soothingly. 'Let's walk, my love. Just like we do in the evenings. Come along, walk with me.'

Matilde looked up. She was pale and thin with wide frightened eyes, still struggling to breathe slowly. She took a few tentative steps towards him and he wrapped the blanket around her shoulders.

'Would you like to hold on?' he asked, offering his arm.

She nodded and slipped her arm through his. After several laps of the yard, she leaned against him as they walked and said, 'Thank you. I don't know what I'd do without you.'

36

IN THE GREY dusk of late afternoon, Hans sat for a moment on the wooden toilet seat lid in the outdoor washroom. The relentless days of monotony and constant tension were affecting his mood. He loved Matilde and knew that he wanted to spend the rest of his life with her, but he wanted more: to show her his home in Germany, to make love with her in a soft bed, to be free. But he knew it was impossible.

Over the weeks in hiding a note was occasionally posted through Adrienne's door, explaining why it wasn't feasible to move them yet: Nazis on high alert, their agent in the south had been arrested, additional roadblocks and checkpoints, plus all new contacts needed to be thoroughly checked and deemed trustworthy before they could be given confidential information.

It was now early December and Hans could see his white breath each time he exhaled. The small window to his left was grimy and cracked, under which sat a lop-sided sill sprinkled with numerous husks of dead flies and a few moths. He stood up and stretched his aching limbs. He was twenty-nine, but lying down for much of the day on a lumpy mattress and being constantly cold, made him feel as if he were sixty.

He grasped the icy metal doorknob, catching a finger on a jagged splinter. He winced and pulled the shard of wood from the tip of his finger using his teeth. While he was sucking it clean, he stopped and listened, finger still in his mouth.

Dull thuds. He opened the door slightly. Raised voices. He waited, straining to see what was happening. Crouching, he ran to the back of the house. With his palms flat against the bricks, he slowly raised his head to look inside the kitchen. He held his breath. His body tensed. Through the smudges of dirt on the glass, he could see the side of Adrienne's face pushed up against a wall by an armed German soldier who was tying her hands behind her back. Her face was turned towards the window where she caught sight of him. Hans saw her eyes open wide in warning. She jerked her head upwards. She was telling him to run. He could hear the stomping of boots running upstairs. Matilde! She had gone upstairs to find warmer clothing when he had stepped outside to take his turn in the washroom. He tried to think. He felt helpless. The house was full of armed men and he knew there would be nothing he could do to save the women. He had to contact Henri and let him know what had happened.

Still crouching, he turned to look for an escape route. The wall at the far end of the yard was a little over two metres tall, but Hans could see a stone plant pot containing some withered stems. He could stand on it and heave himself up. A scream came from inside. They had Matilde. He knew the only way to help the women would be to contact the underground cell, so he had to make a run for it.

He turned then darted towards the trees. He reached the wall. A shout. A window smashed. A German voice yelling, '*Halt!*' He jumped on to the stone container and hooked his forearms over the top of the wall. Gunfire. Another scream. Bullets ricocheted off the brick wall as he heaved one leg over the top, then he swung his other leg over and jumped. In that split second he prayed that he would not fall in front of patrolling soldiers.

Hans landed upright. He was standing in a deserted narrow alleyway. There was no time to rationalise what direction to run in. He could hear men shouting in Adrienne's back yard. It wouldn't be long before they would be in the alleyway that was bordered on both sides by brick walls. There would be nowhere to hide. Speed was his only hope.

Fear gave him impetus. He sprinted along the cobbled alleyway. He'd never been chased before, other than during childhood games. Panting with the effort of pushing his body, he inhaled deeper and faster. He could hear the percussive reverberation of jackboots landing on the cobbles behind him.

Hans reached the end of the thoroughfare and momentarily hesitated. He knew that if he took a wrong turn or made a bad decision, there would be no second chance. He heard the *tac-tac* of gunfire behind him.

He veered left and sprinted across the road, thankful that he was wearing civilian clothing and could mingle with the citizens of Paris. He walked at a fast pace, not wanting to attract the attention of patrolling Wehrmacht soldiers by running. Hans was relieved there were lots of people about. It was Friday evening so he supposed they were escaping the tedium of yet another week of making do, restricting, working and monotony.

Behind him a woman squealed. He didn't look back. Then shouting, a disturbance he dare not turn to see. Hans knew it would be his pursuers catching up with him. He saw a throng of people ahead waiting to get into the Madeleine Cinema. He calmly joined the group. The last thing he needed was to upset someone by pushing and attracting attention. As the movement of the small crowd edged forwards, he read posters advertising the premiere of a film called *Les Visiteurs du Soir*. He lowered his head, walking slowly and falling into step with the others. The ticket office that normally stood outside the building had been moved inside, due to blackout regulations.

Once inside the dim foyer, he took the chance and looked back through the swing doors. The armed soldiers who had been following him, had now been joined by several more Germans. They were manhandling men in the queue, swinging them around or throwing off their hats to look at their faces. He stepped back out of sight, peering outside through a rip in a promotional poster.

'Are you in trouble? Or perhaps hiding from someone.'

Hans swung round and faced two men. He recognised them as members of the secret military police, the *Geheime Feldpolizei*. Running would be a disaster. He had to front it out. They spoke passable French but with harsh Germanic accents.

The second man laughed. 'Yes, are you hiding from your wife or your mistress?'

Using his near-perfect French, Hans tried to act as nonchalantly as possible.

'Neither, gentlemen. I waiting to meet a lady for the first time. A friend of my sister's. It's too early to tell if she will become a wife, a lover or neither.'

The two men guffawed.

'So you're looking to see if she has a pretty face and slim ankles? Very wise.'

Thankfully they were both relaxed and obviously enjoying spending some time off duty; the glasses of wine they were both cradling between their fingers were no doubt contributing to their jovial moods. Even so, Hans knew they would change personality in a split second if he gave them even the smallest hint of suspicion. He forced a smile, desperate to show a casual indifference towards them, despite the adrenalin rushing through his body.

Although he was under intense stress, Hans found it exhilarating to realise that these fellow Germans believed him to be a Frenchman. His love of Paris and study of the country's language during and beyond his education was saving his life. It also helped that his hair had grown longer, he hadn't shaved in several days and he was wearing civilian clothes.

The taller of the two men raised his glass. 'To the fairer sex! Always late, but we men would wait all day if there was a promise of a kiss in the evening, wouldn't we?'

Hans laughed loudly, hoping it didn't sound as awkward as it felt. He knew that the secret police used any sign of fragility as an inlet to surge through and conquer. Luckily alcohol and a night of entertainment had made them affable.

'If she doesn't arrive, there are plenty more pretty faces,' said one of the men, turning and gesturing with his arm to several ladies sipping drinks at a small counter.

'Good idea. I'll wait another five minutes.'

The men moved away and Hans took the opportunity to look around. The foyer took on a sepulchral atmosphere due to the gloomy ambience produced by protective blackout measures. Outside, leaning against the glass, were many sandbags piled high and blocking what little light there was left of the day. Inside, in order to keep the light low, ultra violet light shone on posters and above doorways. Music was playing in the background, no doubt to keep spirits high despite the cheerlessness of the room. Hans thought of Matilde and felt a suffocating thick grief. His body and brain had been running for his life. This was survival or death, and he needed to live so he could help Matilde and Adrienne.

A message through the tannoy system informed them that they should take their seats because the projectionist was due to start the film running. Hans knew it was too dangerous to leave the building, so he got back in the queue to the ticket booth despite not having any money on him. As he was nearing the front of the line, he diverted towards the gentleman's toilets close to the entrance to the auditorium.

'Ticket, sir.'

A young woman held out her hand in front of him. She was dressed in a maroon jacket and knee-length skirt. Hans continued his act of nonchalance.

'My friends are just buying them, but I needed… ' He pointed to the toilet door and shrugged, giving what he hoped was a disarming smile.

The usher turned to see a small group assembled around the ticket booth. She turned and nodded, smiling back at him.

'That's fine. I'll check your ticket in a few minutes.'

With the usher now walking away from him, he slipped inside the auditorium and took a seat towards the back next to an aisle, just in case he needed to make a run for it. As seats filled up the dim light was turned off and the hum of conversation stopped. A beam of light pierced the smoky darkness in the auditorium, and the clicking of the projector began to whirr. The light emitted from the little window at the rear entranced Hans. It wasn't simply a consequence of pictures being cast on to the screen, but an emotional link with pre-war life. A life before forced enlistment, involuntary invasion and mandatory rules and regulations.

37

Matilde and Adrienne were pushed into the back of a canvas-topped truck. Grey-green material was draped down the sides of the vehicle to protect passengers against the elements, although straps held back the canvas at the rear. Matilde tripped as she stepped into the back, but as Adrienne moved to help her, she was pushed away, falling herself. They were manhandled on to opposite sides, flanked by German soldiers.

Blood from a punch was tightening as it dried around Matilde's mouth. She ran her tongue along her lips, feeling a cut in the corner of her mouth. The lorry started moving. She looked out the back of the truck but there was no sign of Hans. Please God, let him have escaped. A tear ran down her cheek, wetting her lips and slightly easing the puckering of dried blood. She looked at Adrienne, her friend's head lowered as if she were studying her wooden clogs. The truck bumped and jostled everyone in the back, causing even more anxiety as the soldiers' forefingers were hooked around the triggers of their guns.

Matilde focused on the streets out the back of the lorry, catching glimpses of gardens, statues and women just like her, queuing for their daily food rations. What she would give to be one of those women now. They entered the 16th arrondissement and drove down the wide, elegant boulevard of Avenue Foch.

Matilde and Adrienne stared in wide-eyed horror at each other. Parisians knew that this broad tree-lined boulevard, bordered on both sides with tall, elegant mansions, was known as the most dangerous street in Paris since the Germans had invaded. Nicknamed Avenue Boche, it stretched from the Arc de Triomphe to a large park, the Bois de Boulogne. The Gestapo had chosen this upmarket area for their headquarters, as they had with many other elegant hotels and buildings around the city.

The vehicle drove along a smaller inner road that gave access to several multi-storey buildings, moving through a tunnel before emerging into a courtyard. They had arrived at a tall cream and grey building, its black iron balconies shadowing the front façade like bruises.

The women were ordered out. Standing in the cold December drizzle, Matilde wrapped her shawl tightly around her shoulders, mindful that her breathing was rapid and shallow. She was intensely aware of her surroundings, looking from left to right at soldiers, vehicles, Adrienne and the building in front of her. They were prodded with guns in the direction of a door and entered the imposing headquarters of Gestapo counterintelligence, rumoured to be the epicentre of a vast web of brutal police, collaborators and informers. A cold insect-crawl of dread crept up her spine. Dear God, what was to become of them?

As Matilde stepped inside the dark interior, she felt as if she were Jonah entering the gaping mouth of the whale. She has no idea why this thought should occur to her; perhaps because she had heard that this building was where prisoners were swallowed up by interrogators before being spat out, damaged and bruised both physically and mentally. And those people had been the lucky ones.

One of their guards spoke with a man wearing a suit underneath a taupe-coloured overcoat. A jerk of the soldier's head informed Matilde and Adrienne that they should follow him. She walked unsteadily, her legs trembling uncontrollably. They stepped inside a lift and one of the men pushed the button to the fifth floor. The door groaned shut. With her head lowered, Matilde raised her eyes and met Adrienne's glance. Her friend's eyes were pleading and sparkled with tears, her skin as pale as milk. The door opened and they were ushered out and along a dimly-lit corridor. On passing one room with its door slightly ajar, Matilde could hear the muffled clicking of a typewriter. Further along the corridor, another door was opened and Adrienne was pushed inside. Matilde's heart sank still further. They wouldn't be sharing a cell.

Matilde was pushed inside an adjacent room and heard the turn of a key locking her in. A single window had been boarded up, so the only light source came from a bare light bulb hanging in the centre of the room. A dirty mattress lay on top of a narrow metal bed, broken springs hanging down like peeling wallpaper. A square metal tub was pushed into one corner, which she presumed was her toilet, and a small hatch has been cut into the door with a hinge and locking system attached. As it was the top of the building, Matilde guessed it used to be the maids' quarters.

Before she had time to settle on her bed, the lock turned again and a smart man entered wearing an elegant suit. He was middle-aged, with greying hair at his temples. If it weren't for the fact that his lips were a little too thin and his eyes slightly too close together, he could have been considered quite handsome. He stood looking at her, interrogating her with his eyes before even speaking a word.

Then he spoke in French, but with a clipped German accent. 'Good evening.'

Matilde nodded her head once.

'Identity card.'

She hadn't carried her card since she'd been in hiding. It was in her bag, which had been left behind at La Coupole. More than likely it was already in the possession of the Gestapo.

'I don't have it on me.'

'Do you understand it is a crime not to carry your papers with you at all times?'

Matilde nodded once again.

'But then again,' he continued, 'I don't suppose there is much need of your paperwork when you're hiding under the floor, is there?'

She swallowed hard but didn't answer.

'Remove your clothes.'

Matilde blinked. She looked at him as if she had misheard.

He raised his voice impatiently. 'Remove your clothes.'

With trembling fingers, Matilde removed her shawl and undid her dress. She slid it off her shoulders and with the absence of any curves on her thin body the dress fell to the floor. Trying to protect her modesty, she folded her arms across her undergarments and looked down at her feet.

The man strode across the floor and slapped her face. 'Everything.'

With her cheek stinging, she fought tears as she removed her petticoat, panties and vest, and in addition to being terrified, she felt acute shame at the condition of her undergarments.

'Follow me.'

Surely he didn't expect her to walk into the public corridor, naked? Afraid of being struck for a second time, she covered her modesty as best she could and followed him. With her head bent forwards and her eyes focusing on her dirty feet, an inane thought occurred to her – she needed to cut her toenails.

To her horror, he turned towards a stone staircase and began to walk down. By now she was shivering violently, both from cold and fear. Her humiliation intensified when two soldiers began to walk up the steps and passed her on the stairs. She didn't look up.

Having descended one flight of stairs, she was led into a tiled washroom. She caught sight of two more pairs of bare feet, which made her immediately look up. Adrienne and another woman stood naked in the middle of the room, also using their hands to hide as much of their body as they could. Matilde exchanged a glance with Adrienne, her friend's face drawn and eyes lost in fear.

The man who had struck Matilde barked an order at the women.

'Shower!'

The three women stepped up onto a square plinth, just large enough for them to stand if they huddled together. The unknown prisoner turned on the shower and they each instinctively gasped at the shock of cold spray hitting their skin. The closest Matilde came to crying was when she felt Adrienne's fingers grasp her hand. Raw guilt stabbed at her chest. Adrienne would not be here if it were not for her.

Not only was there was no soap to wash with, but a regular movement of soldiers coming and going from the bathroom led Matilde to believe that this was a structured source of punishment through humiliation; an ugly carnival metered out by men who used a woman's primal insecurities for titillation and did not care about their distress and degradation. Their nakedness was meant to lower their self-worth and make it easier to think of themselves as worthless, and therefore in defeat, tell them what they wanted to know. One thing she could be assured of was that their nakedness was not for the sexual arousal or gratification of the men who took it in turns to come in to the room to look at them. She could see that she and the other two women had dull pale skin that sagged on jagged bones protruding from their hips, shoulders and chest. Their breasts hung fleshless and wrinkled, their stomachs concave and empty.

Beneath the biting cold of the deluge, a determination grew inside Matilde. A notion burned in her thoughts. She would face whatever fate was ahead for the sake of Hans, the families hiding beneath the city and her loyal group of friends working to fight back against these men. She would endure; she would do her *utmost* to endure.

'Stop!'

Matilde turned off the shower and the three women huddled together shivering violently.

'Follow me.'

They stepped off the plinth and trailed after the man back upstairs. Instead of being separated, the three women were pushed into another room where the door was locked behind them. The room had a double bunk on one side of the room, two buckets and a high window that wasn't boarded up. Three shapeless gowns had been thrown on the bottom mattress. Still dripping and shuddering with cold, they each pulled the rough material over their heads and hugged their bodies to get warm and dry. Matilde could feel her head juddering in spasms and her teeth chattering as she turned to her friend and the other prisoner. Adrienne spoke first.

'I'm so sorry.'

Matilde frowned. '*You're* sorry? What could you have done? We had no warning.' She stepped forwards and hugged her friend, the sacking scratching her chin as she rested her head on Adrienne's shoulder. 'How could we know they would break the door down instead of knocking? It's me who's sorry. I should never have involved you.'

They pulled apart, wiping away tears. They looked at the other woman who was quietly watching them while biting her lower lip. She looked a few years younger. The left side of her face scratched and bloodied, her long black hair was tangled and her round dark eyes reminded Matilde of a nervous field mouse. Matilde stretched her lips in what she hoped looked like a smile.

'I'm Matilde, and this is Adrienne.'

'Bruna,' she replied.

'What have they done to your face?' asked Adrienne.

'They knocked me off my bike when I didn't stop.' She touched her face. 'I was delivering leaflets.'

'Did they find them?'

'Yes. I'd stuffed them inside my coat. I didn't have time to dump them.'

'You're very brave.'

'Why are you here?'

Matilde touched Bruna's upper arm. 'Fighting back. Like you were.'

'Do you know what they're going to do with us?'

'They'll ask us questions. You'll need to be brave. It won't be easy.' Matilde paused. 'How old are you?'

'Seventeen.'

Matilde was shocked; she looked older, but was just a child.

'Perhaps we should rest. You take the top bunk and Adrienne and I will share the bottom one. At least we're all together.'

'For now,' said Adrienne.

38

FROM HER POSITION lying on the lower bunk, Matilde could see the cell's high window. She had no idea of the time, but it was dark outside. Adrienne's head was at the other end of the mattress, but Matilde knew she was still awake, as was Bruna. Every now and again they would sniff or sigh, and more than likely wipe away errant tears, like herself.

'Are you awake?' she asked.

'Yes. I'm scared. My mind's too full of thoughts.'

'Me too,' said Bruna. 'And my stomach hurts.'

'Mine too,' said Matilde. 'Probably nerves and hunger.'

'I'm frightened,' said Bruna. 'I cry if Mother slaps me or if Father shouts at me. I can't imagine tomorrow when… '

Matilde pushed herself to a sitting position and stood up. She reached for Bruna's arm, pressing her palm against the young girl's bony shoulder.

'You're not alone. We both feel exactly the same. We may be a little older than you, but age doesn't take away fear or pain. You're stronger than you think. You rebelled against the invaders, Bruna. You're a brave teenager who didn't hide away; instead you actively helped France.'

Matilde felt Bruna's hand lay on top of hers.

Matilde continued. 'Try to imagine your favourite place. The sun's shining and someone special is with you. It might be your family, or maybe there's a special boy out there waiting for your return.'

'A boy called Pierre kissed me. He's the son of my mother's friend.'

'There you go. What's he like?'

'He's nice. He makes me laugh and he's kind.'

'He sounds perfect to me.' Matilde smiled, causing the cut on her lip to split. She winced and touched it with her tongue. It was bleeding again. 'Imagine Pierre whenever your mind starts to think about tomorrow.'

'I'll try. Good night.'

Matilde gave Bruna's shoulder a gentle squeeze and climbed back into bed, hoping she had sounded more confident than she felt. It was the same dread of interrogation that was keeping her awake.

Adrienne's cold feet brushed against Matilde's arm.

'Sorry.'

'You're freezing,' said Matilde.

'We need blankets. Do you think we should ask?'

'Perhaps we should see what tomorrow brings first. We may be moved again.'

THE NIGHT WAS long, noisy and bitterly cold. The disturbance came from the guards' heavy footfall as they walked past the door numerous times an hour, but not before stopping to open the door hatch and then slam it closed again. Matilde had no doubt that if was done purposefully as a tactic to cause sleep deprivation.

It was still dark outside when they were woken by a guard. He unlocked the door and shouted for them to get up. Matilde's joints ached and she found it difficult to move due to being so cold.

'Bring the bucket and follow me.'

As Matilde was first to stand, she lifted the handle of the bucket, which thankfully contained only liquid waste. The three women stumbled out of the door and into a nearby washroom.

'Five minutes,' said the guard, before pulling the door to.

Matilde emptied the contents of the bucket down the toilet but was there was no facility to rinse it out. On a shelf above a sink were teeth-cleaning powder, a hairbrush and one towel. Each of the women brushed their teeth with their fingers, washed in cold water and in the absence of a mirror, brushed each other's hair. Next, without embarrassment, they each used the toilet while they had the opportunity. Without giving much thought to what she was doing, Matilde took a roll of rough medicated toilet roll and pushed down her gown. She held it in place beneath her armpit and turned to see Adrienne and Bruna looking at her open-mouthed. Before she had time to change her mind, the guard returned and ordered them back to their room.

Back in the cell, she retrieved the roll.

Adrienne couldn't hide a wry smile. 'You do realise that you've just stolen from Germans, don't you?'

'I think you'll find it's French toilet paper,' said Matilde, showing her the label.

'What if they notice?' asked Bruna.

'We haven't had the same guard twice yet, so they won't know what was supplied and what wasn't. Besides, ladies can't be expected to use a bucket without paper in any decent hotel.'

With hands held against their mouths, they laughed quietly, feeling minutely encouraged by this small act of rebellion.

'Look,' said Bruna.

Matilde turned to see three pairs of wooden clogs and three sacking blankets had been thrown onto the lower bunk.

'What did I tell you,' said Matilde. 'This hotel has suddenly become quite luxurious.'

BREAKFAST WAS WATERY porridge passed through the hatch. Despite being tasteless, the three women ate it hungrily. Outside the window was the grey hue of dawn, and in conversation they guessed an hour had passed since they had been woken. Wrapped in blankets and huddled together on the bottom mattress, the women began to feel their fingers and toes once again.

They each looked up at the sound of several sets of footsteps resounding along the corridor.

'No,' whispered Bruna.

A key was turned. The man who had slapped Matilde the day before entered the cell wearing a dark tailored suit. His hair was slicked back, his eyes as emotionless as a reptile's.

'Matilde Pascale.'

With her stomach twisting with dread, she pulled the blanket from her shoulders and slipped her feet inside a pair of clogs. She presumed they were men's clogs because they were several sizes too big, meaning she had to shuffle them along the floor in order to keep them on. She followed several guards along the corridor, down a flight of steps and into a small room, bare except for a framed image of Adolf Hitler on the wall and a single wooden stool opposite a small desk and chair. On one end of the table was a pad of paper and a pen. On the other was the horrific sight of a grimy tray, on top of which sat a set of pliers, a pair of scissors and a length of rope. In the centre of the table, coiled like a venomous snake, was a riding whip. Were they there to intimidate, or to be used?

The suited man sat at the table and a soldier with badly pockmarked cheeks and severely cropped hair stood beside him.

'Please, take a seat.'

Matilde sat on the stool. He picked up the pen and straightened the pad of paper.

'I am Hauptsturmführer Krüger and I work here on behalf of the German State Police. Who are you and where do you work?'

He spoke in broken French, which made him difficult to understand. It was as if her own language was objecting to being spoken by the enemy in order to have it used against her.

'Matilde Pascale. I work… worked at the Jeu de Paume.'

'What was your role?'

'I logged and numbered whatever was brought into the museum.'

He raised his eyebrows in what she assumed was fake interest as surely he knew this information already. She could hear his pen scratch on the paper as he wrote.

'A very responsible role. Kommandant Beitel must have believed you to be very trustworthy.'

'I suppose so.'

'But you're not, are you, Madame Pascale?'

Matilde could hear her rapid pulse pounding in her ears. Despite the chill, her back and underarms felt damp. She had no idea how to answer.

'You're not, are you, Madame Pascale?' he repeated, raising his voice.

'It depends what I'm doing.'

'Or perhaps for whom you are doing it? On this occasion you were involved in very important work for the Reich. The third empire of Germany honoured you with such a role. Was that not worthy enough for you?'

Matilde twisted her hands on her knees. 'I wasn't given a choice.'

'But you did have a choice. You chose to be disloyal. You

chose to use stolen information to try and jeopardise an important mission. That is how you repay us for giving you a job in order to put food on your table. That is your gratitude.'

'You killed my husband. You took our home.'

The pockmarked guard strode across the room towards her and drew back his arm before slapping her face. With head bowed and cool palm against her cheek, she vowed not to cry. Not here, anyway.

'What secret organisation do you work for?'

'None.'

'Who is in this secret organisation?'

'No one.'

'What is your role in this secret organisation?'

'There isn't one.'

A sharp pain to the side of her head nearly knocked her off the stool. She struggled to sit upright again.

'This grieves me, Madame Pascale. There is no situation that cannot be resolved. Are you hungry?'

She was starving but wouldn't show him weakness of spirit. 'No.'

Krüger laughed. 'You are a stubborn one.' He used his pen to push back a cuticle on one of his fingers then spoke as if he were bored. 'What a magnificent meal you must have enjoyed at La Coupole in September. I've been myself several times. I hear you left early. In fact, I'm informed you haven't been back to work since then.'

Matilde remained quiet.

'How long has Corporal Engel been plotting with you?'

The mention of his name softened the edges of her determination. If only she were back in his arms beneath the sanctuary of the floorboards once again. She couldn't bear to think of what was happening to him.'

'He hasn't.'

'So you admit you've been plotting?'

'No. I just mean that Corporal Engel isn't involved in anything.'

'But you are?'

'I thought I could help some of those families. That's all.'

'Who provided your nurse's uniform for you?'

'I found it.'

Krüger sighed. 'Found it where?'

'On a second-hand clothing stall beside the river.'

Matilde watched as he took a photograph from his jacket pocket. He studied it.

'You found a nurse's dress, apron, belt and cap lying in a perfectly laundered condition on a dirty market stall?'

Matilde swallowed.

Krüger stood up. 'My time is valuable, Madame Pascale, and you are wasting it.' He brushed the shoulders of his jacket with the palms of his hands and turned and looked at the image of Hitler. Taking a couple of steps towards it, he straightened the frame a fraction. He faced her once again.

'I *will* get answers, but it's up to you how I extract them. I can spare you pain, ensure you're well fed and kept in improved conditions. Or… ' He walked towards the table where he picked up the whip. Using its handle, he pointed at the wall over her left shoulder. 'Do you see those rings?'

Matilde turned sideways and for the first time noticed two metal rings, about the size of dinner plates, fastened to the wall and set almost two metres apart. She felt sick.

He continued talking while pacing the room and slowly pulling the whip's leather cord through his fingers. 'It's important we understand each other. I have a list of questions I want you to answer truthfully. We can get through this quickly and painlessly, or you will be tied to the wall and we'll extract the information the hard way. You choose.'

Matilde recalled the saying Xavier used; the focus that comes from fear is wisdom in the face of danger. She had to concentrate. She needed to think of a way of answering the questions without giving away names.

Krüger sat back down and laid the whip on the table. 'Let's try again, shall we? What secret organisation do you work for?'

'I work by myself. There's no secret organisation.'

'Who is in the secret organisation?'

'Just myself. It's not an organisation.'

'What is your role in this secret organisation?'

'I just try to help my own people. There's only me.'

Matilde jumped violently when he thumped the table. The pliers and scissors clinked as they bounced against each other. Müller motioned to the guard who strode towards the table and picked up rope and scissors. She held her breath almost expecting the rope to be wound around her neck, but instead he cut two lengths and tied each of her hands. She was manhandled to a standing position and pulled by the ropes towards the far wall.

As the guard was tying one of her arms to a metal ring, she watched him. In addition to his scarred cheeks were white pustules and red patches, and he smelled of garlic sausage. He hadn't shaved that morning and a drip of dried food was stuck to his chin. It was the colour of a flowering dandelion so she decided it was egg yolk. Why was she thinking such absurd things? Please God she wasn't losing her mind.

Having firmly secured one wrist to the wall, he moved behind her, pushing her roughly, causing her to bang her forehead against the concrete wall. He began to tie the other hand to the second metal ring, pulling the rope so tightly that she winced. She could feel her pulse beating beneath the knotted tie and squeezed her fist.

She waited. The anticipation was terrifying. She heard movement behind her and squeezed her eyes tightly shut. Her whole body was tense.

Krüger cleared his throat, his voice menacingly calm and polite. 'I hope not to keep you much longer, Madame Pascale. You can be released within minutes if you're truthful. Let's start again. What organisation do you work for?'

'I… I work alone.'

The whip slashed across her back. The pain was indescribable. She could hear buzzing in her ears. Her legs shook uncontrollably. The shock of intense agony prevented her from crying out.

'Who is in the secret organisation?'

Matilde was trying to catch her breath.

'I repeat, who is in the secret organisation?'

'Just me.'

Her whole body tensed. The whip whistled through the air. It struck her on her shoulder blades. A shriek emitted from her throat. She felt a warm stream of urine trickle down the inside of her thighs. Hans, where are you? Why was she thinking of a German? Why not Xavier?

'What is your role in this secret organisation?'

'To help my countrymen.'

There was a pause. The whip didn't strike.

'You're saying that your role in this organisation is to help your countrymen?'

She pressed her forehead against the cold concrete wall. 'There is no organisation.'

The whip struck again. She screamed. In her imagination she envisaged her skin ripped open, her ribs and backbone revealed. Was it sweat or blood trickling down her back?

Krüger repeated the first question. She answered and the leather coil cracked against her lower back. Her knees gave way as her shoulder joints took the weight of her body. The pain was beyond anything she had previously experienced.

Krüger spoke quietly into her ear. ‘Look at me.’

Matilde slowly turned her head sideways to look at him. He was out of focus but she could see his smile, as thin as a knife blade.

‘Let’s try that question again.’

39

HANS LEFT THE cinema at seven o' clock. The chill of the evening air hit him like a punch after the snug warmth of the velveteen chairs. It had rained and puddles sparkled in the crowd's torchlights. He trailed behind a throng of people who were deep in conversation as they left the building. His mind was alert and watchful, eyes scouring the dark street.

He eventually reached Henri's house just before curfew, having taken two hours. Normally the journey would have taken twenty minutes, but a lot of time had been spent dodging patrols or hiding.

Hans entered the gate and crept towards the front door, feeling along the stone walls in the darkness. The air smelt of damp earth and decaying vegetation. He inhaled deeply, relishing the smells of nature that had been forbidden to him for three months. He had only visited Henri's house once before, around the time they had moved the families into the catacombs. Often, lying beneath the floorboards, he and Matilde would wonder how they were fairing. The thought of Matilde was like a wound.

Matilde. Where are you, my love?

He raised his hand to knock, then hesitated. There was a particular way of knocking to show it was safe, but he couldn't remember what it was. He held a hand to each temple and leaned against the glass window of the door. There was no light inside. He had to knock and hope for the best.

Hans knocked four times and waited. Nothing. He knocked again and a chink of light shone through the glass. Someone had opened an internal door. A man's voice asked who was there.

'It's Hans Engel.'

The person inside hesitated. 'I don't know a Hans Engel.'

'Henri, I understand you don't believe it's me, but the house was raided.'

Another long pause. 'Tell me whose house.'

'Adrienne's.'

'How is her sister, Madeleine?'

'They're not sisters and her name is Matilde.'

Hans waited and was relieved to hear the door unlock. Henri pulled the door ajar and shone a torch on him. Hans squinted.

'Come in. Why are you here? I sent news that we were trying to get you out.'

Hans followed him into his kitchen.

'They knocked the front door down while we were out of hiding. There was no warning. I was outside and escaped, but they've got Matilde and Adrienne.'

He watched Henri clutch his head. He stood like this for several seconds, before taking a deep breath. The colour had drained from his face.

'When?'

'Late this afternoon. I was seen and followed for a while.'

Henri's eyes widened and his mouth fell open.

'No, it's all right,' said Hans, raising a hand. 'That was earlier. They didn't follow me here. I hid inside a cinema for a couple of hours. I was very careful.'

'Were they hurt?'

Hans felt his voice quiver and tears fill his eyes. 'I don't know. I was outside and jumped over the back wall. I saw Adrienne being tied up, but Matilde was upstairs.' He couldn't meet Henri's gaze. He felt ashamed and guilty for having left them.

Henri passed him a cigarette. 'Here.'

Hans took it and leaned forwards while it was lit for him. He inhaled deeply. Not having smoked for months he felt dizzy and grabbed for the back of a dining chair.

'Sit down,' said Henri.

Hans sat at the table and watched Henri walk towards the back door, open it and bend down. He came back with two bottles of beer.

'If there's one thing we can thank the Petain for, that's for not letting the bastards ration beer.'

He opened the bottles, and sat down opposite Hans, pushing one towards him.

'Now, go through it again. What time was it?'

'I went to the washroom about four o' clock. It was just before dusk. I heard noises.'

'What sort of noises?'

'Thuds. Raised voices.'

Henri nodded. 'Then what?'

'I crept to the kitchen window. That's when I saw Adrienne. She was being tied up.'

'Did she see you?'

'Yes.'

'Did she give any sign. Could she give any message?'

Hans shook his head. 'She couldn't speak. She was facing me but had her face pressed against the wall. She made a sign with her eyes.'

'What sort of sign?'

'It's difficult to explain. She widened them and jerked them upwards, as if telling me to go.' Hans lowered his head and sucked on his cigarette, making it crackle. 'I didn't know what to do for the best. I had to make a split-second decision.'

'You made the right decision. What was the point of being arrested too? You'd probably have a dozen bullets in you by now. What happened next? After you saw Adrienne.'

'I ran to the back of the yard. They saw me and started shouting and firing.'

'You didn't see the women again?'

'No. I didn't look back. I knew they would be coming after me. I ran.'

Henri scratched his head. 'Do you have any idea where they'll be taken?'

'From what I hear, resistance prisoners are initially taken to Avenue Foch. They'll be interrogated by the Sicherheitsdienst.'

'Who?'

'SS counter-intelligence.'

'What do you mean by, "from what I hear"?'

Hans took a gulp of beer. 'I normally keep to myself off duty. Stay in my room or go for a walk. But sometimes a colleague would come in to my room to talk. You have to understand, I worked with Matilde either in a remote storeroom in the basement of the museum or I had my own small office for paperwork. Thankfully I didn't take part in patrolling the city and arresting French citizens.'

Henri chewed his lower lip, looking thoughtful. 'We need to establish whether they're still at Avenue Foch.'

'You'll never get inside Gestapo Headquarters.'

'I wasn't thinking of me.'

Hans nodded. 'I'll do it. My uniform is at Adrienne's house, if we can get inside.'

'I wasn't thinking of you, either. We have a contact. There's a French patrolman who's allowed access. That's where Matilde's husband was initially taken on his arrest. This man found the report on Xavier's interrogation and the reason for apprehending him. I'll get in touch with him.'

Hans stubbed out his cigarette, tipped up his bottle and drained his beer. 'I want to help. Tell me how and I'll do it.'

'It's getting late. I'll make contact with this man tomorrow. I can't believe I'm saying this to a German, but we have a spare room upstairs.'

Hans wiped away an unexpected tear. 'Thank you.'

40

MATILDE WOKE UP on the bottom bunk in her cell. Her whole body was one intense persistent ache. Occasionally sharp intermittent spikes of pain made her wince. Her gnawing hunger had now developed into a painful twisting emptiness in her stomach. She tried to move position but her rough clothing was stuck to her back, causing more agonising spasms. A cry escaped her mouth.

She heard the springs on the top bunk squeak. Legs appeared on the rickety ladder and in the next moment Bruna was looking down at her. The young woman's eyes were swollen and her cheeks were dirty and tear-stained.

Bruna knelt beside her. 'Are you all right?' She shook her head. 'Sorry, of course you're not. Was it awful? Stupid question. I'm sorry. I'm so scared.' She began to cry.

Matilde slowly raised an arm and took hold of her hand. Bruna squeezed it.

'Where's Adrienne?' Matilde didn't recognise her own voice. It was deep and rasping.

'They took her about half an hour ago.' Bruna wiped her face, making more streaks of dirt.

Matilde closed her eyes, trying to slip into peaceful unconsciousness once again, but it eluded her. The agony she felt made it difficult to think as her body twitched in painful spasms.

Bruna sniffed and fidgeted. 'What did they do to you? No, don't tell me. What should I do? I don't know what to do.'

Matilde opened her eyes, remembering what the prisoner Sandrine had told her when she was arrested two years earlier. 'Make something up. Tell them something. Anything. They may be lenient if you speak.' She did not want to give this young woman false hope, but even if it eased her fear to some degree or gave her time to imagine a false story, she hoped it would help a little.

MATILDE JUMPED WHEN she heard the door unlock. She must have fallen asleep again. Bruna was no longer standing beside her. She saw the mattress move and dip above her, telling her that Bruna had returned to her bunk. She heard a shuffling sound but was unable to turn and look. After a blur of movement, Adrienne was dragged towards the bed and placed alongside her, her bloodied feet close to Matilde's head. The men left and slammed the door.

Bruna came back down the ladder.

'How is she?' asked Matilde. 'Is she awake?'

'No.'

'Help me up.'

Bruna came to her side and put an arm around her shoulders. Matilde clenched her teeth against the pain. Her movement caused cloth that was stuck to bloodied wounds, to tear away from her skin. She felt fresh blood run down her back.

Adrienne had a cut lip and swollen eye.

'Help me turn her a little,' said Matilde.

The two women gently pushed Adrienne's hip and shoulder to reveal part of her back. Like Matilde, she had been whipped. Bruna took a step back with her hands covering her mouth, but before Matilde could speak, the cell door opened once again.

The guard with bad skin entered, a smirk on his scarred face.

'Bruna Duvall.'

Bruna began to cry and backed away towards the far wall. The man laughed and strode towards her, grabbing her arm. Bruna collapsed on the floor. She slipped from his grasp. He cursed before striking her with his fist. Matilde squeezed her eyes shut as the young girl was dragged from the room.

MATILDE WAS ABRUPTLY woken by a slap across the face. As she was being forced to stand, and despite the pain of the oozing welts on her back, she thought it ironic that at long last she had fallen into a deep sleep when they came for her. At least she had been given no time to panic. Bruna! Had Bruna been brought back? Had she slept through her return? She felt bad for not being there for the young woman.

As she was pushed and marched out of the cell, beams of torchlight flickering in the darkness disorientated her. She had no idea of the time, except it was night.

While she was being manhandled down the corridor, something was pulled over her head. She guessed it was a sack or a hood of some kind. The material smelled putrid, as if it had been worn numerous times before during interrogations. How many people had coughed, spat, bled or vomited in this hood? Had those people talked? Had they survived? Would she?

The sound and vibrations of noise changed. Matilde guessed she was inside a room. Still no one had spoken since she was pulled from her bed. Her arms were jerked roughly behind her back, squeezing the skin on her back and causing her to groan in agony. The pain was like a hot poker piercing the open cuts. She felt her wrists being tied. Footsteps. Then silence. She strained to listen. Was that someone breathing close by?

She tried to escape inside her head. She imagined she was

asleep in her childhood bedroom and her mother was baking downstairs, but no sooner had she envisaged it than a fierce pain struck her feet, immediately dragging her from her place of safety. She screamed and bent double. Someone in the room had stamped on her bare feet with heavy boots. With her hands fastened behind her, she could not reach the pain to hold her toes. She began to sob, silently berating herself for showing weakness.

Someone kicked the back of her legs and she crashed to the ground on to her knees. Before she could call out she was dragged to a different area of the room. The silence was menacing. She was kneeling but her legs were shaking uncontrollably. Her eyes were squeezed tight waiting for the next blow. A hand grasped the back of her neck and pushed her forwards. Her head was plunged into cold water. The sacking stuck to her face. Water pressure was sealing it against her skin. She tried to open her eyes in panic, but it was black. She began to struggle, trying to push against the hand that was forcing her down. Her pulse was pounding in her head, her lungs about to suck in water, desperate for oxygen.

She was pulled backwards, coughing and struggling for breath. The material loosened around her mouth as she gasped for air. Her knees slipped on the wet floor and she fell sideways. Someone laughed. She was pulled back to a kneeling position.

A voice spoke. It was Krüger's.

'What organisation do you belong to?'

Oh God, she thought, despite not believing in Him. I'm not strong enough. I cannot bear another minute. 'I work alone.'

Matilde was prepared this time. As soon as she felt a hand on her neck, she took a deep breath before being plunged into the water once again. He kept her under longer this time. She slowly let the breath out of her lungs, listening to what may be the last breath of her life bubble up around her ears. When she had exhaled, a calm descended. Was this such a bad way to die? In another minute she would be free of pain. She could sleep forever. She could seal her silence forever and die without shame.

Matilde felt her body being dragged backwards. An instinctive breath sucked air into her lungs. She wouldn't be released from the pain just yet.

'I admire you, but in the end everyone talks,' said Hauptsturmführer Krüger. 'But be assured, your friends will die and you will join them if you don't tell me about the organisation that helped Jews to escape from the Vel' d'Hiv. Are three lives not worth a few truthful words?'

Still panting, Matilde listened as he strode around the room like a predatory animal.

'Perhaps you think that anyone could become a member of the SS. Do you really know what an SS soldier is? He is a great man. A warrior. He is a professional chosen personally by Hitler. A soldier whose ancestors are analysed for four generations back before he is given the honour of being allowed to join this elite organization.'

He had stopped behind her and whispered in her ear. 'Don't take me for a fool. It will be the last thing you do.'

MATILDE OPENED HER eyes to see a blurred face looking down at her. She blinked several times. Adrienne came in to focus. Was it night or day? How did she get back to the cell?

'You're awake,' said Adrienne.

Matilde tried to lift her head but a pain shot through her temple.

'Stay still. Don't move.'

'How…?' Matilde coughed. Her entire body hurt. 'How did I get back?'

'They dragged you in at dawn,' said Adrienne. 'You were soaking and frozen. I rubbed you dry as best we could and tried to get your circulation moving.'

'Thank you. Bruna. I was worried about Bruna. How is she?'

'She hasn't come back since they took her yesterday evening.'

It felt to Matilde as if her heart weighed a little heavier in that moment. 'Maybe they freed her.'

'Yes. Maybe they freed her.'

Matilde didn't believe that either she or Adrienne was that naïve.

'They must have struck you with something. You have a deep cut and a lump on your head. Your hair's covered in blood.'

That would explain her pounding headache, thought Matilde, but she would refuse to let those bastards break her. She forced a smile.

'I'll have to book a salon appointment before the dance tonight.'

41

December 10th 1942

THE FRENCH PATROLMAN working undercover for local underground cells had informed Henri of the date the women were to be moved to Fresnes prison. The morning of Matilde and Adrienne's transfer dawned grey and sullen. It has snowed overnight leaving behind a hush to the city. Statues wore a fresh covering of white, although the road was less pristine, criss-crossed with slushy-grey tracks from military vehicles and wagons.

Hans was wearing borrowed clothing and sitting in a car with Henri and Charles. They were parked on the opposite side of the wide tree-lined boulevard of Avenue Foch. Hans looked up at number eighty-four. He saw amber electric lights shining from several rooms inside the building and wondered if Matilde were inside any of them. He scanned the front façade looking for her face, but the window continually fogged up so he held his breath for several seconds at a time. He fidgeted in his seat and turned to Henri in the back.

'Are you sure only the date has been given for their transfer to Fresnes? No time was mentioned?'

'Just the date and destination.'

Hans turned back to face the front, looking through the windscreen at the building. He began to bite his nails.

'Listen, we could have a long wait,' said Henri, leaning forwards and offering Hans a Gauloises. 'You're going to go insane with all that nervous energy.'

Hans accepted a cigarette and thanked him. They had grown to like and trust each other over the past week while Hans had been staying in Henri's spare room.

'Could we have missed them? Could they have left early?' asked Charles.

Hans shook his head. 'It's doubtful. We were here at seven and it was still quite dark. The staff will be too organised and punctual to move anyone before breakfast. The higher ranks love French food and don't like their mealtimes disturbed. It's a private joke amongst the lower ranks that they wouldn't even let Hitler interrupt their meals.'

Hans gave a quiet laugh, aware that the two men didn't join in with him. Perhaps the mention of Hitler had not been a good idea. He had only tried to break the tension.

'What time is it now?' he asked, changing the subject.

Charles checked his watch. 'Nine-twenty.'

Hans lit his cigarette and sucked deeply and impatiently. He exhaled, blowing out two thin silver streams of smoke from his nose. They swirled in front of him making a single cloud that dissipated around the interior of the vehicle.

'Let's run through it again,' said Henri.

Hans concentrated as he recounted what he had been told. 'When we see the truck arrive at the front entrance, you cross the road to ensure that it's Matilde and Adrienne being moved. You make a call from that public telephone,' he said, pointing, 'to Philippe, who will be waiting to receive a call from you in a café in Bourg-la-Reine.'

Henri nodded. 'Then we follow the truck at a distance. Meanwhile Philippe will have notified Pierre and Francis, who will pretend to have broken down on a side road leading to Fresnes.'

'Let's just hope that the Boche don't take a detour,' said Charles.

'There's nothing we can do if that happens, but our informer tells us that the side road is their usual route to the prison. A short cut only used for human deliveries.'

Hans felt sick. What if it wasn't Matilde? He looked down at the Sten submachine gun lying across his thighs. It was one of two that had been given by another underground cell, along with three Walther P-38s and half a dozen grenades. Hans had received training in the use of machine guns, which was why one had been allocated to him. Francis used to be an active member of *la chasse* before the war, so his expertise as a hunter meant that the second machine gun had been handed to him. Francis would also be in front of the truck when it was stopped, hopefully giving him a clear view to aim for the driver.

Hans turned to Charles. 'Do you have everything you might need?'

'I hope so. A contact at Clinique Saint Genevieve gave me some penicillin. I have a good supply of bandages and aspirin but sadly no stronger painkiller. If she has broken bones I can try and set them, but… '

Hans rubbed his palms roughly over his face as if to erase the images the doctor had painted in his mind. He repeated to himself, if she's alive there's hope.

AT THREE O'CLOCK that afternoon, just as the men were worrying about the failing light, a canvas-topped truck was driven to the front of the building and parked.

'Right men. Stay alert.'

Henri got out of the back door and appeared to walk nonchalantly across the road. The snow had melted throughout the day leaving only small drifts clinging to chimney pots and hidden corners. Hans strained to see the front entrance but due to the way the truck had parked, he was unable to discern anything. He watched Henri instead, looking for any response. Henri stopped close to the entrance of the building and lit a cigarette. Delaying tactics. When the cigarette was lit, Henri was seen to tense.

'He's seen something,' said Hans.

'Can *you* see anything?' asked Charles.

'No, the vehicle has parked next to the door. He's coming back.'

Henri climbed inside and shut the door. 'Only one person was carried into the back of the van. It was impossible to see who it was. Do we take a chance it was one of the women?'

'Just one?' asked Charles.

'One person, then the back doors were closed. Quickly, you need to decide. They're moving off.'

Hans and Charles looked at each other.

Hans spoke up. 'This is the date we were given and it will soon be dark. I can't believe they'll make any more trips to Fresnes today. I vote we continue with the plan.'

Charles nodded. 'Agreed.'

Henri nodded. 'In that case, follow at a safe distance.'

Charles followed the truck down Avenue Foch until they reached the Arc de Triomphe. There they turned south. Keeping at a low speed, they passed the Musée du Louvre on their left and pursued the vehicle through the fourteenth arrondissement. Charles drove past Le Jardin du Luxembourg towards the café where Philippe was waiting.

'Were there any clues to who the prisoner might have been?' said Hans.

'I'm not keeping anything from you. One person was laid on a long bench inside the back, but they were covered in a blanket.'

Hans bit a fingernail so short that it bled. Was it Matilde? Was she still alive?

Bourg-la-Reine was only about ten kilometres south of Paris, built on an old Roman road. Hans read the village sign post as they drove past it, and shifted in his seat.

Henri touched Charles's shoulder. 'Nice and slowly. The turning is on the left and not far ahead now. Yes! The truck is slowing down. They're taking the side road, thank God.'

Charles kept his distance and followed the vehicle around the corner. Evergreens grew on either side of the road, with occasional abandoned industrial units tucked in amongst the trees. No one spoke. The only sound was the purring engine as it crept along behind the truck. Occasionally the wheels would snap a branch or crunch over gravel. It was as if each of them were holding their breath. After several minutes, Henri could stand it no longer.

'Can you see ahead?'

Hans leaned sideways. 'No… wait! Yes, there's a car in the road ahead.

'Christ. It's happening.'

'The truck's stopping.'

'Get ready lads.'

Hans took a deep breath. Fear took hold of him. Would his luck hold out another day?

Charles stopped the car fifty metres behind the vehicle. The three men slowly opened the car doors and climbed out. Hans ran and hid beyond the treeline, propelled forwards by adrenalin and the thought of seeing Matilde again. Charles and Henri crouched behind the car.

They waited. The German driver was leaning out of the window, gesticulating and ordering Francis and Pierre to move the car. Hans crept through the undergrowth keeping parallel to the road. He saw Francis pointing to the car and shrugging, luring the soldier from the cab. It worked. The driver opened the door, climbed down and strode towards the car.

Hans was now level with the back of the truck, hidden behind tall, gnarled trunks of pine trees. The German was losing his temper and started shouting. Pierre beckoned to him and a second soldier in the cab, motioning that they should help push the vehicle to the side of the road. Hans smirked. The cheek of Pierre! Perhaps his apparent lack of nerves persuaded the driver and his passenger to help. The second man climbed down from the truck and walked towards the group of men surrounding the vehicle.

Pierre and the two Germans leant their shoulders against the boot of the car and pushed. The car began to roll towards the grass verge and with the help of momentum, it moved off the road with ease. The soldiers stood up straight and turned.

Pffft! Pffft!

Francis fired twice and the two men fell to the ground.

At the sound of gunfire, the back door of the truck opened and two more soldiers jumped out, weapons in hand. Hans opened fire. One fell as bullets hammered into his stomach, blood and guts spilling from his belly. The second man hid behind the far side of the truck. Several rounds were exchanged, some hitting the trunks to Hans's left. He ducked. The soldier turned and ran into the trees on the far side of the road. Henri and Charles set off after him.

Daylight was now fading. All Hans could focus on now was who was inside the vehicle. He stepped out of hiding and edged towards the back doors of the truck. Francis and Pierre nodded to him as they crept towards him. Francis put a finger to his mouth to stay quiet. Another man could be hiding inside. Hans nodded, holding out his arm for a handgun. He handed over his machine gun and motioned for them to stay back. If anyone were to be shot rescuing Matilde, it would be him.

Hans crouched low, gun outstretched. With a quick lunge, he moved forwards, aiming inside the truck. It was empty apart from the shape of a person lying on a bench. They weren't moving.

'Watch my back,' called Hans. He climbed inside and stood beside the figure. His hand was shaking as he pinched the blanket between his fingers, slowly peeling it back. He saw long dark hair and a swollen, bloodied and bruised face. He closed his eyes in bitter disappointment, overwhelmed by the sense of loss. His shoulders sank. Matilde's hair was the colour of autumn leaves.

Francis stood at the door. 'Is it Matilde?'

Hand bit his lips closed and shook his head.

'Who is it?'

'I don't know. A woman'

'Let's get her out of here quickly. Someone would have heard the gunfire.'

Francis stepped up into the back of the truck. 'Come on.'

Hans grasped the woman beneath her arms while Francis lifted her legs. They carried her towards the car at the rear. Two more gunshots were heard coming from the trees. Please God it wasn't Henri or Charles. They laid the unconscious woman along the back seat. By the time they closed the doors Henri was being half-carried towards them, by Charles.

'What happened?'

'He got me in the thigh. I'm okay,' said Henri.

'Did you kill him?'

'I don't know. He fell. We hurried back. There's no time to wait. We've got to get out of here now. Pierre, you drive Hans and me. Francis, you go with Charles. He needs to attend to the woman in the back. Perhaps she knows where the others are. Philippe will be waiting for us back at mine.'

Hans lifted one of Henri's arms around his shoulder and supported him to the car that had been pushed to the side of the road. Pierre dragged the bodies of the Germans to one side and jumped in the driver's seat. Hans helped Henri into the back before climbing into the passenger seat. The car started immediately, turned around and followed behind the others at speed.

Hans rested his head against the cold glass. He felt empty. Bereft. He had prayed that he would find Matilde, but it seemed as if God had turned his back. He felt a hand touch his shoulder.

'I'm sorry,' said Henri.

Hans patted it twice and nodded, not able to speak for fear of crying. He looked up at the clouds gathering in clusters. The sky was charcoal-grey, growing blacker by the minute. A thick darkness swallowed them more quickly as snow began to fall silent and straight on the windscreen. Night descended on them, layer on black layer.

42

IT WAS NEARLY five when the convoy of two drove through the centre of Paris. The red crosses painted on the side of their cars had done their job, preventing the enemy from stopping their vehicles to question the drivers. The relief of being so close to the safety of Henri's small townhouse felt almost palpable.

Hans looked ahead through the windscreen, following the movement of Charles's car ahead. Snow had turned to rain, resulting in a dark, starless night. Disappointment still weighed heavy, leaving him feeling exhausted and numb. He needed a cigarette, a measure of his host's secret stash of brandy and a long sleep.

They turned into Henri's road and Hans shifted in his seat, preparing to get out. The car in front slowed down before picking up speed again.

'What's he doing?' asked Pierre.

Hans heard Henri shuffle forwards on the back seat and could hear him breathing at his side.

'My house! It's floodlit.'

As they approached what had previously been their safe house, they saw several Citroën cars parked on the road close to the gate. Hans's body was rigid, as if paused, while his mind caught up with the situation. His mouth was frozen open in horror.

'Croix gammée flags,' said Pierre. 'Swastikas on the cars. We've been compromised.'

'Keep going! Keep going! Don't slow down.'

They drove past, each straining to see inside the open gate. Just at that moment, lit by a stark white floodlight, they saw Philippe being frogmarched at gunpoint from the garden into a waiting car.

'Fuck!' shouted Henri. 'He must have been followed from the café.'

'Where now?' asked Pierre.

'God knows. Follow Francis.'

Hans realised he was sitting with his palms pressed against the sides of his face. He lowered his arms, slowly shaking his head. No Matilde and no safe house. He felt his luck ebbing away.

The convoy of two snaked its way along the Rue de Rivoli with the ink black Seine on their right. A few citizens were hurrying along pavements, shoulders hunched forwards against the relentless rain. German soldiers gathered beneath awnings that covered restaurant entrances, preparing to fill their bellies with an abundance of food and too much wine. Hans watched them talking and laughing as if they were on holiday, shame adding to his disappointment and worry. A few minutes later as they followed behind Francis and passed St. Augustine's church, Hans knew where they were heading.

'They're driving to the auction house,' he said.

Being on the outskirts of a small industrial estate, the streets surrounding the auction house were quiet. There were no houses or bars in the near vicinity to either patrol or visit. The two cars pulled into Lombard's courtyard, and as they had done previously, drove around the back of the building out of sight from the road.

Without Matilde's keys, Francis and Pierre smashed the window in the back door and fumbled to unlock it from the inside. When they had gained access, Pierre helped Charles to carry the woman inside while Francis helped Henri hobble towards the building.

'I'll keep watch for half an hour,' called Hans, relishing the thought of being on his own for a while.

He turned the collar up on an old coat of Henri's and searched in a pocket for cigarettes. Pulling out a crumpled packet, he slid one out, lighting it with a flip-top chrome lighter. He slipped it back inside the pocket and inhaled deeply. It felt good despite his mood. Hans settled on the floor of a narrow porch leading to the entrance door. He leaned against a wall, knees drawn up against his chest. The cigarette crackled in the silence whenever he sucked on it. The street was dark and empty. He heard a dog bark in the distance and the far-off siren of a police car. Within minutes it was silent again, apart from the tapping of rain against windowpanes or dripping off the roof.

Just as he was stubbing his cigarette out, he heard his name being called in a loud whisper.

'Hans! Where are you? Hans!'

He jumped to his feet and hurried to the side of the building. Pierre held a box torch, its light shining in Hans's face and making him squint.

'Quick! Come here. You're never going to believe this,' said Pierre, beckoning him to hurry.

Hans picked up his pace and followed Pierre inside the building.

'Quick. Follow me.'

Hans was perplexed. What could they have found? He stepped over debris left by the families and through the main auction room, into a side room. Henri was sitting on the floor leaning against a wall, pressing a cloth against his thigh. In the middle of the room, four dining chairs had been lined up next to each other to form a bed. The woman lay across the chairs with a blanket pulled up to her shoulders.

Charles was kneeling beside her and gently washing her face and neck. He looked up at Hans. 'I had to clean the skin and hair to see where she's injured. Look closer.'

Hans frowned. He stepped forwards and looked down at the woman. Her eyes were swollen, bruised and closed. Undamaged skin was as white as milk. She had a cut and large lump on her forehead, scratches on her cheeks and puffy, split lips.

Then he saw something else.

He opened his eyes wider and looked at Charles, not daring to hope. Charles nodded. Hans took another step closer, holding his breath. He slowly knelt down beside the chairs and raised his hand to touch the woman's hair. Where Charles had cleaned her blood-matted hair, auburn strands shone in the light of the oil lamp.

Matilde!

Tears filled Hans's eyes. He lifted the blanket and searched for her hand, cradling it against his chest, kissing it and then cradling it again. Violent waves of rage surged through his body at seeing her in this state, yet at the same time, he felt utter relief at seeing she was alive and at least for now, safe.

'I didn't recognise her, said Hans.

'Don't feel bad,' said Charles. 'I doubt her mother would recognise her at the moment.'

Hans stroked her hand. It was small, cold and bloodied with broken nails. 'How is she?'

'Very sick. Her breathing is shallow and noisy. She either has a chest infection or pneumonia.'

'What can you do?'

'I need to clean her, dress any wounds and try to wake her. She needs to be able to drink water because I only have penicillin and aspirin in tablet form.'

'Let me help.'

'No, you're too emotionally involved, but stay close in case she comes round.'

Hans watched as Charles continued to clean Matilde's neck and shoulders, moving down her arm to her hand. She was wearing a loose, stained, sacking dress, stiff with dried blood. Charles reached for her other arm, still covered by blankets. Hans heard him take a sharp intake of breath so he looked more closely. Cigarette burns dotted the skin on the inside of her elbow, the cross of Lorraine had been scratched into her forearm and three fingernails had been pulled from their nail beds.

'Jesus Christ,' said Pierre, his hand covering his mouth. 'Evil bastards.'

'I need fresh water,' said Charles, 'and bandages from my case.'

Hans couldn't move. He watched as if in a trance as the men fetched water, ripped sheets into cleaning cloths and brought bandages. Charles cleaned and bandaged her arm and fingers.

'We can't stay here long,' said Henri. 'They'll be looking for her. For all of us. If they check her documents they'll be reminded that she used to work here. She'll need moving as soon as possible.'

'Not tonight,' said Charles. 'She's too sick. Help me turn her on her side. That's it. Gently.'

With a blanket covering her lower half, Charles tried to pull up the rough material to reveal her back. Dried blood had congealed on the sacking, making it impossible to lift without ripping her wounds open. He began to sponge the material with water, soaking it from the surface until it softened. He eased it away from her skin before slowly raising her robe.

Each man blanched when they saw the extent of her injuries. Suppurating welts crisscrossed her back and shoulders. Angry red lesions oozed blood from where skin had been ripped from her body by the whip. Everyone was shocked into silence. Francis disappeared into the toilet cubicle from where the others heard him retching. Hans lowered his head and gently rested his lips on Matilde's forehead.

'These need cleaning before infection sets in,' said Charles. 'I have to disinfect the lacerations. Pierre, can you look for something in the kitchen?'

He returned within minutes holding a bottle of vinegar. 'This was all I could see.'

'It'll have to do,' said Charles. 'This is going to be agonising and will probably bring her round a little. Hans, stay by her head and talk to her if she regains consciousness.'

Hans watched him pour vinegar onto a clean rag until it was soaking and dripping. He readjusted his kneeling position and began to carefully disinfect her back.

MATILDE FELT SUDDEN intense pain. Agony ripped through her battered body making her cry out with deep guttural cries. Her body felt broken. She couldn't take any more. 'There's no organisation,' she shouted. 'It's just me. Only me.'

Someone was talking to her. His voice was gentle and kind. Her hair was being stroked. It couldn't be Krüger. This voice was calming. It reminded her of someone from her past.

'It's just me,' she said, more quietly. 'There's no organisation.'

She felt herself sinking once again, willingly relaxing into the sweet oblivion of sleep.

MATILDE WAS AWARE of trying to open her eyes. Her eyelids moved imperceptibly, just enough for daylight to enter her world of darkness. Someone spoke to her, although she couldn't discern what was being said. Something cold touched her lips. Water trickled inside her mouth. She coughed, fighting against being pushed under the water again. 'No! No!'

She was being held down but was also aware there was an absence of violence. That voice again. Kind words whispered in her ear. A gentle touch on her cheek. Drops of water wetted her lips. It felt soothing. Cool. Another trickle covered her tongue and she swallowed. It was like drinking nectar. She tried to raise her head, her lips apart, straining for more. She took a mouthful this time, swallowing it greedily. And another. It soothed her throat. It eased the pain in her lips. She sank backwards and fell asleep.

Matilde sensed the shape of time had distorted. It shifted from light to dark. Hot to cold. Voices to silence. Indistinct memories drifted in and out of focus. She was no longer aware of the boundaries of her body, just an all-consuming vicious pain. She imagined crushed bitter tablets pushed between her lips, followed by water. There was a sense of movement, as if her body was floating. Gentle whispers. Did she imagine a lingering kiss on her cheek? Perhaps it was a breeze? Was she being carried? Matilde tried to force her eyes open as if straining to wake from a nightmare. She smelled a memory of a scent, the haunting aroma of church incense: myrrh and frankincense. Now she was falling deep inside the earth. Passed from hand to hand by saints and martyrs. Lower and lower into purgatory. Muffled voices echoing in the darkness. She willed her eyes to open. A lamp held high. Stacks of bones. Empty eye sockets. Gaping jaws of skulls.

No! She had been carried to the pits of hell.

43

HANS LOOKED AROUND in awe at numerous families settled in between macabre displays of broken skeletons. He had imagined what life would be like down here in the catacombs, but nothing prepared him for the reality. Instead of damp and unpleasant subterranean passageways, these manmade corridors were dry and had an ambient temperature. Above ground, the invasion by his country had reshaped Paris. Spatial, political, racial, social and economic restrictions had been forcibly imposed, but deep below the capital was like a demilitarised sanctuary of peace.

'This is incredible,' he said. 'I had no idea it would feel so comfortable.'

Charles kicked dust and rubble on the floor. 'Comfortable?'

'Perhaps not literally, but it feels safe, peaceful and warm for these people.'

'If only we could have rescued more.'

Hans nodded. 'We must be thankful that these families will hopefully live full lives after this bloody war is over.'

'It was all Matilde's idea. Henri said she was like a dog with a pig's ear after she'd found out about the roundup. She wouldn't let it drop. She's a special woman,' said Charles.

Hans looked to where Matilde was sleeping on a mattress offered by one of the families. She had been brought here in the dead of night for safety, the men not prepared to take the chance of being discovered. She had been drifting in and out of consciousness due to her fever, but thankfully appeared to be less agitated now.

'She is,' said Hans. 'I wish things were different. I wish I deserved… I wish I wasn't… '

'Men should be judged by their behaviour, not from where they were born,' said Charles.

Hans shrugged, unable to answer.

Charles continued. 'Why should you be ashamed of your nationality? It's your leaders and those of your countryman who find gratification in cruelty and murder that you should feel apologetic about. Remember the amount of blue berets persecuting the Jews inside the Vel' d'Hiv? French police betraying their fellow citizens. Evil dwells inside individuals, not countries. In a hundred years' time, every human being in Germany and France will be replaced by others, just like these souls have been replaced by us.' He extended an arm towards geometric patterns of skulls and femurs. 'You are a good man. I believe you are worthy of Matilde if that's what you both choose.'

HENRI, HANS AND Matilde remained underground for a fortnight. Henri's house was no longer safe and he was recovering from his bullet wound. Matilde was too weak to be moved and Hans refused to leave her side.

Christmas and Hanukkah had been quiet affairs. Being an undertaker and skilled at making coffins and general woodwork, Francis had put his hand to carving a dreidel for the children, a small wooden spinning top. He also fashioned a simple menorah to help the families celebrate their festival. The children had loved making paper decorations to dress a small fir tree that had been placed next to a mound of white femurs.

Just before midnight on 31st December, Hans checked his watch for the fifth time in the last few minutes.

'Five, four, three, two, one. Happy New Year, my love,' he whispered.

Matilde took his hand. 'Happy New Year.'

They lay beside each other deep inside the catacombs, just as they had for three months beneath Adrienne's floorboards. Matilde thought of her friend every day, wondering where she was and whether she had survived her interrogation. A feeling of culpability never left her.

'Do you think anyone else is awake? I know it's not their New Year, but… '

'Shh,' said Hans. 'You're always thinking of others. Just relax and sleep.'

Matilde woke to the sound of more than one set of footsteps. She slowly rolled on to her stomach, cringing in pain with each small movement. A lamp lit the faces of Charles, Father Aubrey and Pierre. She nudged Hans who sat up.

'Happy New Year to you,' said Father Aubrey. 'May 1943 bring peace to our country.'

Hans and Henri stood up and handshakes were exchanged. Members of different families joined them, reciprocating greetings.

The priest spoke to each of them. 'Alma, still smiling I see. Joseph, hello. Good morning, Daniel. Martha, how are you? Glad to see you're feeling better, Edith.'

'We've brought food,' said Charles, setting down a basket.

'And here's another box full,' said Pierre.

Henri shook his head. 'Your congregation is incredible.'

'They are indeed. Of course I don't go into any specific details when I ask for donations of food, but I suspect they're aware that I don't sit and gorge myself silly with every delivery.' He chuckled to himself. 'How's your leg?'

'Healing well, thank you. I've still got a limp but I can live with that.'

'How's our other patient?' asked Charles.

Matilde struggled to sit up, wincing as the skin on her back pulled with every movement. 'Still very sore, but I can breathe more easily now.'

'We need to discuss getting you out,' said Charles. 'Your back is going to need more specialist care. Despite the penicillin, not all your wounds are healing. If the infection gets much worse it could be… dangerous.'

Matilde knew he was protecting her. She knew he was going to say, fatal.

Charles checked Henri's bullet injury, saying he was pleased with how it was healing. Next he cleaned Matilde's wounds, dressed them and gave her a second course of penicillin.

'You still have a fever,' he said. 'With my help, can you stand? Francis has an idea of getting you through any road blocks.'

'I can get up but can't stand straight. I walk like a little old lady but I know I need to move several times a day.'

'You're right. You're the perfect patient. The reason you can't straighten is because the skin on your back is healing in some places but not others. The scars are tightening.'

While conversation hummed between the families as they were eating, Charles helped Matilde walk to where Hans, Father Aubrey and Francis were sitting in front of a neat pillar of skulls. An oil lamp on top of the pile of bones shone amber light on each man's face.

Father Aubrey smiled as he watched Matilde settle beside Hans.

'Firstly I want to apologise for my absence on the day we had planned to bring the families down here. I've already explained to the others, but two members of the Gestapo escorted me directly to the hospital and ordered me to give the last rites to a dying Catholic soldier. I had little choice and I'm sorry. Thankfully you came to the rescue once again,' he said, looking at Matilde. 'The auction room was the perfect transition. Right, Francis, you explain the plan.'

Francis nodded, shifting his position on the ground.

'Charles and I have been thinking of a way to move Matilde, and we think we've come up with a workable plan. Remember, they have your description,' said Francis, looking at Matilde. 'Your hair would be noticed immediately, so it will need bleaching. Germans are more likely to overlook the colouring of their favoured Aryan race. We need to make use of what we have available.'

'That's not much,' said Henri. 'Matilde doesn't have any papers. She can't walk, let alone run for her life. Transport will be stopped and the driver questioned. There are still road blocks at the Maginot Line even though the Germans have invaded the south—'

Francis raised a forefinger to interrupt his friend.

'Who can travel without papers? Who is all but invisible?'

Everyone looked at each other and shrugged.

'No one,' said Henri.

Francis looked at Charles and they both grinned.

'The dead,' said Charles.

Francis moved to a kneeling position and became more animated. 'Henri thinks we have nothing we can make use of, but we have just the things necessary to get Matilde to safety. I have a coffin in which we'll drill holes in the base for air. I have funeral make-up that I use to make a corpse appear to be sleeping peacefully. Why can't it also be used to make someone sleeping, appear to be dead? Fish heads and pigs' trotters can be found in markets—'

Hans looked horrified. 'What?'

'As Henri says, there are still checkpoints we have to get through, despite Germany moving into the south. If the Boche want the coffin opened, hopefully the smell of hidden rotting food will repel them from examining the body.'

'No. It's too dangerous. We'll have to think of something else.'

'Hans, I'm a doctor. I know what I'm talking about when it comes to Matilde's health. We either attempt this or… Matilde won't survive down here. It could work. Do you think Francis and I would risk our lives without some chance of success?'

Hans rubbed the bristles on his chin in agitation. 'How is Matilde expected to pretend to be dead while the lid of a coffin is being prised off by soldiers looking for escapees? She'll be terrified. It's impossible. I won't let her be put in such danger.'

'I have chloroform,' said Charles. 'She'll be anaesthetised.'

Hans was silenced. Everyone was quiet. Matilde was aware that she was clenching and flexing her hands, so she folded them across her chest. Her body ached, her head throbbed and she felt nauseous. The men were looking at her but she found it impossible to form a response.

Charles turned to face her. 'I know this plan sounds far-fetched, but you can't stay here. Unless your infection is treated properly, and soon, it will poison your blood. These are far from ideal conditions to live with open wounds, poor nutrition and lack of facilities.'

Hans rubbed his hands vigorously up and down his face in anguish. 'It sounds too… implausible. Too dangerous.'

'It's even more dangerous for Matilde to stay here without medical care.'

'When were you thinking of carrying out this plan?' asked

Matilde.

'Sunday.'

Matilde blinked rapidly. 'That's in two days.'

'Your funeral can be disguised during Mass. Time is critical for your health. This is the only idea we've considered that has a chance of working.'

Matilde let out a long breath and turned to Hans. Would she ever see him again?

'I know you're worrying about leaving Hans behind, but he will stay with one of us. He'll be as safe as the next person in Paris,' said Charles.

'If this crazy plan works and you get past the roadblocks, what happens then?'

'We'll drive to Bourges and stay there until Sunday night. If all goes to plan, we'll deliver Matilde to a trusted resistance group in La Châtre. Over the course of the next two weeks, each underground cell will contact another further south until she reaches the safety of her parents. Throughout this journey, Matilde will be looked after by medically trained resistance members.'

Francis leaned forwards. 'And the Brits and Americans are fighting hard. The Allies have recently attacked Italian cargo ships and almost one hundred RAF aircraft have bombed the Philips' radio works in Eindhoven. If they carry on like this, the war could be over this year.'

Matilde knew that a future with Hans would be impossible if the infection in her wounds grew worse. The penicillin was keeping her stable but it wasn't curing her. Charles had explained that the antibiotic could simply stop working at any time and if she stayed underground, she would eventually die. If she agreed to their plan, there was at least a small chance of a future with the man she loved.

'Thank you. I'll do it.'

44

Epilogue
October 1945

THE CREAKS AND groans of the old building waking and stretching brought comfort to Matilde. She lay in her childhood bed watching shafts of sunlight streak across the room and decorate the far wall. Occasionally the curtains billowed by the open window as if taking a deep breath.

Matilde had awoken in this room ever since being carried into the house in a fevered daze in early 1943. She was subsequently told it had taken two weeks to move her from Paris, transferring her from one underground cell to another, each one transporting her closer and closer to the Mediterranean sea and the house where she grew up. The journey had taken its toll on her health, reigniting a high fever with her body failing. It had taken many weeks for her to recover and when she finally left the haze of delirium and re-entered a lucid existence, another shock was awaiting her.

A swollen belly.

MATILDE ROLLED OVER to where her young son, Raphael, slept. She stroked his blond hair causing him to stir and stretch, rubbing his cornflower-blue eyes.

'Hello, sleepy head.'

The little boy smiled in sleepy recognition and held his arms out to his mother. She drew him close, inhaling the scents of wildflowers and wheat from yesterday's walk. He had fallen into an exhausted carefree sleep the previous evening, even before his grandfather had carried the bathtub in from the barn.

Matilde kissed his forehead and slipped out of bed. She walked to the window, pulling aside the drapes. It was October and the sun was sitting like a molten ball of orange glass in the cloudless sky. In the distance she could see the silver-snaking River Orb and the wooded valleys leading to the sea.

'Matilde! Is that you I can hear out of bed?'

Matilde smiled and walked to the bedroom door. 'Yes, Maman.'

'I have a saucepan of coffee on the stove and I've warmed some milk for the little one.'

'Thank you. We'll be down.'

LOCAL HOTELS AND manor houses now stood abandoned after fleeing Nazis absorbed the news of Hitler's suicide a few months earlier. It was as if their small village and its inhabitants had been holding their breath for years and could now finally breathe.

Time had assuaged some of the fears and nightmares that had crawled through her veins during 1943. Her parents, Rosalie and Yves, were her refuge, her hope and her cure. Her childhood home was a small farm just a twenty-minute horse and cart ride from Sérignan, which meant that food wasn't as scarce as it had been in Paris. They grew potatoes, leeks, carrots and rhubarb. Rabbits were bred for food, chicken for eggs and her father had bought a cow in the summer, his previous one having been requisitioned by the Germans.

Matilde carried her son downstairs into the kitchen, where her mother was creating a melody of chinking cutlery. Above the wide stone fireplace, pots and jugs sat on an oak mantelpiece next to stacks of logs piled high on each side. Several battered and well-loved orange-gold copper pans hung from hooks on beams, reflecting colours, shapes and movement in the room.

Matilde lifted Raphael onto a chair at the kitchen table, and smoothed flat his pillow-squashed hair.

'Breakfast for my little man,' said Rosalie, carrying a pan towards the table. She ladled a mound of scrambled egg onto a plate.

'Blow, Raphael. Hot.'

The little boy puckered his lips and blew a raspberry, making Matilde and her mother laugh. Just then Yves stepped inside the back door carrying a bucket.

'What's all this jollity?' he asked. 'Anyone would think the war was over.'

He placed the bucket on the stove and Rosalie playfully slapped his arm.

'Wash your hands, old man, or there'll be no breakfast for you.'

Yves grabbed his wife, leaning forwards for a kiss, while she giggled and pretended to fight him off.

His laugh was deep and carefree. 'I bring in a bucket of fresh warm milk and I can't even have a kiss?'

Matilde smiled indulgently. They were as in love now as the day they first met at a farmers' market, thirty years earlier. Their happiness made her wistful. She yearned for the feelings she experienced with Hans: anticipation, exhilaration and excitement. She remembered that even the vast space of the museum's basement turned into the most rapturous space when he was present. Her dream was for them to be together and to experience the love her parents shared, but she knew that was a futile fantasy. She wished her feelings for him would fade and disappear like the grazes on Raphael's knees.

Matilde thought back to the last news she had received; a scrawled note, not even written in his handwriting. The message had been pushed under the front door in the middle of the night, she guessed by the local Maquis. That had been just before Easter. Due to the distance the message had travelled and the numerous people it had been passed through, its contents could have been months old. The note had said all was well in Paris. Matilde had no way of returning a message. She had no idea where the regional resisters' hideout was, and they had presumably gone back home to their families now that Germany had surrendered. Besides, she didn't know where Hans and Henri were living due to Henri's house having been compromised. It all seemed like a different lifetime to her.

Her father sat down beside her and rested his hand on hers.

'You're daydreaming, ma cherie.'

Matilde blinked. 'Yes. I was deep in thought.'

'In Paris, maybe?'

'Maybe, Papa.'

Her mother pushed a cup of coffee across the table and shared out the pan of scrambled eggs between them.

'Maybe you will travel to Paris again, one day,' said Rosalie.

'I'm afraid to go back because so many bad memories are waiting for me there. But I know I must go, and I will one day. There are too many unanswered questions. I need to find out what happened to Adrienne and the families that were hiding beneath the city. I need to find out if Hans has gone back to Germany or even whether he's alive. He doesn't know he has a son. I need to retrieve the lists I made of stolen treasures. I hid them in Adrienne's house and need to hand the information to the authorities. I can't bear the thought that everything was in vain: the sacrifices and pain that everyone went through. It can't have all been for nothing.'

'You will see him again, I'm sure,' said Rosalie, spooning a mouthful of egg into Raphael's mouth. 'Who knows? You may even be together one day.'

'I don't think so. He wouldn't be accepted here and this is where I want Raphael to grow up. I think that it will take generations before a German could live here peacefully.'

Yves finished his breakfast and pushed his dish to the middle of the table. 'People here judge how they find. From what we've heard of Raphael's father, it wouldn't be fair to define him by his nationality. He sounds like a kind and sensitive human being and I for one will shake his hand for protecting you and risking his life for you and others. What father could ask for anything more for their daughter?'

'He *was* a good man, Papa. He had hopes and dreams like anyone. He saw beauty in things and was looking for happiness, like we all are.'

'We've lived through terrible years of hardship and everyone's dreams have been paused. We all have memories that cast shadows on our present and future. I will travel with you to Paris, perhaps next year. You won't have to face your demons alone. Your mother will look after Raphael while we're gone. You will find your answers, ma cherie.'

Rosalie began to collect dishes. 'Let's put such thoughts to the back of our minds for now. It's another beautiful day and I have sheets to wash this morning.'

'I'll strip the beds,' said Matilde.

'Thank you. Perhaps we can take a walk down to the river after Raphael's afternoon sleep. We can take the fishing rod your father made for him.'

Rosalie hugged her grandson, kissing his smooth pink cheeks before he wriggled free and plunged his fingers into his egg.

BY LATE-AFTERNOON SHEETS were flapping on the washing line. Matilde and her mother held Raphael's hands as they walked through the orchard towards the river, an intoxicating honeyed-sweetness of decaying windfalls perfuming the air. The fruit trees had produced an abundance of apples, plums, cherries and pears during the summer; Rosalie's infantry of lined jars bursting with pickles and jams laid testament to the fact.

Further ahead, a bonfire of leaves made a purple haze of wood smoke spiral into the air. Wheat stoops stood to attention drying in the autumn sunshine in a nearby field. The day was warm and peaceful; the quiet only disturbed when Raphael squealed in delight. When he was released from the restraints of the women's entwined fingers, he ran unsteadily, chasing cartwheeling withered leaves down the lane.

'We need rain,' said Rosalie. 'Just look at this parched soil.'

Matilde kicked a flinty stone with her wooden clogs. 'Don't you think the earth looks like the top of a cracked and over-baked loaf?' She inhaled deeply, imagining she could smell the aroma of freshly baked baguettes. 'I wonder when we'll have real bread on the shelves again, instead of hard, dark loaves? When we do, I'm going to eat a whole baguette to myself.'

Rosalie chuckled. 'As soon as flour is available, I'll bake you one myself.'

They passed by another field, its splintered crops cut down to stubble. Raphael raised his hands to be carried so Matilde swept him into her arms, planting numerous small kisses on his neck. She pointed out a buzzard circling above their heads and a rabbit darting into the wildflowers at the edge of the path.

The three of them turned left and walked through a meadow that led to their favourite area by the river. White clover, toadflax and poppies brushed against their bare legs as they wafted away flying insects that had been disturbed by their presence. Matilde stopped walking when she heard the sound of water and saw flashes of liquid light sparkling through the pine trees.

'Listen, Raphael.'

Still in her arms the little boy smiled.

'It's water. Water with fish to catch,' said Matilde.

He wriggled to escape her embrace so she lowered him to the ground, but held on to his hand. Rosalie stepped down on to the bank and turned to let Raphael jump into her arms. She swung him round twice and set him down on the shallow sandy bank they pretended was their very own private river beach.

Rosalie ruffled his fine white hair. 'He's remembered, look! He's setting off to the fishing rocks along the bank. Wait for Grandmother, little man.'

'I'll sit here and watch for a while,' said Matilde.

Her mother waved a small fishing rod in acknowledgment and caught up with Raphael. Matilde lay back on the warm sand and closed her eyes. She could hear the distant mumblings of her mother and her son, and a smile played on her lips. Light and shadow flashed on her closed eyelids as leaf-dappled sunlight fell on her face. She could smell the sweet algae covering rocks baking in the sun, the delicate odours of riverside vegetation and the brackish bouquet from eddies of froth bouncing off sunken stones. The sun's rays warmed her skin while the plop of surfacing fish and buzzing insects willed her scarred body to relax. The sounds were hypnotic and the last thing she heard before she fell into a restful sleep, was the sound of laughter coming from her son and his grandmother bonding over a stick and length of string.

A shadow fell over her, blocking the heat and light of the sun. Matilde lifted an arm to her eyes and sat up.

'Papa? You joined us.'

Her father held out a hand to help her to stand, but said

nothing.

'Is everything all right? Is Raph—'

'Everything's fine.'

'Then why are you acting so… strange?'

'A visitor came to the house shortly after you left.'

Matilde became more animated. 'Oh, did they bring a message from Paris?'

'You could say that.' Her father raised and arm and pointed towards the line of trees edging the riverbank. 'I'm going to join your mother for a few minutes.'

'But Papa… '

She watched him walk away. What did he mean? She was confused. Was she meant to go back to the farmhouse to read a note? Is that what he was pointing at?

A movement in the undergrowth made her turn. A man stepped into the clearing. He was wearing a loose white shirt, blue neckerchief and braces attached to buttons on his trousers. She recognised his smile and caught her breath, her hand going to her neck. Her memories of Hans, and their imagined conversations had been her solace for so long, that the thought of seeing him again had simply become a constant wistful ache.

But here he was. Standing in front of her.

Thistledown drifted in the breeze between them. Neither of them moved. His fair hair was no longer short, but long to his neck and pushed away from his face. His skin was tanned. Had he always been so handsome? She whispered his name. It sounded like a prayer on her lips.

He walked towards her and she felt her body move. They stood an arm's-length apart, just looking at each other. Neither of them spoke, but Matilde took the final step and leaned against his body, her head resting on his shoulder. She felt his arms encircle her waist. The warmth of his skin and the shape of his muscles beneath the cotton shirt were overwhelming. They held each other for several minutes, neither wanting to let go. When they did pull apart, she saw tears in his blue eyes.

'You look beautiful, so beautiful,' said Hans. He rested his palm against her cheek, letting his fingers linger.

'You came back to me,' said Matilde.

'There's nowhere else on earth I want to be.'

He leaned forwards and kissed her. A tender kiss on her lips. And another. Then her arms enclosed his shoulders and he kissed her more urgently. She pulled him closer, inhaling his clean, salty, masculine scent, causing a thrill to jolt and disrupt her emotions. Aware her parents might be watching close by, she released her hold and let her arms fall.

'Will you sit with me?' She pointed to the sandy area where she had been lying.

Hans followed her and sat facing her. They held hands, gazing at each other.

'Your father welcomed me. I didn't know what to expect,' said Hans.

'I've told him about you. How you helped save families. And me.'

'How have you been?'

'Good.'

'You look wonderful. When I said goodbye you were so thin and pale. I didn't know if I would see you again.'

'It took a while to recover, but I'm well now.'

'Your back… ?'

'Scarred, but healed. And at least I can't see it when I look in the mirror.' She made a noise that sounded like a reticent laugh. 'Tell me what you've been doing.'

'Henri and I have been living in Francis's funeral parlour.'

Matilde covered her mouth. 'Really?'

'We weren't bothered there. Who wants to enter such a place? We've spent two years feeding the families you rescued.'

Matilde moved to a kneeling position, facing him. 'How are they? Where are they? Did they all survive?'

Hans grinned. 'We had over a hundred down there by the end of the war.'

'No! Tell me!'

'Matya had her baby. A girl. Then we heard isolated stories about Jews hiding in attics, barns and in the woods. Month by month we rescued more people and took them to the safety of the catacombs.'

'You're all incredible. What about Matya's baby girl? She didn't want to keep her baby.'

'She gave birth a month after you left. Only Matya could feed the baby and keep her alive, so she bonded with her daughter. She's called Espère. Hope. That little child brought so much promise, faith and happiness to the families during the thirty-four months underground. I'll miss that little angel.'

Matilde thought of Raphael and how he had helped to save her own sanity. Should she tell Hans now? No, not yet. She needed to know more before she questioned their own future.

'Where are they now?' she asked.

'Free. Making new lives for themselves. Some have gone back to the houses they left, but in many cases other families had moved into their property. When things become more settled they'll have to look into getting their houses back with help from the authorities. Others went to stay with family scattered around France. The celebrations in the streets will be something I'll never forget. I sometimes forget I'm not French.'

'You sound like a Frenchman,' she said. 'Your accent was always good, but now it's indistinguishable from any French person's.'

He smiled then shook his head as if in disbelief, tears glistening in his eyes. 'I wish you could have been there. Espère was walking and talking. Her face… ' A tear fell on to his cheek and he wiped it away with the back of his hand. 'Her face when she first saw daylight. Freedom is the greatest gift anyone can receive.'

Matilde knelt forwards and hugged him. He held on as if he would never let go, sobbing against her shoulder. She knew he needed months, even years of gentle care to help him recover from the psychological and physical trauma he had been through for the last five years. Everyone who lived through the brutality of war needed space to love and heal.

When he calmed, they sat facing the river, leaning against one another.

'I almost daren't ask, but have you heard from Adrienne?' asked Matilde.

'I knew you'd want to know, so I tried to find out for you. She had been sent to Drancy after her interrogation at Avenue Foch. She survived but was very sick with tuberculosis and starvation when they found her. She was in the care of the Red Cross for many weeks.'

Matilde's voice was a broken whisper. 'She's alive.'

'Yes. She's moved back home. I went to thank her.'

She couldn't hold back tears of relief as she rocked in Hans's arms. 'I thought she was… I blamed myself. I thought she was… '

Hans held her and soothed her with words she couldn't hear over the sound of the river, but she could feel the comforting vibrations of his voice as she leaned against his chest. His hands stroked her hair. She felt safe.

After a while, she quietly asked, 'Did Adrienne mention anyone called Bruna?'

'No. Who's Bruna?'

'She was a brave young girl in our cell. They took her one day, but she never returned.'

'I'm sorry. She didn't mention her.'

Matilde nodded against his chest. 'And what about Philippe? When we were in the catacombs you'd said he'd been arrested.'

'He didn't make it.'

She sat up and wiped her eyes. 'No!'

'They shot him when interrogation didn't work. He never gave us up.'

Matilde closed her eyes to the pain she felt at this news. 'I'm so sorry. What a brave man.'

Hans nodded. 'We need to live our best lives for those who didn't survive. I love you and don't ever want to be separated from you again.'

'Never.'

'Tell me, how was your journey here? It was weeks before we'd heard you were safely with your parents. I was beside myself with worry.'

'I remember very little of it. I have hazy memories of kindness shown to me. A woman bathing me. Someone feeding me soup. My dressings being changed. People carrying me from place to place. I have no memory at all of being in the coffin or passing through road blocks.'

'That's not a bad thing.'

'It's not. Tell me about Paris. What's it like now?' Matilde asked.

'The oddest thing is that young men are walking the streets again. It's strange how quickly we got used to seeing women and the elderly making up the population. People are wearing bright colours and the streets are clicking to the sound bicycle chains and children's laughter.'

Matilde gazed into his eyes, which seemed to be looking, unfocused, in to the distance; seeing images of memory.

'All the swastikas have been removed and checkpoints dismantled. German street signage has gone. Jewish shops and galleries have been washed of daubed paint. But the scars remain: bullet holes, broken windows, boarded up homes and fractured statues.'

Matilde nodded, unable to speak. There was a pool of silence between them, deep enough to sink in.

Eventually she said, 'How has it been for you? Have you been able to hide your nationality?'

'I've had no choice but to hide it, but that's fine. I'm ashamed to be German at this moment in time. If anyone knew I'd be arrested and moved into one of many camps where prisoners of war are being forced to rebuild Paris. Although, I'm sure they prefer that to facing death every day patrolling the city during wartime. Henri has been incredible. And the others. They accept me for who I am and my actions, not by my place of birth. They've protected me. Many would have turned their back on me after Germany's surrender. He'll be a friend for life. But for now, it'll be just you and me spending time together and getting to know each other again, without hiding. Doesn't that sound perfect?'

Matilde paused.

Hans looked at her, his brow creased. 'Is that what you want?'

Matilde heard footsteps and splashing in the shallows growing closer. 'I love you, but you will have to share me with someone else.'

Hans looked at her questioningly. 'Who?'

She stood up and beckoned for him to do the same before she stepped to one side, revealing her parents walking back towards them with Raphael. The little boy was ankle-deep in the river, grasping handfuls of water and throwing them into the air while laughing beneath silver droplets raining down on him.

'Our son.'

Hans stared incredulously, his lips apart. He looked from Raphael to Matilde, seemingly unable to move.

'Our son?'

'His name is Raphael.'

'He's our son?'

'Yes.'

Hans's tentative smile spread until he gave a sudden short laugh. His eyes were wide open, as if trying to absorb this revelation.

'When?'

'He was born in July of forty-three. There was no way to get word to you.'

He grasped Matilde and pulled her towards him. She felt his heart racing and his body shaking. His voice broke as he made a statement, not a question.

'I have a son.'

Slowly he released her and walked towards the little boy. Matilde saw her father motion that he and her mother were going back to the farmhouse. She nodded, blew a kiss and watched them walk towards the treeline, hand in hand.

Matilde stood back watching the two loves of her life meet for the first time. She saw Hans bend, take off his shoes and roll his trousers a short way up his calves. He slowly entered the water and Raphael looked up at him. The little boy pointed to the water.

Hans sat on his heels, his toes submerged. He was looking at Raphael with such adoration that Matilde swallowed a sob and rested her fingers on her trembling lips. She saw Raphael nod at something Hans had said and then the little boy struggled to retrieve something from his trouser pocket. His little fingers reclaimed a glossy chestnut shining inside its tufted burr. Hans seemed to be admiring it and said something in return, before touching his son's hair. Then Matilde gasped. Raphael was holding up his arms towards his father, and after initially hesitating, Hans stood up and lifted him into his arms. He turned and walked back towards Matilde with the widest of grins on his face and his cheeks wet with tears.

'He's the best gift I've ever received,' he said.

'Mine too.'

'How could such a beautiful child be created in such a dark and terrifying place?'

Hans took another step closer and held Matilde tightly. Raphael joined in, leaning his head on his mother's shoulder and popping his thumb in his mouth.

'Let's head back for some dinner. We have so much to catch up on,' said Matilde.

'The first meal of a million we'll share together.'

The three of them made their way back to the farmhouse as the autumn sun sank lower, leaving pink ribbons of cloud streaking across the evening sky. They spoke of freedom, a life together and their love for each other and their little boy. Nearby church bells began to chime, echoing over the pine-crowned hills. They were a family wounded by memories of pure evil, but a family who possessed the most powerful force of all. Love.

The End

Dear Readers

Thank you for choosing Spring Breeze out of the thousands of books that merit reading.

I loved researching for this story and even ventured down into the catacombs beneath Paris to see for myself the macabre displays of bones, and to get a sense of the atmosphere in the hundreds of miles of tunnels beneath the city.

The Vélodrome d'Hiver no longer exists, the complex having been demolished in 1959. A memorial was installed in 1994, which commemorates the Jews who were transported from Paris to the concentration camps.

One of the reasons I wrote Spring Breeze was to help keep the memory of what happened, alive. I hope that in some small way, this book enlightens and reminds people about the brutality of war and the millions of lives lost.

If you enjoyed, or were moved by this story, I would hugely appreciate if you could spare a minute to leave a review on the site where you bought this book. Reviews from readers like you are invaluable and make a huge difference in raising a book's profile.

Many thanks in anticipation.

Love Angela x

mybook.to/ASPB

An emotional and beautifully written debut you will not want to put down.

One woman's struggle to fight back against the enemy in order to protect the ones she loves.

When Arlette Blaise sees a German plane fly over the family farm in 1940, she's comforted by the fact that the occupying forces are far away in the north of the country. Surely the war will not reach her family in the idyllic French countryside near to the small town of Oradour-sur-Glane?

But then Saul Epstein, a young Jewish man driven from his home by the Nazis, arrives at the farm and Arlette begins to realise that her peaceful existence might be gone for good …

What readers are saying about Arlette's Story—

~ "My goodness, what an emotional roller coaster ride of a novel."

~ "A superbly written book that brings together the power of love both between individuals and family in many senses."

~ "I read a lot – and have always done so. Many of the stories have stayed with me for various reasons – but only a very few have touched my heart in a way that Angela Barton's story has. She truly has a gift and passion that is not often seen."

~ "I thought this book was quite superb – a love story at its heart, a rural idyll destroyed, an unexpected depth of detail about real events and experiences, combined with a really powerful and totally riveting story."

mybook.to/MHPB

Angela Barton brings you a wonderful and bestselling new novel set in London.

When you open up your home and your heart …

Rowan Forrester has it all – the happy marriage, the adorable dog, the good friends, the promising business and even the dream home after she and her husband Tom win a stunning but slightly dilapidated Georgian townhouse in London at auction.

But in the blink of an eye, Rowan's picture-perfect life comes crashing down around her and she is faced with the prospect of having to start again.

To make ends meet she begins a search for housemates, and in doing so opens the door to new friends and new beginnings. But could she be opening the door to new heartbreak too?

What readers are saying about Magnolia House—

- "This book is outstanding. I finished it in 24hours, and was totally gripped by it. I was actually moved to tears in some sections due to the magical descriptions by the author that allowed me to play out the whole story in my head."
- "Love this journey through so many emotions, heartache, betrayal, loneliness, depression, addiction, fear and of course love and the happiness that it brings."
- "I highly recommend Magnolia House, it's full of warmth, love, secrets, drama and emotion, the perfect combination to a Contemporary Women's Fiction."
- "A fabulous story. I love, love, loved this book."

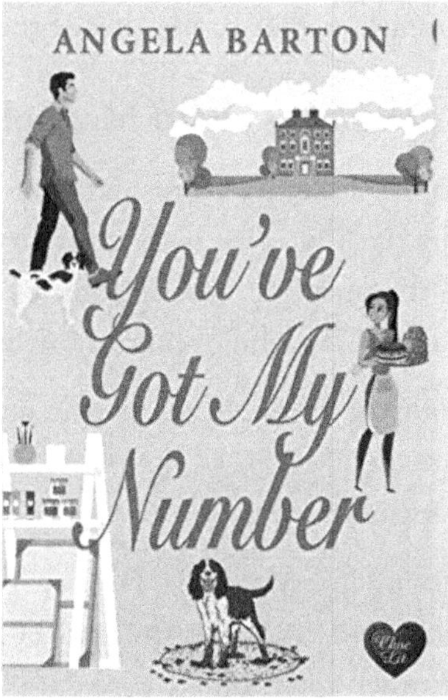

mybook.to/YGMN

An Emotional, Witty and Unputdownable book from the author of Arlette's Story.

Tess Fenton should be happy. She has a job at The Blue Olive deli. Yes, it may be dull, but at least she gets to work with her best friend. She lives in a little cottage in the pretty village of Halston, and she's in love with her boyfriend, Blake. Isn't she?

It's said that eavesdroppers seldom hear any good about themselves, and that's what Blake Snipes discovers when he overhears a conversation. In response, he decides to tell a lie. A lie that grows and spreads, until it affects the lives and loves of those around him.

Daniel Cavanagh is an artist living at the manor house in Halston. He blames himself for two past tragedies, resulting in an obsession with the number three. Whatever happens in his life, he's determined not to be the catalyst of a third catastrophe.

Love isn't always as easy as one, two, three.

What readers are saying about You've Got My Number—

- "I gorged on this book, devouring every word."

- "Romance, lies, twists, secrets and humour make this a story to keep you reading!"

- "This book is the definition of an uplifting romantic story."

- "Angela writes wonderful characters with depth and relatable flaws/dilemmas that just warm your heart."

About the author

Angela Barton was born in London and grew up in Nottingham. She has three grown up children and loves to spend time with her eight-year-old twin granddaughters and a new baby granddaughter born Christmas 2021.

Angela is passionate about writing both contemporary and historical fiction and savours time spent researching for her novels. She lived in France whilst writing Spring Breeze and explored Paris and its miles of catacombs stretching out beneath the city.

In 2018 Angela signed publishing contracts for three of her completed novels. She is a member of the Romantic Novelists' Association, a reader for their New Writers' Scheme, a member of the Society of Authors and also Ellipses and Ampersands' fiction critique group.

Angela is busy writing her fifth novel set in France during WW2. Her next story takes us away from the capital to the Pyrenees bordering Spain.

In addition to writing, Angela also relaxes by making landscapes using free motion sewing on a machine and has a small online gift business at

www.buttonmooncreations.com.

Book links:
Arlette's Story: mybook.to/ASPB
Magnolia House: mybook.to/MHPB
You've Got My Number: mybook.to/YGMN

Social Media links:
Website: angelabarton.net
Facebook: facebook.com/angela.barton3
Twitter: twitter.com/angebarton
Pinterest: pinterest.co.uk/abarton3862
Instagram: instagram.com/authorangelabarton

Printed in Great Britain
by Amazon

24409668R00202